KNIGHT
OF STARS

Book Three of The God Fragments

TOM LLOYD

MIX
Paper from
responsible sources
FSC® C104740

www.gollancz.co.uk

For Fiona, with all my love

Soldiers of Anatin's Mercenary Deck

	SUN	STARS	BLOOD	SNOW	TEMPEST
PRINCE	ANATIN		TOIL*		ATIENIO*
17	Foren		Aben*		
16			Paranil*		
KNIGHT	PAYL	TESHEN*	REFT	SAFIR*	SUTH*
14		Dortrinas	Silm	Layir*	Finc
13	Fashail		Brellis	Aspegrin	
DIVINER		ESTAL*	HIMBEL		LLAITH
11	Haphori*	Rubesh		Colet	
10		Hanva			
STRANGER	VARAIN		ULAX	JOAS	LYNX*
8	Darm				
7			Sethail	Ylor	
MADMAN	CRAIS	KAS*		BURNEL	
5	Fael	Brel			
4				Ismont	
JESTER	SITAIN*	LASTANI*	DEERN*		BRAQE
2			Hule		
1					

*Cards marked with white tattoos by the stone tree of Jarrazir

What Has Gone Before

Stranger of Tempest – Honour Under Moonlight – Princess of Blood

Once, Lynx was a soldier – an idealistic young man in the warrior state of So Han. As a commando lieutenant he was at the spearhead of So Han's attempt to conquer all the land west of the inland sea Parthain, but refused to engage in the atrocities being committed. After killing his commanding officer in a duel he was sent to the brutal To Lort prison and forced to labour in the mines there.

A decade after the end of the war, he finds himself joining a mercenary crew called Anatin's Mercenary Deck – the Cards – on a rescue mission to the city of Grasiel. On the way, Lynx frees a young night mage called Sitain who elects to hide in their ranks. The job turns out to be protecting Toil, an agent of the city-state of Su Dregir, who has just assassinated the ruler of Grasiel before he can make an alliance with one of the most powerful Religious Militant Orders, the Knights-Charnel of the Long Dusk.

Matters are complicated by the rescue of Sitain and one of the Cards selling her out, so they find themselves pursued out of the city by elite Charneler troops. In an attempt to escape, Toil leads some of the party into the ancient Duegar ruin of Shadows Deep. Crossing the city, they are beaten to the only remaining bridges across a huge underground rift by the Charnelers.

In desperation, Toil wakes a beast of legend that inhabits the lower levels of the rift, a golantha, a monster that feeds on magic. The Charnelers are massacred, but the Cards manage to lure the golantha on to the bridge and use their mage-guns to drive it over the edge.

They eventually are reunited with their comrades and complete the journey to Su Dregir, where Toil reports back. While waiting for the next job, Lynx, who has fallen for Toil, gets caught up in an underworld conflict as one of Toil's employees makes a power play.

Not long after, Toil receives word that an academic in the city of Jarrazir, on the northern edge of Parthain, a great inland sea, is close to solving the riddle of the Labyrinth that lies beneath Jarrazir. The Labyrinth is a Duegar construction that has never been opened in recorded human history, but is rumoured to contain a great treasure. As an experienced relic hunter, Toil goes to offer her services, taking the Cards as back-up, but the Labyrinth is opened before she arrives and ghostly guardian spirits kill many citizens as multiple entrances appear across Jarrazir.

Having long prepared for such a day, the Charnelers send their own relic hunter, Sotorian Bade, ahead of an army and he uses the Labyrinth to cripple the city's defences. The Charnelers fight their way into the city as Toil takes a team after Bade, a man who abandoned her in a city-ruin years ago. They each negotiate the puzzle-box of the Labyrinth and end up in a shoot-out at the lowest level. Bade escapes with a huge cache of God Fragments, the source of magic used to power mage-guns, but Toil and her team discover a hidden chamber. Inside is a stone tree surrounded by a strange moat and when a mage called Lastani touches it, something happens to them

2

all. Every member of the party wakes to find themselves with white tattoos on their skin and the three mages in the group are immeasurably more powerful.

They escape the Labyrinth and pursue Bade to his paymaster's command post. There they find themselves in a stand-off, but their mages prove the tipping point. Toil triggers an explosion, gambling that their mages can protect them while the others are killed. They hide from the subsequent inferno that rages, emerging later to discover the Charnelers have retreated in disarray.

In the days that follow, the nearly indestructible God Fragments are dug out of the smoking ruin by Jarraziran troops and a grateful Monarch agrees to discuss an alliance with Toil's employer. Several new members are co-opted into the Cards after getting marked with the magical tattoos and, as the company celebrate their survival with a days-long bender, a message reaches them that a new mission awaits in the southern Mage Islands.

Interlude 1
(now)

'We're here to drink beer an' fuck people up, but we ain't halfway through the beer yet. You want to join us and hear the many tales o' our exploits, darlin', you sit that fine arse right here beside me.'

There was silence as the locals went as still as rabbits. Given the Cards were in a disreputable corner of Caldaire, heart of the former pirate haven known as the Mage Islands, this wasn't the best of signs.

'Darlin', is it?' said the woman he'd addressed.

Deern cackled. 'Now there's a tone o' voice all treacly and thick with menace. Hoy, Llaith, how long's it been since we had ourselves a good old-fashioned bar-room brawl?'

Llaith sighed. 'Oh, who can remember? All fades in the dimness of days long departed.'

There was a growl from one corner of the room. 'It's been four fucking days. I've still got the bruises.'

'Four days, that's it!' Deern brightened. 'Good news then, darlin'. We're probably still in practice.'

The woman pulled over a chair and sat in one neat, graceful movement. She and Deern were of the same height, but there the similarity ended. With light brown skin and a muscular frame she was clearly still in her prime, despite the grey threads in her hair and a weathered complexion. Deern by contrast was pale, scrawny and difficult to imagine as ever having had a prime. Between the sleeves of the woman's shirt and the traditional shawl around her neck any tattoos were hidden, but she was clearly a crew leader of some renown.

'From what I hear,' she said in accented Parthish, 'only one of you has much talent for brawling.'

'Oh I've got all sorts of talents,' Deern replied. 'Buy me a beer and we'll see if we can't lay some of 'em out for you.'

'I'll cut off anything you lay out. You're not the one I'm here to see.'

'You're here for one of us?' Deern turned to address the rest of the company. 'Hey, who ordered the mean, pretty lady? Was it you, Lynx? That's your type, right?'

Lynx made an obscene gesture in reply.

'I'm the boss here,' Anatin drawled, a crooked grin on his face. The mercenary commander was slumped against Reft, cheeks flushed from the heat and the booze. 'Can I help you, darlin'? See something you like?'

'That badge on your jacket,' she said, looking round at the others. 'The Prince of Sun? You look short of a full deck.'

Anatin snorted. 'You ain't the first to suggest that.'

He made to stand up and after one false start succeeded. 'All the same – that's me. The one and only Prince of Sun,' Anatin said with a wobbly bow that ended up with him falling back into his chair. 'Commander of Anatin's Mercenary Deck. Two and forty men all fine, upright, honest and true – 'cept for those who're women of course. Mebbe only half are actually honest and true, come to think of it. Mebbe a tenth could be described as fine, so long as the light's poor. But there's two and forty of them, of that bit I'm almost certain.'

'Any upright?'

'Not really. Forty are definitely drunk and the other two are indifferently sober. But still, they're at your service, Mistress Whatever-yer-name-is. Come to hire the handsomest mercs in all the Mage Isles?'

'Merely come to see what you're made of.'

Anatin pointed at the slim dagger she wore. 'You're gonna need a bigger knife in Lynx's case. The boy's kinda padded.'

'You Parthish mercenaries are all the same – drinking everything you can get your hands on and laughing in the face of danger.'

'Hey, we've been known ta do a whole lot more than that,' Anatin protested. 'Sitain back there will puke on it quick as you like. I won't tell you what Deern does to danger if he finds it with its britches down. It'd likely haunt ya next time you're getting naked with some upstanding citizen.'

She ignored the grin on his face, somehow immune to his charms. 'That was good work you did over in Nquet Dam, quick and clean.'

'Compliments are always appreciated, but why do you care? The sash around your waist says you're from Vi No Le district. How's it your business what goes on in other parts of the Mage Isles?'

She gave him a small smile. 'How many people wearing crew colours do you reckon are welcome in other districts?'

'Just the one,' Anatin said after a pause. 'So you're the queen of all that's nasty in this city?'

'The undisputed champion at least. That means I get to stick my nose in everyone's business – make sure no little dispute blows up into something more disruptive.'

'Ah right, you're the law in this lawless pirate den?'

'Only if it threatens trade – we're a free port and don't stand for anything getting in the way of business.'

'No problems there then,' Anatin declared. 'We've finished our contract, it's cake and medals time for us. Any nastiness to follow isn't our problem. We're open to offers though.'

'There will be no offers,' she said gravely. 'We have our own way of settling disputes round here and it doesn't involve rabbles of hired guns.'

'My Cards are a crack team, specialists the lot of 'em!' Anatin declared in mock outrage. 'Some just also specialise in eating all the weird foreign muck they can get their hands on. But make no mistake, they're an elite fighting unit always ready to take the gold o' some new employer.'

'This I believe.'

'Hey, if it's really necessary we'll do the job too.'

'Take no further job,' she said firmly. 'You will be watched until you leave the city. Make that soon or I make an example of you.'

The woman didn't wait for a reply, just swept out of the room and let the door bang shut behind her. The quiet that followed was broken by a voice from the back of the room.

'Ah blackest hells.'

They all turned towards Teshen, tucked into one gloomy corner of the bar.

'Problem?'

He gave a nod. 'Yeah.'

'You know the mean, pretty lady?'

'Once upon a time.'

Deern gave a bark of laughter. 'Did you fuck the mean, pretty lady?'

'Aye.'

'Break her heart?' Anatin asked.

'Something like that.'

'Sure she recognised you?'

'Yeah.'

'Shitting hells, Teshen, are you certain? I didn't see her skip a beat.'

'She saw me. That last bit was as much for me as you.'

Anatin reached for his drink. 'See, Toil?' he muttered. 'Were you watching? That's how you spot someone from yer past and don't set fire to the whole fucking city.'

'Just 'cos it's not in flames yet,' Toil pointed out, 'doesn't mean it won't be.'

'Aye, shit, you're right.' Anatin slumped back. A grubby deck of cards spilled on to the floor, ignored by all. 'Gods-in-shards! One easy job, that's all I asked for.' He waved a hand in the direction of the door. 'Go on then, man, get after her.'

'Eh?'

'Teshen, my friend, my Knight of Stars! In all the years I've known you – all those times we got fuckered an' maudlin together – I ain't never heard about a lover every bit as scary an' cold-nerved as you are. That tells a story all of its own. Get after her.'

'And do what?'

'Romance her or cut her throat. I don't much care which, but we don't need this coming back to haunt us, okay?'

'Okay.'

Teshen stepped forward and opened the door, looking as hesitant and conflicted as Lynx had ever seen him. 'This ain't going to end well.'

'When does it ever?' Anatin growled, draining his cup. 'One time, you bastards! One easy job. How hard was that? What's wrong with you all?'

'At least it's not my fault this time,' Lynx chimed in.

'I still blame you. We all do.'

'Yeah, I know.'

Chapter 1
(two weeks ago)

Everything was on fire, but given they were the ones to start it this shouldn't have been a great surprise. What to do next, however, seemed to have the Cards stumped. For a while they stared in dumb confusion as the flames rose higher. The sudden force of heat drove them back, but still no one spoke, as though whoever mentioned it first would get the blame.

A splutter of outrage erupted from the rear of the barge. Men were shoved out of the way, women dodged, and the air was thick with obscenities. The words themselves were so garbled it was only Toil's tone that conveyed her message and her anger.

'Which one of you witless apes set the shitting boat on fire?' she yelled finally. Behind her the bargemen were howling and scrambling for buckets. The crowd of mercenaries barely moved. 'Who did it?'

Again there was a moment of silence. Then they all pointed at Haphori.

'It was him!'

'Haphori did it!'

'We tried to stop him!'

'Man's a bloody menace!'

The easterner growled and swung a punch that caught only air as the others abandoned him to his fate.

'Gutless bastards,' he snapped, dropping the mage-gun that hung loose in his hand. 'Weren't my fault, it's my bad arm. The flathorns flushed some ducks an' I got the wrong cartridge.'

'In the name of all the broken gods, what's wrong with you?' Toil roared before turning to the rising flames. 'Lastani! Lastani, where are you?'

'Here,' the young woman called, slipping through the crowd on deck. 'I'm on it.'

'Thank you.'

Toil watched stonily as the white-haired woman approached the front of the canal barge – currently wreathed in flames along with the canal wall behind it. She held her arms out and a haze of ice magic filled the air, smothering the flames.

'Do I have to add this to the list of things you bastards should already know not to do?' Toil said once Lastani was finished.

'Might help, yeah,' muttered someone from the safety of the back of the crowd.

'Look at my fucking face!' she snarled. 'Do I look like I'm in the mood?'

They looked at her face. It was scarlet – not quite as red as her hair, but one fitting her Princess of Blood badge.

It hadn't taken Lastani long to put the fire out, but enough for the willow-pattern tattoos on several Cards, Toil included, to pulse with white light. The nearest two bargemen who'd been approaching with buckets of water stopped dead, staring openmouthed at the diminutive young mage. Behind Lastani, black soot marked every surface, but not even the ropes appeared to have anything more than superficial damage.

'Do you people not understand?' Lastani said. 'Is everything a game with you?'

'How's about you rein in the whole "you people" talk, little miss blonde?' Haphori demanded.

'What? I . . . no, wait—'

'Relax,' Toil broke in. 'He's either fucking with you or he's trying to distract me from being as pissed off as I have every right to be. Either way, it's not going to work when "you people" mostly consists of white folk.'

Still the young mage's cheeks pinked, her anger spent. Toil let out a breath and took a step forward. Haphori flinched, but Toil just raised her hands placatingly.

'Now,' she continued in a quieter voice, 'do you not see the problem here?'

'Yeah, I get it. No setting the boat on fire.'

'For once, that's not actually my biggest concern. I mean, it's not good, not by a long shot. Even a member of the Cards should know that if there'd been a cartridge case anywhere nearby, you could have blown the end off the boat. But. Still. There's a second problem.'

'Magic?'

Toil nodded. 'Magic. Even if I pay off the barge-master and his crew, there's no guarantee they don't tell stories about us. Stories we don't want being spread to certain ears. Given some people have "opinions" when it comes to murdering witnesses, unless I fancy putting up with Lynx's disappointed face, that option's been taken away from me too.'

The middle-aged veteran soldier contrived to shuffle his feet. 'Right. Yeah. Sorry.'

'Good! See, that wasn't too hard now, was it?'

Haphori shook his head. Before he'd finished, Toil had kneed him in the balls with all the force she could muster. He toppled but Toil had him by the scruff of the neck before he hit the ground and dragged him towards the gunwale. Slamming him against the side, she punched him in the face.

'Don't—' she snarled, punching him again. 'Set—' more punches. 'The damn— Boat— On fire!'

Blood spurted from his nose over the wooden deck. Safir stepped forward to grab Toil's arm, but she'd already released Haphori. The injured man slumped back with a groggy moan – nose broken, lip torn. Safir and Toil exchanged a look then both stepped back.

'Easy there,' Safir said. 'No one here asked for these tattoos and all the shit that comes with them, remember?'

'Nor did I,' Toil said. 'Doesn't mean we can pretend we don't have them though.'

Safir nodded in agreement. 'Just remember who we were following when we got the damn things, yes?'

'Ah, Princess?' interrupted Anatin. The commander of the Mercenary Deck stepped forward from the crowd. 'Did we not have an agreement regarding discipline within my company?'

'Yeah, I recall something o' the sort,' she said, inspecting her knuckles. 'Honestly though, I didn't think your book of regulations would cover the eventuality.'

Anatin smirked. 'That's because you've not spent enough time around these dumbshits. Forel?'

The company quartermaster bobbed his head. 'Ah, yes. Page six I believe, sir. Use of heavy ordnance on the ship, building or anything similar that members of the company are occupying at the time.'

'And the punishment?' Anatin asked with an eyebrow raised at Toil.

'Ah, well.' Forel gestured to the bloody groaning mess on the deck of the barge. 'Pretty much exactly what she did. But with all due procedure first.'

'Really? Bugger. So much for my moral high thingy.'

'With the usual caveats of course,' Forel added.

'Which are?' Toil said.

'Company commander reserves the right to shoot the offender in the head should any of his stuff be damaged or there's an unsatisfactory level of alcohol within easy reach.'

Anatin coughed. 'We prefer to think of that as more of an unwritten rule, don't we, boys and girls?'

The rest of the Cards said nothing, no one willing to become the focus of this conversation. When Toil gave Anatin her sweetest smile those nearest Anatin edged slightly away.

'But Forel's actually written it in, hasn't he?'

''Course he hasn't!'

'I . . . well. It's pretty much the first rule o' the company, sir,' Forel said. 'Seemed only right to write it in.'

'Oh for pity's sake.' Anatin shook his head. 'Fine, lucky guess from you, Toil. Point is, they're my troops whether or not you're currently paying the bill.'

She nodded. 'High time, then, that they learned my first rule. I don't give a damn what they get up to, except when it gets in the way of what I'm paying for. Paying damn well too – maybe *too* well given all the new clothes and jewellery I see all around me. But what you all need to learn is that I'm buying something for my money – the tough-as-nails unit I need to complete my mission exactly as I need it done. That includes not drawing attention except when it's called for, certainly not waving pissing flags to any of our recent acquaintances who might be looking for us. Am I understood?'

No one replied, but Toil didn't wait for a response. She stalked her way back to the rear cabins and the Cards cleared her path with unusual haste. Lastani scuttled along in her wake, not meeting anyone's eye. Once they were gone, Safir cleared his throat.

'Anyone got a piece of paper?'

'Why?' Anatin demanded.

Safir clutched his hands to his heart. 'She called us tough as nails. I need to write to Mother and tell her! She'll be so proud!'

Anatin snarled and punched him. A great cheer rose up from the rest of the company and the deck descended into a brawl.

Chapter 2

As the afternoon turned a lazy eye towards dusk, Lynx felt his eyelids sinking. Long streaks of cloud stretched across the sky, now tinged pink and orange against the bright blue. The skyriver, faintly thinner as they headed south, was a wisp of gold and grey overhead. Below it the wilds stretched into the dusty distance unbroken by forest or hill.

Dun savannah ran for miles, marred only by clumps of wild rose and wedge-shaped anthills angled to avoid the afternoon sun. Closer at hand, fronds of creeper hung in broad sheets over the edge of the canal. Fat bell-shaped flowers looked up to the sky as bees hummed all around and the lowest leaves trailed in the water.

Lynx groaned and shifted his feet off the gunwale to sit more upright. 'Is it time to start drinking yet?' he called over his shoulder.

The comment drew idle laughter.

'Fancy-pants Hanese bastards,' croaked Varain from the piled crates behind Lynx. He gave Lynx's chair a kick. 'Too good to drink all day with the rest of us, eh?'

'Better'n most of you lot, aye,' Lynx said. 'Shame that doesn't mean shit by normal human standards.'

He felt something bump his shoulder and turned, squinting into the setting sun until he saw a battered pewter cup and Sitain's face behind.

'Aha, knew we'd make a proper merc out of you yet, Sitain!'

He settled back in his chair, adjusting the long mage-gun in his lap so he wasn't about to shoot off his toes before taking a mouthful. The beer was sour, lukewarm and gritty, but Lynx wasn't feeling overly fussy. Not about drink anyway, and there was sod-all food worth getting excited about on the barge.

Sitain settled in beside him, shunting the chair forward until she could put her feet up. The young woman had her new jacket on, fitted to her frame and unbuttoned in a way that certainly wasn't for Lynx's benefit. On her head was a large maroon hat against the sun, but now evening was come she had tilted it at a ridiculous angle to shade her eyes.

Lynx looked around at the other mercenaries on deck, noting with amusement the sudden rash of respectability among them, or at least something above the usual air of vagrancy anyway. Deern lounged next to Varain; scrawny and half-naked, but with a half-dozen charms and pieces of jewellery hung round his neck in addition to the ghosts of willow leaves tattooed on his skin.

Layir sprawled on top of the flat cabin roof behind them, looking for all the world like the exiled nobleman of Olostir that he absolutely wasn't. He wore a glittering smile, golden necklace and rings, and a crisp white shirt; carelessly and effortlessly handsome in a rakish sort of way. The image was enhanced by the merc beside him, Brellis, who seemed as delighted with Layir's smooth muscled skin as he was himself.

Layir lived and looked the man he intended to be, Lynx reflected with no small amount of envy. Lynx had never managed that trick. His past was clear to read in the tattoo on his cheek and the scars on his back, even if he had a fine new coat and boots back in his cabin.

Most of the others on deck also showed similar signs of wealth and contentment. Even Varain wasn't looking too dishevelled, the gruff veteran wearing a red silk scarf around his neck and a neatly repaired tunic.

'Getting paid suits us,' Sitain commented, following Lynx's gaze.

'Aye, say what you like about Toil—' Lynx scowled and raised a hand. 'Shut up, figure of speech that was. We don't have time for your list of grievances. Anyway . . . yeah, say what you like about her, she pays well.'

'Not much choice there,' Sitain reflected. 'A third of us are marked and she can't afford to lose us, Anatin will know that.'

'I don't care,' Lynx said. 'I've had enough jobs where I never got paid at all. Everyone got a bonus after Jarrazir and she saw to the death-pay for our lost. Whatever her reasons, she chose the better path when I'm sure there were less friendly options in her head.'

Sitain hmmed. 'Doesn't sound much like her, come to think of it. Was it your idea? Something you got her to promise while she was purring in bed?'

'Um, yeah, let's go with that,' Lynx said with a laugh. 'Happy to take the credit.'

'Oh gods, I just pictured it,' Sitain said with a shudder. 'Go get me another drink!'

Lynx smirked and finished his own. He passed the gun to Sitain, gave her a suggestive look that actually did seem to make her queasy, and stood.

The view had hardly changed this past week, but had yet to become dull after too much excitement in Jarrazir. Their journey had been a long one; ten days on the Ongir Canal out of Jarrazir and crossing the inland sea known as Lake Udrel, now over a week on one of the longest Duegar canals on the continent, the Shrelan Canal, which worked a zig-zag path south-west.

There wasn't much in the way of civilisation out here until you reached the coast, just backwater fiefdoms and lost villages.

Far to the north was the Greensea and, beyond that, Lynx's homeland of So Han, but the wilds here saw few humans. Canal water wasn't great to drink or use for crops so there were few waystations or settlements. Where there were waterways on the great continent of Urden, there were tolls, but most days had been a peaceful glide through the empty land between pockets of civilisation.

Lynx had observed life out there though, as he let the jangle of bloody, brutal memories from Jarrazir start to fade. Much of it seemed unbothered by the gentle passage of a barge train – hauled by teams of flathorns that had once grazed free on these plains. Great clouds of butterflies could often be seen crossing the landscape, pursued by birds and flying lizards. Huge black bees attended the flowers at the canal side and many-legged things scuttled through the undergrowth. The further they went south-west the more flying lizards were common and now the sun was setting, canal martins darted all around the barges, feeding on the insects.

Lynx looked up as he poured more beer from the deck's keg. There were four roosting boxes under the eaves of the barge-master's station – years of plying these waters teaching the bargemen that the voracious birds were a blessing.

As he returned to his seat, more mercenaries emerged from the low cabins. The barges were built with a central cabin running the length of it and wide cargo platforms on either side. They were hauling wool and cotton for the main, but also precious blocks of paper and more wine and beer than was safe around Anatin's Mercenary Deck.

It was enough to justify the journey, but most of the barge-master's profit would come on the return where they hauled oil, precious metals, spices, medicines, and tobacco. The hub of the Mage Islands was called Caldaire and it straddled the entrance to the Shrelan Canal. That position allowed it to dominate trade from all parts of the Callais Sea, being the only route to the silk lands west of the Hanese Mountains. For that return journey, the Cards wouldn't have to pay for passage, the value of almost fifty guns coming into its own.

'It starting yet, Sitain?' Anatin called as he emerged into the sunlight.

'Not long,' she replied.

More Cards appeared, Toil among them, but Lynx was already settled back beside Sitain, waiting for the show to begin. It had unsettled them all at first, but now they mostly looked forward to evening. The barge-master still thought it an ill omen, but the mages of the Cards claimed otherwise and at least two of them were expert enough for their word to carry weight.

The shadows lengthened with every passing minute and for once the Cards were content to sit together in silence. To Lynx that seemed like a minor miracle in itself, but after some of the things they'd seen together, it hardly registered.

Beside him, Sitain had a small glass ball in her fingers. She held it up to the fading light to inspect it. From where Lynx was sitting, it looked dully grey, but no doubt to the eye of a night mage it was rather more interesting. He knew they were mage beads – not as powerful as the cartridges in his gun, but easy for most mages to make.

A supply of glass beads and a modicum of control was all a mage needed for a basic weapon. Cartridges were made with God Fragments, the crystal-like shards that were all that remained of the five gods, used to focus and concentrate the mage's magic. It was strange to think of the Militant Religious Orders using holy relics on a daily basis, but profit and power had somehow worked an exception to the usual reverence.

'Fancy making me some of those?'

She gave him a sideways look. 'Why?'

'Why do you think? Not having to kill people can be useful.'
He shifted in his seat and looked at his comrades. 'I realise
not everyone 'round here understands that, but I thought you
would.'

'Is that what all the noise is in Toil's cabin? You explaining
about ethics and stuff?'

Lynx coughed and glanced back at Toil. The sometime
assassin caught his eye and gave him a quizzical frown. He
grinned awkwardly and looked away.

'Aye, absolutely. The woman's a fool for lectures on morality.'

'Good to hear. The answer's no, I'm afraid, not yet. Atieno
says I shouldn't trust any I make at first. Once I've done fifty
or so, mebbe they're worth keeping, but not before.'

'How many you done?'

'Including those I broke?'

'No.'

Sitain looked away. 'Not fifty, put it that way. These ones
felt better though.'

'Tested 'em?'

'I was waiting for Deern to say something really stupid.'

'Let's toss 'em now, see if we can't start the show?'

Sitain gave Atieno a guilty look, but the tall mage's attention was elsewhere. Atieno now wore the Prince of Tempest
badge on his chest – about as cheerfully as Lynx had adopted
the Stranger – but it was more of an honorary position. Along
with about a dozen others, Atieno had been marked by the
stone tree hidden beneath the Labyrinth of Jarrazir. They still
didn't know what had been done to them, but their futures
were bound together now.

The pale willow-leaf pattern was more obvious on his darker
skin, but whenever any of the mages drew much magic they
would all glow faintly white. Distance didn't seem much
hindrance either, from what modest tests they'd done, so

striking off on his own wasn't sensible even if that was his natural inclination. The Vagrim brotherhood was a solitary one, made up of men and women who'd seen enough of this life to prefer their own company.

Lynx and Atieno both wore the Vagrim ring, a simple silver band with three diamond shapes, black, grey and white. They both followed the Vagrim code and as a result felt an obligation towards another who'd been dragged into all this. Lynx could see it in the way Atieno acted around Lastani, although the young academic seemed less resentful of that than Sitain did.

'Sure, why not?' Sitain said at last. 'What could possibly go wrong?'

'Hey, it's mages doing mage stuff – nothing much for the barge hands to gossip about there.'

'Not compared to Haphori setting fire to the barge anyway.' She chewed on her knuckle for a while then came to a decision. 'Screw it. I need better control over my magic as much as I need to understand what these leaf-marks mean. Hold my beer.'

'Words that always herald success,' Lynx muttered as he took the tankard.

Sitain leaned forward and rested one hand on the gunwale. The far bank of the canal was only twenty yards away since they were travelling under the barge's small sails. On the other side the team of flathorns trudged all in a line, unhitched from the barge but too big and heavy to be loaded on board. The beasts were the height of a horse but twice as wide, each huge leg the size of a man. The grey skin reminded Lynx of the maspids they'd seen in Shadows Deep, but the flathorns were powerful and placid rather than swift and savage. There was little stopping an enraged flathorn, but they turned only rarely and always with reason.

Just as well, looking at that damn shield, Lynx reflected. *Even an earther would need to hit it dead on.*

Running the length of each flathorn's head was a raised protrusion, like a horn that had been somehow hammered into the shape of a shield. Its wide-set eyes couldn't see directly in front of it, but three tonnes of muscle and bone meant that wasn't a good place to be. They weren't as fast as horses, but they could haul a barge all day for months on end.

'Ready?' Sitain asked. She didn't wait long, hurling the glass bead high in the air. The mercenaries watched it sail over the calm canal waters and crack against the stone side. There was a twitch of something in the air, a momentary wrench of shadows that made Sitain gasp, and Lynx saw a tiny shape drop down into the water.

'Did you just knock out a bee?' he said, pointing.

Sitain gasped. 'Oh gods, did I?'

'Looks like it.' He couldn't help but chuckle. 'Reckon it works then. Don't worry, bees are renowned for their ability to swim while unconscious.'

Sitain cursed under her breath and thumped his shoulder, but didn't hesitate to pull another glass bead. This one she threw long and nothing happened. A third cracked against the side but did nothing more that Lynx could see. The fourth worked, but that was the last of what she had. Sitain sat back as the last of the sun's rays receded from the plain before them.

'Here we go,' whispered someone reverently.

A small smile on Sitain's face told Lynx the speaker was correct, but it was a while before he caught the flickering movement they were waiting for. In the gloom of twilight it was hard to make out, so fast did it move. Lynx had seen this up close before, but still his breath caught in his chest.

Two shapes, or rather collections of shapes, flickered uncertainly through the low undergrowth. Angular and ever-shifting, some just a grey suggestion and others obsidian black. Sharp angles, twisting shards of shadow that bore no relation to anything alive, yet somehow moved with a will and purpose – night elementals.

It still wasn't clear what they were doing, but there was a complex movement that to Lynx resembled a dance, as though the elementals were greeting the twilight. Certainly they matched the sedate pace of the barges for a long stretch, sometimes vanishing entirely only to reappear a few yards away. Entirely silent and otherworldly, the shadowshards achieved the near-impossible by rendering the Mercenary Deck dumb, and they were only one aspect to the remarkable show out here in the wilds beyond civilisation.

High in the air behind them a faint white light suddenly streaked across the sky, cutting a path that was quickly joined by two others. There was a collective intake of breath from the watching Cards as flashes inscribed the evening. With the first pinpricks of stars only now dotting the eastern horizon, there was no mistaking them for shooting stars. Two streaks of light wheeled and danced with long swooping motions – as high as mountains perhaps, cutting a path beneath the skyriver before spiralling north then vanishing from view while the third looped lazily towards the sun.

'Gods-in-shards,' breathed someone down the barge. 'What are those?'

Heads turned towards Lastani and Atieno. The white-haired academic shook her head, while the man beside her remained impassive as he watched.

'They've no name that I ever heard,' Atieno said at last in the gravelly voice of a man past his prime. On his neck there was a willow-leaf mark, pale against his dark skin, that told a different story. He'd grown used to his modest skills with the most perilous forms of magic, tempest, only to have that wax just when it should be starting to wane.

'How do you know they ain't firedrakes?'

'Because firedrakes do not dance,' Lastani interjected. 'They do not fly high in the sky and tend to be more wreathed in flames. That is not a fire that scorches the sky, it is light itself – pure and crisp.'

'The Duegar gave them a name,' Toil pointed out. 'There was that glyph in the lower level of the Labyrinth. You didn't recognise it, but it must have represented light elementals. There was one for wind too.'

'Can you translate it?'

She shook her head. 'Not in a way that makes sense.'

'Lastani, can you tempt 'em closer?' Lynx asked.

'Closer? Why would you want that?'

He shrugged. 'So we can get a better look. Magic attracts elementals doesn't it?'

'If one of us was a light mage, perhaps. The shadowshards doubtless attend Sitain, the leviathan we saw once was just passing through. There are old magics buried in the canal walls to keep them standing and Sitain's presence calls the shadowshards, but I cannot see why the light elementals would come close.' She shook her head. 'Hopefully it's just coincidence.'

'Why?'

'Because I have only read scant accounts of light elementals – this is quite unlike the dance of the thunderbird, lighting up the clouds of a storm. It is incredibly rare for even a mage to witness some yet there they are, unless we are mistaken.' Lastani glanced at Atieno before continuing. 'We do not know what others may also exist.'

Atieno nodded. 'If there's more magic in the world, elementals might become more common than ever since the days of the Duegar. And if you think firedrakes are bastards, imagine what destruction might be wrought by the embodiment of tempest as it pays me a visit.'

Several of the Cards started to edge away from Atieno. Most of them hadn't seen his corrupting, twisting, magic at work, but everyone had heard stories. They were likely the true inspiration of horror stories about dark mages. Even if those were all lies, tempest magic remained wild and dangerous. He might have more control than ever these days, but Atieno would be the last to trust any tempest elemental.

A hand suddenly shot up, Kas's voice breaking the silence. 'Wait — what's that?'

All heads turned back as they scanned the sky in momentary panic. It wasn't a swirling storm of an elemental bearing down upon the barge, however, but something in the distant sky.

There were shapes moving against the deep blue, black specks in the distance but moving fast and more than Lynx could easily count. It resembled a murmuration of starlings, not quite that fast-flowing cloud of birds, but many creatures flying high. High enough to be moving only towards one thing – the dancing light elementals.

'What are they? I've never seen a flock fly so high,' Kas said. 'And what would they want with the elementals?'

'Oh gods,' Toil said after a few moments. 'That can't be good.'

'What? Why not?' someone demanded. Deern.

'Remember Shadows Deep? The golantha?'

'What about it?'

'The thing fed on magic – the shadowshards feared it, Sitain said.'

'So?'

'So the wilds out here run for three hundred miles, but in the heart of them is a place not so different to Shadows Deep. More to see from the surface so I've heard, less of the deepest black, but home to all sorts of strange creatures. Might be they're hunting.'

'Hunting elementals?'

'Why not? They're both drawn to the places of magic and we know there are creatures that feed on it.'

'But we're on a place of magic. We've got elementals following us too. Oh.'

A collective gloom settled over the Cards. Up until now they had been enjoying the calm passage and warm spring of the south, their numbers enough to ward off the threat of raiders even out in these isolated parts. For a long while they could only watch in silence as the great flock surged towards the dancing ribbons of light. They moved closer and closer without the elementals seeming to notice. Only when the haze of creatures was upon them did the elementals dart away, scattering in a flash of movement.

The flock pursued only one, spiralling to follow it west – pursuing even when its light faded. The streaks of light came only in bursts, sprints it could not sustain and the flock chased even when the elemental was invisible to the ground. It turned one way then another without Lynx being able to see anything of its quarry, before a thin blade of white betrayed its presence and showed the flock closing.

Three times it turned, the flock stuttering and changing direction, but all the while its formless shape evolved and changed as others led the pursuit. Then it broke into two groups. One smaller part peeled away and let the larger herd the elemental towards it. They converged no more than ten seconds later, a single flash of white appearing at the heart of it all and then nothing.

Lynx looked away as someone gave a small cry of dismay. The shadowshards were still with them, winking in and out of sight in the low cover at the canal side, but dusk was coming on swiftly and he could barely make them out.

What are you really? Animals? Beings closer to the gods than anything of flesh? Does anyone alive even know?

'Have we just happened to witness something so rare accounts of it have never reached any book I've ever read?' Lastani breathed in wonder. 'Or has this been almost unseen in centuries for a reason?'

Her only answer was Anatin standing abruptly, the ageing commander snapping his orders like a wary dog. 'Extra guards on every shift. At least one of the marked Cards on duty each night, watching the sky.'

As the grumbles started he gave a loud bark of anger. 'Any of you don't like it – tough shit. Anyone want to cast blame for this, there she is – your employer. Good luck with it.'

The one-handed mercenary turned and stamped away to his cabin, waving Payl on with him. Lynx looked around at the remaining faces on deck, but it was mostly alarm he could see. Extra guard shifts were hardly a rare thing at the best of times and they'd at least had time to recover since Jarrazir's many excitements.

Now the Cards were reunited with their greatest love, beer, and heading to the source of half the continent's more exotic drugs. No one was about to complain too hard at the woman putting so much money in their pockets. Not until the monsters came for them anyway. Still, they all kept their guns a little closer to hand. The holiday was over.

Chapter 3

The hunt of the light elementals left the Cards in reflective mood and for once the posted guards were alert through the night. Their passage down the canal remained peaceful, however – lazy, quiet days punctuated only by brief moments of alertness as they passed barges doing the return journey. Most were in trains of three or four and known to the barge-master and his crew. Ambushes were rare in any case, despite this being too far south to have a Militant Order presence. With the mage-guns of the Cards on show, it was the other crews moving warily.

News was exchanged, some small trade done and then the barges would continue on their way. Once, the hour and friend-ship had prompted an impromptu party of barge crews, but it remained reserved. The barge folk were a disparate, extended family much like the Cards, but godly in a quiet fashion. They despised the fanaticism of the Militant Orders and abhorred violence, however much they recognised the need for guards out in the wilds. They moved cautiously around the Cards as a result, but even the troublesome members of the company wanted a quiet journey.

The street fight against the Charnelers had been swift and brutal, ten Cards dead by the end. During the days and nights that followed, Jarrazir had witnessed a surge of drugs and illicit booze sweep through the shocked, scarred city and the Cards had led the charge. It had been a spent and grieving company that was herded on to barges for the long journey to the Mage Islands.

One bright light for them had been the return of a former Card, Colet, who'd spent six months recuperating from a wound. Suth, the new Knight of Tempest, had brought on a few Jarrazirans to help cover the losses too, after much discussion between Toil and Anatin. As the days passed and the Cards had little to do beyond talk and gamble, the new members settled in well. With nothing to serve as baggage the way Lynx's Hanese heritage did, even Deern could find little to complain about skilled veterans boosting their numbers.

Only when the barge-master announced they were four days from Caldaire did the Cards begin to stir from their quiet haze of drink, mourning and some of the more sedate Jarraziran drugs. Anatin passed the word for a company muster on deck of the biggest barge and by fits and starts the mercenaries gathered. As they did so, the barge crew drifted away, abandoning their posts after Anatin made it clear he didn't want them near.

Anatin had, of course, taken the greatest share of the company's pay and the grey-haired mercenary had kept one Jarraziran tailor busy until the day they departed. While he had hardly become a dandy in the last few weeks, Anatin now cut a fine figure of a mercenary captain with a silk-lined jacket of green draped rakishly over one shoulder. Pearls adorned one ear and emeralds his throat, while his beard was perfectly trimmed along with his hair. Lynx wasn't the only one to notice the jacket covered Anatin's missing hand, but the loss seemed to be less of a burden now.

'Ulfer's ragged arse-beard, just look at the state of you all,' Anatin began, casting his gaze over five suits of mercenaries. 'Three weeks of idleness and all form o' martial prowess fades in the sun. Even our employer there, shattered gods – is she wearing a damn dress?'

All heads turned to the prow where Toil lounged behind the assembled mercenaries of Blood, indeed wearing a sleeveless cotton dress. With deference to her nature, however, close inspection would reveal it was not adorned with flowers, but coiled serpents. With a lazy flick of the wrist she made a gesture that got Anatin roaring with laughter.

'A dress! Oh dear me, how the terrifying have fallen.' He paused. 'However, you are the lady with the money, Toil, so I guess you can wear whatever you damn well want. Squeeze yourself into Deern's old underwear for all you like – I would merely ask Himbel to repeat some of his many lectures on filthy diseases one might pick up in foreign parts.'

Again Anatin paused, this time for a faint theatrical shudder that saw an empty cup tossed at him.

'Oh yeah, that's right. We had to burn all your smallthings, didn't we, Deern? Nonetheless, the lady wears what she likes. The rest o' you bastards, however . . . well, we've needed some down time to say our prayers and stitch our wounds. I don't begrudge you that, but the lady pays for quality and I don't see a lot of it round here.

'Some o' you are new so here's a few rules to safeguard how much I'm getting paid. Anyone who's decided Lynx has the sort of figure all mercs should aspire to, yer wrong – even if our employer does have a weird kink in that direction. None o' you could argue that the state o' Varain's liver is ideal, but I've seen the stock tallies. They tell their own story so from now on, the fun's over.'

While he was waiting for the chorus of boos and insults to end, Anatin pulled out a cigar and lit it with a match that spat dirty black smoke into the sky.

'Such enthusiasm,' he purred once the Cards had quietened. 'Such fire and determination, my boys and girls. That's the company I assembled, hidden somewhere behind the overweight sots I see. But have no fear, my friends, my mostly trusted comrades and almost entirely loyal troops! I will bring that part of you to the fore – I will reforge you all into the weapon all of Urden shall come to fear. A force of keen and hungry . . .'

He stopped and pulled hard on his cigar. 'Oh sod it. It's too early and I need a drink so I'll go with the short version. Those of you who don't get to give orders, the holiday's over. It's time to work. The booze is cut off and you'll be taking shifts in walking alongside the flathorns until the poison's sweated out.'

'And the job?' Estal asked. She was a white-skinned veteran who wore the Diviner of Stars and doubled as the company seer. Her grey hair was tied up on top of her head to reveal jagged scars down one side of her neck overlaid with white tattoos. 'Some of us were marked by the last job, we could all be hunted because of it. It's only fair we know what we're heading into this time.'

Anatin nodded. 'Yeah, I get it. This one's actually as simple as it sounds though. Unless things go to shit and o' course that'd never happen to us, right?'

'I ain't trying ta piss on your toes here, Toil,' Estal said, turning to look at the red-haired woman, 'but since when are you interested in simple?'

'I like simple,' Toil said with a smile.

'In yer men, sure, but for your work? We all know now who we're working for really and no one minds that, but the Mage Islands are a long bloody way. Your war's to the north so I don't see what quick job could be worth your time out this way.'

Toil pushed herself up and moved to the front, kicking a few of those too slow at getting out of her way.

'The job,' she said at last. 'Well, it is a simple one, I promise. It *does* call for a crack company of mercenaries though, so if any of you could recommend one that'd be helpful. No state secrets this time round, just the usual caution. So far as the rest of Urden goes, we're escorting a party of mages to meet with the guilds then looking to secure work somewhere sunny. Given these tattoos, that's more'n halfway true.'

'More please,' Estal said grumpily.

Toil nodded, acknowledging her tone. 'The good news, as some of you may quietly agree, is you've got a new employer.'

'So why're you still here?'

'Oh I'll stick around a while longer. As you can all imagine, I spent many of my formative years dreaming of being a princess. Now I am one, I wouldn't want to give up this badge.'

There were more than a few sniggers. The whole company by now knew Toil's father was the founder of the Red Scarves mercenary company. Most companies had an official home that ranged from a single tavern, in the case of the Cards, to the greater part of a town for larger ones like the five-hundred-strong Scarves. As only daughter to the commander there might have been something regal in Toil's upbringing, but not very princess-like.

'Your esteemed commander has found himself a contract with the Whitesea Banking Consortium. By happy coincidence the job's a long way away from any retribution the Knights-Charnel may hope to dish out. And just perhaps, my employer might have an interest in the Consortium's bright future.'

'Banking? What the fuck use are we to them?'

'High-level banking,' Toil clarified. 'We're not talking a small loan here, we're talking a mid-level kabat.'

'Kabat?'

'Used to mean a pirate captain in the Mage Islands, now it's what they call any local figure of power. The politicians and rulers there don't have many delusions of respectability. They're folk of business first and foremost but aren't averse to emulating their pirate ancestors. You've heard of the saying that war is politics by other means?'

Estal folded her arms. 'Nope.'

Toil sighed. 'Well it *is* a saying, I promise. Anyway, at this level an elite merc company can be called bailiffs by other means.'

'What other means? Most bailiffs I ever met had mage-guns and knives. Some real nasty bastards too.'

'You're not helping me make my point here.'

'Wasn't trying to.'

'Yeah, I noticed.'

Toil gave Estal an overly broad and cheerful smile. It didn't quite have the effect of Reft's golden shark-like grin, but Estal got the message all the same.

'You'll get final orders once we're in the Mage Islands and have met with the bank's local agent but suffice to say, they don't like lawyers in a pirate haven. The locals don't respect a contract with the enthusiasm a bank does.'

'So assets haven't been handed over,' Anatin broke in. 'That's bad for the bank's reputation and cash flow when they're already out a huge sum. Between the kabats, mage guilds and trading consortiums, you can't hire anyone local for the job without getting betrayed and screwed over. Instead we go in, hit hard and bugger off out again. The Consortium present the Court of the Kabats with a done deal and they all remember they're pirates who don't give a shit about each other—'

'Fuck it up and fail to get it done clean,' Toil added, 'then things get sticky. The other kabats either remember their treaties or sense an opportunity.'

'It's a pirate kingdom,' Teshen called from the back of the crowd. 'It's where I grew up. Might be no more pirate fleets any more than there are kings, but don't let that fool you. They smell blood in the water as fast as sharks.'

Toil nodded. 'And as we all know, there are nastier things in the Callais Sea than sharks, so let's not screw up, understood?'

'Ever get the feeling you're wasting your time?'

Kas raised an eyebrow at Lynx. 'What? Pulling guard duty when everyone else is on deck and carrying a gun too?'

'Yeah, that.'

She grinned. 'If you were looking for sense, you're in the wrong job, my friend.'

Lynx nodded and lapsed back into silence. As the gloom of night drew further over the sky and night elementals flittered through the canal's shadows, the darkening sky was spotted only by clouds. Solitary trees punctured the view out on the plain beyond with great skirts of darkness, their close-weaved leaves spread like canopies high above the waving grasses.

As they walked side by side back down the barge, bow and mage-gun on their shoulders, Lynx felt a prickling sensation and glanced around. On the other side of the barge, the third member of the evening guard duty, Colet, was watching them. She was a former Card who'd been convalescing since before Lynx joined and even now carried her right arm awkwardly. Colet hailed from somewhere way east of Parthain if Lynx's guess was right, with skin like pale coffee, wavy brown hair and bright green eyes.

'Aw, you two are adorable,' she laughed, seeing Lynx scowl.

'What now?'

'You two – walking in step, as close as an old married couple. It's enough ta warm my jaded heart.'

'We ain't—'

'She knows,' Kas interrupted. 'The woman's just soft in the head. Bloody pagan who gets all sorts of foolish notions and says each and every one out loud.'

'I've missed you too, Kas love.' Colet beamed, crossing the deck. 'And I didn't say you two was bumping uglies, just that

33

you made a lovely pair. Deern already said you broke Lynx in on behalf of the company. Kind o' you to welcome him on his first day like that.'

'Hadn't joined up by then,' Lynx said gruffly, unsure which of them was the focus of the needling.

Colet's voice went furtive. 'Does that bring some sort of finder's fee from Anatin? 'Cos I could see—'

Kas slapped her on the arm. 'Rein it in there, crazy-lady, I'm pretty fond o' your husband remember?'

Colet scowled. 'So're the new serving girls back home.'

'He'd never!' Kas protested.

'Aye well, I ain't getting any younger and they seem to be. Doesn't seem to mind them flaunting themselves around him.'

'Not good for business to mind that,' Kas scoffed. Seeing Lynx's blank expression she went on to explain. 'Her man's a groom at the livery stable that adjoins the Hand o' Princes, where the company's based. He tells anyone who listens how he's got a gentle touch with even the most skittish of mares, which is how he got Colet to marry him in the first place.'

Colet's expression fell. 'He didn't sign up for this, though,' she added bitterly, raising her right arm to chest-height. The limb looked barely under her control, her fingers twitching fitfully as she moved. 'He's been good about it, but what man wants a broken wife, eh?'

'Sparker?' Lynx asked, having seen the injury before.

'Yeah, fried the nerves in my arm and damn burns got infected too. Took me months just to lift it this far, but Himbel says if I keep moving it things'll improve.'

'Good time to work on the babies then,' Kas said, 'instead of being out in the shit with us.'

'Fuck that! 'Colet slapped the mage-pistol holster on her left hip. 'Spent the last six months learning to shoot with this hand. You ever tried that, Lynx? Damn expensive to practise

34

each day, but I'm a merc. I'll play the doting aunt when Kas has a brood each as beautiful as her, but it ain't for me.'

'You'll be waiting a while then,' Kas laughed. 'Not many o' this lot are husband material.'

'Come back to Ei Det with me then. We'll find a man for you so beautiful it'll make yer heart ache. Mebbe other bits too.'

'Aren't the Orders still trying to blow the shit out of Ei Det?' Lynx asked.

'Ah, only a bit of it. Ei Det's a big country.'

Colet spat over the side and looked east as though she could feel the call of her homeland from so far away.

'Plenty o' work for a fighting woman and plenty of space to get away from it. The Orders haven't made ground in years, food and water's pretty scarce round there. If any one o' them commits the resources necessary to take Ei Det, they'll get swallowed up by another. That's the fun thing about being deranged fanatics, your friends are real shitbags.'

Before Lynx could say any more there was a commotion on the other side of the barge where a dozen Cards were assembled. The trio exchanged a look and raced around the central cabin to where chaos had descended. For a moment Lynx thought something had come out of nowhere and attacked the barge, but then he realised the chaos was just panic. Beers were tossed aside as a dozen mercenaries tumbled off their seats and crashed into each other. Half were fumbling at their cartridge cases, mage-guns being waved in all directions.

In the middle of it Teshen roared orders that only he was ready to enact, but Lynx barrelling forward seemed to shock some into readiness. Kas and Colet appeared in his lee, making the most of the path he'd made and readying their weapons. For a moment the three of them stared blankly at the twilight beyond, the shifting cloud of dark shapes eluding them at first. Not thousands, Lynx saw, not like a flock of starlings, but scores of something much larger.

'Oh shit.'

'Yeah,' Teshen growled. 'Let's hope they ain't like that golantha in Shadows Deep. Bunched up like that, we need our sparkers and burners to work.'

'Fuck, how many of them are there?'

'Enough.' Teshen tightened his gun against his shoulder. 'Anyone with an icer, take aim – fire!'

The mage-guns crashed out into the night. Seven or eight white streaks tore through the evening sky straight for the oncoming flock. In the fading light it was hard see what hit, but the creatures broke and wheeled, one of their number spiralling down. The Cards gave a brief cheer until Teshen roared at them to shut up.

'Least we know they don't like it,' Lynx commented as he reloaded. 'Given 'em pause for thought.'

'Ready – fire!'

All the guns spat a second volley and another of the creatures broke away from the re-formed group – not dead, but clearly hurt and abandoning the hunt.

'Reload! Lynx, hold back – get a burner ready.'

As the third volley was readied, more Cards appeared on deck. Lynx distantly heard boots hammer on the wooden deck and Toil yell at Lastani and Sitain to get back below, clearly not wanting the tasty mage treats on view.

Above the plain, the creatures were close enough to make out slender wings and a pale hide. Against a darkening sky, Lynx could see long sinewy necks supporting a horned wedge-shaped head. The wings looked leathery like a bat's, with hooked claws clearly visible down the arm. A broad, kite-shaped tail trailed out behind them, cutting at the air as they manoeuvred – forty or fifty at least and each bigger than a man.

There wasn't time to count properly. A stuttered pair of volleys hammered the ghostly shapes at fifty yards, killing several, and this time the flock broke up. Diving fast towards the barge, they split into five or six flights that spread and spiralled down towards them on all sides.

Lynx tried to take aim but couldn't get a fix on the moving shapes. After just a second of trying he pulled the trigger more in hope than judgement. The creatures parted in a flash away from the roaring spear of flame, while elsewhere one of the largest creatures led three others in a swooping raid.

The Cards scattered and threw themselves to the deck. Grasping claws tore splinters through the cabin roof and there was a howl of pain. Lynx glimpsed a thrashing figure be dragged a few yards along the deck before the claws ripped free of their clothes. White lines stabbed in all directions as the Cards fired in panic. The handful of mercenaries on the following barges had more success, calmer shots winging one and killing another. The creature crashed to the deck, a massive lump of grey-white that clipped the gunwale and pinwheeled into the side of the cabin. Deern howled as the corpse slammed right on top of him, the scrawny wretch disappearing under a tangle of limp limbs.

For good measure Reft jumped forward and hacked an axe into the creature's back, just below the neck, but it failed to even so much as twitch. Leaving Deern where he was, Reft hefted his mage-gun again and clipped another of the beasts with an earther. The shot snapped its wing like a twig and the creature plunged twenty yards off the stern.

More strafed the deck, looking to snatch up prey, but those they did snag were heavy and flailing. The effort of lifting them proved too much for most and was abandoned. One or two persisted, only to present large, slow targets for the mage-guns around them.

Lynx slid a sparker home and readied his gun, waiting a few moments to get several in his sights until he pulled the trigger. A jagged burst of lightning scattered them but, even as they wheeled, the lightning's claws leaped out to embrace them. Sparks wrapped around three, one falling and the others barely avoided crashing into the water before they recovered and limped away into the sky.

Several Cards ran to the edge of the boat and fired icers down into the downed creatures, one screeching piteously until it was finished off. The bodies lay crumpled on the surface of the water as the others broke away, the fury of their hunt broken by gunfire. Whether or not they fed on magic like the golantha in Shadows Deep, they couldn't shrug off gunfire so easily. Their losses had been severe with little to show for it, with luck they'd not risk the barges again.

'Himbel!' came a yell from the other side of the downed creature. As the yell came up the dead thing's wing began to move. Several Cards almost shot it again before Deern's scratched and dishevelled head popped up from underneath.

'Just fucking leave me here then!' he shouted at Reft. 'Don't worry, damn thing didn't hurt when it dropped from the gods-burned sky on to me!'

Reft merely shrugged and hauled the creature all the way off Deern as Himbel hurried past. The company doctor knelt at the side of another man wearing a Blood badge, but in moments Lynx saw him shake his head. Reft stepped over, as sergeant of the suit, while Deern stood and swore profusely as he realised who was dead.

'Anyone else?' Anatin called.

A few people reported injuries, but the Knights of each suit did a swift count and all Cards were accounted for. The dead man turned out to be a taciturn veteran called Silm. Lynx had barely said two words to him, but even Deern looked upset at the man's loss. In brisk fashion, Anatin ordered the stinking pale corpses kicked off the barge, ignoring Toil and Paranil's efforts to sketch and inspect the unknown monsters.

Before long they were clear of the beasts and the barge-master had pulled to the side of the canal while Silm was wrapped in cloth. A pyre was swiftly built on the shore. As soon as yellow flames began to reach into the sky, the full ranks of the Cards assembled at the gunwale, the barges moved on.

It was late to keep going, but no one wanted to be near the dead monsters or whatever might be attracted by their corpses. Toil had been pushing them for days now, deciding they were running behind the schedule she'd set for herself, but no one was arguing.

The death, Lynx realised, was a reminder to them all. The holiday was over, the mourning of their lost was over. It was back to the violence of their usual lives. The putting of grief aside until the job was done. It was a cold way to live and broke many a good man, but warfare was a cruel and sense-less calling.

'How many more of these will we get?' Lynx muttered to Kas and Teshen as they watched the pyre recede into the distance.

'Not many,' Teshen said, impassive as usual in the face of death. He had tied his long hair back for once and quickly turned his face south. It looked like he was searching for something on the horizon, but in the advancing gloom Lynx could see nothing.

'How do you know?'

'We're close to the end of the canal, close to the Etrel Cliffs.'

'So?'

Teshen gave him a strange look. 'So something else hunts in the skies above the Mage Islands, remember?'

Lynx hesitated. 'Tysir?' He'd only read about the Mage Islands, never visited, but some things were famous.

'Tysarn,' Teshen corrected. 'The biggest ones don't fly, but I doubt anything's going to want to hunt within twenty miles of the coast.'

'Are they really man-eaters?'

Teshen shrugged. 'Not often. If you go in deep water you've only got yourself to blame. But yeah, some. A pack o' smaller tysarn are more dangerous – once they get to the size of whatever those are, they don't play well with others. If you're hurt and alone though, you'll get 'et.'

'Fond memories o' home, eh?'

'Some,' Teshen said, looking south once more.

Kas clapped a hand on Lynx's shoulder. 'Reckon you'll like the place anyway, whatever's flying in the sky.'

'How's that then?'

'The food, Lynx, the food. Spices from east and west, plus a few you won't find anywhere else, and more'n a thousand different things you can eat from the sea.'

Teshen nodded. 'The lagoon's so full of life, you won't believe your eyes if you ask an islander cook to surprise you. On feast days they catch and roast tysarn too. Of all the world, Lynx, the Mage Islands is the place for you.'

Lynx nodded as his stomach growled its approval. 'So probably the worst place for me to visit alongside Toil – Princess of Chaos and Making Enemies?'

'Yeah,' Kas laughed. 'Make the most of this trip – we won't be welcome again!'

Chapter 4

The following days saw a steady change in the landscape and weather. The vast open plains gave way to hills and rocky outcrops as they headed towards the broken coastline of the Callais Sea. The crumpled terrain was scattered with copses of low trees that looked as though they were hunkering down against some onslaught, while the huge isolated canopy trees of the plains dwindled and were left behind.

Just half a day's travel from their destination, the canal merged with another that ran south-east through the Greensea towards the Hanese Mountains. They reached the junction not long after midday, a human-built tower on a wedge of land to dominate both branches. Lynx found himself staring at it as they came closer, a nameless bubble of tension building inside him. When a hand touched his shoulder he flinched, almost stumbling as he moved away.

'Whoa, Lynx – where were you?' Toil said, startled.

'Huh?'

'You were lost in thought.'

She looked towards the tower as he released his mage-gun, feeling foolish. He'd been holding the weapon so hard his knuckles were white, his wrist aching.

'Oh,' she said, 'I see.'

'Nothing to see,' he replied, feeling himself grow angry, then even more so as he railed against his own stupid reaction. *Gods damn it,* Lynx told himself, *get a grip on this.*

'Not yet,' Toil agreed, 'maybe on the other side of that though? Not much trade coming that way in recent years, so I hear, but some still.'

'Don't worry about it.'

She sighed. 'Sure, I know. All the same, we could all do with reaching Caldaire. The company needed this down time, but right now we're a bunch of brawlers crammed on to a boat or made to run alongside it. Neither of those is fun, 'specially when half this lot are experts at getting on people's nerves.'

'Yearning for your freedom?' Lynx said, far more snappishly than he intended.

Toil nodded slowly. 'A bit of space would be nice.'

He forced himself to nod. 'Aye, right. Don't get me wrong, I ain't complaining about the cabin or . . . well, anything else. It's just, ah . . .'

She laughed. The sound both lightened his heart and made him instinctively tense, but Toil just leaned forward and planted a kiss on his cheek.

'Don't worry, it'd never occur to me that a man would complain about *that*. But you're getting scratchy. Too much time trying to be nice, it's not good for you.'

He shifted his feet. 'I ain't so good at nice, not for days on end. Too used to being alone.'

'We're not so different there. I'm exhausted and I'm not the one who's a maladjusted loner.'

Lynx snorted. 'Sure about that?'

'Aye, mebbe,' Toil admitted. 'But I hide it better, even if that's not saying much. Sharing *my* space, however, that's not so easy. I've got my own issues there. Might be a growling semi-feral cat isn't the biggest intruder my private space has seen recently, so I'm touchy on that subject.'

Lynx nodded, remembering the skyriver festival in Su Dregir. Toil's apartment was surprisingly personal and understated

– her sanctuary in a chaotic and violent world. That had been violated by the assassins sent by one of Toil's employees attempting an underworld coup. Any disruption after that would leave her more prickly than usual.

Steadily they closed on the toll-fort. The barge-master had told them it was part of a local fiefdom that encompassed a handful of villages in the hilly ground beyond. Nothing problematic, but Lynx's concern was the unseen waterway beyond. The economy of So Han, his former homeland, was still a shambles after the war and two subsequent famines. Even so, Lynx didn't fancy meeting any of his countrymen coming this way.

While his prison designation was covered by the tattoo on his cheek, anyone he met was likely to be nosy – either rich and therefore arrogant, or ex-soldiers keen to work out the pecking order. Lynx didn't give much of a shit what they thought of him, but he knew how such things would go, given the average Hanese soldier and his own short temper.

As they reached the junction and were flagged to a halt, he couldn't see all the way round but there appeared to be nothing tied up at the toll-fort and he felt some of the tension slip away. Tolls were common enough on the canals and no great nuisance. They kept their demands modest to avoid merchant factions hiring someone like Anatin to deal with the problem. This far south-west they would bear no allegiance to the Militant Orders. As it turned out, they were as keen to buy cartridges as they were to extract a toll. The barge-master was carrying some and drove a hard bargain for them, but Anatin refused to sell any of the company's stock.

The continent's mage cartridges mostly came from the north, from Militant Order heartlands, so prices were very high in Caldaire. The western silk lands past the Hanese Mountains paid a premium to supplement a small local supply, importing through Caldaire because the mountains were largely impassable to trade. Warfare took a different form both there and south across the Callais Sea. That region was a storm-ravaged wasteland few bothered to venture into, with just the savage ocean beyond. No great market for the Militant Orders' wares despite the small kingdoms and pirate states that dotted the coastline.

As they passed the toll-fort, Lynx wasn't the only one to stare down the small, empty stretch of water that led in the other direction. He felt Sitain appear beside him too. The half-Hanese woman said nothing as he very gently edged to one side to lean against Sitain's shoulder. She had never visited the country of her mother's birth, Lynx knew that. But while it contained the horrors of Lynx's memory, for Sitain it was the place of monsters her mother had fled long ago.

'One day, puss,' Toil said behind him. 'One day.'

Lynx gave a cough of surprise. 'One day what? I ain't going back there!'

She tilted her head and gave him a sly look. 'Oh I don't know about that, there's probably one thing that could tempt you there.'

'If my dad's still alive, I'd only bring him trouble.'

'Not what I meant.' She sighed and lowered her voice a touch. 'There's a war brewing. I'd put money on someone like me being sent that way, looking for experienced troops to hire.'

'You're fucking mad if you think I'll play recruiter,' Lynx said. 'Drag a whole new generation of stupid kids to die or end up like me? No chance.'

'We don't need kids, we need veterans – something So Han's still got a lot of. Mebbe scratchy and bad-tempered some of them, gone to seed round the middle even, but with skills you can't teach youngsters so fast.'

'Veterans who'd never leave or come to any sort of agreement while the Shonrin is still . . . oh. Oh. Shit.'

She gave a nod. 'There he goes.'

The realisation hit him like a punch to the gut. 'Fuck,' Lynx breathed. 'Fuck!'

'Quite the challenge, eh?'

He gasped. 'It's an impregnable mountain-top fortress filled with elite fanatics. That's a suicide mission unless you've got someone on the inside.'

She shrugged. 'Or you could *get* someone inside.'

'Inside the fortress up a mountain? Um . . .'

'I always wondered about that bit. You Hanese aren't really famed for your construction skills. I mean, you're plodding and determined in your own way, but bloody-mindedness doesn't get stone halfway up a mountain.'

'They say the Duegar built it, or at least some of it. So what?'

'So, my little painted cat, the Duegar never once built on top of things.' She turned away, patting him on the shoulder as she went. 'They always started much lower down. If you recall, low down and dirty is something of a speciality of mine.'

'Oh.'

She laughed. 'Don't worry – that's a mission for another day, assuming we even get that far. It's not the job we've been given, so let's keep our eyes on this one.'

'Sure, let's make sure a bank gets its money back so it can finance a nice big war.'

'Can you think of an alternative?'

'No.'

'Let me know when you do.'

Long before the barges reached the canal's end, Lynx could smell salt on the wind and see the great hump of rock known as the Etrel Cliffs. From this direction the cliff seemed nothing special, a steady rise in the ground over tens of miles that steepened abruptly. The canal walls now rose above them on both sides, sheer blank stone marked by the centuries. The long, uneven slope above the cliffs continued west for more than a hundred miles, while Caldaire and the canal stood at its eastern end. The coast in the other direction was lower, a frayed edge of channels and peninsulas blurred by a huge mangrove forest too dense for large settlements.

Up on the cliff's back, long stretches of bare rock and earth were marked by abrupt gullies and pale clumps of bone-grass. It looked desolate and empty for miles. The distance was too far to hear the mournful clatter of the bone-grass, but Lynx knew the sound all too well anyway. The stuff made anywhere seem more desolate, not least because it was poisonous. The rattling seed pods gave off some sickly sweet vapour that lured creatures closer, but would kill them if they lingered.

The far side of the Etrel Cliffs was more impressive, so every tale claimed. Deep inside the caverns, far from daylight, had once been Wisp settlements. History told of occasional trade between the species, who interacted only very rarely, but for unknown reasons it had tailed off and ended in recent generations. Nowadays the entire cliff face and nearer caverns were occupied by the largest of the flying tysarn. Lower down, at the water line, the caves housed great beasts that had grown too big to fly and employed their four wings in the sea instead.

A large defensive fort blocked the way to the very mouth of the canal. Iron gates spanned the water itself between a squat pair of rounded towers topped by grenade throwers. Lynx saw dark shapes circling against an overcast sky as they reached the fort. Not as large as the creatures that had attacked the barges, but there were several dozen on view and doubtless many more above the islands themselves.

As one wheeled and came closer, gliding along the canal towards them in search of fish or eels, Lynx could see four wings, the fore pair slightly bigger than the rear and all frilled with claws. They moved in a strange rippling motion that ran through its whole yard-long body when the tysarn beat them, dagger-like head turned down to scan the water below. Pale green in colour, its wings bore clear markings of yellow and as it closed he realised there was a strange noise in the air. Deep croaking calls, almost like the sound frogs made, but each sound was elongated and proportionately louder.

Lynx walked a few paces across the deck and waved a hand to attract the attention of the Knight of Stars. 'Hey, Teshen, can we eat those ones?'

There was a smattering of laughter from the Cards on the deck, followed by a few catcalls in reply that Lynx chose not to listen to. The burly Mage Islands native paused in the process of shaving his scalp and shook his head.

'Too old, it'd be like chewing leather.'

Teshen had let his beard grow since hearing their destination and had now sculpted that into a strange design that left his chin and neck bare. For some reason he was now dressed like Anatin's piratical younger brother in a shirt open to his navel and red silk pantaloons. Many of the Cards went shirtless in the warm weather, but Teshen had decided to become something of a dandy instead, sporting voluminous sleeves turned back at the cuff with gold-headed pins.

'Is this all necessary?' Lynx asked in a more serious voice.

'Probably not,' Teshen said, though the tightness of his lips said otherwise.

'Someone might really be holding a grudge all this time?'

'Like I said, probably not. But we're here to do a job, makes sense to take some precautions while I've got nothing better to do.'

'Your face was well known in the city?'

'Some districts, aye. Adventurers in the silk lands wear their beards like this. Being outsiders they have to have their heads shaved 'cos hair length is a status thing out there. Lots o' Mastrunners head out that way to make their fortune. Warriors in those parts are big an' thick-limbed so we make good scouts. Those that survive to return tend to be tough as nails, so the crews give 'em a wide berth.'

Lynx scratched his cheek. 'I'm starting to think this'll be a nice change of pace.'

Teshen eyèd him darkly. 'Why?'

'Anatin being pissed off at someone else 'cos it's all gone to shit.' Lynx grinned. 'I'm not saying it definitely will, o'course, but I've been around you lot for a while now. So it will. Probably five minutes after we step on to the dock.'

'Unless the city's changed in weird ways, it shouldn't be a problem, but. . . remember Toil's reaction when she saw Sotorian Bade, back in the great hall of Jarrazir?'

'That bad?'

Teshen gave a wry laugh. 'Not so much wrath o' the gods, mebbe, but there's a few people might not care for the sight of me. If it starts a fight in the street, we've all got a problem on our hands and we burned our Steel Crows insignias after Grasiel. Until we get a new set to masquerade as, best we don't have the name Anatin's Mercenary Deck on everyone's lips. Which will happen if we start firing mage cartridges out here.'

Lynx nodded as the barges were waved forward, the bargemaster having apparently satisfied the fort's commander of their peaceful intent. He paused and glanced back at Teshen.

'Have you trimmed your eyebrows too?'

Teshen laughed. 'That's not part of the disguise, I just look really pretty this way.'

'Pretty creepy more like.'

'Do I look like me?'

'No.'

Teshen nodded, satisfied. 'Good enough. Now fuck off and go stare in awe at the Mage Islands like a good little landsman.'

'Feeling pride in your home at last?' Lynx said as he turned to face the way they were heading. A stretch of two hundred yards and three barge trains was all that stood between them and the huge building of yellow stone standing on the eastern bank of the canal.

Beneath it was a wide harbour that sported several docks and a long beach running up to the huge pillared space underneath. The clothes and faces of a dozen different nationalities went about their business there, a zig-zagged stair cut into the rock leading up the side of what Lynx knew had to be the Casteril Trading Hall.

The docks could handle three dozen barges he guessed and one corner was given over to boatyards, while small houses perched on shelves of rock on the hillside and a tavern led on to the main dock. The main activity was the swarm of labourers and merchants around the Trading Hall. Six storeys high and mage-cut from the rock of the hillside, goods were bartered, sold, inspected and stored there. On the ground floor of that, the open space behind the pillars, Lynx glimpsed massive furred creatures hauling goods-wagons on a track towards the other side.

A covered bridge ran across the canal from two-thirds up the side of the hall to a sheer outcrop of rock on the far side. From that, two dozen different flags hung almost to the top of the gates – obscuring their view of the city beyond. The curve of the bridge meant that those in the centre were the largest. Lynx guessed it was some sort of ranking for the kabats of the city – which according to Teshen's description were a curious mix of pirate captain, merchant prince and local lord.

'Pride?' Teshen said thoughtfully. 'Nope, not especially.' He glanced up at the sun that peeked through a tattered cloud and nodded to himself after a moment's thought. 'The sound o' tysarn on the wind now, that brings back a few memories.'

'What then?'

'Ah, just a guess. Some folk say the city's quite a sight, first time you come here. But you're a grizzled veteran and a seasoned traveller, I'm sure you'll take it all in your stride.'

Chapter 5

'By all the broken shitbastard gods, look at it!'

Lynx's mouth hung open. He could only nod in dumb agreement with Deern while Teshen chuckled away in the background. They had swept through the water gate with practised ease, two more boats ferrying the remaining Cards into the softly shining green-blue waters of the lagoon at the heart of the Mage Islands.

'Told you it's a sight,' the now-bald Knight of Stars said.

'That's all you got to say?' Deern continued. 'Jog on with the ice-cool act, we ain't biting. Trying to tell me that's not a fucking amazing view?'

'Must be amazing if it's got you acting like a ray of sunshine.'

'Get fucked, ya toad-sucking eunuch.'

'Ah – that's better. The majesty's worn off.'

Lynx still said nothing. Lynx had read the city – or rather collection of districts that comprised Caldaire – resembled a huge wheel, but the sight was rather more than that. It was a vast circle of rocky ground, a broken ring of islands that had been entirely mage-carved to suit its inhabitants. They created an undulating wall of pale yellowed rock punctuated by greenery and skirted by island-gardens.

Some of the islands rose like mountains, windows and hearth-smoke showing that they were inhabited right to their peaks. Even the lower islands were on multiple levels, the local mages having used the sloped ground as a guide for their work, but not a constraint. Most dramatically, however, at the heart of the lagoon were dozens of small islands, ranging in colour from dark, dead brown to startlingly green, all around three huge chimney-like rock columns.

'The hellmouths!' Teshen called, pointing at the peaks. 'One o' the seven entrances to the underworld – so legend says anyway.'

'And the truth?' someone asked.

He gave a callous laugh. 'Climb up there you'll find your way into the afterlife, sure enough, an' it won't be pretty.'

They had disembarked at the docks, their kit transferred to boats with teams of rowers to take them into the city while the barges were unloaded. Their crew seemed a typical mix of locals as the order was given to pull away. Many looked like Teshen, tanned skin, fair hair and cold grey eyes, but they ranged all the way to the slim, dark-skinned and green-eyed rower nearest to Lynx.

The men all wore loose pantaloons and sleeveless shirts with a headscarf of thin cloth as protection from the sun, most with a variety of metal and bone necklaces and earrings on show. The women were similarly dressed, but wore their hair long and mostly uncovered, with a light shawl around their neck and shoulders. Lynx glanced at Teshen with his newly shaved head. Without displaying his own crew tattoos, he wouldn't be able to dress like the local he was. Instead he was forced to highlight that he didn't belong here now.

The boats steered away from one of a pair of rocky pillars that rose twelve feet out of the water ahead of them. By the colour of the water Lynx guessed they marked the deeper water used by seagoing ships. He couldn't tell how shallow the rest of the lagoon was, but some people were standing waist-deep off the shore to his left.

The pillars marking the channel had some sort of metal and glass contraption at their top, perhaps to light the way at night so trade never had to sleep. They followed a regular arc between the outer ring of city streets and the strange central islands which ranged from several hundred yards across to a few dozen.

The spice islands, Lynx remembered they were called just as Deern recognised them too.

'Can we go there?' Deern called to Teshen, rat-face shining with excitement. 'That's where the drugs come from, right?'

'Yup,' Teshen said with a curt nod. 'But if you cross the inner markers you'll get a warning shot in the head.'

'Just for looking?'

'They don't mess around with their drugs. Some can only grow here. Every damn spare inch of ground there is used, intensively farmed with help of mages – it's the only way.' Teshen pointed. 'See that reddish one? Looks like it's a whole island of dead bracken or something? That's rust-eye. You set foot on that island you're likely to stir up the spores and overdose before you get ten steps. O' course they don't care about that bit, only that you'll mess with their profits.'

The hellmouths protruded from the heart of that central cluster. A mile or so away, Lynx could only see they were unevenly yellowy-grey stone, streaked with black and smears of green creeper somehow clinging to their almost sheer sides. Right now they were imposing, about two hundred yards above the bushes and trees of the islands around them, but Teshen had hinted they would only get interesting at dusk.

The outer ring was where the people lived and worked. It was skirted by small island-gardens dotted around the inner shore, all covered in vegetation. The rest of the city was a haphazard sprawl the likes of which Lynx had never seen – sloped cliffs and hills that had been so extensively mage-carved it was hard to tell what the original line of rock had been.

There were a few open plazas and markets near the shore, but much of the district he could see – Casteril, the largest of the city's five districts – was like the Trading Hall but on a far bigger scale. One main section was a good mile in length and sported so many balconies, walkways, staircases and windows it was impossible to even count how many levels were inside it.

Where there was open space, there were plants and small trees, while odd alcoves had been colonised and creepers threaded an eccentric path down the rock. Most of the city was the same pale yellow-grey rock as the rest – with painted shutters, awnings and the clothing of its inhabitants a stark counter-point to the uniform stone.

On the near shore Lynx finally caught sight of the furred beasts of burden he'd glimpsed in the shadows beneath the Trading Hall. They were not quite so broad or powerful as the flathorns that pulled the barges, but taller, with longer limbs and loose hanging hair – looking more like twelve-foot-high sloths than anything else Lynx had ever seen. As he watched, one pulled itself up a wide stairway with long, ponderous movements, untroubled by the baskets affixed to its back and following the fluttering flag of its handler with placid acceptance.

He looked over the edge of the boat. The lagoon was so shallow here he could see the yellowy-green bed through the clear water, a multitude of small creatures swimming and scudding beneath the water's surface. A small octopus darted from its lair to snatch up something, fish scooting away from the movement. A blurred cloud of what might have been prawns parted briefly as an eel wriggled through while insects skimmed the surface above.

A shove jolted him forward. He flailed as he started to tip towards the water and had to grab the edge of the boat.

'Don't be too eager to get stuck in, Lynx,' Llaith laughed as he dragged Lynx upright. 'Wait 'til they've cooked the fishies first!'

One of the rowers chuckled as Lynx recovered his balance. 'Tysarn eat you!' he said in broken Parthish.

Lynx frowned. 'Here?'

'Here. Eat men who fall.'

'Don't believe him,' Teshen said. 'You don't often get tysarn in the lagoon, not the big swimmers anyway. See the flags?'

He pointed to a tall flagpole that stood on its own outcrop of rock extending out from the shoreline. Currently it flew a white banner with no decorations visible. Lynx could see more in the distance, all white.

'I see them.'

'When a big one's sighted in the lagoon, you'll hear a horn sounded and the flag turns to red. Tells people to stay clear of the shore where the water's deep enough for a tysarn to swim up.' Teshen laughed. 'Keep an eye out for the flags and you're more likely to get eaten on land than in the water.'

'Eh?'

'If a pack of smaller tysarn decide you're too helpless to fight back you'll get et, but you'd have to be really shit-dribbling drunk. Everything eats everything round here,' Teshen added expansively, 'it's the pirate way!'

Passing between a pair of small islands covered in fruit bushes, Lynx saw a mage gather a glittering stream of water from the lagoon and deftly scatter it like rain over the island. They all watched the young man in fascination, even the mages of the Cards themselves, and he responded by sculpting complex shapes in the air with the water as he went about his work.

Then they were past and the boat nosed into a berth at a small dock. The mercenaries eagerly jumped out, most happy to feel solid ground under their feet again. The other two boats came in right behind, while Lynx started to heave bags to Llaith on the shore.

'Hey look, a pub!' Llaith called as he slung his bag on to his back. 'I'll race you, Varain.'

'Hold up, we're on the clock remember?' Anatin shouted from the last of the boats.

He nodded towards the three mages still in the boat, surveying the district. Sitain, Lastani and Atieno were all now dressed like respectable citizens of some wealth. Behind them lurked Paranil, Toil's tame academic who was playing their manservant far more convincingly than he would a mercenary.

With an exaggerated gesture Anatin extended his hand to Sitain to help her off the boat, seemingly delighted by the scowl he received as she accepted it.

'Right now, ladies and sir, shall we secure you accommodation?'

Lastani inclined her head. 'Do so,' she said in a curt voice, in case there were any curious faces watching.

Lynx couldn't see any, but with a busy street and three crews of rowers, he could only imagine how many people there were happy to pass on any interesting titbit. Anatin gave Teshen a nod and the burly man set off for a street that cut towards the sea-shore.

Lynx was about to follow him before reminding himself that he wasn't part of Teshen's suit any more. The mercenaries of Stars slouched along behind Teshen, Kas fairly dancing along with delight at the sights of the city. In comparison to her the rest looked about as surly a collection of mercs as Lynx had ever seen, slowly moving away from the tavern.

'Pub now?' Llaith suggested hopefully as he wandered back from begging a coal off a street vendor. 'Since we've got some time to kill?'

A few of the Cards had already started to drift towards a tavern Lynx guessed was called The Three Robbers by the painting beneath the name. Llaith puffed away at a cigarette as he walked, a sigh of contentment escaping his lips.

The Diviner of Tempest was one of the long-standing members of the Cards, a drinking crony of Atieno's from before Lynx had even fired a mage-gun.

'Can't we just enjoy the sunshine?' Anatin demanded. 'Bask in the warm air and drink in the sights of a wonderful new vista?'

'What in the name o' the deepest black for?'

Anatin laughed. 'I'm only joking, ya damn fool. Let's sink a few. Master Atieno, Lady Lastani – can we escort you to a genuine slice of local charm?'

Atieno gave the pub a grave look. It was three storeys tall, with a raucous-sounding common room down on the lower floor but a stair leading up the side to an open terrace at the top.

'Have some wine brought up to us,' he said at last. 'Ladies, shall we?'

'Toil,' Anatin called over his shoulder, 'you're on duty.'

The red-haired woman gave a snort and gestured for Atieno to lead the way. 'Lynx, Aben, look after the kit.'

'Why, what did we do?'

Lynx looked around at the bags piled on the dockside, a handful of thin-limbed urchins surreptitiously watching them. They weren't the only ones watching either. A pair of teenagers had also stopped to look, but they were armed and seemed more interested in the Cards than their belongings. One set off at a trot as he watched.

'Looks like our presence has been noted,' Toil said. 'Things must be twitchy here if they're reporting on every merc that docks. To answer your question though . . .' She pointed towards the street vendor Llaith had taken a coal off for his cigarette. 'I don't know what he's frying in that cart, but I'm guessing it won't matter much to either of you. Don't worry, we'll send out some beer just as soon as we remember.'

Lynx shrugged. 'Guess life could be worse,' he said to Aben, who shared his enthusiasm for any impending meal.

'That's what worries me,' Aben said, kicking the bags into a closer heap. 'This might be as good as the job gets.'

'Quick and simple, what's what she said.'

'It's what she always says. Never bloody true though, is it?'

'Don't, you'll spoil my appetite.'

Chapter 6

It started to rain as Lynx and Aben waited on the dock for someone to remember them. The clouds drifting in from across the sea cast a pall over the strange circular city and even a bowl of rice and garlicky tentacles didn't improve Lynx's mood much. The traffic around the lagoon was near-constant, while children fished near the dock and the occasional tysarn dived in after anything edible. There were seabirds too, red-eyed gulls watching for any scrap of food and sleek, dark shapes soaring above, but it was the tysarn that seemed to rule the air here.

'Here you go, boys,' called a voice behind them.

Llaith and Safir joined them on the dock, each carrying two large clay mugs of beer. Lynx pulled uncomfortably at his britches, the warm weather making them sticky and binding even though he only had moccasins on his feet. For once, the kilt Safir wore looked practical, but Lynx kept the thought to himself in case Llaith started to wear one. Having those puckered white legs on show all day was likely to put him off his food.

'Turns out this place can brew something pretty decent!' Safir said, waving a beer towards Lynx.

'Pull up a pack then,' he said, gratefully accepting the mug. 'Hopefully this one ain't either of yours?' he added, pointing at the pack he was sitting on.

Safir squinted at it. 'That's, ah, Deern's I think.'

'All the better. Something went crunch when I sat down.' Lynx wriggled around to get extra comfy then raised his mug in toast. 'Here's to not getting shot.'

'First rule o' the Cards,' Llaith said, grinning and clunking his mug against Lynx's.

'There's a lot of those,' Aben commented after he'd taken a swig. 'First rules I mean. Few people getting shot too, I guess. Is it none o' you lot can count properly, so everything's a first rule?'

'Something like that,' Safir agreed. 'Some of us had a proper education, but most amaze me that they don't blow their own heads off.'

Lynx eyed the former nobleman. 'We've all ended up in the same place, though.'

'Some of us, my tattooed friend, made some bad choices along the way,' Safir said with a smile and a nod. 'Many of us, no doubt.'

'Others are just bone-deep idiots,' Llaith chuckled. 'Look at Darm – man's got the brains of a flathorn.'

'But put the company in a pub and all sense goes right out the window, often with one of the locals.'

'Ah, but that's honouring a time-honoured tradition,' Llaith protested. He paused and looked around before speaking again. 'Still, best we find some real geniuses,' Llaith said in a more serious voice. 'Put more than a couple of you next to each other and that light tattoo is all the more obvious. Safir, don't linger between Kas and Atieno until we get that fixed, yeah?'

'I would never stand between Kas and any man,' Safir said with a wink. 'Layir, of course, may need more of a warning on that front. I believe my young ward is holding something of a candle there, despite screwing Brellis every chance he gets.'

'Given Kas and Layir might both light up at any given time, let's keep the sparks dampened down, eh?'

'At least this must be a good place to find answers,' Lynx said, always keen to steer conversations away from the affections of their female comrades. 'I doubt that's a coincidence.'

'You really reckon there is a cure?' Aben brushed the faint outline of willow leaves on the back of his hand – left there by the Duegar stone tree hidden beneath the Labyrinth of Jarrazir. 'Is it even something that needs curing?'

'I'll settle for understanding it,' Lynx said. 'Don't much fancy serving as some sort of power reserve for our mages – glowing when they draw more magic than any human's supposed to – but we're all still healthy at least. I've rarely felt better than after wading through that weird water around the tree, but *something* happened beyond fixing every tiny cut and bruise. Best we know what that is.'

'Ah, now look at them all,' called a voice from the tavern doorway. 'Gossiping about girls no doubt.'

Toil sauntered towards them, her concession to the weather being light cotton britches, a tunic embroidered with the Princess of Blood badge and bare feet. Unbidden, the memory of her figure-hugging Jarraziran wrap of green and grey appeared in Lynx's mind. The image forestalled any clever reply, despite Toil at the time having been brandishing a knife and swearing like a grenadier with the clap.

'As it happens, Princess,' Safir declared with a bow, 'we were – just not about you.'

'Don't think you'll win friends with that attitude, oh noble Knight of Snow. If I'm not occupying all o' your thoughts, I demand to know why not.'

'Flash a bit of leg more often and we'll consider it.'

She laughed. 'I'll leave that to you. The ladies of the company consider them among your better attributes. All discussed in genteel and discreet fashion of course.'

'I've met the ladies of the company, remember? But their enthusiasm is gratifying. I try my best.'

'Really? That's your best? I better have a quiet word with Estal then, she's too much of an optimist.' Toil walked around the group to clap one hand on the shoulder of Aben, her long-time friend and comrade, as she adopted a more serious tone of voice. 'Now – Teshen should return soon so we'll be back to business.'

'Which is?'

'Getting ourselves settled, getting the lie of the land, then finding the best place to become quite heroically drunk.'

'Eh?'

She winked at Safir. 'See all these young toughs watching the dock? Kabat spies no doubt.'

'So?'

'So – if I was a kabat in hock to a bank, I'd be watching out for foreign mercs who arrive quietly, trying to avoid too much attention.'

Safir looked at the others. 'Anyone else follow her?'

'Time for a little misdirection – the one piece of subtlety this Mercenary Deck is capable of.'

'You want us to pretend we're as far from a group of professionals on serious business as it's possible to be?' Lynx wondered aloud. 'Hah, "pretend".'

'Exactly! The cover story is that we're a company who've fulfilled our contract. What would we do to blow off some steam before moving on?'

'Get shitted and start a fight most likely. Oh.'

'Like I said.' Llaith grinned. 'Some things are just a time-honoured tradition.'

Much later that afternoon, in a quiet corner of Auferno district in the south-east of the city, the three mages and Teshen sat on an empty balcony and looked out across the Callais Sea. A steady breeze rolled in off the sea, hauling white curls of water on to the long rocky shoreline that broke the worst of the sea's strength before it hit the city.

'Do you want to get started tonight?' Teshen asked in a quiet voice, eyes never leaving the great expanse of water.

Their view was narrowed by more islands that stretched twenty miles or more down the coast. None were as populous as Caldaire's districts but they were still important components of the Mage Islands. The chain ran south-east from the city, sheltering the mangrove shore from the worst of the sea's strength. Away to the east, the high pale face of the Etrel Cliffs overlooked a line of mostly desolate islands for as far as the eye could see.

There was little more to see here, Auferno having no sea-facing ports because this shore bore the brunt of the wind's constant assault. Two tall-ships made for the lagoon entrance and the dark bulk of a huge, water-bound tysarn lurked close to shore. The breeze whipping over them carried only the sound of the waves, nothing of the city behind.

'Is there time?' Lastani asked, nodding towards the descending sun.

'We can get there before dusk, aye. Won't be admitted of course, but that's not 'cos of the hour. Best you can hope for is leaving a respectful message at Shard's Rest, see if you pique their interest.'

'The current Shard is a woman if I recall correctly?' Atieno said.

Teshen nodded and gestured inside. 'So our friend who runs this fine lodging house tells me. I'd heard the last one had died, but no more than that. Doesn't matter much, does it?'

'It is always worth knowing as much as we can before we try to impress anyone.'

'Well, mage politics ain't really my thing. I can tell you some about the last one, but this new Shard I never heard of. Ambor Urosesh's her name, but like in Jarrazir, you call her by her title.'

'Shard?' Sitain said, as much wanting to be part of the conversation as anything else. 'Mistress Shard? Guildmaster Shard?'

She knew so little about her magic and was feeling increasingly out of her depth. Lastani had tried to teach her some basic principles, but all the words in the world couldn't describe what Sitain felt running through her body.

'Just Shard, or Shard Urosesh if you really feel the need. She's a guildmaster too, but there's a few o' those. Think of her as the first among guildmasters – she speaks for 'em, but don't expect a lordly ruler. If she gives an order, most of 'em will pretend not to hear it, or argue, or twist the words to mean something else.'

'Then what's the point?'

He gave a bleak smile, the usual sort she saw on the Mage Islander's face. Teshen was one of those Cards Sitain couldn't read at all. To her he was like a snake – unnervingly different and remote. The only thing she could be sure of was the bite.

'Point is, she gives an order and the rest will listen to it. That's more'n you get from most mages round here. And the kabats listen to her. The Shard maintains the balance in the Mage Islands, just the right side of chaos and well clear of some bastard pronouncing themselves king.'

'Should I write a letter to be delivered if we're not getting in anyway?'

'Nah, they appreciate a little humility. Walking to a man's door here show's you give a shit and they should too. Doesn't mean you're getting inside, but that's only prudent. There's a lot o' big talk in this city, a lot o' bluster. It's only a threat if you're knocking on the window.'

'That sounds like the voice of experience,' Atieno said.

'Me?' Teshen laughed. 'As meek and gentle as a lamb I was, in my youth. Anatin's just a bad influence.'

'Then why did you leave?'

'For reasons,' he said, all traces of humour vanishing. Teshen cocked a head at Lastani. 'Thought about what you want to say yet?'

'We offer an exchange of information. Access to their libraries in return for a first-hand account of the Labyrinth.'

'And that'll do?'

'To a leader of mages, it'll be valuable. She may demand more of course, but that will either be calling on our skills or something Toil can arrange.'

He stood. 'Come on then, let's get to it.'

Sitain gave a snort. 'Never thought I'd say this, but I've grown used to having all the Cards around. Especially since what happened, an armed escort seems more important than getting away from that bunch of idiots.'

Teshen patted the pistol at his waist. 'You've got an armed escort – any more than me, people start wondering if you're rich and important. These are the Mage Islands, remember? Your kind made this place and the Militant Orders aren't welcome. They've long since stopped sending snatch squads round here, the kabats are wise to all that. Come on, we're taking the scenic route.'

They left the lodging house and found themselves in an overlooked street, where balconies and narrow bridges loomed on either side. Teshen headed for the nearest stairway, a switch-back of narrow stone steps that took them up to a wide shelf of rock where doorways opened out on the right-hand side.

'This is not a city for the lame,' Atieno huffed as he followed at a steady pace. 'A few weeks ago this would have been beyond me.'

He still didn't look steady on his feet by the time they got to the top, though the consequences of his Tempest magic had diminished since Jarrazir. His foot was not back to normal, but the gradual ossification of his bones there had been retarded hugely.

'We could go at sea level,' Teshen called back. 'But if you want to see the city properly, best to climb.'

Sitain said nothing. She was still marvelling at the huge rocky outcrop that had been carved over the generations into a place fit for humans. Stained yellowish stone comprised every wall and most roofs in addition to the dirt-smeared ground underfoot. Windows and doors were brightly painted wood for the main, except for the occasional wealthy house where the seaward windows were bulges of mage-blown glass.

It was all human-proportioned at least, albeit otherworldly. The daylight kept it from reminding her too much of Shadows Deep, but still she felt a little jumpy at every corner. Sitain wasn't looking forward to getting to dusk much, in case the nightmares returned in force, but the sight of children playing and adults going about their daily lives restored some reality.

The road snaked left and right through a cleft in the rock then opened into a fork overlooking a small market. Teshen led them up again, deep stone steps taking them through an archway flanked by shrines to Ulfer and Insar that streamed incense from two dozen sticks. The wind began to tug at their hair as they headed along a high-sided stone bridge above a training ground where youths in green sashes sparred. On the other side of the bridge Teshen beckoned them all together and pointed out towards the lagoon, talking loudly over the wind.

'Look.'

Sitain narrowed her eyes, peering in vain across the water to where Teshen was pointing. For a moment she saw nothing, though Lastani beside her gasped. They had a fine view of the spice islands at the heart of the lagoon – great clumps of green heaped around the forbidding peaks that rose from their centre. Only then did she see it – no individual creature but a cloud of what almost looked like smoke rising. Movement poured from the top of each peak – shadowing the sky behind.

Not peaks, chimneys, Sitain said to herself, trying to smother a gasp. She couldn't see inside them as they were taller than any structure in the city, but it was clear now the top was no flat plateau.

'Shattered gods, you weren't joking about that being a hell-mouth! Tysarn?'

'Young ones, aye. Tens o' thousands of 'em, meat eaters all. They mostly feed at night on the insects of the islands and the eastern forest, but the smell o' blood will bring 'em racing. In the dark they run less risk of getting eaten by their kin.'

In the distance she heard a faint addition to the cries of seabirds and long, low bellows of the large tysarn. It rose like an onrushing tide, thousands of high voices merging into an undulating pulse of sound. It reminded her of the calls of jack-daws when flocks of them would circle the fields back home.

'Are they dangerous?' Sitain asked. 'In those numbers?'

Teshen shook his head. 'Nah, don't worry. Storytellers might claim different, but we love the young ones round here. Without them this place would be a misery, overrun with every sort of biting pest you can imagine.' He shifted the direction of his arm, now pointing down the long curve of the encircling city districts.

'That's where we're going. The Shard's Rest is there, though mage guildhouses are spread throughout the city. See the round roof? That's the Rest. The block below it is the Shard's private residence – one o' the few places no Masts crew will wander. Hidden behind the next island is the greater channel, where ships come in. Just one bridge across it and real high up, but a rope or two you can use to swing if you're feeling adventurous. Far side of the channel is Nquet Dam district, with the biggest temples and open ground. Vi No Le is round behind the spice islands – don't go there until you've stopped getting lost in Casteril is my advice.'

'Masts?'

'Aha, that's a sight for another day. If you hear a big ship's bell ring out, keep your eyes open. You're not in any danger, but it means there's a game starting. You'll see folk in sashes jumping roofs or climbing walls as they chase each other. Some of the fights are legend now.'

'Vi . . . Vinolay? Does it go all the way to the cliffs?'

'Nah, that part there is Cliffbase, an island just in front of the cliff front. There's a channel separating it from the cliff that the large tysarn make use of when they're spawning. See the darker patch in the cliff face? That's a tunnel, once a Duegar canal they say, but only the tysarn use it. No person gets more'n a hundred yards inside before they're et. Less of a district is Cliffbase, more a slum. There, folk do get picked off by the bigger tysarn from time to time.'

Teshen waved them forward, across a shorter bridge and past a run of ten tiny homes before they descended to a lower level. The street there was wider, but still they had to wait for a pair of the huge shambling sloths to pass. The beasts were twelve feet from broad muzzle to stubby tail. Trailing fronds of hair brushed the ground and claws the length of a man's hand clacked against the stone as they walked.

They negotiated the stairs and twisting alleys of the stone city with a languid grace, despite the wooden frames on their backs. The boy leading them couldn't have been more than ten years old, his dark hair as long and matted as his charges, but they responded to every twitch of the ragged flag he carried.

'They can swim too,' Teshen commented, nodding towards the beasts.

'Now you're just taking the piss,' Sitain muttered, prompting a bark of laughter from the local man.

'I swear it, you'll see some for yourself. Most roam the plains in the wild, but some feed in the sea itself. The water-bound tysarn hunt them sometimes. It's quite a fight if you're lucky enough to see one. The tysarn are big and nasty, but sloths are damn strong and those claws . . . mostly they're for digging up roots but piss one off and they'll punch through armour.'

Once the way was clear Teshen led them down a long stretch that skirted the upper reaches of a market. It was a confusing section of the city that led to a rope bridge from the island they were on to another, fifty feet in the air and swaying alarmingly in the breeze. On the sea-side of the islands Sitain spotted four or five prominent rocks that the waves were breaking upon, some sort of great netted pens strung between them in the water. Her questions elicited no answer from Teshen. Either he didn't hear or was keen to press on before darkness came.

Sitain hesitated before following, despite her alarming position. A flitter of movement caught her eye out on the water. For a moment she thought it was some sort of falcon skimming the waves and racing around the rocks that anchored those pens, but it was too fast and elusive even for that. She caught Lastani's eye who smiled and nodded. That made Sitain's breath catch. She looked again – knife-sharp blurs of movement that circled and jinked like swifts hunting, barely visible in the fading evening light. Without form even, just an outline of movement delighting in the surging air.

Wind elementals! Sitain thought with excitement. She didn't know if they had any other name, but surely here where mages would have drawn such things for centuries, they would have one. *Every kind of elemental might be drawn to such a place. Those are the sights I want to see, not lizards or ancient ruins.*

Even up here, the sun was only just visible above the headland. When she turned back to follow Teshen the western horizon was a smear of orange and yellow that hurt her eyes.

I hope we return a different route, she thought desperately, thinking of how this swaying bridge with open slats underfoot would be after dark.

Fortunately Teshen descended soon after. A broad street of detached houses led to a wide stone bridge and beyond that, a large dual-temple complex unlike any Sitain had ever seen before.

From the way Atieno stopped dead, she guessed he was just as surprised. A central courtyard opened out towards the open sea, embracing the wind into the space between two weathered, copper-clad domes. Great seashells had been set on pillars in the courtyard, each one emitting a different moan as the wind ran through them.

One dome was dedicated to Ulfer, god of the seasons, but to their surprise the mirror of it was a temple to Banesh, lord of change. Further north, such a thing would be unthinkable even outside of Order-controlled states. Banesh was more often described as the great enemy or betrayer of the gods in the Riven Kingdom and even where the stance softened he was not worshipped in the same way. Here they seemed to have no such qualms.

The sea-facing side of this island was a high ridge with two levels of streets on its inner side. It sheltered a spine of raised streets down the centre of the district, but aside from that it was all largely at ground level. Abutting that was the Shard's Rest, a massive circular assembly hall with a modest palazzo branching off one side and a high perimeter wall around the rear half. Its meniscus roof sported two dozen gargoyles around its edge, each one holding a flag of three colours.

'I've just realised. There are no proper uniforms here, not soldiers or watchmen anyway,' Sitain commented as they entered the square in front of the Shard's Rest. 'Who—'

The mages all stopped dead, realising there were pale figures all around them. Statues surrounded them, but not on plinths – each was sitting on one of several dozen stone benches around the outer edge of the square. Some stared forward, others seemed in mid-conversation with each other. One or two had a living person sitting beside them, seemingly entirely at ease with their stone companion.

'Uh, what're they?'

'Former Shards,' Teshen said. 'Some old tradition or other. The mages live apart from the rest of us, most of the time. As for the uniforms, this is a pirate city – standing armies ain't so popular.'

'So Mastrunners wear the colours of their district but aren't soldiers?'

'Nah. Might be they keep the peace on some streets, but mostly they're the powerbase and honour of a kabat. To call yourself kabat you need to run a crew and take part in the honour games. The senior kabats take those seriously so their underlings treat it as a matter o' life and death. Masts is about capturing the banners o' the other crews, though. It's a game played out on the streets, so no mage-guns allowed. Mastrunners often die, but it's rare civilians do.'

'They've still got crossbows,' Lastani pointed out. 'Those can kill just as well.'

'Mostly they use blunt arrowheads that mages can charge,' Teshen said. 'Not just crossbows either, staves too. Sometimes a useful edge in a fight – spark-charges, light-bursts or sleepers packing just enough night magic to put a man out. All very easy in a city of mages and glassblowers, but cartridges are damn expensive and no one wants the city torn up just for a game.'

'No guns at all here?' Sitain asked.

He gave a snort. 'There are guns – the kabats have guards for their compounds and palaces, but it's a last resort when you've got dozens of armed Mastrunners whose lives are cheaper than a gunbattle.'

It was a wealthy area they'd walked into. A mage was charging the sea-glass heart of a street lamp, one of a dozen they'd passed that emitted a soft glow across the stone street. The windows of restaurants and coffee houses cast their own light on to the square, while the mage-carved equivalent of large townhouses occupied the south face. Four Mastsrunners in green sashes had patrolled the street they'd come here by, but the guards of the Shard's Rest were mages in black robes, she could sense the magic coming off them. They wore thin strips of three colours down one side of their robe, leaving Sitain to wonder if that was a designation of ability or guild allegiance.

The guards were alert but not hostile as the group approached and Teshen stepped forward. He spoke a volley of words in the local dialect and Sitain could catch none of it, nor the guard's growled response. The man was a burly white thug with a full sandy beard, while his younger comrade was a black-skinned youth with green eyes and quite startling eyebrows.

'Your powers,' Teshen translated. 'You need to prove them before you get in.'

Immediately a swirl of cold wisps appeared around Lastani's hands and the man grunted, nodding. Sitain followed suit, sluggish grey trails following her fingers as she embraced her power and waved her hand left and right, while Atieno merely sniffed.

'Tell him I'm tempest.'

When Teshen did so, the man's eyes widened a fraction and he gave another grunt before he offered a small bow and lifted the latch of the door.

'Here's where we part company,' Teshen said as the door was opened and the guards gestured inside. 'I'll be waiting out here for you. No non-mages in the building unless we're specifically invited.'

'But we don't speak the language!' Lastani protested.

'They'll speak Parthish, lots of 'em anyway. You'll do fine.'

Lastani frowned but said nothing more as Atieno stepped inside. He peered around at the entrance hall within as Sitain followed and the young academic had little choice but to follow. Once inside, the door was smartly closed behind them, but by then Sitain was caught up in the opulence of the hall.

Tall mirrors hung on every available wall, casting a dizzying array of reflections into the far distance. The doors and ceiling bore intricate spiderweb scrollwork in gold leaf and overlapping woven rugs covered the floor, while a polished mahogany table stood at the centre bearing some sort of ornate glasswork. The grand double doors ahead were flanked by polished black statues of Insar and Catrac, also picked out in gold.

'The Court of the Shard, I assume,' Lastani murmured, looking forward. 'A seat for every mage in the city, so my teacher, Mistress Ishienne, used to say.'

Before Sitain could reply, a tall white man in a formal coat stepped out of one doorway and spoke to them in the local language. White-haired and moustached, he blinked at the blank looks he received and took in their appearance before smoothly continuing in richly accented Parthish.

'My apologies, I had thought you guild members, but I see you are new to our city.'

Lastani glanced for a moment at Atieno and nodded. 'We are visitors, we seek an audience with the Shard.'

The twitch of the man's whiskered cheek made Sitain expect him to burst out laughing in their faces, but instead he merely gave a bow.

'I am afraid the Shard is most busy, she is unavailable.'

'I understand,' Sitain said, warming to her role. 'We wish to petition her or a deputy of hers perhaps. My name is Lastani Ufre.'

'I, ah, I'm afraid I do not know that name.'

'If the Shard does not, I believe she soon will.' Lastani took a step closer to the man, her voice lowering. 'News of events in Jarrazir have reached the Mage Islands?'

'Events? We, ah, have heard some fanciful rumours, it is true.'

'I am here to provide the Shard with a first-hand account, information she will not hear through her sources there.'

'And your petition?'

'Access to her libraries and records, should she be satisfied with the account I provide. I am confident she will feel she profits from the exchange.'

The man cocked his head at her. 'What do you seek?'

'Answers – if I find them, I will share them with the Shard but I would not waste her time with conjecture and half-formed thoughts in advance.'

There was a long pause while he considered her words. 'Very well, I shall inform the Shard of your offer. Where do you lodge?'

'I . . .' Lastani's cheeks pinked. 'I cannot pronounce the name. May we perhaps return here tomorrow instead to hear her decision?'

'As you wish,' the man said, adding somewhat gnomically, 'privacy is something many mages in this city wish for. My name is Tegir, Fen Oe Tegir. I am one of the Shard's stewards and advisers. Ask for me when you return.'

Lastani bowed. 'Thank you, we shall return tomorrow.'

Sitain blinked. 'What, that's it?' she whispered to Atieno.

He gave her shoulder a shove. 'Aye, it is. Time to go.'

'But—'

'Move,' Atieno said firmly. 'We gave our message, but you don't hurry the senior mage of the city.'

'I could have stayed with the others and be well into my second drink by now.'

'But you chose a higher calling,' the older man said, smiling down at her. 'The path of enlightenment and civilisation.'

'I'm regretting it now.'

'We both are.' Atieno sighed. 'Come on.'

Chapter 7

Of all things, it was the whip of wings that started memories cascading through Teshen's mind. He'd steeled himself against the more obvious aspects of returning home; the deep croaks of the larger tysarn, the warm, familiar scent of the lagoon or the chatter of voices in his mother tongue. But a young tysarn hunting had blindsided him all the same. The distinctive zip of its wings as it chased a midge, like a razor being sharpened, had instantly dragged him back through the years.

He walked without seeing, leading the mages through Auferno's shadow-wrapped streets as the past descended like dusk. He'd never seen the tysarn that night, only caught the blur of movement that he'd first thought was a dart. Somehow he'd frozen – not dived aside or even flinched. After years of training and a lifetime of brawling in these stone streets, he had simply done nothing.

It had been late in the evening by then. Both his knives were bloodied – it had been no game that day. What had played out on the streets of Vi No Le had been swift and savagely real. He had seen friends cut down, some butchered without mercy, while he in turn had killed plenty. And in that one long moment he had thought he was already dead.

It was only the lack of movement that had saved him. Looking back he could see that. He'd surprised her by not reacting, by not pulling the weapons he had left and attacking while she was vulnerable. They stood on the upper level of the Sath Eil, a corkscrewed warren of cramped housing and tunnels where it was near impossible to be pursued.

'Why?' Sanshir had asked after hauling herself over the ledge.

She'd been tired after it all, chin-length hair pinned back and soaked in sweat. He remembered the blood on her tunic, a flash of alarm for her despite everything. Then he realised it was arterial spray running across her shoulder, her kill not her injury, for all there were deep scores in one leather shoulder-patch.

'You know why.'

Sanshir had shaken her head. 'That's a stupid reason – I can't accept it.'

'It's all I've got.'

'You threw away everything for that?' she'd spat, more contemptuous than furious. 'You threw away us?'

'I gambled,' he had said simply. It had been true. Not a good reason, but the real one. Life had been a gamble then. A high-wire walk in the wind, every step a challenge he couldn't refuse.

Quick as a flash she had her crossbow levelled, the light-weight weapon tipped with red. 'You. Fucking. Gambled,' she repeated in a level tone.

The lack of anger had chilled him. Few had known her as well as Teshen, or rather the man Teshen had been before he took that name. He felt the heat of rage coiling inside her, but she'd always been the controlled one of the pair.

'You wouldn't have joined us.'

'How long did it take you to make up your mind? To betray all of us?'

Sanshir had paused just a fraction, but Teshen had known it wasn't the 'us' that really mattered in this. The game was a game, politics little more in his book. There had been only one thing that had given him pause and even then, it hadn't been enough.

'To betray me?'

He bowed his head briefly. '*Long enough.*'

'*Would you have killed me yourself, if it came down to it?*'

'*No.*'

She had been so beautiful in that moment. Proud and strong; mistress of them all, with a dark gleam in her eye. It was how he remembered her, that very last sight. The day she fulfilled all the promise within her and he'd failed to.

Despite the blood and the bruises, the stink of sweat and dirt, and all he'd thrown away. The hours and days and weeks they had spent together – desperate and brutal and tender too. Neither held back when they sparred. No one else in their crew could match the ferocity they unleashed upon each other.

Even before they had become lovers, long before, they had been a pairing of some sort. There had been a connection between them that went beyond respect. Before they had first fought, each had recognised something in the other just by the way they stood. Young Mastrunners grew up assessing poise and balance as well as anyone. The good ones could read their opponents in a heartbeat, but it had never been about rivalry between Teshen and Sanshir. Never anything so mundane.

'*The others are dead. If Kelerris isn't already, he won't make it out of the city.*'

'*I know. It's over.*'

She lowered the crossbow and let it fall to the ground. Teshen still hadn't drawn any weapons and for a moment they stood facing each other, hands empty but poised at their knife handles.

'*Go then. You can make it alone.*'

Teshen watched the tiny flickers of emotion on her face. Part of him had wondered if it would come to blood between them, if what he'd done might have finally pushed them over that cliff edge. But in that hush of breath while the skyriver shone down upon them, he knew that would never be.

They had nothing to prove to each other. He'd turned his back on her, but perhaps it had always been a duel. One would win, the other lose and there would never have been another outcome. Perhaps that was why he'd chosen this path, even, recognising one day it would come anyway.

The faction he'd backed had meant far less to him than she did, but it was done and neither could see any value in going to the death. There was no returning from this. He'd lost and always would have.

'Goodbye.'

As dusk turned to dark, Lynx followed a narrow sloped path down to the lagoon's edge. The whole inner shore was dotted with tiny mage-created islands that resembled smallholdings. Most had a low perimeter wall and contained narrow rows of crops, bushes or fruit trees. Everything about them was small, regulated and neat, in contrast to the chaotic tangle of city behind them. With fertile ground at a premium, even with the abilities of the city's mages, there clearly was no space for disorder if the people were to be fed.

The scents of seawater, flowers and earth mingled strangely with spices and meat cooking nearby, but Lynx was fast growing used to it. Much of the stink and refuse of a normal city was washed away or carried by wallowing barges across the channel to dump in the water around the spice islands. Apparently it kept the insects breeding in their millions there and those fed the young tysarn that helped fertilise the islands themselves.

Out on an oval jetty, overlooking one of the wider channels between the crop islands, was a ramshackle tavern of sorts. A battered wooden hut served wine to tables placed wherever there was room all across the jetty. The patrons themselves looked fairly well-to-do and as Lynx secured a cup of surprisingly good wine he heard talk in three or four languages. Bulbous white paper lanterns hung on poles all around and he could see the small tysarn darting through the pool of light as they hunted.

'You speak Parthish?' Lynx asked the woman at the bar once she'd finished dealing with a customer.

She looked like she had Hanese blood in her, Lynx thought; short and round, with pale skin and long, lustrous black hair. The notion reminded him that he actually had no idea what they thought of his people round here. The armies of So Han had not invaded or come anywhere near this way during their campaign of conquest, but were hardly famed for making friends wherever they went.

'Of course, this is a place for merchants. A little Hanese too, if you like?'

Lynx shook his head and checked around again, feeling uncomfortable. He realised one further aspect of the bar – or tavern or whatever the hells they would call it here – was that it was separated from the rest of the city. Most of the walls here might be made of stone, but echoes carried and there might be rooms above and below. Confidential business might actually be better served out in the open, where you could see the face of every person within earshot.

'I was asked to leave a message here.'

'That is a service we provide.'

'Good. The message is for the lesser cousin, if that means anything to you?'

'It does,' she said gravely, blinking at Lynx with long, dark lashes.

'Glad it does for one of us,' he muttered. 'Well then, tell this lesser cousin, his package has arrived. He can collect it tomorrow morning.'

'Very well, I shall inform him, ah – unless you would like to tell him so yourself?'

'He's here?'

'Indeed.'

Lynx shrugged. 'Not much point, I'm just the messenger.'

'Very well.'

He tipped the remaining wine down his throat, gave the patrons seated all around a cursory look, and nodded to the bartender. Making his way back up the slope again, Lynx felt eyes watching him all the way and had to fight the urge to hurry. Returning to shore he set off down a narrow street and rounded a corner, heading for an oddly domed tavern a hundred yards off.

There were several turns in the road and Aben lingered at one of those. He nodded as Lynx passed and continued on to the tavern. The sign outside rather grandly called it the Old Court. From the uneven shape of its dome, Lynx could see why the locals referred to it as the Odd Egg.

Inside he found Toil, nestled in a dark corner of the upper level. The tavern had a round central bar, at the back of which a pair of wrought-iron staircases curled up to the mezzanine. It was a narrow strip that ran around the inside of the dome, cramped if you were tall and barely three yards wide. An ornate iron railing around the inner edge meant they had a fine view of the drinkers below. Lynx sat and helped himself to a drink before surreptitiously following Toil's gaze.

'That lot our winners then?'

'They'll do. Lots of booze already down them, lots of talk and dick-measuring.'

'We'll outnumber them.'

'I'll only fetch a dozen Cards, we wouldn't want to frighten them off. So long as we've got Deern to start the fight and Reft to end it, it'll serve.'

'Who are they?'

She wrinkled her nose. 'They're speaking more languages than I know, so it's hard to say. Badge looks like a bird, probably a raven or something. It's pretty bad though so I'm calling them the Ugly Sparrows.'

'Who needs Deern? Just go and introduce yourself.'

'Oh, you know I don't like to get caught up in trouble.' Toil winked at him. 'That's what I pay you people for.'

Lynx leaned on the table and took a longer look at the mercenaries below. 'Are those tattoos?' he said.

They were from somewhere on the Callais Sea he guessed; tanned or dark skin and only a few among the fifteen-odd men and women were carrying pistols. A lean and muscled lot though, Lynx realised. They favoured sleeveless shirts to display faintly luminescent markings around their biceps and forearms in addition to torcs and bracelets. Most also wore several rings at least, not the most practical thing in combat but they would add a nasty edge to any punch.

'It must be some sort of mage or alchemical thing,' Toil agreed. 'I've not seen it before, but I think we might want to find out, no? In case we start showing our own colours?'

'Couple of big bastards down there,' Lynx said. 'Could get nasty.'

'Oh sure, because the Cards are a cuddly little family who all just want to get along. I could name half a dozen who'll do it for a laugh. Probably as many who just haven't kicked anyone in the nuts for a few days and miss the feeling.'

'That's not what I'm saying.'

'I know – but you're mercenaries. I pay you to fight when I say, that's literally your job. Some of you are proper soldier types, I know, others are pure bastards who like to spit blood once in a while. I've got a use for both. I say this fight is worth having and so it is. You want to give me odds on them not picking a fight tonight anyway?'

Lynx scowled. 'Aye, I know.'

'Right then.' She stood. 'You and Aben wait here while I go round up a few happy volunteers.'

'It ain't that I don't like it round here!' Deern insisted, gesturing around the room with his tankard. 'Weather's nice an' all, everyone's free with their affel . . . affcec, affections. Thass ma whole point!'

Varain's battered face screwed up in thought. 'Eh?'

'What?'

'There was a point?'

'Dunno.' Deern paused, took a long drink and then threw his arms up, flinging most of what was left over his shoulder. 'Yeah! Tha wassit, is too nice. Don't get proper fighters growin' up round here. Ya need mud an' cold an' starvatin' to make real soldiers outa folk. Here, they's too busy screwin' an' drinkin' in the sunshine. Can't blame 'em mind, but . . . Eh? Yeah?'

He squinted over his shoulder where a man glowered at him, a trail of beer running down his face. 'Watch your beer,' the man said in broken Parthish, before adding a few extra words in his own language.

'Easy there, fella,' Deern protested. 'Night's a bit young fer that talk, me old asazhka.'

The other mercenary paused. Like most of the Cards he was a fair bit bigger than Deern. He ran one hand over his head and swept off the now-damp scarf that covered it, exposing the cropped stubble of scalp.

'Vehlom,' he said after wiping his face. He raised his own drink and Deern cracked his tankard against it.

'Here's one in yer eye,' Deern said to the man, reaching out and brushing another drop of beer from the side of his head. 'And anywhere else you fancy,' he muttered as he headed back to the tables occupied by the Cards.

Without a glance back, he and Varain deposited the latest

round of beers, courtesy of Toil's purse, to a smattering of cheers from the assembled Cards.

'That looked all a bit friendly,' Anatin said as he sat down. 'Little too friendly, frankly. We're not here for that, remember?' he added with a sideways glance at Reft. The big man didn't react, just took another drink as he watched Deern.

'Pah – too early ta get cold-cocked,' Deern said with a shrug and a wink at Reft. 'Best to get 'em all hot first, eh?'

'Fuck off – you just bottled it,' Aben laughed.

'Like shit I did!' Deern said, keeping one ear open for the buzz of chat at the tables behind them. 'I got a plan, but it's far too early.'

'A plan? It's a fucking fight,' Aben hissed. 'How hard is that to start?'

'Hey, there's a gods-damned art to a proper bar fight,' Deern scoffed. 'I don't lecture you about . . . ah, whatever the deepest black Toil gets you to do, sittin' on folk most likely – you don't try and teach me how to start fights. I always say a good fight is a lot like a good hard fuck.'

'Oh yeah, say that a lot do you?'

Anatin cackled from the end of the table. 'To be fair, he really bloody does,' the commander laughed. 'With more detail than anyone'd like.'

Anatin had taken off most of his jewellery, just in case he got caught up in things, but with only one hand he wasn't planning on wading in once Deern worked his magic. There were a dozen of the Cards there, fewer than the Ugly Sparrows, but Toil, Lynx, Safir, Kas and Sitain sat on the mezzanine above. Four as reinforcements, one to put the whole room out if things turned bad.

'Catch 'em too early an' it'll be over in one quick tussle,' Deern explained. 'Too late in the evening an' things go all weak and limp. Got to get the blood flowing, get yer bits all pumped up an' ready while the booze dulls the senses an' the sense.'

'What are we talking about again?' Estal asked, cheeks pink. 'Fuck it, I'm up for either now! Where'd Safir go?'

'Please tell me you didn't bring any o' those grenades you picked up on the way here,' Anatin said, wincing at the thought.

'Left 'em behind,' Estal confirmed with mock sadness. 'I feel all naked now.'

Anatin snickered. 'Sorry, love, but I don't reckon that'll be enough to start a fight. Mebbe a panic?'

Estal made an obscene gesture and knocked back her drink. 'The expert suggests more beer,' she said. 'I best follow orders.'

The next round came and went with great enthusiasm. Even the more quietly dedicated drinkers were happy to act as obnoxiously loud arseholes for the evening and with every drink Deern felt a tingle of anticipation building. It was all he could do not to drag Reft off and out of sight for a few minutes, but he had finally been given a job he was perfectly suited to. He intended to make it part of the company's legend.

That in itself was enough to let him ignore who was the one giving him that job. No doubt Toil was a bitch of the highest order, Deern was often the first to suggest that. He had more than a little to fear from her too. She was the only one to figure out why the Charnelers had been after them from the outset in Grasiel – but at the same time she was *his* sort of bitch. No apologies, no stepping back, no handwringing like that fat cockscraper beside her, just a 'fuck you' to the world if it didn't fall into line.

Deern grinned and knocked back another mouthful of beer. He could respect that much at least.

I ain't ruling out killing her still, he admitted to himself, *but not this week I reckon. Not till she's finished paying so well.*

Chapter 8

Reft watches. All around him there is noise and movement, jostling and shouting. The beer is flowing, the tankards emptying and are replaced at a determined pace. Reft is a big man – he drinks his share and more besides, but every night in the pub starts this way. It hits the others faster than him and while he's with them, he's also apart – too big to ignore, too huge to throw his weight around.

He's a silent man and used to being separate from the rest. Even as a child, it had been that way. Large from a young age, silent his entire life, how else could it have been? In the Cards they did not joke about him in the way his peers had – there was no fear in their words, no malice. This acceptance means much to Reft, even if he cannot join in fully.

He ignores the stories of his prowess that inevitably are told around newcomers. His size demands that some explanation of his presence be given as the legends of the company are recast once again. All the while the voices grow steadily louder, the gestures more expansive. Their cheeks become flushed, movements less steady. He can feel the warmth in his belly as the booze takes hold, but the beast awakens slowly and all around him it is stirring. Varain and Deern lead the others in a dance, their curse words growing louder and sharper as the hours tick by.

Estal and Braqe are more than willing to snap back, while

Anatin's sharp tongue flickers like a snake's, his cruel wit restlessly drifting. The others are all boisterous too. A tide of laughter and anger flows over them, but Reft can see Deern's hand steering it all. There is a deft touch – no one is singled out, no one is ignored but Reft himself.

The attractive man whom Deern had first teased is careful not to look over as much as his friends. Only once did he catch Reft's eye, a brief and guilty glance that makes Reft wonder, but now he is drinking harder than the rest.

The Ugly Sparrows, as Anatin has insisted on referring to them once or twice, do not wish to be goaded. All the same Reft can see it happening, inch by inch. They will not allow themselves to be chased from the tavern, pride dictates they last as long as the newcomers. On such fertile ground, Reft knows what crop Deern will reap. His partner knows the many flavours of anger intimately, as though he could read it in subtle shades of a person's aura.

Flashes of annoyance spark around the Sparrows and are smothered, but only just. There is no single moment that has forced them over the edge, not yet. Reft can sense Deern waiting, tasting the air, enjoying that shiver of anticipation and teasing it out a little longer. Reft is not a peaceful man. He is normally placid, though, and it comes as a surprise to most when he does stir to violence.

More people come into the tavern. Locals in plain head-scarves, wary at the noise but pointedly ignoring it. They have been fetched by the owner, Reft guesses, and arrive in groups of four or five. Ten, then closer to twenty of them. Green sashes around their waists, cudgels hanging from their belts.

A local Masts crew, come to play watchmen in their district just as Teshen had predicted. Reft tries not to smile at this. The tavern is large. With just the mercenaries there would be too much space for a proper fight. Too much room to swing a chair or think about drawing a mage-gun. Or swing a cudgel for that matter.

The remaining locals have cleared out. They can sense the danger in the air and the mercenaries have the place to themselves. Too much space, too much time to think again. But with the Masts crew there is a press. When Deern decides to take the first swing – or more likely, receive the first swing – there'll be little room for anything full-blooded. Instead there will be just chaos and grappling, men and women barging each other and heads and elbows more use than any weapon.

Anatin announces a game of Tashot. Reft sees almost relief on the faces of the older Sparrows. Cards means a focus, a contained circle of concentration – or it would in most circumstances. Anatin is as much a master at this as Deern and his words can be as inventive as insulting. Some people can ignore a stranger's words, others can shrug off the laughter those words might provoke, but few are immune to both.

Anatin roundly curses the manhood of all those men who refuse to join him in a game. It takes him a while but he is an orator of no modest skill when the beer is flowing. He mostly insults Cards, but some of the Masts crew and the Sparrows are still left with pinker cheeks than before. He takes a small diversion to insult the womanhood of some of the women present too – a colourful and highly specific description that paints its own picture.

Reft understands this only at a remove. He's never taken enough interest in the subject to fully picture women in all their apparent glory, but its effect is startling. For a moment the voices falter. Only Varain and Deern are so immune to Anatin's verbosity that they chuckle their way through it. Even the men of the Cards are briefly taken aback. Even the serving staff who are keeping their heads down all stop and look.

The quiet is broken by a roar from Braqe that Reft knows is not feigned. Still, she remembers the job well enough to toss her tankard aside before hurling herself at Anatin. The tankard casts a neat arc of beer through the air before it hits a Sparrow. Anatin howls with laughter as Varain restrains Braqe. Braqe kicks wildly behind her as she struggles and catches one of the Masts crew in what appears to be a genuine accident.

What she lacks in vocabulary, Braqe makes up for in heartfelt rage. She curses Anatin then Varain, yelling things that no man wants to hear and Deern isn't the only one jeering her. More beer is thrown. Most of it misses and there's a growl from the Sparrows not far behind.

Braqe almost ruins the moment by rounding on one man as Varain lets her go, shouting with such vehemence that the Sparrow stops in his tracks. Fortunately she calls him a cunt in the next breath.

Deern swoops in to the rescue, a masterful touch Reft feels. By then he has established himself as the loudest mouth in the room, the one they all know because his name's been used most often. There's a mocking grin on Deern's faces as he smooths ruffled feathers and drags Braqe from the stranger's grip.

Reft sees the other Sparrows move closer, the Masts crew too – all drawn to this flashpoint by some inexorable force. Yet somehow Deern manages to calm things, to quieten voices as everyone leaves their seat and there's a press of bodies in the centre of the room.

All eyes are on Deern as he hands the Sparrow two tankards of beer as recompense. He makes sure the man's hands are full and unable to grab Braqe again. He makes sure the room is near silent as Deern turns away, one had pressed against Braqe's chest to keep her still. There is a twinkle in his eye as the quiet allows him to be heard all the more clearly.

'*Cunt.*'

The anger is still building on the Sparrow's face when Braqe punches him. She's a career merc, but not the biggest and knows not to break her hand when she's hitting someone. The Sparrow isn't felled. Instead he staggers back, arms thrown up and hands full of beer that flies behind him. Reft watches and a smile spreads across his faces as the remaining Sparrows surge forward. One of the biggest Cards there, Darm, puts his shoulder into the closest Sparrow and drives her across the others. Half of them trip, but there are more coming.

Deern howls with laughter and hurls himself into the mass, grabbing hold of one man and hauling him round. Estal and Layir follow him while Anatin chucks his tankard to encourage the others. Then the rest of the Cards pile in. The Masts crew charge too, but the Sparrows are full of fire and fury now. There's no space for sense in their heads and a chair sends the first of the crew sprawling across a table. The locals don't even pause. They lay into both sets of mercs with utter abandon and the tavern descends into a magnificent broiling mess of bodies and shouting.

One man steps towards the Cards' table, seeking some space to raise his cudgel. Reft frowns and reaches forward. Cudgels are not in the spirit of fun. When the man makes to hammer it against Haphori's skull, he wrenches his shoulder hauling on a stick that does not move. The man yelps in pain, the sound lost in the bedlam, and Reft tosses the stick away. The man finally sees who's taken his cudgel and gasps as he takes in the size of Reft, but before he can recover his wits Reft shoves the table. It knocks him back into the fray where he collides with a Sparrow and the two fall, tangled about each other.

Even Anatin has thrown himself into the fray now. The attractive Sparrow has him by the collar, dragging him in a circle to keep Anatin off balance and punching him in the gut at every opportunity. The man catches a stray elbow from one of his own and Anatin, ever the opportunist, plants a knee right between the Sparrow's legs.

Reft heaves a regretful sigh as the man's legs wobble. Haphori barges into Anatin before the commander can damage Reft's hopes entirely however, locked in a grapple with some local woman. He's stronger but she's slamming her knee into his side and he's unable to do much about it. The sweat's pouring from his face, the thick hair of his eyebrows, beard and neck glistening in the lamplight.

'*Reft!*' he hears Deern yell. '*Dammit, what are you doing?*'

His partner's pale face pops briefly out of the crowd. There's blood smeared around his mouth and his cheek is purpled, but Reft can tell Deern's enjoying himself. Two Sparrows hang on to him like dogs tugging on a piece of meat, getting in each other's way more than anything else. Reft raises his drink at Deern and the smaller man ducks, hooking one of his assailant's legs.

The man tumbles and Deern falls on top of him, slamming an elbow into his neck as he falls. The other, a woman, sprawls across Deern only to have him grab a fistful of loose hair. He uses that to push himself up to his knees as he drives her face into the floor. There he pauses for a moment and Reft tenses. He sees the dark thoughts that are crossing Deern's mind, but then Deern releases her head and hops up.

Deern gives the woman a perfunctory kick on the ribs and then he snags a chair, drawing it around as he surveys the brawl before him. There are Cards everywhere. Reft sees that Deern can't take a swing without likely hitting one, but still Deern considers it. Then he just shoves it forward to trip one Mastrunner throwing a punch at the Sparrow he'd been tussling with.

The brawl ebbs and flows. For a moment Reft thinks he's seen the bald head of Brols in the centre of it. Then the bloody smile in a freckled face becomes another man's, someone Reft doesn't know, and Brols is dead once more, his body left to quietly rot in the Labyrinth of Jarrazir. He takes another drink and ponders the thought as Estal drags a man's arm from around Layir's throat. She snaps a finger or two by the shriek that pierces the hubbub. In some strange maternal moment, Estal plants a big kiss on the cheek of her man's adopted son. In the next they part company and return to the fight.

Reft nods approvingly at the sight. Death, life, fighting and fucking; all inextricably bound together in this world. A local has Darm by his red hair, dragging him back before landing a thunderous punch that lays the big man out. Just behind them Crais is busily and methodically smearing a Sparrow's nose across his face.

From somewhere over the noise Reft hears Deern yell again. *'Shift yourself! The fuck're you waiting for?'*

The voice is drowned out by the wordless yells and noises of the brawl.

More people slip, more people fall or are laid out. The blood's flowing now, they're all bloody and battered. Clothes are torn, headscarves dislodged and trodden into the dirt and blood. The attractive man is still on his feet, Reft notes, but he's looking woozy. Anything more than fending off stray blows is beyond him now. The Cards are certainly not winning; Darm is out cold, Crais and Burnel down too from what Reft can see. Anatin's slumped back in a seat, exhausted and unable to fight for long at his age.

Varain's too stupid to know when he should go down and drinks so much he can't feel pain, so he's still trading blows. Deern's bloodied grin darts in and out of view still, while Braqe's basic level of anger can never be quenched. Half the furniture in the room is smashed. There's blood and staggering figures everywhere. Reft is pretty sure Toil will be happy that her instructions have been carried out.

He finishes his drink and pushes himself upright. With one hand Reft lifts the table and sets it on end to give him a clear path. The nearest Sparrow sees this and is gawping as he's backhanded across the room. Reft surveys the heedless mass of people still fighting. He's almost a head taller than any of them. With slow, deliberate movements he rolls his shoulders and flexes his hands. His great muscles tingle slightly as he's been sitting for an hour or more, but in moments the feeling fades.

Reft grins, gold canines flashing in the light. He steps forward and bunches his fists. The time for watching is over.

Interlude 2
(now)

Outside a different bar, four days after Reft's dramatic inter-vention, Teshen felt the cool night air like a slap across the face. He blinked and felt the fog of beer start to fade from his head. Behind him the sounds of the bar continued; Deern's grating laugh, Kas's musical laughter, Varain's gravelly voice raised in song.

The sky was a blaze of stars, a great glittering whorl overlaid by the thin blade of the skyriver. Lower on the eastern sky, the moon was almost full and startlingly bright. This close to the equator, the skyriver cast no more light than the moon, but the two together provided more than enough to see by.

'You can come out now,' Teshen called softly. 'I can see you.'

There was a long moment of silence in which, distantly, there came the peal of a bell. The sound provoked a pang in his heart and quickened his blood.

'Do you feel it still?' she replied from the darkness away to his right.

'Not dead yet.'

The bell was the signal for a game of Masts. They often took place at night if the moon was full, fewer citizens around to get in the way. Some of his greatest moments in this city had been under the moonlight, feats witnessed by one other at best, but worthy memories all the same.

'One last game?'

Teshen gave a snort. 'That's all behind me now.'

'True, you've put on weight.'

'I've learned how to enjoy life. Turns out that's one of the side-effects.'

She came out into the moonlight, darkness smoothing out the faint lines around her eyes and masking the grey in her hair. The effect was as good as a punch.

Teshen gave her a small bow. 'Kaboto Sanshir,' he said in greeting.

'That must have hurt to say.'

'Not so much. Like I said, I've learned to enjoy life a little more. And I'm mindful of the last time we met. You won, I lost. I'm old enough to honour that.' He glanced to the side. 'Aren't your friends going to come out to say hello?'

'So this is the Bloody Pauper?' answered a voice from the shadows.

Six heads popped into view and a tall man stepped forward. He was half a head bigger than Teshen, with parallel scars down his cheek. Dark skin and fine features announced a south-shore heritage, but his accent and the stray braid of hair creeping out from his black headscarf were all Vi No Le.

'Once, perhaps,' Teshen said. 'No longer. I'm just Teshen now. The Bloody Pauper is dead.'

'Unlike the death sentence he left behind. That's still got life in it.'

'I'm careless.' Teshen looked Sanshir in the eye. 'I left a few things behind.'

The man unsheathed his long knives. 'This one's been waiting for you.'

Teshen snorted. 'Your new First Blade, Sanshir? Times must be tough.'

The man took a step forward, but Sanshir raised a hand. 'Calm yourself, Bolereis. Now isn't the time to test your blades.'

Bolereis gave a snort. 'Whatever his reputation, it's long behind him now.'

'He's not so far gone he can't draw that mage-pistol at his side,' she pointed out. 'And the man I used to know was always ready for trouble. It's likely a spark-bolt in there.'

'Still sharp I see,' said Teshen, who'd totally forgotten he was wearing the gun until he got outside, and he certainly hadn't remembered to swap out the icer.

'Sharper still now,' she corrected.

'And a blunt instrument to hand when needed,' Teshen said, nodding at Bolereis. 'We all have our roles in this life, I suppose.'

'And what's yours?' Sanshir said as the tall man growled.

'A humble mercenary, nothing more.'

'Humble?'

'Most of the time.' Teshen grinned. 'Compared to the rest, certainly.'

'Hired by whom?'

He sighed. 'You know already, our job's finished. Why ask questions you're not going to believe the answers to?'

'Because truth hides in the strangest places.'

'Aye well, truth means nothing to an enemy, if we're swapping empty sayings.'

She cocked her head at him. 'Is that how you see me?'

'Nah. Your crew, mebbe, but never you. I can't say more'n Anatin did back there, though. We've no employer from these parts, just a standing contract from elsewhere that doesn't affect any o' the Mage Islands or the kabats.'

'He's lying.'

Teshen turned to Bolereis. 'Back in my day, First Blades weren't so chatty. The grown-ups are talking now, so button it until your mistress calls.'

The man actually drew a knife at that, but Teshen only laughed and slipped a hand around his pistol's grip.

Well, look at that, he thought as Sanshir forestalled Bolereis with an angry wave of the hand. *Turns out I do care who's First Blade after all. I'd gladly kill this knife-spanker given the chance. Death by nostalgia, that's a nasty way to go.*

'Like I said to your commander, it's time to leave the Islands.'

Teshen shook his head. 'Not so simple as that.'

'What then?'

'None of your business.' He took a breath. 'San, this is me, remember? Not some fool come to visit. Vi No Le hasn't changed so much a crew of forty could tip the balance against you. The Siym were ripe for the taking, everyone knew it. The Jo-Sarl family falling to an outside force, though? Not so much.'

Even as he spoke, he could see the memories in her eyes. The day he'd attempted just that, supporting a cousin of the Jo-Sarls in a coup.

'A man of ambition might try it,' Sanshir said. 'A commander of no small opinion of himself might, especially when he's got mages in his company.'

'Making last night just a pretext for being here? Mercs like to live long enough to get paid, they're not fanatics.'

'Mercenaries are easily led.'

'Not by me.' Teshen felt his jaw tighten as he spoke. 'I ain't in command, I'm not even Anatin's second. You were there the night I found out I wasn't the best at giving the orders.'

She inclined her head as he felt a pang in his gut, shameful memories welling up fast. He thought he'd done his best, but it hadn't been anything like enough back then. Things went south mostly because of Sanshir and the kaboto of the day, but enough time had passed since then. Teshen no longer kidded himself about his own failings.

'I was there,' Sanshir said. 'I remember that day as well as you.'

Without warning she turned and walked away. Her crew went to follow her, Bolereis last to go. The tall man fixed Teshen with a crooked grin and pointed at him with his knife.

'You're full of shit, old man, now and back then. Remember my face, I'll be there to end you when the time comes. By my reckoning, it's coming soon.'

Teshen looked the man in the eye. He was younger, but not so young he wouldn't remember that day. Might even have been a novice in training when it all went down, dreaming of Masts glory then finding blood all over the streets.

'Don't worry,' Teshen said. 'I'll remember your face.'

Chapter 9
(four days earlier)

Temples were not by and large a place Lynx spent much time. He didn't have a lot to say to the gods under any circumstances and with a hangover they became even less enticing a prospect. The fact that this one served food was a big point in its favour, he had to admit, but for some reason the bastards hadn't gone so far as to include coffee.

The morning was unexpectedly, insultingly beautiful. A brilliant blue, cloudless sky was marked only by the pale halo of the skyriver. Below it the lagoon sparkled with sunlight. The breeze was a soft caress on his cheek, enough only to lift the tang of salt water and carry the sweet, earthy scents of the spice islands. It was early still and the morning progressed calmly around Lynx while he slouched at a wooden table in the pillared courtyard of the Water Temple.

Before him was a now half-empty bowl of deep-fried dough sticks that had been sprinkled in sugar, beside an untouched plate of raw fish in lime juice. There was only thin tea to drink and he'd received startled looks when he asked for bacon, but slowly the horror of the early hour was fading from Lynx's mind.

Protruding out from the shore, the Water Temple occupied one of the few small, mage-built islands that were not given over to crops. A shallow causeway connected it to the mainland, one apparently designed to get the ankles wet as you crossed. It was fantastically decorated in honour of Ulfer's watery aspect as god of the seas. The tiled floor bore bright mosaics of huge tysarn amid a host of strange fish and crustaceans, all shaded from the glare of the sun by vines strung across the courtyard.

Only half of the tables were occupied. Lynx and Toil had arrived just as the temple was starting for the day. At first Lynx had assumed his hangover was to blame when Toil had woken him and dragged him from his bed to go to temple. It had taken a burst of blind panic to get him upright, but that'd been just Toil's cruel humour as she asked him to make an honest woman of her.

'Isn't this better than lounging around in bed all morning?' Toil sighed, stretching her arms up to brush her fingers against one trail of vine that had slipped its binds.

'No.'

She laughed and plucked a sugar-stick from the bowl, chomping thoughtfully on it as she looked around the other patrons.

'Just think of the good you're doing,' Toil said after a few moments more.

'No.'

All the same, Lynx glanced towards the small crowd of beggars who had gathered at the temple entrance, some of whom sat on the rocky shore of the island and ate the same food as Lynx and Toil. The temple charged a high price for breakfast to rich locals and hungover foreigners alike, but fed half a dozen for free as a result.

'Doesn't it make you feel just a little good?'

'No.'

'Still feeling delicate?'

'Bugger off.'

Toil smirked. 'How's the fish?'

Lynx gagged a little and said nothing, but that didn't dissuade Toil from removing the dish and helping herself.

'Delicious,' she declared. 'I may get some more.'

Lynx frowned and squinted at one of the beggars being served. 'Is that cornbread? Some sort of pancakes? If there are eggs and no one's told me I might just burn this whole shitting place down.'

'Calm down,' Toil sighed. 'I think they're fried corn cakes. There's no need to shoot anyone, we can order some.'

'Yes.'

'Yes what?'

'Yes I'm going to get some,' Lynx growled and pushed himself to his feet. He lurched a little before finding his balance and staggered over, fumbling at his purse. A combination of aggressive pointing and waving money around secured a stack of the bright yellow discs and Lynx tottered back to the table to discover a stranger seated opposite Toil.

'The fuck's he?'

'Good morning,' the man said in a pleasant voice. 'I hope you don't object if I intrude on your breakfast?'

'Yeah I fucking well . . .' Lynx broke off as Toil kicked him hard on the shin. 'What?'

'You don't mind,' she said.

'Bloody do.'

'Shut up, sit down and eat,' she snapped.

Lynx shut up and sat down. After a glower at both of them he began to eat. The stranger was not a local – Lynx could tell that much from his accent, though he wore a headscarf. Somewhere on Whitesea Sound would be his guess, though the man spoke perfect Parthish.

He was an overweight merchant's clerk-type; a little older than Lynx with pale skin that had caught the sun and small brown eyes. Not a rich, deep brown, more of the runny shit variety. That coupled with the fastidious little pursing of his lips before he spoke and a hangover made Lynx take an instant dislike to him.

Hey, Whitesea Sound? Weren't we meant to meet with someone from there? Oh.

'As I had just intimated to your commander here – my name is Hezhi Voronay. I represent the Whitesea Banking Consortium here in the Mage Islands.'

Lynx let the commander thing slide. For one, he wasn't sure what he was meant to call Toil and for a second, she'd been ordering him around for months anyway. At some point you just had to give up.

'You have been hired to ensure the bank receives what it is entitled to, no more and no less.' Voronay offered a short slip of folded paper. 'Here, I have prepared a brief description of what holdings the contract confers upon the bank.'

'Ain't we a bit beyond contracts here?' Lynx asked.

He received a startled look. 'We are never beyond the terms of contracts,' Voronay said gravely. 'However much we must accept that enforcement often requires alternative means, it is the bank's strict policy to never overstep its bounds.'

'Oh really? What with you banking types being all moral.'

'Morality is irrelevant,' the man said in a chillingly practised way. 'There is no column for morality in a bank's ledgers. We prefer certainty. It may be that we drive a hard bargain, but without the sanctity of what is written down there can be no certainty for either party. Our business will suffer if we gain a reputation for overreaching.'

'Lynx, shush,' Toil warned. 'We're here to do a job and the validity of that job has been confirmed. Their debtor took one shit load of money and is refusing to repay it or turn over the holdings.'

'We regret it has come to more direct means,' Voronay added, 'but this is the Mage Islands and lawyers are not respected here.'

'So who's the lucky winner of our gentle affections?' Toil asked.

'A kabat of Nquet Dam named Fioril Siym. As you will see there,' he said, nodding to the piece of paper, 'she is heavily invested in drugs and spices, holding the title to four islands and importation bonds with several foreign parties. Her goal was to develop an overland route to the states of Whitesea Sound for these mostly lightweight, high-value goods.'

'Does that need lots of money? Surely you just need mules or whatever?' Lynx interjected. He received a pitying look.

'The mules must eat, also drink at safe waterholes. The caravans must not be slaughtered as they travel so there must be treaties with the locals. The carts must also have a road of sorts to travel on, part of which required mages to raise a road through the mangrove forest in order to prevent it disappearing every season. This is a distance of several hundred miles through largely unclaimed territory, a route that would be used by many parties if it could be established as safe.'

'But it wasn't,' Toil stated baldly.

Voronay shook his head. 'Not sufficiently. In another life perhaps you would have been hired to wage war upon a particularly troublesome clan, but the combination of a pest infestation on one island and a drought elsewhere meant the Siym finances took a hit at the worst possible time.'

'How important is Kabat Siym to the rest of the city?'

'Enough that the others will still come to her assistance if there is a fight raging. She's sold what she can quietly to ensure her Masts crews don't abandon her. The other kabats are biding their time until they can pick apart the Holding's assets without a fight. The bulk of her debt is to us and the extent of that is unknown to most of Caldaire. Should there be time to summon other crews you will be hugely outnumbered, but there is a window of opportunity prior to that happening.'

'But you don't want her dead?'

'Merely control of her holdings long enough for our officials to be established.'

'How?' Lynx found himself asking in ghoulish fascination. 'If the other kabats don't want to accept you and we're not there to be garrison?'

Voronay inclined his head to acknowledge the point. 'They are highly pragmatic people, the kabats. Presented with a threat they react accordingly. Presented with a fact they may choose their response. The Siym Holdings will be ours to dispose of as a result of the default – additionally, once the head of the snake is removed, the body remains. Loyalty can either be earned or bought, after all, and a bank is extremely adept at buying things.'

'So you keep on the staff and guards at a better wage, kick out anyone named Siym and bribe the other kabats to accept it. Why not do it all yourself though? All banks have enforcers.'

'We have the Courier Division, it is true, but to muster sufficient forces would leave us vulnerable elsewhere. Additionally, any identification of bank-sanctioned forces makes the actual enforcement harder. Siym is prepared, but cannot live in a state of siege. I am not currently the bank's official representative in the city. That dubious honour falls to another and he is engaged in diplomatic efforts still, while under constant surveillance. The bank has lost patience, however. As a gesture of goodwill to the Consortium, Mistress Toil's employer suggested an elite company suitable to the task.'

'Speaking of whom,' Toil said, standing, 'we should probably go see if they're sober enough to be bailed out of prison.'

Voronay looked startled. 'Prison?'

'All part of a clever ruse,' she said with the full force of her glittering smile. 'Not at all because they're drunken lunatics. Ninety per cent at least. Maybe eighty-five. Will you be joining us on the action itself?'

'I . . . no. I am no soldier. Give me instructions as to when and I will be nearby, ready to enact the more legalistic part of the plan.'

'Time frame?'

'As soon as you are able.'

She nodded and gave Lynx a kick. 'Best we get on surveillance then. You about done with breakfast?'

Lynx smothered his natural instinct to growl and hug the bowls of food to his chest. 'Do I get a choice?'

'Oh, but you wouldn't want to miss out on seeing the others, would you?'

Lynx brightened for a moment then felt a flicker of suspicion. 'Oh gods, they're not going to be naked again are they?'

Toil's bark of laughter echoed briefly around the temple. 'Not at my doing, but I wouldn't put anything past them! Come on, it's time to work.'

Much like its military might, the civil authority of the Mage Islands was a nebulous thing. There was no single state but a collection of financial interests and a sense of cooperation born from centuries past when the islands were a haven for the sea's pirates. As Hezhi Voronay had already reminded Lynx that morning, the law was fitful at best.

Lounging outside the stronghold of Kabat Shen Ategeo, principal kabat of the Auferno district, Lynx reflected that in most circumstances a bar fight would be nothing remarkable here. Laying out most of the tavern, however, including a decent number of Mastrunners sent to quell the trouble, was a little more serious. Do that and clearly someone felt they had to step in.

The stronghold was a large square tower that loomed over the rest of the plaza. A bulky statement of power that overshadowed the shoreline palazzo from which Ategeo ran his textiles empire. When his Mastrunners had arrived it hadn't been to break up a fight and fortunately none of the Cards had pushed their luck. Mage-guns were rare in the islands because of the expense, but the kabats that ruled each district were vastly wealthy. Mage-guns were a good way to make a statement to the lesser kabats, and woe betide any foreign mercenaries who let themselves be made an example of.

When the combatants had been picked over and checked for signs of life, there had been only three Cards really able to stand. One of them was Reft, however, and it had been clear to Lynx that they were arresting the winning side on general principle. It seemed no one was dead, which was a bonus, and most were simply battered and bruised. Dazed, drunk and exhausted, the Cards were carted off to the gaol in Ategeo's tower to sleep it off.

Toil was in the stronghold, attempting to secure their release, but Lynx had decided a quick doze in the sunshine was more his speed. The stink of booze oozing from his pores was already bad enough. A gaol with all the usual accompanying smells and the likelihood of shouting meant he couldn't face going inside right now.

'Gods-in-shards!' called a voice from his right. 'Look at the state o' you!'

Lynx jerked around and immediately regretted it as black flowers burst across his eyes. When they faded the view wasn't much improved by Llaith's grinning face. The Diviner of Tempest was a tall greying white man with disease-scarred cheeks, hardly the most handsome even when he wasn't looking darkly gleeful. Behind him were the elegant figures of Safir and Kas – looking almost perfectly matched but for the decade difference in ages.

'No coffee, no bacon,' Lynx growled.

'None? Broken gods, let's burn the city down.'

'Pretty much the conclusion I've come to.' Lynx squinted at the three of them. 'Why're you here?'

'Figured there might be some walking wounded,' Kas said. 'Plus it's a nice morning and I wanted a walk.'

He blinked at her. There was something strange about Kas, but it took him a long time to work it out. Just as realisation hit, Llaith laughed.

'You've been with us too long, Lynx! Time's come it looks odder that Kas is in a skirt than Safir!'

Kas did a twirl, showing off her firm brown legs in a way that made Lynx blink a few more times. Not to be outdone Safir performed a mock-curtsey, although if Lynx was to be honest the man had better legs than half the women in the company.

'I own skirts,' Kas added. 'Well, one skirt. But we're not often in warm parts so one's enough. Estal's even talking about getting a dress, which I don't hold with unless it's got some bloody pockets, but she's always been dainty.'

Lynx coughed at the idea of stocky, scarred Estal being dainty. When he tried to form proper words, however, they got lost somewhere in his throat.

'Aye,' Llaith said, 'that's pretty much what the rest of us said when Kas started going on about her warm parts. Don't worry, it'll pass.'

'She's not the only one who's dressed up,' Lynx noted at last. Llaith wore a fine new shirt with a bright band around the throat, and a pale blue tunic, elaborately decorated and hanging artfully open.

'Ah yes, the other reason we're here,' Safir added. 'The Mage Islands have no courtesans but no institution of marriage either, so Llaith has pronounced it the best city on Urden. He wants Layir beside him to distract the rich ladies at some fancy gathering.'

'How do you even find out about these things?'

'I avoid pubs where mercs get into fights,' Llaith said with a shrug.

Lynx chuckled. 'Good luck with your plan. I've not seen him today, but I'm pretty sure Layir got more'n a few smacks in the face last night.'

Kas made a dismissive noise. 'Llaith's going to have more of a problem with Brellis, who's decided to adopt Layir as her own private sex toy.'

'True enough.'

Before anyone else could speak there was a ragged cheer from the stronghold. They turned to see the battered face of Deern split into a wide smile as the main door banged open and he was admitted through.

'An adoring crowd waiting to give their heroes a welcome?' he crowed.

'Come to finish what that lot couldn't,' Kas corrected him cheerfully.

At that Deern raised his fists as though ready to box, but Lynx saw the man wince even through his humour. Quickly Deern dropped his hands again, clutching his shoulder and Reft half-swept the man up as he came out of the tower ahead of the rest.

'Bit sore there, Deern?' Llaith asked. 'Did you have an accident?'

'Piss on you,' Deern said through gritted teeth, rubbing his shoulder a few more times before he straightened. 'Didn't even notice it happen neither. Feels like a mule's kicked me.'

As for the rest, there were more than a few swollen and broken faces following along behind. Layir was indeed heavily bruised all down one side of his face, his left eye bloodshot in what little was visible past the swelling.

Haphori had lost a few teeth and couldn't put any real weight on one leg, Toil helping him to walk. Darm's face looked misshapen even ignoring the scarf around his chin and Estal's scarred face was unsmiling and ashen as she clutched her ribs.

'Victors indeed,' Safir muttered as he stepped forward to inspect his adopted son's injuries. Layir winced but smiled as Safir took hold of his head then slapped him on the back.

'You should've seen the other lot,' Layir croaked.

'Hardly seemed fair,' Anatin said, 'keeping Reft in reserve until they're tired. Was pretty sore too, reckon I might be getting too old for this shit.' He straightened all the same and beamed at the others. 'But deepest black, I do love the sight of our beautiful white monster tearing through a bunch o' arseholes!'

Lynx nodded, despite the protests from his head that had found their stride now. It had been quite a sight, Reft wading into the press and felling men and women left and right.

'Llaith,' called Toil. 'Go find a boat to hire.'

'Eh? What for?'

''Cos I say so.'

The look on her face was enough to make it clear she didn't want to debate out in public so Llaith just turned away, heading for a short road beyond which the lagoon's waters sparkled in the distance. Like the shambling dead the battered Cards left the tower and its guards slammed the door behind them.

'You made friends then?' Lynx said, nodding towards the door.

'Yeah, they made it clear how pleased they'd be if this happened again,' Toil confirmed.

'And the boat?'

'Darm and Estal, they could do with seeing a healer. How about you, Layir? How's the eye?'

'Fucking hurts, don't it,' Layir growled.

'You too then.'

'Himbel's back at the tavern,' Lynx pointed out. 'Sitain too.'

'Payl will send 'em on once they're out of bed.'

'On where?'

She gave him a broad smile. 'This is the Mage Islands, they've got proper healers here!'

'Sounds expensive.'

Toil nodded. 'Enough to make me wince, yeah, but I owe 'em as much. Coming?'

Lynx paused. 'If the alternative is to have a hangover around Deern?'

'True. Stupid question.'

Chapter 10

Sitain met the three injured Cards plus Lynx, Toil and Llaith in the bowl-shaped courtyard of a mage guild complex of Nquet Dam. It was located on the spur of the district's smaller, central island where a massive, high-sided stone bridge partly sheltered it from the easterly breeze. Three-quarters of the bowl was mage-carved stone, apartments or offices on four levels above the courtyard floor. As Sitain entered, she turned full around, surprised by the grandeur.

A cloister ran around the courtyard, scalloped pillars bearing engraved prayers all draped in vines that grew from great troughs of earth after every fourth pillar. The open quarter of the bowl had ropes strung between two pillars and the side walls, from which hung an array of flags. Those alternated between green banners that seemed to bear the guild's symbol and a whole range of others. Personal crests, Lynx guessed.

'I assumed this magic was rare,' Lynx commented as Sitain joined them, her eyes bright with anticipation. He pointed to the green-robed mages and novices of the guild, both in the offices that adjoined the courtyard and on the terraces of the upper levels. The men's headscarves and women's shawls were all white with symbols picked out in green, but less decorative than those they'd passed on the way there. 'There's loads of 'em here.'

'There's no healing magic,' Toil explained. 'They're all of various disciplines.'

'Like what? How can you tell?'

'Why would they bother to advertise? Green's the guild colour, that's all anyone needs to know.'

'What then?'

'Earth and stone mages mostly,' Sitain broke in, unable to contain her enthusiasm. 'A few light mages, who're rare enough, and a handful of tempests too. That's for the healing itself though. There'll be night and fire mages here too.'

'But only you came?'

'Atieno didn't want to,' she said with a nod. 'Says he's had the hard sell from a healer guild once before, didn't much care for another.'

'They teach here?'

'Bloody hope so! I ran most o' the way.'

'Well you ain't missed much.' Lynx gestured all around. 'They've been mostly looking at us like we're something the cat sicked up.'

'Are you surprised? Can't you smell those three?' Sitain demanded, pointing at Darm, Estal and Layir.

'Aye, fair point. Mebbe you could do some magic though, wake these shitweasels up a bit?'

As though the mention of magic had been enough, a tiny black woman in a green robe that reached her ankles exited a shuttered room off to Lynx's left and walked over.

'Unerna Toil?' the woman said in an imperious tone to Toil. The Princess of Blood nodded and replied haltingly in the same language.

'We may speak in Parthish, Mistress Toil,' the tiny woman said in a thick accent.

Her black hair had turned white, but she wasn't too far past forty, Lynx suspected, with skin like creased leather and a faint dusting of blue on her eyelids. She held her hands across her belly, cradling one in the other almost protectively.

Toil grinned. 'That's lucky, only other thing I know how to say is "more wine".'

The woman gave the mercenaries a sideways glance. 'You teach this to your friends?'

'Something like that.'

'My name is Olen Siere,' she said before turning to where eight others had gathered, five women and three men of various races that showed just how far the renown of the Mage Islands reached. There was even a Hanese man, something that got both Lynx and Sitain blinking, his features clear to see despite the headscarf. There seemed to be few Hanese in the Mage Islands, unusually few given the direct route between the states, but to find one in a healer guild seemed doubly unlikely.

'My colleagues and I will assist your friends. You have enough money?'

There was a sceptical tone to her voice that Lynx understood. They were clearly mercenaries who'd been hurt in a brawl. That Toil would have the money for healing was in itself unlikely – that she'd waste it on common mercs just as implausible to most. Fresh meat for the companies was rarely difficult to find in any city. Round here mercs could be replaced more easily than the mage-guns they carried.

Toil offered a piece of paper, which Lynx glimpsed enough of to see it was a promissory note from the Oderich Bank – an institution that was largely owned and controlled by the Knights-Defender of Shain. Siere's nose wrinkled with distaste, but she took the note all the same.

'This will have to be verified.'

'Of course, but that won't take long so we can get started, no?' As though to punctuate her point Toil slipped the mage-pistol from her holster and offered it forward. This Siere took also before giving Lynx an enquiring look. He sighed and handed his own gun over, which elicited a curt nod.

'Very well. Do you wish to wait?'

'I want to watch!' Sitain blurted out. 'I . . . I mean, if that's okay?'

Siere gave her a level look. 'You are a mage?'

'Yes!'

'Very well. Your craft?'

'Craft? Oh, right. I'm a night mage.'

'Ah yes. And you?' she said, looked at Lynx.

'No magic here. Got any coffee?'

'Perhaps,' Siere conceded, eyes darting to the promissory note.

'Gods-in-shards, I'm all yours then!'

Lynx was careful not to pay any attention to the foul look Toil was giving him. He wasn't really prepared for cheeriness, but the mention of coffee was a bright spark amid a dismal mood.

Siere gave a curt nod. She called over a passing mage, handed the young man the mage-pistols and promissory note before sending him off for coffee. 'Do you wish to observe your countryman's work? Lan Ifir is a very fine healer.'

Despite himself, Lynx felt the cheeriness evaporate. 'No offence to him, but I'm done with my countrymen.'

'I understand. Many feel this way.'

'Tell me about it,' Toil muttered. 'Can we get moving?'

The mage nodded. 'I will take him then,' she said, gesturing for Darm to follow her. 'Healing is painful and he must not shout. You may be useful.' Two of the other mages stepped forward to direct Layir and Estal to other rooms while Sitain, Darm, Lynx and Toil all followed Siere. The remaining mages split up without needing instructions, two following each of the patients.

The room was a bare and functional stone box, just the door and a shuttered window looking out on to the courtyard. A long surgeon's table surrounded by chairs occupied the centre of the room, but unlike some Lynx had seen this was scrubbed clean of any bloodstains. Water and clean bandages occupied a side table next to a tray bearing the usual brutal tools of surgery.

Siere directed Darm to sit on the table and her two attendants helped him lie down.

'His name?'

'Darm.'

Siere gave a curt nod. 'Very good. Darm, this will hurt and you must try not to move. This is difficult, I know, but healing is not strong if a night mage makes you sleep.'

Darm managed a grunt and accepted a leather strip between his teeth with a wince. As the mages sat around him, Siere at the end of the table, Lynx pulled up another chair and offered Darm his hand.

'You're gonna need something to squeeze down on by the sounds of it.'

Darm grunted again, gratitude in his eyes as he clasped hands with Lynx. There was a spark of fear in his eyes too now. While the company were losing their fear of Sitain's night magic, strangers performing something painful to your face was a whole other kettle of fish.

'I will perform the work,' Siere announced, more to Sitain than Darm. 'My colleagues will contribute their power for me to use.' She reached forward stiffly, using her left hand to place her right against the side of Darm's jaw.

Lynx gasped as he got a better look at her hand. The fingers and wrist were rigid, frozen at rest, and the skin was pale – greying at the tips of her fingers.

'You're a mage of tempest!'

'Yes. This is problem?'

'No, I . . . no, nothing. I just realised.'

'Few recognise the signs. You know a tempest mage?'

113

'We . . .' Lynx coughed, remembering that Atieno had clearly wanted to avoid this place. 'We met one, not long ago. His foot was going.'

'It is our curse.'

Sitain leaned forward. 'So your tempest magic can change the others?'

'Correct. Pagarith there is earth mage,' Siere said, nodding to the blond-haired man with a bushy moustache. 'His energy is of, ah, things you hold. Saolas there is light mage.' The round-faced woman with black hair and narrow eyes gave them a cheery smile. 'Her power is of movement, energy. I combine these with change and some damage can be healed. Not all, but the first days of injury are hardest.'

Without waiting for a reply she bent over Darm's face, gently probing the line of his jaw to feel the bone underneath. Darm stiffened under her touch, but that was all. Before long she sat back, satisfied that the line of the jaw was as she needed. Siere nodded to the two other mages and directed their fingers so each had placed their index and middle finger either side of the break.

Darm's jaw was badly swollen after a night of not being treated, but Lynx guessed an approximate location was enough. Once they were in position Siere set her own fingers to the jawline and closed her eyes. A soft glow began to emanate from the light mage's skin, illuminating all they were doing. It made the grey ossifying flesh of Siere's right hand all the more obvious, but beyond that Lynx could see little happening.

Siere held her position for a full minute, her face lit from below. The skin of Darm's face or the air around it, possibly both, trembled faintly. Only once was Lynx sure of movement, not least because Darm almost broke his hand as the broken part of bone shifted into alignment.

Once that was done, Siere broke off her efforts and sat back, flexing her fingers and scowling at the sensation in them.

'All done?' Toil asked.

'No. We rest now.'

'He needs to rest already?'

'*I* need rest,' Siere corrected her. 'The more magic I draw, the more damage to my body.'

'Oh, right.'

'Two or three more times we must do this, then he will be able to eat and speak without pain, if he is careful.' Siere raised an eyebrow at Lynx. 'But first, we drink coffee, yes?'

Lynx unpeeled Darm's fingers and rubbed his half-numb hand. 'Coffee,' he agreed.

Chapter 11

As evening fell, the mages set out again for the Shard's Rest. The weather had turned over the course of the afternoon, thick cloud rolling in on a chilly breeze. It was a different city they walked through now. There was a gloom that seemed to mute even the mage-lit lamps, and the taste of a sea fog lingered on the air. The party made better time as Teshen took the sea-level route and arrived just as rain started to patter down. This time they were admitted without delay and the Shard's steward, Fen Oe Tegir, was waiting for them in the grand hallway.

'Come, be welcome, friends,' the man intoned, bowing. 'The Shard has agreed to hear your request. Your guide may wait here, should he so wish, but no non-mage is permitted in the Court of the Shard itself.'

'The Court of the Shard?' Teshen asked, sounding surprised. 'Not somewhere private?'

'The events of Jarrazir are of interest to many guilds. First-hand accounts are a rare luxury for the news we receive so several guild leaders have requested to attend. The Shard is representative of the court, I remind you, not its ruler.'

The big mercenary shrugged. 'Guess that makes sense.' He waved the others forward and headed for the most comfortable-looking chair, shrugging off his Knight-of-Stars-emblazoned jacket. 'Good luck. Don't be too long or you can find your own way back.'

Lastani and Atieno exchanged looks while Sitain just tried to quell her own anxiety. The finery of the hallway was just another reminder of how out of place she felt. The reflection each of the grand mirrors presented were of a girl pretending to be a mercenary and that only worsened the feeling.

Not a proper merc, not a proper mage, Sitain thought. *Neither one nor the other, just stuck in the middle and fairly useless to both.*

She swallowed and took a step forward. 'Let's get this over with then, eh?'

Atieno broke a rare smile and put a hand on her shoulder. 'Shall we leave the talking to you?'

'What? No!' Sitain gasped. 'Ah, you're joking.'

'I am,' Atieno confirmed. 'Apologies, you are nervous. I did not mean to make that worse. But of course – you've not met many mages before and are now presented with the Court of the Shard.'

'Shut up and get in there, grandad,' Sitain muttered. 'Go do your job.'

Atieno sighed and inclined his head before extending a hand, offering Lastani the way. Lastani, not much older than Sitain, just looked startled. When she didn't move, Atieno advanced on the great doors to the court, opening them himself.

Sitain and Lastani followed in his wake as the older mage headed into a large, well-apportioned meeting chamber that smelled of incense, leather and polished wood. There were raised tiers on either side and tall windows ahead – a bank of four behind a large trio of solid wooden seats at a long desk. Those weren't quite thrones, but close, and the woman in the centre one was a worthy occupant.

The Shard was a dumpy woman in her fifties with chocolate-brown skin, hair cropped close to her skull and eyes like dark diamonds. She sat awkwardly to one side on her pretend throne, not lounging but hardly comfortable. There was an expression of irritation on her face, but Sitain didn't get the impression it was at the newcomers and she recalled Teshen's words about the obedience of mages here.

The Shard was in fact the least formally dressed mage there, aside from Sitain herself. She wore a plain shirt and the usual Islander loose-fitting trousers. If it wasn't for a long coat of hundreds of strips of coloured silk, presumably incorporating the colours of each guild, she could have just as easily stepped off a fishing boat.

A dozen mages attended too, in clumps of two or three dotted around the tiers. They were mostly old, but of as great a mix of races as she'd seen at the healer's guild. While none of them were dressed the same, they all seemed to follow a formal style of clothing that she was starting to associate with mages here in addition to tri-colour markers that Teshen had said indicated their guild.

Sitain took a breath and found the air warm and dry in her throat. For a moment she thought it was just nerves – her throat really was dry, after all – but then something else occurred to her. She'd never been in a room with so many mages before. They all drew magic from the air around them, it was present always and flowed through them naturally, but in the presence of so many, was there less power in the air here than she was accustomed to?

'Be welcome to the Court of the Shard,' called a small man with olive skin, rising from his seat to the left of the Shard's. 'Enter as free mages, leave as brethren.'

Atieno grunted and nodded, but instead of replying he stepped to one side. Sitain almost had to stop dead to avoid walking into him. Lastani hesitated a fraction longer then remembered she was the expert on the Labyrinth of Jarrazir. She was the one who had to tell the story.

'Mistress Ufre, Mistress Sitain, Master Atienolentra – be welcome in my court. I hear you have a tale to tell us,' the

Shard called in flawless Parthish. 'Entertain us and I shall entertain your request for access to our libraries.'

Sitain blinked at the Shard. It took her a while to realise that in the Mage Islands, the chief mage would hardly be without intelligence sources, but it was a surprise to hear her own name there still.

'Shard, I thank you for hearing us,' Lastani said, bowing. 'I am Lastani Ufre, former pupil to Ishienne Matarin of Jarrazir.'

'Her name is known to us all and her loss is grieved,' the Shard replied. 'Mistress Matarin was a scholar of great renown, I believe she contributed several works to our library.'

'She did – and considered it an honour that they would be housed here.'

'You have my personal sympathy and that of all mages in these islands for her loss.'

That made Lastani falter for a moment. She bowed her head, clearly remembering that fateful night, but after a few seconds continued.

'Thank you, Shard. I was present when Mistress Ishienne opened the Labyrinth, as was Atieno here. We assisted in the operation and barely survived the attack of its spirit-guardians.'

'And your companion?'

Lastani glanced back and Sitain swallowed. 'I'm just a mercenary, um, Shard. Well, almost a mercenary. Sort of anyway.'

'Just so long as you're sure,' the Shard replied with twinkling eyes. 'What is your part in all this?'

'Sitain is part of a mercenary company in the employ of a relic hunter. That hunter had been informed by her contacts of what we were to attempt. They travelled to Jarrazir to offer their services and be involved in any exploration.'

Sitain gave a small snort at the word *involved* given how Toil had gone about it, but aside from a curious look the Shard allowed Lastani to continue speaking.

'Part of the mercenary crew escorted us into the Labyrinth after matters . . . well, the situation deteriorated.'

'Deteriorated?'

'Went to utter shit,' Sitain found herself saying. 'Some of which was our fault, some of which was the bastard Charnelers.'

'You will find no friends of the Knights-Charnel here, girl,' the Shard said. 'But most of this I have heard – as indeed I have heard that a cache of God Fragments was recovered from the Labyrinth. So what exactly do you offer for the privilege of accessing a library unmatched outside of the secure vaults of the Militant Orders?'

Lastani cast around the room for a moment, then pointed to an old man with leathery skin off to her right. 'You, you're an ice mage.'

The man inclined his head, unsurprised that Lastani could sense it.

'Then please attend,' Lastani said in a teacherly tone.

She raised her hand and began to draw hard on her magic. Sitain could sense the rush of power tighten like a net snagging a huge fish. It even pulled on the power inside her own body as Lastani continued the flow. She couldn't see what Lastani was doing in her hand, only the haze of white, but, as the surge of magic continued to build, the willow-pattern tattoos began to glow.

In seconds they were blazing with light. The temperature of the room dropped like a stone. Sitain saw her own skin start to glow as the large oval room became an ice house. Glittering motes of frost sparkled in the air all around Lastani. She held it a few moments longer, long enough for the skin on Sitain's face to prickle with cold. The mage lamps in the room started to flicker and falter and tentacles of frost spread out across the floor from Lastani's feet. Before long Sitain felt the sharp bite of winter on her cheek and frost started to form on clothes and furniture alike. Only then did Lastani break off, dismissing the magic as she turned to the old man.

He croaked and flinched under her imperious gaze, the blood drained from his face. Pressed back into his seat, it took him another few seconds to recover himself and form words.

'She . . . spirits of the deepest black, how is this possible? This young woman . . . She's the most powerful ice mage in the world.'

'What?' Sitain yelped. 'What do you mean? Don't be so fucking stupid!'

All eyes focused on her for a moment and the room fell silent. Despite the urge to edge behind Atieno, Sitain was too astonished by his words to move.

'Stupid or not, young lady, I am the highest authority of ice magic in the city and among the foremost in all of the Riven Kingdom,' the man said at last. 'I know every ice mage in Caldaire; Mistress Ufre surpasses them all. I doubt anyone on the entire continent of Urden could be so powerful and escape our notice.'

'We three have all been changed by the Labyrinth in this way,' Lastani confirmed.

'Screaming shits,' Sitain muttered. 'Stronger yes, but the most powerful on Urden? All of us? But I've hardly even started to learn what I'm doing.'

'And still we witnessed what you were capable of, almost without training,' Lastani reminded her.

'Indeed?' the Shard said in a thoughtful purr. She brushed at the sheen of frost covering her desk's top and leaned forward to peer closer at Lastani. 'You have my interest, Lastani Ufre, oh indeed you do. Tell me more.'

Chapter 12

'What's with the face?' Kas said as she appeared at Lynx's table. 'Black dog got its teeth into you?'

Lynx scowled and tried to ignore the fact he'd flinched at her arrival. He'd been lost in the view over the balcony, or rather staring blankly into space. A slim, well-worn Hanese novel lay unopened beside his hands.

Nquet Dam was a bustling, attractive district – wealthy in these parts and ostentatious too. The hard lines of the city's mage-carved stone were softened by brightly coloured awnings and flags, red, ochre and yellow. There were swirls and circles of script on each: prayers, Lynx assumed, despite the more relaxed approach to religion in these parts. Where he would expect to see wells or statues in the street there were raised beds of earth instead, supporting lemon trees and vine-laden pergolas. Every sheltered corner above street level was similarly colonised by greenery, the early season fruit bright against the leaves.

'Just hungover,' he muttered.

'Sure,' she said, patting Lynx on the shoulder as she sat alongside him. 'If you say so.'

'What's that supposed to mean?'

Kas sighed and took his arm. Lynx tensed and quietly cursed himself for it, but Kas made no sign of noticing. She leaned against him in a sisterly way and reached for the plate in front of him, teasing up a strip of sticky pastry. She popped it in her mouth and licked her fingers clean before answering.

'I've seen you hungover, remember? Seen you naked too, and sleeping. More'n any man I've ever known, you always look like there's a black dog after you. Especially when you're dreaming.' She squeezed his arm. 'Sometimes the fucker gets too close and takes a bite, there's no shame in it. This life we lead is hard on the sunniest o' folk.'

In the street ahead a winding column of the sloth creatures, all bearing laden bamboo frames on their backs, cut a path across their view and blocked the street for a minute. It didn't take long for the shouting to begin, pedestrians and traders yelling at the squat beast-master leading the sloths. More faces soon appeared at balconies to watch the fun. Several of those yelled their own contributions to the impromptu street theatre while the sloths drifted back and forth in confusion.

'I like dogs,' Lynx said at last. 'I never think of it as a dog.'

'No?'

He shook his head. 'Dogs come in three types. They love you like all the world, they're not interested, or they want to rip your face off. My demons,' he tapped the side of his head as he spoke, 'the bastards that claw all sense from my head, they ain't dogs.'

'What then?'

Kas kept where she was, gaze away from him and sharing the view of the tangled stone streets. The Siym Holding compound was just about visible from there, the heart of Kabat Siym's modest trade empire, encompassing six narrow streets that were sealed off from the city at night.

Lynx willed his shoulders to relax, to accept the warmth of that weight on his body. Kas kept still, just a companionable presence that meant he didn't end up staring too deeply into those beautiful brown eyes. Like this, he could almost believe he was just talking to himself.

He glanced down as best he could without moving his head. *Fuck, I'm an idiot, aren't I?* The breeze caused the awning above him to flutter sharply, rattling its agreement, but he shook the feeling away.

'My demons are cats,' Lynx began. 'It's a black cat that lurks on the edge of eyesight. You only catch a glimpse – you don't hear a thing, but suddenly it's there. Gentle at first, worms its way in under your guard. Then it sinks its claws in, all sharp and hot and it's too damned late.'

'True enough,' Kas conceded. 'Bastards act like your friends right up to the point they're drawing blood.'

'Exactly. If a black dog was hunting you, you'd be able to choose – to run or to fight it. There's no fighting the black cat, it just appears. All you can do is hold your breath and wait to see what it decides to do. Mebbe it acts nice, mebbe it plays with you and draws a little blood just for fun. Or mebbe the claws dig in deep.'

'So how do you chase the cat away?'

'Fucked if I know. Being in a stone city don't help much though. Reminds me of Shadows Deep more'n I'd like.'

'Yeah, you're not alone there. Happy memories, hey?' He felt her hesitate, poised on the edge of speaking. 'Don't take this the wrong way, okay, Lynx?'

'Uh, sure. I'll try.'

'All this.' Kas waved her hand towards the view ahead. While she just made a general gesture, Lynx knew what she meant. 'Does it make things worse? Should you be sticking around?'

'Yes and no,' Lynx said eventually. 'There's good and there's bad. I've lived with these demons long enough to know that much.'

'Violence, terror and a woman who's got you always off-balance?' She held up a hand. 'I know, but I'm talking as a friend here. You don't know where you stand with her – that's who she is as much as how she plays. Her life ain't simple, never going to be.'

'I don't do simple, really,' Lynx said. 'Not without screwing it up. But yeah, I know. Some days all you can do is keep moving, make it hard for the black cat to catch up. Have a job, have a goal, have a problem you've got to work round. Boredom's bad. Boredom gives you time to hear the scratching in your head. This ain't perfect, but some o' you are decent company. There's usually something to focus on when I need a focus.'

'Even if it gets you killed?'

'I got to earn a living somewhere, somehow. In the Cards I do it around folk who'll hold me back when the scratching stops me thinking clearly.'

Walking the streets somewhere ahead of them were Toil, Teshen, Payl, Safir and Llaith – each one tasked with making a few observations they could then pool. Kas had been doing the same, but the job called for them to never linger so she'd stepped away. Lynx was there as back-up. His job mostly comprised eating enough to justify sitting in one place for two hours. That part he'd liked, but it had turned out to be a bad morning to be left with his thoughts.

'Right you are,' Kas said with a nod. 'Start thinking then. From here, how'd you want to do it?'

'Not my call.'

'No, but I'm asking. You were a gods-damned Hanese commando, you led strike missions.'

'You don't need me to work it out, you know your shit already.'

'Shitting gods, Lynx, I'm not asking for your help. I'm asking you to use the brain of yours to distract you from your black cat.'

'Oh. Right. Yeah, fine.' He took a long breath. 'Not knowing what the others will come back to say? I'd do it the Hanese way – hard and fast.'

125

'For the sake of this conversation, I'm going to let that one pass,' Kas purred, 'but we're going to have to come back to mocking that statement later, okay?'

'Dammit. See? Not thinking clearly.' Lynx shook his head. 'Anyways, their strength is their position and their Masts crews. They've got the numbers, but we're better armed. So we get there when the crews are asleep or unprepared. Kill the sentries and we're inside before anyone reacts. With luck they'll see they're beaten and surrender.'

'Could turn into a street fight. The guards in the mansion just need to hold out long enough for other crews to appear.'

'True. We need a second breach team for the mansion. Everyone's looking one way while they slip in the other. Atieno can bust open doors, Sitain can put any guards down. Once they're inside, Suth's quickest on the draw and all the marked Cards see better in the dark after Jarrazir.'

Kas nodded and sat up, helping herself to more of the remaining food as she considered his idea. 'I like it,' she said finally. 'I was going to go in to the offices, use it as bridgehead.'

'Using an earther to breach the gate? Surely there'll be some sort of rattle-cage behind each one?'

'Using Estal. She knows her grenades. We get her to rig something for those big hinges and pull the gates down.'

'Risky. Anything slows you up and it becomes a prolonged fight.'

'Hey, I didn't hear your idea to actually breach the wall – what was that again?'

'Fair point.'

'Thank you.' She paused and leaned forward to look over the remaining food. 'Hand me those prawns, would you? You know what, I don't think I've ever seen so much unfinished food on a table you're sitting at.'

That made Lynx crack a smile. 'Then you didn't see the four plates they've already cleared away. Stuffed squid cooked in wine, fried rice balls, some sort of little red plants that tasted like nuts, and smoked fish and samphire in a pot of garlic oil. Try the soup too, there's slivers of some sort of meat in it even I can't work out. Might be it's tysarn I guess, but sweetened somehow. And who says I wasn't going to finish it all in my own time? I'm just pacing myself.'

'Your famed Hanese way, eh? Hard and fast with a soft finish?' Kas laughed, waggling her eyebrows at him as she reached for the soup. 'If one of us had needed back-up, would you even be able to move?'

'I was mostly planning on rolling to the rescue, then vomiting as a distraction. Toil inspired me with that brawl ruse.'

'Smart, very smart. You should probably drink lots of wine to add authenticity there.'

'Way ahead o' you.'

She smiled and raised a hand for a waiter.

Chapter 13

The administrative offices of the Siym Holding were modest affairs, sparsely populated and possessing a near reverential hush. Despite the reach of their interests, only eight clerks attended an elderly couple who had devoted their life to the day-to-day running of the Holding. Uncle and aunt to the kabat, Quelo and Udar Siym had been a couple for close to fifty years – the initial decision made out of pragmatism more than infatuation. Each loved order and sobriety of thought and mind. They cared nothing for the rule of the house other than it was done well.

Sparrow-thin and permanently draped in a neat formality all of their own, the couple mirrored each other in almost every way. They dressed almost identically each morning, ate the same food and often would pace the offices shoulder to shoulder as they inspected the work of their underlings. Quelo was darker-skinned than his partner, but such was their neat co-existence that small cosmetic differences were all that differentiated the two of them. They had no children and could not abide the presence of anything so chaotic, but worked tirelessly on behalf of their extended family. What one was told, the other would know. What one decided, the other would agree with.

Ferociously intelligent and masters of their small domain, they barely needed the rooms of ledgers stored on the floor above, but were also scrupulous about their records. When a fist hammered on the door early one morning, the pair had not yet retired to their office and were the only ones in the room not to jump at the sound.

'Foolish mice,' Udar muttered.

'As if Whitesea Consortium enforcers would knock on a door,' agreed Quelo after a phlegmy cough.

'Why do you all stare?' Udar demanded. 'Back to your work. Junior Scribe Sarams, see to our visitors.'

The Junior Scribe jumped to his feet and scampered to the door. He had barely begun to open it before the person on the other side decided even this task was beyond his ability. Sarams gave a squawk as he was swept up by the door. Even with the impediment that was the Junior Scribe, the door was flung back and Sarams half-crushed against the wall behind. The woman who stepped through the door seemed entirely unsurprised by the howl that resulted and looked around the room with a self-satisfied expression.

Udar and Quelo exchanged a look. They had seen this type before. Vain and convinced of her own intellect, she would no doubt equate a loud voice with acumen.

'Who's in charge here?' the woman demanded in Parthish, the language of thugs so far as the Siym were concerned, but thugs with money.

All heads turned towards the elderly pair who said nothing. If the question needed answering, the visitor had no purpose here.

The woman stepped forward. Her clothes were intricate and fussy; a flowing dress of layered silk, grey and blue, inlaid with pearls and embroidered with pictures of fish. Her cloak had a fox-fur collar, her silk shoes were laced with blue ribbon of all things and her long red hair was pinned with a dozen silver clasps set with sapphires.

Or perhaps blue glass. To present herself here in such a way, how important can she be?

'You speak for the Siym family?' the woman said, advancing on them. She was tall and muscular, hardly the image of noble Parthish wealth one might conjure from the stories told of that inland sea.

'We are Siym,' Udar acknowledged.

'Excellent, my name is Iliatory Esber. I wish to buy from you.'

'Does this appear to be a shop, Mistress Esber?'

'What's that got to do with anything?' the foolish woman said. She pointed back behind her where they saw two figures. 'We wish to establish a business relationship, not purchase goods.'

One of her companions was dark-skinned and dressed in similarly foolish fashion, the other was an easterner, Olostiran by his colouring and skirt. They took a long look at each other. All three were handsome, self-assured and entirely comfortable in unfamiliar surroundings. None looked like the Siym's usual trading partners.

To underline that fact, they had come armed to the compound gates, a detail which marked them as newcomers to the city and grossly ignorant of all its customs. The women wore now-empty holsters at their belted waists and the man an empty rapier scabbard.

Like a dirty afterthought, a fourth stranger appeared at the doorway. This one was clearly just a guard, albeit dressed in better clothing that the usual mercenary. She was a tall woman with a scowl on her face who did not enter, no doubt under instruction from the guards who'd taken the women's mage-pistols.

'And what do you seek in this relationship?' Udar asked finally.

'We represent a consortium of interests in Sha Sain,' the foolish woman said. 'One of our city's more creative apoth-ecaries has developed a new use for one of your drugs – a use that has proved most popular.'

'And we export to Sha Sain,' Quelo said.

Esber muttered something in her own language then took a breath. 'I am well aware of that. The problem is who you export it to.'

'The drug is?'

'Yellow-spore.'

'I fail to see the problem. Humble Inshir is a man with whom we have a long-established and steady business arrangement.'

'Humble Inshir is a—' The woman broke off into her own language and unleashed a torrent of abuse that went on for quite a while. Quelo and Udar exchanged a look of boredom.

Quelo raised a hand. 'Master Inshir is our client in Sha Sain,' he said after the bluster and noise had lost its initial burst of energy. 'Should you wish to buy, I'm sure he is willing to sell to you.'

'Only on unacceptable terms!' Esber protested. 'We want to buy ten times what he offers and he demands the process our apothecary has devised, so he may cut us out entirely.'

'That is hardly our concern. We do not trade with strangers. Good day.'

'What? Don't be damned fools – we're willing to pay above what Inshir is and in far greater amounts.'

'On what assurances? The drug cannot be produced in much greater numbers, it is delicate to transport and we still do not know you. Why would we restrict supply to our established partners in the hope that you have the funds to pay on delivery and continue to pay?'

'Money talks, in my experience,' Esber snapped, pulling a sheaf of paper from inside her jacket pocket. 'To prove our position we're willing to pay well above the current rate. In advance.'

Again Quelo and Udar exchanged looks. They rarely needed to make a business decision out loud, but these were unusual times. The Siym finances were strained to say the least, but as a result this offer could prove suspiciously fortuitous.

'What quantities are you seeking?'

'How much can you supply?'

Udar sucked her teeth. 'Three crates, a hundred weight each.'

'How frequently?'

Quelo blinked. 'That is all until next year, after the spore is harvested again.'

'I'll take it.'

They blinked. 'Perhaps you should come in to our office while we inform the kabat. Such an arrangement may complicate other business arrangements and, as such, there must be a ruling.'

She wrinkled her nose. 'There? Is there nowhere else?'

'You have an objection?'

'I have a . . . condition. Somewhere outside?'

'What sort of condition?'

'Does it matter?'

'It is an unusual request,' Udar said. 'One that comes in conjunction with an unusual offer.'

The woman sighed and pursed her lips. A twitch of the shoulder showed her trying not to glance back at her companions. 'The smell of ink,' she admitted in a more muted voice. 'It is making me nauseous.'

'Nauseous?' As practised as they were in Parthish, the language of trade for all their northern clients, that word was unfamiliar to both.

The woman shrugged. With an impatient little gesture she mimicked vomit coming out of her mouth. Both Quel and Udar took a small step back.

The foolish woman's male companion took a pace forward, a broad smile on his face. 'You're pregnant?' he asked. 'This is, ah, most pleasing news, Mistress Esber.'

'Quiet.'

Quelo pointed to a side door. 'This way.'

Udar led the way out into the central street of the Siym compound while Quelo issued instructions to the Junior Scribe and the strangers exchanged a flurry of whispers. Esber abruptly broke off the conversation as she followed Udar outside. With quick steps and a lace cloth to her lips, she hurried outside.

For a while the foolish woman merely strode up and down a short stretch of street, face turned skyward and taking long, deep breaths as she cleared the nausea. Quelo and Udar watched her cautiously. They knew such sensitivities could occur in pregnant women, though Esber was clearly not far along.

The Olostiran man cleared his throat as they watched her recover herself.

'Perhaps, the trees?' he said, indicating the small grove that stood at the end of the office building. 'We may wait there for word from the kabat?'

Quelo nodded and they set off side by side, leaving the others to follow. Passing the wide street that led to the Siym palace, where Quelo and Udar had modest apartments, the strangers naturally paused to appreciate the sight.

The south wing of the palace was by far the larger of the two. Built in typical Nquet Dam fashion, the main wing was composed of linked blocks, bridges and walkways, six storeys at its highest and set around a central courtyard. A large hall abutted that, linking it to the three-storey curling north wing, from the broad balconies of which leaves trailed down each flank. Hidden by that was the inner shoreline, the kabat's private garden on one side and the docks the other.

Continuing, they passed a round watchtower that overlooked the western wall and the Mastrunner quarters beyond. The grove itself was a square of greenery protected by a ridge of stone, twenty yards across with a tall silver leaf fig tree in the centre and the unlovely bulk of warehouses on two flanks.

The group had to step aside to allow a trio of laden carts past, the five Mastrunners leading them each signalling their respect to Quelo and Udar as they passed. While they waited, Quelo noticed their male guest staring all around at the Holding. Aware that there were clear signs of disrepair and disorder, he pointedly cleared his throat.

'Might I enquire how a man of high standing from Olostir came to find himself as part of a trade consortium in Sha Sain?' he said.

The man smiled. 'There, ah, there was a mistake with a pig.'

Quelo blinked. 'A pig?'

'Indeed.'

There came a coarse laugh from the white woman, Esber. 'Was it pregnant?' she called.

'It was not,' he replied with a raised eyebrow at the woman that conveyed nothing to Quelo, but elicited a gesture he assumed to be insulting from Esber. 'My mistake was not the same as my colleague's. My mistake was how loudly I likened it to a . . . a kabat, you would say here.'

'Would that not result in a duel, from what I understand of your homeland?'

'Normally yes.' He gave an embarrassed cough. 'The accuracy of the statement did not help matters, nor in whose presence it had been made. There were other, regretful, incidents that followed too.'

'Oh?'

'Public denouncements, retainers brawling, business deals falling through. Her lover being pinned to a wall by a rapier through his scrotum – we both came to regret that. The theft of her most valuable possession, however, well. Only one of us was unhappy there.'

Quelo said nothing in response. The shifting piratical state of the Mage Islands meant such deeds were hardly unheard

134

of, but they were senior clerks who lived in a palace. No doubt the kabat would have been amused, found some witty response even, but the whole subject was beyond both Quelo and Udar.

They sat on stone benches under the fig tree while the foolish woman paced theatrically around the grove. Without further small talk to distract them, the prospective trading partners continued to survey what they could of their surroundings. The Holding was situated on the larger island of Nquet Dam and enjoyed one of the largest private shorelines. From their jetties, Siym boats could travel almost directly through the garden-islands that dotted the shallows and across to the spice islands they controlled.

Refreshments were brought by one of the clerks. They drank red tea in polite silence until at last word came back from the kabat, or as it turned out, the Holding's Chancellor, who spoke with Kabat Siym's authority. The Chancellor's principal secretary spoke quietly into Udar's ear while Quelo caught enough to understand.

'You request is accepted,' Udar informed the Sha Sain trio. 'There is an elevated initial price, however, given the unusual circumstances, which will be reduced should an ongoing relationship be established.'

'How much?'

'Three times the wholesale price with transport fees on top. There are further conditions, naturally, those will be included in the contract. Principal among them is the advance payment.'

'How much?' Udar asked again, but warily now.

'Fifty per cent in advance, the balance of funds to be released upon consignment delivery.'

The woman laughed, but there was murder in her eyes. 'Such a price is insulting.'

'Nevertheless, that is the price.'

'Ulfer's horn it is!' Her bark of anger drew the attention of two passing Mastrunners but Udar waved them away. 'Three times the price and half up front means you'd make your usual profit without even letting it out the door. I'll pay a fifth when we sign the contract, the balance on departure of the barge. You get more in advance than you would normally and still have the incentive to deliver.'

'This is not how we do business.'

'Me neither,' she said with a fierce grin. 'Someone tells me to my face they're going to fuck me, I don't care what profit I might make next year.'

'We are not ignorant,' the Olostiran man broke in. 'This price is not usual in any circumstance and it confirms rumours we have heard.'

'Rumour has no place here.'

'Oh but it does. The Siym are short on their loans, this is known. This deal shall be lucrative for us both, but we are not the ones in need of improved finances.'

'You overestimate the impact of one deal,' Quelo said, the mere mention of their loans provoking a bitter taste in his mouth.

'Then add another condition to your contract,' Esber said. 'Next season's entire harvest of yellow-spice – what weight would that be?'

'Twenty crates, should we choose to renege on all current contracts.'

All three members of the Sha Sain consortium smiled widely.

'Interesting,' Esber said brightly. 'Suggest to your kabat the following – a fifth upon signature of our contract, release of remaining funds upon consignment delivery. In addition a down-payment on next year's entire crop at double your standard rate, let us say another fifth, also released to you.'

'Triple the usual price,' Quelo said before adding, 'assuming the kabat approves.'

She shook her head. 'Double. I am not here to fix your finances and if I buy such bulk, I require a better price.'

'She will not agree to double,' Udar said. 'There are too many agreements to breach. Double and one half is our best assessment.'

'Agreed. We will return in two days.' The less-than-foolish woman stood and placed a hand on her belly. 'Now if you will excuse me, I have some surprising news to pass on.'

Chapter 14

Shit, mebbe I am becoming one of the Cards.

Sitain carefully removed her hand from her holstered mage-pistol and hoped no one had noticed. Outside the lodgings there was a man – several in fact, but only one had made her want to start shooting. But her last target practice had been on the barge and had left Lynx grinding his teeth with frustration. The stranger was probably the safest person there, but that didn't stop her urge to shoot him in the face. None of their usual watchers were in sight. Whether they'd given up or run off to report was anyone's guess.

The newcomer was extremely tall and thin – not ill but elongated somehow. He reminded Sitain of the Wisps they'd encountered in Shadows Deep. Pale skin told its own story in this sun-drenched sailor's city, while long luxuriant black hair billowed in the breeze. It was his predatory eyes that made her want to kill him though.

'Good morning,' he said with a deep bow. 'Mistress Lastani Ufre, I presume?'

He was a mage, that much was obvious from his coat. Lightweight, long and grey, it hung off his frame and flapped like a scarecrow's. Three long stripes ran down his right side, two purple and one white. His companions, standing like guards behind, wore tunics of grey bearing the same stripes.

'I am,' Lastani said, slightly stiffly; probably also trying to restrain the urge to kill everything in sight. Or not, Sitain accepted upon reflection. She'd not spent as much time around the Cards. 'May I assist you?'

'Quite the opposite, my dear,' the man said, beaming with all the warmth of a lizard trying very hard to replicate a human smile. 'I am Guildmaster Tanimbor, I have heard great things about you all.'

'All? Like what?' Sitain found herself saying.

Tanimbor blinked at her, his expression not changing at all. 'That you investigated the Labyrinth of Jarrazir, that you discovered something unexpected down there, and that you are quite remarkably powerful now.'

'Oh.'

He took a step forward. Tanimbor looked to be about fifty, his guards half that.

Strange for a mage to come with guards, Sitain thought. *Is he that powerful or got that many enemies?*

'I have come to offer my assistance, should you require it.'

'Would that not be better offered at the Shard's Rest?' Lastani replied. 'That is where we are going.'

'I am, ah, unwelcome there. The politics of this city is a game of self-importance, one I choose not to play.'

'Refusing to play gets you banned from the principal mage forum in the city?' Atieno said with a frown. 'Or deciding to break the rules?'

'Some rules cry out to be broken.' Tanimbor shrugged. 'You will no doubt hear many lies about me, should you trouble yourselves to ask. I am the Shard's principal opponent among the guilds and gossip is everything to the mages here.'

'What assistance can you offer us, then?' Lastani asked. 'Does your guild have a private library you mean to open to us?'

'Unfortunately not, it is a young guild and does not amass such things. No – instead I offer you sanctuary, should you wish it. I know how they play their games, how they control and manipulate. They do not like unaffiliated mages here. I am sure you will see that all too soon.'

'I've heard as much, but what sanctuary can you offer from the guilds when you lead one yourself?'

'It is my concession to politics – my guild is not run like the others.' He gave a fussy little cough of amusement. 'Some joke that it is the guild of misfits and I embrace that label. We are a haven to those who choose not to conform to the roles they impose. The discipline and loyalty they demand.'

'Are you saying they will demand we join a guild?' Lastani shook her head. 'We won't be staying in the islands that long.'

'All the more reason – influence beyond these shores is as attractive as the power you apparently wield. They will compete for your affections I have no doubt, offer you great things so long as you become one of them.'

'And you stand apart from such games?'

'I choose not to play the way they would like,' Tanimbor clarified. 'I have other goals. My concerns lie with magic itself and those who practise it.'

'How very noble. I thank you for your offer.'

He bowed once more. If the man heard her edge of sarcasm he chose to ignore it. 'I shall delay you no longer. Should you wish to speak to me again, you will find me in the shadow of the cliffs.'

He pointed as he spoke without looking, indicating somewhere beyond the humped coil of buildings that occupied the far side of the street. Sitain frowned for a moment before realising where he meant.

'The island beneath the Etrel Cliffs? I thought that was a slum?'

'So some prefer to think of it. The people are poor certainly, and our guildhouse is no grand palace, but it serves our needs. You would be welcome to visit and see for yourself, should you choose to do so.'

Lastani cast a look at Atieno, but the older man was impassive. 'I thank you for your offer, Guildmaster.'

'I hope you find what you are seeking, Mistress Ufre.'

With that he turned and left. Once Tanimbor had vanished from sight, Lastani faced her companions.

'Does anyone else think we've walked into some sort of conflict?'

'Perhaps,' Atieno replied. 'But some young fool says we're the most powerful mages in the world. It may be we can spark a conflict by our mere presence.'

Sitain laughed. 'Gods-in-shards, we really are proper members of the Cards now!'

'It appears so.' Atieno sniffed and eased his weight to one side, wincing at the result of standing still on his bad leg. 'One thing is for sure, I do not like that man.'

'Oh no, that bastard's going to try and kill us before the week's out.'

Lastani blinked. 'I think that's being a little dramatic, don't you?'

'Nope,' Sitain said. 'I've been hanging round with Lynx long enough to suspect it's true in most circumstances – and Toil long enough to know my friends will probably start it.'

That brought Lastani up short. For a little while she didn't speak, unable to argue on the basis of everything she'd seen of the Cards. 'Let's get our answers quickly then,' the mage said at last. 'The longer we stay in this city, the faster trouble will find us.'

'Cheer up, old man, you should be happy right now.'

Anatin scowled at Toil. 'Yeah, why?'

'Tonight we get to test your life's work,' Toil said.

'What are you on about, woman?' He shook his head and looked back towards the Siym Holding. They were watching the main gate now, counting guards and waiting to see what happened as it was closed up.

'Don't pretend, not to me. This job, tonight – it's perfect for your crew. The life of a merc is hard and bloody. Anyone who's seen a battlefield knows what a screaming pile of misery that is. Your deck of Cards ain't an accident, too many expensive hires for that. Most merc crews are bigger and half-full of gun-fodder, but you've almost no dead weight – just proper soldiers and specialists. On top of that, the nationalities run far and wide, giving you local knowledge all over. With the recent additions, I bet this is the elite crew you've been planning a long while.'

Anatin was quiet for some time. 'It's close,' he finally admitted. 'Not like I've got a shopping list, mind, but we could cover most unusual jobs.'

It was late afternoon and the shadows were starting to lengthen. The heat of day was still enough to make them sweat, but the midday lull had passed and the city was getting about its business again.

'So what does the man with the plan say?'

Anatin glanced over, a hint of amusement on his face. 'Oh, you'll be letting me plan this one?'

'Scale's bigger than I'm used to,' Toil admitted. 'Plus we don't want sharp and quiet. It doesn't have to be a bloodbath, but we want the whole city to see. Otherwise some bastard might think to move in as soon as we're gone.'

Anatin smirked. 'A subtle balance, that's what you get when you hire the Cards.'

'Better be, this time round.'

He nodded. 'Three teams. Safir takes the lead with Snow and Tempest. You take Blood and Sun while Teshen has Stars. On the north wall there's a watch-tower. Sitain puts them out then we rig a grenade to blow the wall. That's the signal. Safir leads his suits in and uses Sitain to put the crews out in their beds. When you hear the grenade you take the main gate, have Atieno break its hinges. Secure the guardhouse and move on the palace. They'll have mage-guns so you put them down hard.'

'And Teshen?'

'Scales the south wall. Might need to pass those who ain't light on their feet to Safir. Teshen's team need to climb and run. He goes straight for the kabat – quiet, fast and bloody while you draw all eyes, occupy the office then fight inward as best you can.'

Toil nodded. 'I like it. How about you?'

'I'll hang back with Foren and Paranil. Your boy's useless outside of a library and Foren can run messages for me. I drop my mage-gun half the time when I'm trying to load it so I'll be keeping a strategic eye on things with our friend from the Whitesea.'

'Any contingency?'

'You assign someone with a burner to guard the gate, Safir does the same with that tower. Any more than that and we risk failing the main job. Whatever troops the Whitesea have got stashed in readiness can follow up and sweep the ground outside the Holding.'

'Want me to pass all that on?'

He shook his head. 'You stay here, pick holes in the plan – you're the one who's seen inside the place after all. I'll rally the troops and ferret out the mages. We go once honest folk have gone to bed, assuming we can find any of those in this place.'

'Your little demonstration has attracted some attention,' the Shard said with a smile. 'For the sake of my sanity, I would ask you to spare them an hour or two later, Mistress Ufre. You know what academics are like when something excites their interest.'

Sitain looked back at the heavy doors between them and the clamour outside. The Shard's steward, Tegir, had been forced to bring an escort to make a path for them. The hallway and Court of the Shard were both full of old men and women – all keen to make their acquaintance and unused to being ignored.

'I shall try,' Lastani said, her eyes already on the books. 'There is much I have to do, however.'

'There, I think I can help you.'

'Oh?'

'Having heard your tale and knowing what I do, I believe I can direct you to some of the more relevant texts. I have explained the matter to our custodian of the books.' Here she indicated a man in his thirties with a hunched back, dark skin and bright blue eyes who was waiting off to one side. 'Between us our knowledge is extensive and should narrow your search.'

'I thank you, ah, Shard Urosesh. However, I'm not yet sure what it is I'm looking for.'

Her words seemed only to amuse the Shard further. 'Because you've not found it yet. But remember, I have read a large proportion of these works already. I can give you a lecture if you prefer – it would save you time – but you would have to take my word for much of it.'

'Works for me,' Sitain muttered as she moved around the room.

It wasn't large, just three bulbous alcoves of mage-carved rock around a central pair of tables that sat beneath a trio of round Duegar spheres. 'Hey, we've got some of those!' she added, pointing.

'Do you now?' the Shard asked, eyes glittering. 'From the Labyrinth?'

'Yeah, you should see the Monarch's throne room now, a copyist's wet dream it is.'

'Clearly we know different copyists.' The Shard cleared her throat and gestured around the clover-shaped library. 'In any case, acquaint yourselves with this at your leisure. I have business to attend to, but can return in an hour should you want my assistance.'

'Thank you,' Lastani said. 'I, ah, I must admit I am surprised.'

'That I don't have better things to do with my time?' The Shard smiled. 'Oh I do, but your news was remarkable. It warrants greater attention, I believe, and what would be the point of being in charge if I couldn't, once in a while, do something I'm interested in? The implications for all mages could be profound, I believe. Something has changed with the flow and availability of magic on Urden, that much cannot be denied. Better to risk wasting my time helping you than ignore the bigger picture for all mages.'

'You're taking quite a lot on faith still,' Atieno said.

The Shard raised an eyebrow. 'Not as much as you imagine. This is the Mage Islands and I clawed my way to the leadership of its guilds. I'm not an easy person to fool. To do so when I have a greater knowledge of magic than any fraud, the means to verify details and, of course, the means to effect a horrible death to those who cross me . . . Well, anyone that stupid isn't the best con artist to start with.'

She gave all three of them a brief beaming smile and headed out, calling over her shoulder, 'Custodian Surrildir has prepared a selection of works you may like to peruse first. Enjoy.'

Chapter 15

'Of course I'm not fucking pregnant, you slack-brained Hanese grunt! Have you never had to tell a lie before?'

'I'm just saying, it's a weird lie to tell, ain't it?'

Toil ground her teeth in frustration, anger rendering her momentarily speechless. Finally she exploded again and he felt the full force of her yell from no more than six inches away.

'No! It's a fucking easy one to tell. Gods-in-shards, you're as bad as the rest of these damn fools. Spend five minutes graphically detailing ways you're going to brutalise each other and you lot just snigger. Mention even the possibility of a baby and the room falls silent while all your balls shrivel up!'

Lynx paused. 'So that's a no?'

'Ask me one more bastard time, I dare you!' Toil yelled, pulling a mage-pistol and levelling at him. 'One more gods-burned time!'

'Okay, okay!'

'Touchy,' muttered someone from the safety of the room behind them.

'Aye, pregnant ones get like that,' said someone else before Toil whirled around to aim her gun at the other Cards in the room.

She could feel the heat of anger in her cheeks, not least because that last comment had come from a woman. She knew they were gleefully piling on, but restraint wasn't her finest quality at the best of times.

'Speak up,' she commanded. 'Anyone got something to say, tell it to the whole bastard class.'

None of them spoke, but still it was all she could do not to fire into the crowd on general principle. Deern, Llaith and Varain all wore their best shit-eating grins, while she knew Braqe was always happy to stir the pot in any situation involving Lynx.

The moment she turned her back, however, there was a small cheer from several of them, congratulating Lynx on his lucky escape. He grabbed a tankard and raised it in reply, only to have Toil spin around again and catch him in the act. The urge to throw something was almost overwhelming, despite a loaded mage-pistol being all she had to hand. In the next moment, sense and realisation crashed down like a rattle-cage.

'Dammit, you got me.'

Half the room fell about with laughter and even Lynx risked a small smile. The clash of emotion on her face was clearly something they were relishing. That only deepened the embarrassment she felt, remembering the last time she'd lost her head. At least she wasn't in the great hall of Jarrazir's Bridge Palace now, but in other ways it was worse with all the Cards watching. Toil was a woman who liked to win and be in charge. To find herself suckered in quite so easily left her more than uncomfortable – all the more so for how rarely it happened.

'Right from the start?'

Lynx hesitated. 'Well, you ain't the sort to toss out that piece of news on the job.'

She narrowed her eyes. *Nope, not buying it. You panicked, I saw it in your eyes.*

'You realise I'll have to find some way to exact a terrible revenge for this?' she said quietly.

The grin on his face faltered a touch. Lynx's shoulders

tightened visibly as his usual hunted air returned. She felt a pang of sympathy for him there, not because of what she'd said but just his instinctive reaction to most things in life.

'That's pretty much my life anyway,' he joked, rallying.

Toil hissed in frustration and grabbed Lynx by the shirt, kissing him hard on the lips.

'It's not all there is in your life now,' she said huskily. 'And all this baby talk's reminded me how you make them. We've got an hour or two to spare yet.'

Lynx's eyes widened as she hauled him away in the direction of their room.

'I just hope the subject doesn't put you off your stride,' Toil added as she went. 'This lot can be so very cruel when they think something's funny.'

The cheers followed them all the way to their room and, by then, Lynx's grin was firmly wiped from his face.

'I hope you have passed a pleasant day?'

Sitain looked up to see the Shard standing in the doorway. She had her hands folded like some sort of damned priest and wore a fittingly smug little smile.

'Stuck inside with a bunch of books?' Sitain asked. 'Turns out even the Cards are better company.'

Lastani dragged herself away from the page she'd been bent over for an hour. Her eyes sparkled.

'It's been wonderful!' Lastani breathed.

Sitain snorted. 'First bloody thing she's said since you left.'

'Yet you stayed?' the Shard said, gliding into the room. Her coat of ribbons hung almost to the ground, a riot of colour even in this dim library.

'They reckon I should know more about all this, since I'm tied up in it. I've mostly been waiting for you to get back and give us the quick version.'

The Shard inclined her head and swept around one high-sided chair before settling into it. She ran her fingers over her cropped scalp with a faint rasping, but all the while her gaze never left Sitain. Rarely had she felt more like a bug under scrutiny.

'The quick version is not all that quick, I must admit.'

As she spoke, the Shard reached inside her robes of office and brought out a slim packet of thin cigars. Delicately picking one out with her neatly painted nails, she lit it from the candle that Atieno offered over and sat back again.

'How quick?' Sitain asked as the silence stretched on.

The Shard nodded towards Lastani. 'For you or for her?'

'What's the difference?'

She tossed her head back and laughed at that, not some politician's trill either but a full-throated bark of amusement. 'We are talking about the most significant event since Jang-Her.'

'I've heard of that one! The conclave of the Militant Orders where all those God Fragments in one place made people dream about the gods and speak Duegar?'

'The very same. What you did was perhaps only second to that in terms of magic itself. The weaponisation of God Fragments has significance for human history of course, but the results of your little expedition are yet to be fully felt.'

'What in piss are you on about?' Sitain said. 'Significance to human history?'

'Surely you have felt the change?'

'To what?'

'To magic,' Atieno broke in. 'To the wind and the sky and the earth itself.'

'Nope.'

The Shard coughed. 'Not at all? You are that new to your powers?'

'It wasn't exactly something to advertise where I grew up. The only change I've felt happened in the Labyrinth.'

'Very well. The rest of us, your colleagues included, have felt a difference – gradual, but continuing. While you three have become massively more powerful in yourselves – well, put simply, there is more magic available for all of us.'

'In what way?' Sitain blinked around at the other mages. 'That tree created more magic?'

'Unleashed,' Lastani corrected. 'If what I am reading is true.'

'So far as we know, yes. The clues have been there for decades, but we've been unable to do much about it beyond encourage the more relentless academics in Jarrazir.'

'You knew about Mistress Ishienne's work?'

'Of course. She and I corresponded infrequently over the last decade. I believe at least one work was copied from our library for her. Let me be clear, we did not know what lay beneath the labyrinth. It was just one of several likely locations for something we believed to exist.'

'Which is?'

'A reservoir of power.' The Shard gestured in the air with her cigar. 'I will forego the details – suffice to say that the Banesh Heresy is likely to be broadly correct.'

'And what's that then?'

'Dear me. Do you not even know the myths of the gods?'

Sitain shook her head. 'I grew up in Knights-Charnel territory. Anything with the word heresy attached got stamped on pretty hard.'

'Very well. Some believe that Banesh was once a mortal Duegar who became a god with one purpose only – to kill his fellow gods.'

'Why?'

'Magic is power. There is a distinct problem with concentrating so much in four individuals. A section of Duegar society reacted against the rise of their gods, as more and more power was drawn to them. Whether they were responding to

150

despotism or a more fundamental problem with the balance of the world remains up for debate, but their answer was two-fold.'

'Killing the gods wasn't enough?'

The Shard shook her head. 'Power finds a way; new gods would rise. The priesthood or secret society or whatever it was, they also created the Labyrinth of Jarrazir – possibly more than one. Within these they drew vast quantities of magic; bottled it and stored it away from those who would be gods.'

Sitain scowled. 'Until some bunch of idiots came along and pulled the stopper out?'

'That part was not included in the plan,' the Shard admitted. 'Perhaps it was inevitable, but we had hoped to have more time to study the Labyrinth before the tree was accessed.'

'So this is as much your mess as ours?'

At last Sitain saw a flicker of discomfort on her face. 'Many of my colleagues would disagree, but yes. It is our mess too.'

'A mess that makes you all more powerful,' Atieno pointed out. 'A mess that makes the mage guilds all the more significant across the continent.'

'And the woman at the top of that particular tree all the more significant too,' the Shard added. 'The self-interest hasn't gone unnoticed I assure you, but frankly I am powerful enough for my tastes and could do without this.'

'Do without it?'

'I am the head of the largest collection of mage guilds in the Riven Kingdom and beyond,' she said without enthusiasm. 'I'm pretty powerful already. As much as I would like to improve the lot of all mages everywhere, I prefer not to be looking over my shoulder each and every day.'

'Tanimbor?' Atieno asked as Sitain tried to remember the strange guildmaster's name.

'Is the greatest of those annoyances,' the Shard conceded. 'He has approached you, then?'

'In a fashion, yes.'

She sighed and took a long pull on her cigar, the smoke curling from one corner of her mouth as she thought. 'Guildmaster Tanimbor is the most ambitious of my rivals, the most devoted to improving the lot of mages everywhere. He was hungry for this robe long before the state of magic changed across the continent, but as our position improves so more mages become interested in taking my position.'

'For a leader beset by rivals, you're remarkably open with us.'

'As we've established, you are a major consideration for me now. I will not hide my interest in having you as allies, what would be the point of doing so? But in the spirit of openness, may I ask you a question?'

'By all means,' Lastani said.

The Shard gave her a thoughtful look. 'Very well. What did you leave out of your story?'

'Excuse me?'

'I think you heard,' she said. 'I have no doubt you told us the truth when you spoke to the Guild Court. Equally, I have no doubt you held some things back. I have offered you a good measure of hospitality, I hope you would agree. In return I would like to hear some things that the others did not.'

'I . . .' Flustered, Lastani turned to Sitain and Atieno. 'We have told you about the tattoos, the tree and the events surrounding it, what else is there to share?'

The Shard's stare was as hard as granite, though her voice betrayed no anger or hostility. 'No one gives the full story, by accident or design.'

'The shields?' Sitain suggested. 'Did we mention that? We each held off a volley of gunfire while the Cards did their thing.'

'A logical conclusion of your increased abilities.'

The Shard rose, grimacing and putting one hand to her hip as she did so.

152

'I do not wish for this to be a confrontation. I'm sure we will speak again and soon – at which point perhaps you will recall something further. If not . . . well, I have already offered my assistance and will remain true to my word.'

She smiled at Sitain. 'An understanding between us will yet prove valuable in the months and years to come, I believe. I remain a woman of optimism, despite having to deal with men such as Tanimbor. However, for today I think it has grown late and I am tired. Steward Tegir will see you to your escort and welcome you back as you choose. Good evening.'

Chapter 16

Deep into the night, Sitain lingered in the shadow of a pillar somewhere in Nquet Dam. Strips of cloud overlaid the light of the moon and the skyriver, laying slashes of white across the city. The air was blessedly cool after a hot day. Fitful rain scattered across the district while the slim dark shapes of tysarn flashed through the air. Something bit her on the neck while she waited. Sitain slapped her hand hard against it, the sound echoing through the night. She froze, feeling a squirt of blood under her fingertips, but the noise attracted no attention.

The smell of blood brought a pair of small tysarn swirling down from the levels above. She watched them warily, able to pick out almost every detail with her unnaturally good eyesight and wishing she couldn't. There was an evil look to them, even when just a hand span across. A rapacious tilt to their spear-shaped heads and the strange double movement of their two pairs of wings that unnerved her.

As the tysarn circled, her mage-sight wavered until she blinked it away. For a moment she wondered if the insect had a poison bite, but the warmth in her belly told another story.

Maybe that last nerve-steadier wasn't the best idea, Sitain reflected. *But at least I don't feel sick with fear now. That's probably an improvement.*

She walked unsteadily on, rounding the corner to find the

Siym Holding's perimeter wall up ahead. There was no one in sight this late at night. The district wasn't quite silent even at this hour, but honest folk were at home and the dishonest tended to keep well away from any kabat's domain.

Well, 'cept us of course.

She couldn't see any guards on the wall or in the tower, but she was careful not to look hard. If they had spotted her they didn't seem to care. One young foreign woman walking drunkenly home was hardly a threat and if they suspected a distraction, they should be looking elsewhere anyway.

Surprise is our chief weapon, she reminded herself. *Surprise and overwhelming firepower.*

There were no windows within reach, of course. The locals weren't total idiots even if most of their fighters were Mastrunners. Teshen had tried to explain Masts to them but it made little sense to Sitain; halfway between a gang raid and a codified sport. All that mattered was the guards here were good in close combat and worked well as a team. It also meant they had a set way of thinking about fighting.

We mostly just want to kill the other lot as quick as we can, she remembered Teshen saying. *That gives us the early advantage because that's not their first instinct, but any drawn-out fight might bring the other crews of Nquet Dam and then we're shafted.*

She stopped at a bulge in the line of the wall and looked up. The lower half of the tower was blank, just a curved section of stone that ran for two storeys until a pair of cross-slit windows broke the uniformity. There was a platform above that, sheltered by a stone roof with only a narrow gap between. If you were really good you might be able to throw a grenade inside, but you needed to get it right first time.

So here's me, Sitain thought tipsily. *A gods-damned human bloody grenade.* She grinned. *But Lastani says I'm one o' the most powerful ones in the Riven Kingdom, so at least there's that.*

She checked around. There was no one in sight, not even the Cards who were meant to be following.

If they ain't and this is all one big joke on me, I'll probably walk away without being shot. Which is nice.

Sitain placed her hands on the wall and summoned her magic. The power wasn't bursting out of her these days, not like those first hours in Jarrazir, but the more she learned to control it the more she realised how much stronger she was. It came easily now, a cool sensation that washed through her veins and sharpened her eyesight even more. She breathed out, luxuriating in the sensation, while the lines of tattoos on her hand traced a white outline of willow leaves. In moments that became a blazing light and she looked up, summoning a wave of power before sending it up through the tower.

There was no result. Possibly something that sounded like the scuff of a shoe, but the stone walls were thick. A horrible thought occurred to Sitain. This could all be for nothing if there was no one in the tower, if they'd decided to ignore the rain and patrol the wall elsewhere for a while.

I really might get shot then, oh gods.

She looked around, feeling a moment of panic as she stood exposed on the street, but aware running away would only be more dangerous. Caught in a moment of indecision, Sitain did nothing. She was still trying to work out what came next when the sound of trotting feet reached her. Out of the shadows of an alley facing the guard tower came Estal, serving as the company's grenadier on the basis that Anatin trusted her not to be so much of an idiot as the rest.

'All done, girly?' Estal called.

'I . . . I think so.'

Estal cocked her head at Sitain. 'How's that work then? You did it or you didn't.'

'I did it. Dunno what happened though.'

'Don't worry, we were watching. They were inside it all right. If you've done your thing, it's over.'

Without waiting for a reply Estal went to the stretch of wall to one side of the tower. From a bag at her hip she withdrew a wrapped pouch of clay and slapped it against the wall. With a little prodding she nodded then gave Sitain a look.

'Might want to step back a bit now, in case I drop something.'

'What?' Sitain scrabbled backwards even as Estal snickered.

The woman didn't respond as she focused on pulling a grenade from her bag. She didn't bother inserting a pin to prime the bomb, they were going to break the magic-charged core a different way. This she pressed into the clay and worked at the edges until she was satisfied. She removed her hands gingerly and Sitain held her breath, but the grenade held.

'Come on,' Estal said, retracing her path. Sitain didn't wait a second longer and had overtaken the woman by the time they'd gone ten paces. She rounded the nearest corner and almost slammed into Safir. He caught her arm just in time and pivoted her away. Estal slipped around the corner and snatched up the mage-gun she'd left propped against a wall.

The bulk of Snow and Tempest were huddled in a hexagonal piece of ground, ten yards across with wooden beams strung between the buildings that occupied three sides. Those beams supported a healthy spray of vines that gave a fair amount of cover from prying eyes.

Sitain blinked as she looked around the assembled troops. Clearly the vines didn't just provide cover for them. Lynx was busily popping grapes into his mouth even as he loaded his mage-gun one-handed.

'Seriously? You're eating *now*?'

He shrugged and crunched one last grape before discarding the rest. 'Was hungry.'

'Get ready,' Safir hissed. 'Sitain, you bring up the rear. Estal – do it.'

'Said yer prayers?' she asked with a smile.

'A short word, yes.'

Someone snorted in the shadows, Braqe by the sounds of it. 'Quite a few short words, aye. Just as well Lastani ain't here, she shocks easy.'

'I'll come up with some more if we're standing here much longer,' Safir growled.

'Aye, sir.' Estal levelled her mage-gun. 'Time to see which grenade I ended up pulling out of the bag,' she muttered as she took careful aim.

There wasn't time for anyone to object. Estal pulled the trigger and Sitain saw her jolted back by the force of an earther, staggering under the recoil. The deafening sound made Sitain flinch, but was swallowed a moment later as the entire world seemed to shudder around her.

'Now.'

Teshen's whisper came before the great rolling boom had ended, but it was all that was needed. Kas was first around the corner, fletching already drawn back to her ear. Suth stepped around her, leaving the first shot to Kas, Teshen ready behind. The cloud cover left little for them to see by, but all three had been changed by the magic in Jarrazir's labyrinth. There were a few worrying implications there, but right now everyone bearing the light-tattoos were glad of their unnatural night vision. Even in the dark the heads of two sentries on the wall were clear against the clouds behind.

An arrow slammed into the first while he was still looking back towards the flames and noise of Estal's grenade. He pitched down off the wall without a sound. Kas had a line on the second before he'd even worked out what was happening.

But the arrow skipped off the stone wall and all she got for her trouble was a yelp of alarm.

'Go,' Suth ordered those behind her, one eye closed.

The whipcrack of her icer split the night. A faint cloud appeared around the guard's head as it burst open. Teshen was already moving, hauling forward the pair of ladders they'd brought. The wood clattered against the wall and then he was scrambling up – one hand on the ladder, the other levelling a gun.

The years seemed to fall away, though the curses and grunts of the Cards behind would never have been tolerated in his old Masts crew. The rush was still the same, that sprint and leap over mage-carved stone. He'd been bigger than most Mastrunners, but great slabs of muscle weren't so useful when you needed to sprint and climb from level to level.

Age would catch up with him soon enough, Teshen knew that, but for now there was only the hunt. It prompted a faint ache in what passed for his soul. A remembrance for times past. One last game before he never returned to this place. One last victory to remind the city of his name.

Best I send the city a note though, Teshen thought, chuckling inwardly. *Make sure I'm bloody miles away first, just in case.*

All was still up on the wall. One guard was dead on the walkway, the other on the dirt floor between the wall and houses. There were a few voices coming from the houses, but most would be employees of the Holdings – few fighters among them.

'Go, that way,' Teshen hissed as his troops followed him up. His directions would take them straight down an alley behind the waterfront, a near-direct route to the palace. But this was Caldaire and the houses were packed close together even inside a kabat's domain. The path of a rooftop run lay invitingly before him. Teshen patted his long knives in their sheaths, hefted his mage-gun and grinned in the dark.

One last run for the Bloody Pauper. Let's make it a good one.

*

Lynx ran, his heart quickening with every step. Safir was ahead of him, Layir leading the way across the rubble of the explosion. The wall was breached and pieces lay all around. There was barely space for two people to enter abreast, but Layir thumped one jutting chunk with the stock of his gun. It fell inside with a crash to open the way for those behind him.

Ahead of them was a tall skeleton of a half-finished building, the Mastrunners' training ground. Beams and ropes crisscrossed the thing, four storeys of scarred stone that jutted like ribs in the dark. The barracks formed three sides of a square behind the training ground and great lumpen warehouses sat beyond.

There was a shout and the flash of movement off to the left. Lynx ignored it as Safir peeled off, driving on towards the barracks with a familiar growl in his belly. He'd missed this. Right now, in this dark moment, he let himself admit that. Not the killing, not the fear or fatigue, but that rush of onward movement. The precarious line between success and death, the unthinking, unrelenting charge that had been So Han's success.

It was part of him, his heritage perhaps. Lynx had turned his back on his homeland, but some piece of it lived on inside him. He honestly didn't know if it was some savage part he'd adopted to stay alive in To Lort prison, or whether this was within all Hanese.

Sitain doesn't have it, a treacherous voice at the back of his head reminded him. *She's tough, but she doesn't have this killer instinct. This is just you, this is what you were long before the prison broke you. They made you a commando because they saw what you really were.*

The first Mastrunner emerged from the barracks, a tall woman carrying some sort of a long hooked axe. Lynx shot her before she'd even cleared the door. The familiar kick against his shoulder prompted his feet to stop, his knees to bend as he reloaded and others overtook. An arrow flashed out from a first floor window and sliced Braqe's shoulder as the woman stepped ahead of Lynx. She hissed and snarled as she returned fire with an earther. The shot blew out the window and a foot of wall beside it, roaring up through the roof behind in an explosion of splinters.

'Hanese bastard,' she muttered as she knelt to reload and Lynx advanced.

'Thanks,' he whispered, firing again at movement by the doorway.

Braqe didn't answer as his return shot produced a scream. The cry was immediately drowned out by another earther being fired into the building. It smashed through a beam and brought down part of the ceiling. More shouts, more cries as icers snapped out all around them.

More arrows were returned, mage-tipped this time. Safir got hit by something in the side of the head and he quietly folded up, limp on the ground. Another Card caught a second – a flare of fire bursting around her arm as she shrieked in pain and fear. The Card's return burst was devastating and the Mastrunners hunkered down. Sitain ran forward with Layir close beside as Lynx reached the doorway and fired a sparker inside.

The explosion of jagged light threw stark shadows across the hallway and room beyond, bringing cut-short screams from the silhouette of contorted figures. He dropped his long gun and drew his sword, his orders being to defend the doorway. It was a nasty place to stand for any length of time, within the killing ground of this courtyard, but it wouldn't last that long.

Under Layir's guard Sitain drew again on her magic. Again Lynx felt his own tattoos warm in response, the power singing through his bones built and then snapped away. In one burst she hurled the magic up and out, as though she stood at the base of a funnel. Lynx saw the magic go, a darkly glittering wave that surged up while he reeled from the force employed.

'In!' Layir roared, kicking open a door on the other side.

Lynx pulled his pistol and led the way, falchion-tip leading though it was a chopping weapon. Any sort of a point with his strength behind it would be enough here. The confines of the barracks were too close for any clever sword play. He barged straight into a man coming the other way and somehow failed to stab him. They slammed together, faces meeting with a stinging slap. The smaller man staggered while Lynx blinked, still half-stunned from the impact, then Llaith shot the man.

Together they pressed on, stepping over bodies as they went. Through a doorway Lynx found himself in the mess hall. Long empty tables and benches provided cover in the near-pitch black. The clunk of crossbows greeted them, two icers crashed back in response but the other Cards couldn't see as well. Lynx shot one Mastrunner who was still aiming her crossbow then threw himself across a table at the ones who'd fired.

They barely saw him coming in the gloom. Lynx slashed one down the shoulder and bore the other to the ground. He slammed that one against the floor, grabbing him by the neck to smash his head against the tiles. The other pulled a knife, but froze as Llaith fired on someone else, the icer flash illuminating the room.

The hesitation gave Lynx time to dodge the slash that followed. Long-haired with dark tattoos down each arm, the Mastrunner looked like a veteran fighter, but the icer had ruined his night-sight. Lynx thrust his sword into the man's throat to finish him as fast as he could while more gunshots rang out.

'Anyone awake up here,' he heard Braqe yell from the corridor, 'stay down or I fire a burner and you all die nasty!'

Lynx picked himself up and wiped the blood from his sword. 'Hope they speak Parthish,' he commented to Llaith.

The ageing mercenary shrugged. 'Fucking dead if they don't.'

Lynx went to fetch his mage-gun from outside. Safir was still down, Layir crouched over his adoptive father.

'Dead?'

'No,' Layir replied. He took hold of Safir's collar and dragged him over to the Mastrunners' barracks. 'Just out cold. Must've been a night-arrow.'

'Lucky, that.'

'Lucky for us the easiest way to win at Masts is to put the enemy to sleep.'

Lynx loaded another sparker and pointed to the barracks. 'Does that mean I'm in charge? Shit. Right – lock this down and set a guard. I'll take a look around then meet you on the other side.'

'Thought you didn't like being in charge?'

'I like getting shot even less.'

'Mewling Hanese wimps!'

'Yeah? Well you're . . . ah shit. I got nothing.'

Layir grinned and headed into the barracks. 'Old people are funny,' he called over his shoulder.

Leaving the ready wit of the young behind, Lynx let the shadows swallow him up and old habits took over. Layir's laughter vanished, replaced with the commando's instinct. There was gunfire not far away, the heavy boom of earthers and crackle of sparkers. It had to be Toil's group.

There won't be any other company in the Riven Kingdom who can use a Tempest mage in battle. Wonder if Anatin's realised that and jacked his prices up a bit?

With a rattle-cage attached to the back of the gate, an earther couldn't breach it effectively. The rattle-cage was an interlocking set of chains and bars that would mostly warp and tangle under the impact. But with Atieno making the hinges and chains crumble to rust, the gate could be pulled down. Most likely.

Lynx flinched back into the shadows as a door jerked open in front of him. A pair of Holding guards peered out. Neither looked keen for a fight despite the mage-guns they carried, twitching at the continued bursts of gunfire.

'Hands in the air!' Lynx called from the cover of darkness.

The guards flinched and looked around, trying to see the speaker. When neither of their guns were pointing at him Lynx stepped forward. On instinct one of them jerked back, bringing his gun up. He never had the chance to realise his mistake.

Lynx fired and an explosion of lightning and gore burst around the guard's head, lashing his comrade in the process. That one managed a cut-off scream then all was silent. Not wanting to leave mage-guns lying around for the Holding's youths to make a fatal mistake with, Lynx made his way cautiously to the dead men.

There seemed to be no one else watching so he pulled their cartridge belts and emptied the guns, using one to load his own. It didn't take him long to skirt the area, but there weren't any more guards on the narrow streets. He doubted they were getting much in the way of pay if the Siym finances were on the brink of collapse. Loyalty only went so far when you had a family to feed.

He worked around to the rear of the barracks, careful to announce his presence and avoid an icer from his own side. There he found Layir surveying their path alongside Llaith and Estal. Sitain was kneeling beside the burned Card, whose name was Aspegrin. She'd put her out, the burn bad enough she wasn't going anywhere. Braqe emerged from the barracks a moment later, wincing at the cut she'd taken on Lynx's behalf. Safir was also stretched out with another man of Snow, Ylor, beside him. He'd taken an arrow in the leg.

'Braqe, you good?'

'Fuck you.'

'Right then. Ylor and Burnel, you're on guard duty. Watch our injured and put a burner in the barracks if they give you trouble, right?' Lynx said this in a loud voice in case there was anyone awake in the upper floor to listen. 'The rest of you, follow me.'

'Who put you in charge?' Braqe demanded, bristling as usual. 'You ain't senior here.'

She pointed at Llaith as she spoke, but the ageing fighter wearing the Diviner of Tempest shook his head. 'All o' you, follow Lynx's lead.'

'Ah right,' Braqe spat. 'That's how it is, eh?'

Lynx frowned at her for a moment but it didn't take him long to remember what the problem was. Braqe had fought the Hanese herself and lost her brother to them. Seeing Lynx at the head of a swift and bloody night strike would bring up some nasty memories for her.

'That's how it is,' Lynx confirmed with all the calmness left to him. 'Walk away if you don't like it. I'm going to back up our friends.'

'Fuck you.'

He turned away. 'Glad we got that sorted out. Come on, at the double.'

Chapter 17

Teshen ghosted along the rooftop. Old habits reawakened inside him as his feet chose a path all on their own. On the ground below he glimpsed the flash and crack of Suth leading the way. The compact Jarraziran was perfect for this work, light-stepping and lithe with a remarkable aim. If she'd had any major personality flaws, she might have found herself as a Card years earlier, rather than a Jarraziran soldier. Instead it was the light-tattoo that bound her to Anatin's Mercenary Deck and simultaneously made her even more lethal in the process.

Keep your mind on the job, dammit, Teshen reminded himself. Still his eyes drifted towards Suth. She looked nothing like Sanshir, but there was that cold razor's edge to her all the same. Here and now, the similarity caught something deep inside of him.

They closed on the palace quickly, two guards on the shoreline dispatched and one Card tasked with guarding the shore. The palace was the biggest structure in the Holding by some way. The south wing rose to six storeys and looked out over the lagoon. This was the biggest risk, Teshen knew. There were simply too many people in there to contain easily. How many guards was anyone's guess, but probably only a handful. The bigger question was whether he'd be cutting a path through civilians, armed or not, or wandering the halls trying to track down the kabat.

Fortunately the Whitesea folk are good for more than just finance.

Their contact had provided some information on the target – coupled with Teshen's own memory it might prove enough. He would lead his team inside and roll the dice once they were there. Four had light-tattoos and they'd make short work of the guards, but still they would have to get lucky. He didn't have the numbers to cover every possibility.

A few lamps shone in the palace's upper windows, one voice echoing out from the central courtyard. The spires of the south wing overlooked much of this district and the kabat's private quarters was a raised section on the shore side. A large terrace projected from the front. It was the easiest way to reach the kabat and everyone knew it, so likely she wouldn't be there now.

The mage-carved rock was done with greater precision here than the rest of the Holding. Bands of colourful tiles ran around the building and outlined each door and window, bright and gaudy by the standards of the mage-carved city. Water-spirits formed the gutter-outlets and every terrace, bridge and walkway was flanked by sweeping arches – while every section of wall included alcoves for iron lanterns or statues.

Stretching from the private quarters to the shore were the kabat's gardens, where the only cover was a single building and low stone walls. Tiers of gravel and shrubs led down to the water, ornamental fruit trees and a long vine-draped pergola breaking up the open ground. There was just one guard in there, an older woman who was trying to see what was going on in other parts of the Holding. Teshen crept up behind her and broke her neck before she even heard him coming. Once all his remaining troops were gathered around him in the garden, Teshen surveyed the path ahead.

'Now where?' Suth whispered.

'Now we've got a choice,' Teshen replied, glancing back at his remaining six. 'I don't see any guards outside, do you?'

'No. Either they're waiting at high windows or they're all with the kabat.'

'Likely both. Kabat's not going to last long if she looks scared by an attack. They've heard mage-guns and know this isn't another kabat making a move, so what do they do?'

'You asking or thinking in a loud way?'

Teshen grinned. 'Thinking, so shut it.'

'Screaming hells, that's the first time I've seen you really smile,' Suth said, ignoring his instruction. 'Born to this shit, eh?'

'Damn right.' He nodded forwards. 'They're expecting a straight assault, how the Cards would normally do it – hot an' heavy right up the front.'

'Tease. I suppose that means you want to slip quietly in from the back?'

Kas muttered something to the Card beside her. He gave a filthy chuckle as Teshen continued. 'The kabat can't hide in her quarters. Likely she's got every gun in the palace ready to meet Toil's assault. We go in the north wing and cut across. Follow my lead.'

He set off, moving quick and low across the gardens, trusting the others to do the same. As they reached the north wing he could hear voices drift out through the shuttered windows. The keening of children and parents trying to sooth them. The wing formed a gentle curve overlooking a low rocky cliff, below which a pair of seagoing ships were berthed.

The ground rose up beyond it. There a steep and treacherous slope came to an abrupt and windswept point half the height of the north wing. It was bare and unused, a recognised border line between the Siym Holding and another kabat's domain that was left unclaimed by either.

Teshen began to climb up to a small balcony in an unlit section, halfway down the wing. Listening at the tall shutter doors for a moment, he heard nothing and put his shoulder to it as Suth and Kas climbed up behind him. The wood broke open easily and he half-fell into the room beyond. A thick rug muted the sound of his boots as he checked around, hands on his knives, then went to pull the others up. Suth slipped past him like a ghost, mage-pistols extended left and right.

The room was square and doors led off either side, presumably to bedrooms, while the one ahead would be to the main corridor. Dark imported wooden furniture gave it an elegant air, but even in the dark Teshen could see the slight shabbiness and chaotic sprawl. Sketches covered one whole table, an easel with a half-finished seascape stood beside the balcony door.

Suth checked one bedroom only to quickly emerge and head to the other. That one, Teshen saw, was still dark but Suth paused for longer as she looked. Eventually she closed the door quietly again.

'Old lady,' she whispered. 'Still sleeping. Smells of rum.'

Teshen nodded. He'd chosen this wing partly because it was where the lower-ranked Siym lived. He doubted anyone here would own a mage-pistol and any fool who came after them with a knife would be easy to deal with. Opening the door to the main corridor, he peered out. There were voices out there, sounding scared and worried rather than guards trying to maintain order.

He glanced back. All of his Cards were ready.

'No killing unless we have to,' he said softly.

Kas moved up alongside him, bow at the ready and four arrows in the fingers of her draw hand. She gave him a nod and Teshen jerked the door open.

No one noticed them at first, walking fast and soft. The corridor was clear and just a few doors were open, the inhabitants scared to emerge. They knew what was going on, or at least could guess something close to the truth. They weren't in danger unless they got in the way. Loyalty to the family was one thing, facing down armed killers was another.

Teshen was at the end of the corridor before the first cut-off scream came from a room he was passing. His head flicked around in time to see the door bang shut so he kept on going, breaking into a trot in case any guard investigated the shriek. Long slanted shafts running down between apartments brought a little moonlight in but that was all. The occasional oil lamps he passed were dark and cold, the extravagance of keeping them burning at night too great to maintain.

At the end there was a wide double-stairway, leading down on the left and up on the right. Teshen slowed to let Kas overtake. At the bottom of the stair, illuminated by a dancing yellow light, was a guard at a window. Kas paused a moment then shot him. The guard staggered, his cry as much of surprise as pain, then a second arrow took him in the heart and he crumpled backwards.

There was a shout of alarm from the hall. Teshen bounded down the steps to meet two Mastrunners coming the other way. He kicked the first square in the chest, throwing her back against the wall. The other tried to bring his crossbow to bear but Kas fired again and made him flinch. In the next moment Teshen was on him. His knives carved a bloody path through his defence before punching into his chest. He dodged to the side in case the woman was on him then went on the attack again. Catching a hasty swipe of her crossbow Teshen drove a knife into her side. The second went into her chest and then he cut her throat.

Suth ran past him, pistols level as she peered into the hall beyond, but soon lowered them.

'Empty,' she reported, glancing down as Teshen's handiwork before crossing the hall.

She ignored the tall peaked door to outside and checked the open doorways on the far side. One was a short antechamber, the other a grand stairway with a wooden rail down the centre. Teshen led the way once more. In moments they were through a door and into the opulent private apartments of the kabat and her family. It was then that the shooting started.

Lynx skidded to a halt and scrambled back around the corner. Icers burst over the stone workshop walls. Sitain thumped down beside him a moment later as the others scattered.

'Veraimin's breath! Is this how you commandos used to do it?' she called over the sound of chunks of stone burst. 'There's more hiding than I was expecting!'

Lynx winced as shards of stone pattered around him. 'Not really how it went, no.'

'Ah, well you're old now,' she said. 'Probably a bit rusty.'

'Is this your version of helping?'

Sitain shook her head, eyes wide in the dark. 'Nope, just too scared for much else.'

Lynx snorted. 'Learn to shoot straight and you might be less frightened!'

She cringed as an earther boomed out and caved in a wall just yards away. Lynx turned away to protect his eyes.

'Pretty sure I won't!' Sitain yelled in his ear.

The gunfire died down and Lynx had a chance to look around. They were not in a good position, little cover to evade or flank their attackers.

'How about that shield thing you did in Jarrazir?'

'Is that going to be your answer to everything?'

'Every time someone's trying to shoot me? Good chance o' that, yeah.'

'Shit. I . . . I can try it. It won't last long though.'

Lynx tried another look around the corner. There was an

171

open stretch of ground twenty yards long, then some sort of sunken water garden surrounded by foliage. Past that was the palace, the nearest block of which had suddenly erupted into gunfire when he appeared.

'Quick is all we need,' he muttered. 'They won't have much ammo. Hey, Layir, get an earther ready!'

Lynx loaded a burner into his own gun. He took two quick breaths and nodded to Sitain. The tattoos on his skin flared white immediately. He could see the glow from his cheek even as Sitain began to blaze. She stood with arms raised, buoyed by the sudden roar of power inside her. Lynx followed at a crouch, ready to fire but anticipating the gunfire she'd have to endure first.

The air ahead of Sitain was a smoky haze, a shapeless and shifting curtain of shadow that billowed as she moved. She cried out as the first icer struck, some strange mingling of terror, shock and exultation. Before too long he couldn't hear her as icers hammered into the shield in rapid succession. Some small part of his mind counted the shots before a pause, seven, eight, nine, while he scanned for their source. Then the gunfire faltered and Lynx yelled Sitain's name.

The shield vanished in an instant. Sitain dropped to a crouch as Layir loomed at her shoulder. Lynx sensed him there as he drew a line for his shot, waiting for Layir. The boom of the earther hammered at his ears when it came, but Lynx was ready for it and followed the dark path with his eyes. Layir's shot smashed into the rocky wall of a second floor and burst through. The windows on either side crumpled and shattered as Lynx fired next.

A stinging scent clawed at his nose as the burner tore through the night. There was the familiar sour taste of dread in his gut as the wrecked palace windows crumpled. Flames bloomed before bursting out from the other windows. The roar of fire met screams

172

of people and merged to one, but Lynx didn't wait to inspect his cruel handiwork. Burners were a necessary horror, he knew that, but he'd seen too much of their effects over the years.

'Back!' Lynx yelled, he and Layir dragging Sitain safely back around the corner.

The anticipated return volley didn't come as Lynx reloaded. Just as he was getting ready to skirt to the other side of the building there was a flurry of gunshots. This time none of them struck the workshop. He looked at Layir who shrugged and gestured for him to step out in the open.

'Oh thanks,' Lynx muttered. He stood there a little longer, but before long he started to feel a bit silly so he edged back to the corner.

This is how I'll likely die, Lynx thought as he looked around it. *Getting shot to avoid feeling stupid.*

The first gunshot made him yelp and scrabble back around while Layir chortled behind him.

'Ulfer's horn, didn't think you'd actually do it!' the young Olostiran hissed.

'Do it again,' Braqe urged from further back. 'Slower this time.'

'Anyone want to be ordered out there instead?' Lynx snapped. Before there were any volunteers a loud voice broke the temporary hush. Lynx paused. 'That Teshen?'

'Nah, Teshen don't speak foreign,' Layir said.

'This whole city speaks foreign,' Lynx replied. 'He was born here, remember?'

'Oh, yeah – probably Teshen then. Sounds like him.'

'Are you drunk?'

'Not one drop of booze has crossed my lips,' Layir said solemnly.

Lynx listened to the words unspoken there and decided he didn't want to know any more. If it was Teshen talking, this was over. Most likely. His suspicion was helped by Kas yelling for him to come out of hiding.

'Come on,' Lynx grunted, mage-gun raised as he went.

The others let him step out before moving, but he chose to ignore that, advancing on the palace in the faint light of the skyriver. He saw more Cards emerging off to his right. Toil was at their fore and the pale face of Reft loomed over her.

In several windows he saw locals with mage-guns, tracking his path but snatching glances towards the part Lynx and Layir had laid waste to. There, in the wrecked window, were Teshen and Kas either side of an older woman, presumably Kabat Siym.

The kabat had light brown skin with the same sandy hair as Teshen, although hers was shaved up the sides and the remainder put in a topknot. Somewhere past fifty, she was tall with a strong build. She probably would have made a good fight of things had Teshen not been pressing a mage-pistol behind her ear.

'It's over,' Teshen called, repeating the same in his native language. What followed was, Lynx guessed, the local dialect for 'throw down your weapons' but it didn't elicit any response.

Old instincts prickled at Lynx and he dropped to one knee, lining up a shot on one of the guards at the windows. The scuffle of feet behind him suggested the rest of his small command were doing the same.

Or they've just run away, the treacherous voice at the back of his head suggested.

The stalemate didn't last long. Teshen said something to the kabat and with a scowl she called out to the guards, saying something not unlike Teshen's words. There was a pause then the guards put up their weapons.

A couple tossed theirs from the windows, making Lynx wince though the cartridges didn't go off, before they turned away from their windows. Presently, Holding guards and a handful of fetish-adorned Mastrunners emerged from the main doorway. Behind them was Suth, a pistol in each hand and such an assured saunter Lynx couldn't help but wonder if she'd gone to the same school of arrogance as Toil.

He put up his gun and they waited for Teshen to come down. A few Cards collected the remaining mage-guns, corralled the resigned Siym fighters and helped themselves to every mage cartridge they could find. The Mastrunners bristled at such treatment, but in the face of Varain's grinning belligerence they wisely chose not to pick a fight. Beyond their red sashes and tied-up hair, they had no uniformity in their appearance. Two sported dozens of tattoos, but most just had crew markings on their upper arms like Teshen.

'The Siym Holding is now under the control of the Whitesea Banking Consortium,' Toil declared as Teshen and the kabat appeared. 'The Holding is forfeit in its entirety for the non-payment of loans.'

She waited a while as Teshen translated, looking up at the various windows around them. Most of the Holding's inhabitants were too far away to hear, but Lynx could see a good number of faces creep to the windows. He guessed this was enough of an audience to get the message across.

'All employees and Siym who wish to stay will be paid any overdue wages recorded in the ledgers. The Consortium intends to continue running the Holding – the title of kabat will be added to the ancillary honorifics of each Consortium Principal and their Factor will direct affairs here.'

There was no word of protest, no anger or complaints, but no obvious resentment either. The Siym looked resigned to their fate, the guards more relieved than anything else that they hadn't been shot yet.

'Additional guards will be brought in temporarily,' Toil went on. 'There will be a curfew for five nights and anyone who breaks it or takes a weapon to any Consortium employee may be shot. Any guard who molests the Holding's inhabitants will be dealt with harshly.'

She paused and nodded to Teshen as a sense of alarm welled up inside Lynx. Before he could move or call out, the Knight of Stars put his gun to the kabat's head and pulled the trigger. A cloud of pink and white exploded into the light of the skyriver, the kabat hurled sideways by the icer's force.

Lynx looked at the guards and the faces at the windows. Several had flinched, some even looked away, but none appeared even remotely surprised.

Just me who didn't see this coming, he realised. *Shit.*

Teshen said something more out loud then reloaded his mage-pistol and turned away, leaving two guards to hesitantly advance on the body. Toil nodded to them and the pair set about taking the kabat away before the dark knife-winged shapes circling above could descend.

'So it ends,' Toil said in the same tone as Teshen, but more to herself than any others.

She spared Lynx one brief glance that he couldn't interpret then turned and headed back the way she'd come.

As easy as that? Lynx asked himself. Certainly from the faces around him, it truly did seem over. The Siym knew when they were beaten.

Is this how business is done round here? Everyone gets on with life again once victory is declared?

He stood there a long while, until the small tysarn ventured down to the ground to lap at the blood on the dusty floor. Feeling a knot in his gut, Lynx left too.

Chapter 18
(now – two mornings later)

Lynx opened his eyes and immediately regretted it as something landed in one. Blinking and cursing, he tried to roll over, but his body was less than cooperative. One arm was pinned to his body by the tangle of bedsheets, the other was numb and ungainly. More thumps came from the ceiling, another scattering of dust drifted down.

He flopped around until his arm was free, then did his best to get the dust out of his eye while a growling Toil yanked the sheet back over her body.

'Fuck's that noise?' he muttered, to himself as much as Toil.

'Reft an' Deern,' came the muffled reply.

'Eh? Oh.'

Lynx shook his head gently, dismay momentarily overcoming the hot thump of hangover. The pair had the room above them and apparently the ceiling was struggling to contain them.

'Don't get any ideas,' Toil added a few moments later. She emerged briefly from the covers and squinted up at him, red hair plastered by sweat across half her face.

'Already got 'em.'

She hesitated. 'Are they about food or coffee?'

'Yup.'

'Good puss, now bugger off and let me sleep.'

Lynx eased himself around on to the side of the bed and fumbled at the discarded clothes. He could feel the warmth in the air already, bright lines picking out the slats of the window shutter. The room lurched around him as he stood to pull up his britches, but a steadying hand against the wall was enough to fix that. He spared a glance for Toil, but she was already snoring faintly despite the continued enthusiasm upstairs.

The lodgings Teshen had found them were typical of the city from what Lynx could see – tall stacks of narrow rooms around a central courtyard. It was on high ground at the seaward side of Auferno district so there were no south-facing windows but, as Lynx emerged from his small room, he could feel there was little breeze that day anyway.

Instead, a sparkling blue sky peered down through the ropes strung between the four towers of mage-cast stone. Through it all was the faint white line of the skyriver, marred by a single grey spot the name of which escaped Lynx.

The calls of seabirds and deep croaks of tysarn echoed around the courtyard as he leaned on the rail and blinked away the throb behind his eyes. The sun was up, but once Lynx could see properly he realised it was still early. The buildings blocked the worst of its glare. Judging by the light and the pair of old women tugging on the ropes to pull an awning across, the sun's full force would soon be cast down into the courtyard.

Lynx headed down a narrow stone stair that headed away from the rising sun, pausing only to test the door to Llaith's room. The greying mercenary was fast asleep. He just grunted in his sleep as Lynx lifted the man's tobacco pouch, while Himbel in the other bed only opened one eye long enough to roll over and fart noisily. Lynx retreated and made his way to a wide terrace that faced the sea.

To his surprise, however, he wasn't the first there. Teshen sat on a bench in one corner, leaning on the surrounding wall's smooth top and staring out at the open water. There was a battered tin samovar on a table behind him, steaming gently though the small bowls beside it were all empty.

Lynx poured a bowl of tea and sat on the next bench, cradling it in his lap as he started to fumble with the tobacco pouch.

'Anything to eat round here?' he said conversationally as he started to roll thin cigarettes, knowing Llaith would expect to see some waiting once Himbel's stink drove him from the room.

'Go whistle at one of 'em,' came the reply.

Teshen didn't bother to turn as he spoke which made Lynx hesitate. Normally, Teshen was always wary, always alert, so clearly there was something wrong. Lynx's priorities kicked in first and he set the tobacco aside to go and catch the attention of one of the old women unfurling the awning. He pantomimed eating at her and her prune face split into a gap-toothed grin as she nodded.

Lynx retreated to the terrace where Teshen still hadn't moved.

'She grinned,' he complained as he resumed his hesitant rolling of cigarettes.

'So?'

'Makes me suspicious.'

'Probably Uver for breakfast.'

'What's that?'

'Spiced fish in fried bread.'

Lynx's heart fell. 'Fish?' Normally he had no objections, but the previous night's victory celebration had been enthusiastic and stretched well into the early hours. His stomach was less than impressed with fish for breakfast anyway, throwing in spices and a towering hangover wasn't going to improve matters.

'Uver means "fist",' Teshen continued. 'Shaped like one and it packs a punch.'

'Shattered gods,' Lynx sighed. 'That's all I need.'

'You ask her nicely, mebbe there'll be some baked gull eggs with rice.'

'Nicely? I can't even say a word she understands.'

'Wave money around, she'll get the message.'

Teshen rose so abruptly Lynx thought for a moment he was going to take a swing at him. Instead, the shaven-headed mercenary headed for the samovar and poured himself a bowl of tea. Lynx watched him do so and offered over a cigarette as Teshen retook his seat. The Knight of Stars shook his head and went back to his contemplation of the sea. Two dozen small fishing boats were already out, hauling in their catch off a sandbar, while the sails of several larger ships could be seen on the horizon.

From this angle Lynx could see the half-dozen islands that made up the western chain of the Mage Islands. There was one settlement of white buildings crowded around the sloped sides of a bay, but most of the islands were smears of green and brown. The great jagged line of the Etrel Cliffs loomed behind them, stretching as far as Lynx could see.

'The woman?' Lynx ventured after a few more minutes fumbling with the cigarettes.

Realising he'd forgotten to find a coal to light them off, Lynx drank some tea to fortify him for more pantomiming to the old lady. Thin with a yellow-green tint, it was basically bloody hot water but right now he couldn't care. It was safe to drink and made him feel a tiny bit better, so that would have to do.

'The woman,' Teshen confirmed eventually.

'I don't remember you ever talking about women,' Lynx said. 'Or men, or anything. I'd kinda assumed you weren't interested in the subject.'

'There've been a few.'

'But none like her, eh?'

'You met any like Toil?'

'Good point.'

They lapsed into silence for a while, during which the old woman brought a wide bowl of golden-brown Uver. He sniffed at them while Teshen spoke to her in the local language. They smelled both delicious and revolting at the same time, his stomach caught between growling and lurching. He left them well alone, keeping a suspicious eye on the bowl until the woman returned with a clay pot that smoked fitfully. Inside was a coal from the fire, hot enough to light a cigarette off. Between that and the tea, Lynx found himself finally able to appreciate the view.

'She going to try and kill us?' he asked after he'd finished his cigarette.

Teshen shrugged. 'It's been a while.'

'Did you shaft her when you left?'

'Tried to.'

'Despite whatever was between you?'

'Ambition and pride can get in the way of most things.'

Lynx snorted. 'Never found much use for 'em, myself.'

'One of them sent you to prison,' Teshen pointed out. 'So there's that.'

'Aye,' he said after a pause. 'I guess there's that.'

Lynx drained his tea and went to fetch more. 'Anatin was talking about moving the company to the Siym Holding,' he said as he did so. 'It's sounding more sensible now.'

'Wouldn't stop her.'

'Shattered gods, just how badly did you screw this woman over?'

Teshen shifted in his seat, a discomforted action Lynx had never seen from him before – and one that worried him far more than the smell of spiced fish. 'Enough. Looks like she's kaboto of the Vi No Le crews though, basically the general of the army. The kaboto don't act on a whim or pick up old grudges.'

'That's good, right?'

'Sure, but it wasn't personal what I did. I don't know what's gone on in the district since I left. That's why I didn't want to be recognised. Always a risk it would stir up old arguments.'

'You didn't even see her when you followed her out?'

Teshen paused then shook his head. 'She didn't want to be seen, means nothing.'

Lynx lit another cigarette as voices began to echo down the passageway behind them, the inimitable bickering of hungover and hungry Cards.

'It's all enough to make a man stock up on cartridges, whatever the prices down this way.'

'Aye.'

'O' course, that might also get interpreted the wrong way.'

'Aye.'

'Bugger.'

Kabat Jo-Sarl was a large man whose presence filled the room. Unlike his peers and the lesser kabats of the four districts, he dressed simply. A gold chain, bearing the symbol of Veraimin, around his neck was the only symbol of wealth he displayed, a plain tunic of dark blue silk all the luxury he permitted himself.

Broad-backed with a lion's mane of dark hair, he had been quite the fighter in his day despite his size and privileged background. His time on a Masts crew had been short because he was destined for greater things, but Jo-Sarl had embraced it with the same ferocity he met every challenge. Sanshir had been too young to spar against him, but she knew even the man now calling himself Teshen would have struggled against that power.

She kept quiet, leaving the kabat to his musing. From the window came the sound of a baby crying, rising up from the lower levels of this great round tower at the heart of Vi No Le. This was a small and private office he kept, well away from prying eyes and ears of the Jo-Sarl court.

'Why didn't you wake me?' he said eventually. There was no anger in his voice, just a question despite the difficult subject.

Sanshir knew the trust between them ran deep, in part because of who they were discussing.

'They were drunk, it was no ruse.'

'So?'

'So whatever they have planned – if they have something planned – it wasn't happening last night. I've seen enough drunks in my time. That crew won't have been able to walk in a straight line before dawn.'

'And of course you'd just seen him. The element of surprise had been lost.'

'Exactly. I made sure the crews and guards were bolstered, but no need to disturb you.'

'What did he say? He calls himself Teshen now? Hah.'

Sanshir nodded and related Teshen's words again.

'Believe him?'

She shrugged. 'It's been a long time. People change. He was never easy to read anyway.'

'But you did, didn't you?'

'I saw no lies.' She hesitated. 'But it's *him*. My judgement may not be sound.'

Jo-Sarl leaned back in his chair and looked up at the ceiling. Sanshir saw a grin appear on his face, the hunger of a man who perhaps had been a little bored in his comfortable life. A kabat's lot was far from simple but it was mostly business, rarely a challenge.

'So, the Bloody Pauper comes back to town.'

'I've made enquiries. No one has disappeared, no sign of messages coming into the compound overnight.'

'And they're staying in Auferno?'

'For the time being. An anonymous lodging, defensible but what mercenary company would choose otherwise?'

'The Siym Holding brings them much closer,' he said, still looking up. 'Safer for them, but more aggressive towards us.

If you were in his position, and you meant to cause mischief, what would you do?'

'With Mastrunners I could cross the city faster than any news of my coming, but they're outsiders. Auferno is too far to be effective.'

'No doubt the Siym would have said the same.'

'We are not the Siym.'

'Just so. All the same, we must take precautions.'

'Do you want certain people confined?'

Jo-Sarl gave a snort. 'And send the message that I've gone soft?'

'I understand.'

He held up a hand. 'Best not to send the message I'm paranoid, however.'

Sanshir ventured a smile there. 'I shall exercise restraint.'

'Good. And the man himself? You said he was looking like some Silkland pirate?'

'It rather suited him actually, except for the eyebrows.'

'Veraimin's breath! That's hard to picture, my memory of him is more wild, hair and headscarf flying in the breeze.'

'We've all got old and tired,' Sanshir said. 'I guess it even had to happen to the Bloody Pauper.'

'I never thought it would.'

She paused. 'No. Perhaps disgrace and exile was the best thing for him. We'd have come to blows one day. I knew I would be kaboto one day, but he'd have seen it as coming second . . .'

'And that was something he'd never have lived with,' Jo-Sarl finished for her. 'Do you think that's why he did it? Threw his lot in with my cousin?'

Sanshir nodded. 'Doubt he saw it that way, but yes. He was never a Mastrunner though, not truly. He liked to fight too much.'

'The Bloody Rose says this?' Jo-Sarl laughed, incredulous. 'You were quite the pair as I recall.'

'I like to fight, I like to win. Him? Fighting was more than that to him. The other crews fear to go up against me because I win – because I take the fastest route to victory no matter who's in my path. If *he* didn't kill everyone in his path, it was only because he was in a hurry.'

'I'm sure the years have mellowed him,' the principal kabat of all Caldaire allowed. 'But a few quick deaths within my family would be only prudent. To make sure.'

Chapter 19

While the rest of the Cards slowly roused themselves, Sitain stayed in bed. She shared a room with Lastani, the magic at their fingertips apparently making them natural roommates. While Lastani heaved herself up and set about dressing, Sitain lay quiet. It wasn't that she disliked the bookish young mage, but Sitain found herself resenting the woman too.

The bonds of gender, age and magic made some things easier, but Lastani was at once fiercely intelligent and utterly brainless. There was so much Sitain could learn from her, but for some reason she shied away from doing so.

'Are you feeling ill?' Lastani asked, catching sight of Sitain's open eye.

'No.'

'Do you want me to bring you some food?'

'I'm fine.'

Lastani sighed and sat on her own bed, across from Sitain. 'Then what is it?'

'Who says there's something wrong?'

'I do. I may not be some fierce mercenary, but I'm still a person with eyes.'

Sitain scowled and rolled over. She lay facing the wall for a moment then sat up. 'It's nothing you can fix,' she said, wincing slightly at her hangover.

Lastani's voice softened. 'I never said I could, but if you

want to talk about it, I'm here. I . . . Look, you're not the only one who got uprooted and tethered to these fools.'

'And still, it looks like you belong here,' Sitain said, gesturing around generally. 'The Mage Islands I mean. You'll be a guild-master soon enough, got the pedigree and such. Me, I'm just a curiosity to them.'

'You think I'm staying in Caldaire?'

'Well aren't you? No Knights-Charnel here. Cold hells, you'll become Shard in ten years.'

'Don't you want that?' Lastani asked.

Sitain grabbed her clothes and started to get dressed while Lastani stared at her in confusion. 'I want my family,' she said at last. 'Or rather, I don't. Village life wasn't much, but at least I belonged there. Not saying I want to live out my life there, but the thought I can never go home is eating away at me.'

'There's a life for you here too, if there's one for me,' Lastani said. 'It's your magic that's valuable, not how many books you've read. The healing guilds will teach you, they'll throw money at you most likely. Yes, they might prod and poke at your tattoos from time to time but digging in fields year in year out gets dull too.'

'And get caught up in their games for the rest of my life? Get talked down to by educated folk all the time and run in circles when I try to think for myself?'

Lastani shook her head. 'You underestimate yourself. I don't think the Mage Islands are prepared for someone like you. I wouldn't bet against you myself.'

'What about the Cards and these tattoos?'

'A trial we have to endure first, perhaps. You say there's a place for me here, but I disagree. Life with the Cards might be more dangerous, but staying in one place and making a name for myself is just asking for trouble.'

'Teshen said they're wise to snatch teams round here.'

'Normal ones yes, but I think the Militant Orders might make an exception for us. We're special, remember?'

'Yeah. And can you think of anyone worse than me to be special?'

Lastani's brow furrowed. 'Plenty. If I threw a stone out of that doorway, I'd likely hit one.'

She stood and straightened her dress, embroidered with linked circles in the local fashion. Lastani looked nothing like a mercenary now, bar the short sleeves revealing white tattoos on her arms. Sitain guessed that was the point and resolved to buy herself some alternatives too.

'Come on,' Lastani said, waving Sitain forward. 'The sooner we find answers to our questions, the sooner we get our lives back.'

Sitain gave a bitter laugh. 'Those are never coming back. The best we can hope for is the chance to control what comes next.'

'Let's do that then,' Lastani said, jerking open the door.

On the other side was Toil, frozen in the act of knocking. The relic hunter blinked once at Lastani then gave them a suspiciously wide smile. Behind her slouched Paranil, her tame academic, who bobbed his head, and Aben, Toil's burly lieutenant, who offered a crooked smile.

'Just the pair I was looking for.' She beckoned and started walking away down the boarding house walkway. 'Sitain, Lastani – heel!' Toil called over her shoulder.

'Ah yes,' Sitain muttered. 'Controlling my own destiny, that does sound nice. How does it go again?'

Toil headed to the south terrace where, by the noise, it was clear half of the Cards were stuffing their faces. Leading the pack was Lynx of course, but she'd seen the company attack breakfast after a hard night's drinking before. The rest were hardly any more elegant in their approach.

'I need some volunteers,' she announced to the group. When the laughter had died down, Toil looked to see who seemed least likely to puke the moment they stepped on to a boat. The selection wasn't great, but she only needed two.

'Teshen and Layir, finish up and get your kit. We've got work to do.'

Without a word Teshen stood, his expression tense and distant. Layir on the other hand groaned loudly.

'Why us?'

Toil smiled. 'I only really need Teshen given I've got Aben to watch my back already, but you're coming as window dressing.'

'Didn't think I was your type, Toil!'

'I like a man in a skirt as much as the next girl, Layir. More important though, I need Teshen to hear what the locals are saying and give me a nod if there's anything amiss. You just need to look pretty beside him so it's not obvious Teshen is listening in.'

The young man gave her a crooked smile, squinting as the sun reflected down the centre of the lodging. 'I feel like I should be offended by the waste of my talents, but at least you admit I'm pretty.'

'Whatever gets you moving, boy. Jacket, gun and sword, on the double.'

'Aye, Princess!'

As Layir heaved himself off his seat and sauntered back to his room, winking at Toil as he passed, Lastani set herself in front of the woman.

'What's going on? We were due back at the Shard's Rest today. There's plenty more work to be done there.'

'Like I said, we've got other work to do right now.'

'More important than understanding these tattoos?'

'You remember you're part of the Cards now? Meant to follow orders?'

'Don't give me that, this isn't part of the arrangement.'

Toil scratched her cheek as she considered Lastani's words. It looked an unfair match-up between them, Toil being taller and bulkier, but while Lastani was no fighter, she'd proved herself quick on the draw. Life with the Cards had brought home to her just how potent a weapon her magic was and the young mage was shedding her meeker self.

'You say that but dammit, little grasshopper, if you aren't acting just like the rest of these pig-headed mercs. I've not forgotten what you are, just as you shouldn't forget who I am and what the Cards are doing for you.'

Toil took a step forward and pointed a finger at Lastani's face, ignoring the sudden drop in temperature that followed. In the background, the mutter of the Cards lowered too as they stopped to watch the confrontation.

'We're all in this together,' Toil said, 'and like it or not there's an army that would love to kill or capture us. So long as you're enjoying the protective company of the Cards, you better accept that sometimes you need to make like a soldier and follow orders.'

Lastani's eyes flashed white. 'Just so long as you remember that we're not normal soldiers and we're not to be hired out like them.'

'Girly, at some point you should probably accept I'm not a fool and don't care enough about money to take any random job. You may not get the how and why, but I don't act on a whim. I've got a job to do and sometimes that's going to need your involvement. If you don't like it, walk away. Until then just remember who's in command.'

Lastani didn't speak for a while, but then she nodded and the chill in the air vanished again. 'Very well. I agree we're all in this together, so don't let your agenda drive us apart.'

Toil gave her a wolfish smile. 'If my agenda fails, you're every bit as screwed as me. Spending the rest of your life in a Charneler sanctuary is the best you could hope for there.'

She stepped back and glanced at Sitain who was quietly watching them from the side-lines with Toil's two long-time employees, Aben and Paranil.

'Now we've got that all sorted, let's get to work.'

Collecting Teshen and Layir, Toil led her party through the winding streets to a ferry dock on the lagoon. A line of five huge sloths moved with deceptive speed alongside them, keeping to the brisk walking pace of their handler without seeming to hurry their long limbs.

As the sloths were being unloaded on to a barge, Teshen set about securing another for passage across the city. Sitain watched him only idly, more interested in the bustle of commerce going on around them. Auferno was the smallest of the four main districts of Caldaire with dozens of small and mid-sized Holdings or Consortiums. It looked like candles were being unloaded from the sloths, but she could also see a Masts crew guarding a shipment of silver, while bundles of linen, jars of oil, and parchment, all stood on that small dock.

Their watchers were back, Sitain also noticed, and not making any great effort to remain unseen. It was a pair of women this morning, an older one with braids in her hair and a Vi No Le sash at her waist alongside a teenager with untattooed arms. Both were armed with staves, the red tips indicating mage-charged balls could be inserted.

The sight made Sitain look down at her new belt, one that she'd picked up a few days previously. In a city of mages it hadn't been difficult to find a leather-worker with one for sale, six metal pouches worked into the belt's design. She hadn't yet mastered the technique of charging the balls, not reliably anyway, but three of the pouches contained her own efforts, Lastani and Atieno donating the rest. When he'd seen the belt, Lynx had waddled off to buy one for himself. It was empty as yet, but Sitain had promised to sell him some balls when she could.

Before long, Teshen was waving them towards a narrow barge with a six-man rowing crew. They settled in while Toil spoke quietly to the barge-master, a slender, whiskered man of sixty at least. He raised an eyebrow at what she said, but didn't pause before barking orders at his crew and pushing off. Once the barge set off into the lagoon, Lastani broke her silence at last, asking where they were going.

'Cliffbase,' Toil replied, eyes on a tysarn that was circling just ahead of them.

There were off-shore gardens on either side, a channel of water leading out into the open lagoon. Once they were clear, the crew pulled hard until they were out in the current and could ride it towards a pair of great stone pillars that marked the deep water shipping lane.

'The slum?' Lastani called.

She didn't get a response at first. Both Sitain and Toil watched the tysarn, a full metre wingspan, drop suddenly into the water and vanish from sight. Only when it returned to the surface, fish in mouth, did Toil seem to remember what they were talking about.

'It's not like these districts,' Toil admitted, 'but there are people with money there all the same.'

'Not much money,' Teshen said. 'Not many who've got it.'

'One's enough.'

Sitain exchanged a look with Lastani. They knew well enough who in Cliffbase had the money to hire them, but neither was keen on working for him.

'Is this why you didn't tell us until we were on the boat?' Sitain asked.

Toil's wolfish grin told its own story as the tysarn flailed for a moment on the lagoon surface, then hauled itself up in the air. The double set of wings had been a strange sight at first, but there were so many of the beasts, big and small, in the air around Caldaire, Sitain was already getting used to it.

'It wasn't clear what the job is,' Toil said eventually. 'I received a note with his guild's seal, but most likely I've got you to thank.'

'Me?'

'All three of you. What you told the Shard must've made an impression.'

'What she told us about Tanimbor also made an impression,' Lastani said icily. 'Why take the job? You don't need the money.'

Toil glanced back at the white-haired young academic. 'It's not about money. I'm in the business of spending that, remember? If I'm not interested I'll pass and we'll head back.'

'The ambitious master of a mage guild will just let us say no and walk away?'

Again the wolfish grin. 'When the seven of us are doing the saying? He'd better.'

She broke off as they reached deeper water, standing high in the prow of the barge and staring forward. Sitain followed her gaze then gave a yelp as a dark shape moved through the sun-kissed lagoon.

'Shattered gods! Are we going to hit it?'

The barge-master laughed loudly at her animation, saying something in the local language that had no need of translation. Ten or more yards long with great blade-like wings pushing at the water, the beast was clearly deep enough that the barge could slip over it without either disturbing the other. Still Sitain held her breath the entire time and had to fight the urge to draw her gun.

'Don't worry, they're in the lagoon most mornings,' Teshen said, scratching his shaved head before settling a cap over it to protect it from the sun. 'Making for the sea hunting grounds. It's rare they stop for a snack on the way.'

'Piss on you,' Sitain muttered, 'don't even joke about that.'

He laughed. 'I ain't joking. Cut your finger and trail it through the water if you don't believe me.'

Sitain snatched her hand back from the edge of the boat and stared into the distance, trying to ignore the warmth that filled her cheeks. The barge made good time to the deep-water channel and darted straight across, fifty yards ahead of a large merchantman that was making for the sea. Sitain looked over towards their destination, but it was still hidden by the foliage of the spice islands. The great chimneys in the heart of the lagoon dominated everything, but they were barren and lifeless.

She found herself more fascinated by the great ring of city blocks that comprised Caldaire. The high outer perimeter that deflected the worst of wind and waves rolling in – and the strange network of mage-carved stone. Yellow rock studded with dark shadows and patches of green, overlaid with flashes of red, orange and blue. The skirt of garden-islands dark against the bleached pebble beaches and pale blue lagoon shallows. The tysarn dark against the sky.

The narrow shore of the Siym Holding soon came into view, hired guards in Consortium livery patrolling the beach and overseeing loading and unloading. It looked peaceful enough, the lifeblood of trade once more able to flow as debts were covered.

Teshen's former home of Vi No Le was a huge multi-level district punctuated by vast stone tors that had been hollowed out in generations past. Even from the lagoon, she could hear the increased babble of sound as they skirted Vi No Le, the population there bigger than any other district. Teshen's face was stony as he regarded his past. Whether he was looking for threats or looking for that crewleader, Sanshir, she couldn't tell.

Man's always been a closed book, she thought, *but there's got to be something going on in that head, right? He must feel something, whatever Llaith says.*

The steady progress of their barge quickly brought the Etrel Cliffs around to view, Cliffbase district little more than an afterthought beneath them. The huge rocky wall towered over the city, running for many miles south-west from the cut-away of the canal.

The cliffs were a sharply-sloped slab of whitish yellow, the shattered face of an enormous rise of land. Having arrived down the Duegar canal, Sitain had seen how far that rise went – an abrupt finale to the leagues of savannah of the north.

The entire city of Caldaire could fit a dozen times inside that great outcrop she guessed, perhaps more given she could only glimpse how long the cliffs were. Caves peppered the cliff face itself. From those the tysarn emerged or sat on high shelves of rock to sun themselves, but it was the dark maw of the great cave that dominated the entire view – a black opening that looked all too familiar for Sitain's taste.

'That's really a Duegar canal? I hadn't heard they built them in tunnels.'

Lastani nodded. 'It's believed so. There is a near-exact tunnel mouth in a nation called Ael Diu two hundred miles north-west of here.'

'They don't know for sure?'

'The long dark,' Toil called from the prow. 'That's what Wisps call it. I've heard relic hunters call it the entrance to the underworld, which I guess it is so long as you don't mind the fact you'll die horribly on the journey. I don't know of anyone who's attempted it in centuries.'

'Is that why we're here?' Sitain asked alarmed, but Toil only roared with laughter.

'Gods-in-shards, do you really think I'm that mad?'

Sitain hesitated, seeing by the looks on their faces that her comrades weren't entirely sure either. 'Um, no?' she hazarded.

Toil continued to chuckle, she was glad to see. 'Okay, I'll give you that one, but the answer's no. The Labyrinth of Jarrazir, by the seven hells yes! Once I'd got someone likely to open it I was there as fast as I could, treasures or no. It was dangerous, but danger's just a problem you need to fit into your plans. The long dark though? That's gods-burned suicide – everyone says so and I've never read a thing that suggests different.'

'So we're not going there?'

'It'll be a short fucking conversation if your friend does want that. I'll wave him off myself, but the biggest tysarn inhabit that and probably all sorts of other nasties besides. I've heard tell of wreckage coming floating out, but that's all. No one has ever come back, not in recorded history. Not even the Wisps come to trade with Caldaire these days, the shore is too dangerous.'

Sitain shivered, despite the dark places she'd survived in the last few months. She felt the tunnel mouth's presence even as she tried to focus on where they were going. Cliffbase was a district of two islands. Separated by a channel wide enough for shipping, both were oddly flat compared to the rest of the lagoon city. The right-hand island had two small rises where she could see homes and streets on multiple levels, but nothing here was even as tall as the palace of the Siym Holding.

While the buildings were mage-carved, few extended above two storeys. But still there were people and small boats docked at jetties, the shoreline still half-obscured by garden-islands. What she couldn't see was holdings, however, nothing that could indicate the presence of kabats in charge. Two or three larger houses faced the lagoon with some space or a perimeter wall between them and their neighbours, but nothing to indicate real wealth.

The barge-master took them past the smaller of the two islands and across the channel that led to the long dark. All heads turned briefly towards it, Sitain noticed, even those of the rowers. As they passed, the crew put in an extra burst of effort, as though some horror might burst out of that wide, empty place. Sitain flinched as something did all of a sudden, but it was just a large tysarn flying out of the darkness and climbing well above their heads.

The barge turned in behind a small copse of fruit trees, no more than twenty in all but all heavily laden with oval pinkish fruits and tended by a pair of mud-spattered labourers. Behind it was a small bay, shallow judging by the clear pale water, flanked by two wooden jetties. Sitain saw a multitude of creatures in the water beneath them. Octopuses darted through the fronds of green or red plants while long blue claws could be seen protruding from burrows. Small clusters of silver fish swarmed around it all, while more than a few bones lay discarded and half-buried in the sand.

The barge pulled in at the jetty on the right. Sitain looked up from the water to realise with a jolt that two of Tanimbor's mages were waiting for them. The pair stood oddly formally amid the dirt and chaos of the dock, hands behind their backs and wearing long grey coats of thin silk that bore the colours of their guild.

'Mistresses Toil and Ufre,' one called, 'welcome to Cliffbase.'

Chapter 20

The nearer mage offered one hand to Toil, his other remaining tucked behind his back. After many years as an agent of Su Dregir and more than a few bar fights, she just eyed him suspiciously until he withdrew it. In her book, any man who offered one hand and kept the other hidden was asking to get a knife in the eye.

Once Toil had stepped up on to the jetty, Lastani did take the man's hand. Both of the Cliffbase mages were handsome and scrubbed clean compared to the dock workers. Square-jawed and young, one was white with long sandy hair poking out from under his headscarf. The other was shorter and dark-skinned with noticeably pointed canines, a feature of one of the tribes in these parts, Toil knew. In this one's face at least, it was oddly enticing.

'The guildmaster thanks you for your prompt arrival,' the first mage said as Layir waved a hopeful hand in the mage's direction. 'He will be especially pleased that you chose to assist us, Mistress Ufre.'

'Don't get ahead of yourselves,' Toil replied. 'We've not taken the job yet. Tanimbor's note lacked any details.'

The mage bowed. 'Of course, Mistress. If you would follow me?'

He led them down a wide market street where the morning's trade was in full force. Most people looked poor, but it was hardly the slum Teshen had made out. There was little of the colour and variety of dress that you'd see elsewhere, but the throng was full of working people rather than beggars.

Toil watched the faces as she passed, but it was curiosity not fear they displayed as they stepped aside for the mages. Clearly Tanimbor's guild held great sway here, but there was industry too by the sounds and smells – many of the more noxious professions tucked away from the richer parts of the city.

Set back from the busy thoroughfare was a wide street of glassblowers and other craftsmen. The mage turned down this without a backward glance at his charges. It was a short street and dominated by the building at the far end – squat and defensible, three storeys high but set in a dip of ground, as though it pre-dated the rest of the district. A conical roof rose from the rear section, strangely out of place in a city of blunt curved stone or terracotta peaks.

A low wall and curling iron railing interrupted the street about halfway down. The dwellings beyond had been co-opted by the guild it appeared, though Toil could see more than just grey-coated mages inside. A trellis framework stretched across the nearer section, almost swamped by climbing plants that offered shade from the morning sun when they reached it.

Once inside the guild grounds, it was clearly a newer and less ornate affair than most Toil had seen. Some of the guilds were ancient and even in passing it was possible to see the detail and refinement in their surroundings. The finest mage-carvers honed their talents both as advertisement of their work and symbol of their position amid the city's structure. Here most of the work was of a more functional nature.

Ushered directly inside, the mage stopped in a large refectory where four long tables stood, empty but for a jug of wine and four brass cups.

'Your guards may wait here,' the mage indicated.

Toil shook her head. 'Not a chance. They come with us.'

'It is tradition that non-mages do not enter guilds,' he said with a pained expression. 'We are already making an exception for you, Mistress Toil.'

'Does it look like that interests me much?'

He paused. 'I will have to speak to the guildmaster.'

Toil nodded and turned back the way she'd come. 'Try to catch us before we reach the barge then.'

She was almost at the door when a voice called her back and Guildmaster Tanimbor himself appeared at the far end of the hall.

'Mistress Toil, leaving so soon?'

She paused. 'We got invited then told we weren't all welcome. Make up your damn mind or come visit me in future.'

'My apologies. I hoped you might consider a small concession to local custom. After all, it has not been so long since bounty hunters and kidnap teams were sent by the Orders to seize slaves for their factories.'

Toil nodded. 'Any of those teams get specifically invited in?'

'Who knows? As I'm sure you are aware, those who work in the wilds, above the law, can be devious.'

She smiled at that and raised an eyebrow at Aben. 'I think he's talking about people like us.'

'We're above the law?' Aben replied. 'That's good to hear.'

'I cast no aspersions . . .' Taminbor paused. 'Perhaps we could speak in a more civilised manner, however. Talking to your back isn't the most productive start to negotiations.'

'Are we all welcome?'

A sigh. 'Very well. Perhaps you would at least concede to leave your guns down here?'

'Nope.'

'You are a most inflexible woman, Mistress Toil.'

'Aye well, I'm not so young as I used to be. Some of the Cards were discussing that very detail, late one night, but I'm confident they came to regret the matter.'

Aben nodded. 'Varain's balls didn't work right for a month, so he said.'

'Quite,' Tanimbor said, the one word conveying faint revulsion. 'As you wish, Mistress Toil. Please, follow me.'

She turned and bestowed her best dazzling smile on the man, which had precisely zero effect. 'Please, lead on, Guildmaster.'

The Cards followed him back through the door and up a wide staircase. The walls were carved in all sorts of strange ways – almost the entire face of stone altered in a bizarre variety of styles.

'Our younger mages,' Tanimbor explained with one finger pointing at the wall, though he'd not looked back. 'It has become a small tradition to experiment with their skills in this way. I feel we all benefit from a reminder of youth's creativity. There is beauty in the process, in the quest for knowledge and artistry, do you not feel?'

Toil looked over the curious, overlapping array of stone-carvings, many incorporating the work of others in inventive or ridiculous ways.

'There's something to be said for that,' she conceded. 'Some of it's just shit though.'

A bark of laughter was all she received in reply. Tanimbor led them past a startled pair of novices and along a corridor to a wide set of doors. He entered a study where a pair of expensive-looking desks stood beyond a round table of polished mahogany.

The question is, are you a true spiritual leader of these people, pretentious manipulator or some crazed fanatic? Toil wondered as she followed Tanimbor in.

On the table was a strange device made of brass, glass and silver. It sat on a circular frame with eight thin pipes curving down from a central glass container, all resting on runners so that it could spin about the centre.

'Please, sit.'

Tanimbor idly pushed one of the runners where a small tap sat above a brass bowl.

'A relic of my people, back before they came to the Mage Islands. The custom is to take a cup and pour yourself the wine,' he added, plucking a cup of silver-chased horn and demonstrating. 'An overly ornate method of hospitality perhaps, but the ritual pleases me.'

He held the cup under one tap and opened it with a twist of the fingers, wine tricking down until he closed it again. The Cards playing guard, Teshen, Layir and Aben, took up positions while Lastani, Sitain and Paranil spread around the table. There were no other mages in the room, a curious detail Toil thought, but inside their guildhouse that was not quite the same as safe.

She spun the contraption around and selected one pipe at random, pouring herself a cup. She raised it in toast, waiting until the others had done the same before speaking.

'Of course, your people were notorious poisoners, well practised in inuring themselves.'

Tanimbor smiled at that, thin and reptilian but that was just him, Toil didn't think he'd been caught out. 'A student of history, Mistress Toil?'

'Just Toil, none of this "mistress" rubbish,' she corrected him. 'And I know a bit of history, but I'm certainly a student of poisoning. You never know who you might end up sharing a drink with.'

'Indeed. However, the task I have for you requires all of your faculties and vital functions to be intact.'

'And the task is?' Lastani broke in, her cup full but untouched. 'Toil wasn't exactly clear on that front.'

'I gave few details,' Tanimbor admitted. 'However, I believe it is something you are uniquely suited to.'

'Me or her?'

'You, Mistress Ufre, perhaps with her assistance. Were I certain, I perhaps wouldn't need your assistance.'

'Why us anyway?' Toil asked. 'We're new in town and haven't made many friends.'

'Aha, not within the established powers no, but that is to your advantage in my eyes. I am not a man content to follow the herd. I believe in a more dynamic way of life and you, Toil, with your Mercenary Deck, are clearly no strangers to upsetting the balance of the world.'

'Hah!' Sitain muttered. 'Oh hells, did I say that out loud?'

'We've been known to upset a few applecarts in our pursuit of truth and justice,' Toil continued smoothly, 'but that's beside the point. Now we're here, what's the job?'

Tanimbor inclined his head. 'Tell me, Toil, do you notice anything unusual about this room?'

She looked around. There were wall hangings and wooden-framed windows, plain rugs on the floor and not a lot more beyond the empty-topped desks. At last she noticed what he meant and kicked herself for not seeing it sooner. There was a door leading off to the right – not in itself strange but the proportions were unusual. It was a double-door, which for a side room was strange, but if anything it was wider than the one they'd come through and the stone surrounding it was old and wind-scoured.

'Oh!' she said. 'Interesting.'

'What is it?' Sitain asked.

Toil pointed at the door. 'That's not human-carved, the frame I mean. Look at the stone, that was outside in the wind and rain for a long time.' She got up and bent to inspect one corner. 'It was engraved at one point too. What did it say?'

'There is no record,' Tanimbor replied. 'The job I have for you lies within.'

'Ulfer's broken horn,' Sitain muttered. 'Not some new bloody Duegar death-trap? If so, you can count me out.'

'Somewhere, deep down, there will be, but I imagine it's flooded,' Toil said. 'This is just the very top – the peak of the tower. What was it, do you know? Some sort of outpost? Something bigger? The tunnel canal must have come to a staging point at very least.'

'We do not know,' Tanimbor said. 'There are several small relics of the Duegar in the Mage Islands, but this I uncovered only recently. There is no path down to be found and I agree the most crazed of relic hunters would not go there.'

'Well she's here now,' Sitain said, 'you can ask her.'

Toil shot Sitain a look and the sour-faced young woman finally shut up. 'I don't know about that, but *this* relic hunter's expert opinion is that it's either flooded or teeming with tysarn.'

Tanimbor nodded. 'Either way, it is of no great concern. The room, however, is not merely some sort of Duegar attic. There are markings that I believe match the few scant records we have of expeditions into the tunnel itself.'

'I thought no one ever made it out?'

'Not entirely true, but given how much has been explored, the prevailing wisdom is that it's safer for all concerned to say no one ever survives.'

'I'm guessing you're not a man who agrees with prevailing wisdom,' Toil said.

He smiled to concede the point. 'In this case, I made the exception. The furthest anyone has ever ventured was a few hundred yards before their ship was wrecked. The greater tysarn are bad-tempered and hungry, but occasionally they miss a few people. Two women and one man have survived to wash out with the wreckage of their expedition and give a record of what they saw.'

'Dark and full of monsters?'

'Close. There was very little to see, but some garbled attempt at symbols remain. It was nothing of particular interest until I discovered something similar in the room next door.'

'Discovered?'

'As a young man I indulged in a little stone carving myself,' he explained. 'I was investigating the floor as a canvas when I found something different. Further explorations produced something interesting.'

'But you don't know what it is?'

'I am a mage with some modest schooling, but I am no relic hunter. My knowledge offers a clearer shape of what I cannot see.'

Toil thought for a moment. 'But you can't bring this to another, more learned guild. Not without offering your secrets up.'

'Nor without the risk they would lie about what they see. You understand my dilemma.'

'Better to trust outsiders then,' Lastani said.

'Mercenaries have very clear interests,' Tanimbor said by way of agreement. 'They like to be paid and they like to stay alive. You have few friends in the city and while I would not risk my mages in a direct conflict, you are likely to leave soon. Sell my secrets to the highest bidder and I am willing to repay that in kind.'

'Meaning?' Sitain snapped, forgetting her promise. A part of Toil sympathised, but it was a different part to the one that wanted to clip Sitain around the head.

'Meaning setting the Orders on us,' Toil said in a level tone. 'Let's put the threats aside for a moment though. I'm more interested in discussing the price of successful business, not the cost of broken promises.'

'I have never hired a relic hunter before,' Tanimbor said. 'I do not know what fees you command, only what a mage of unusual abilities may expect. I warn you that our finances are limited. As you can no doubt see, we are not a large or powerful guild.'

'Money's dull,' Toil said, feeling a slight quickening in her blood. 'It's just a way of keeping score, once you've earned a decent amount.'

Tanimbor raised an eyebrow. 'You are a rare mercenary then.'

'You've no bloody idea. What's just as valuable to me is information.'

'And the cost to me of giving that information?'

'Modest.'

'In which case you have my interest.'

Toil grinned. 'Thought I might! All I want's a name. I know there's a guild secretly manufacturing cartridges here in the Mage Islands, I want to know who.'

He blinked at her. 'Do you now? Such information is indeed valuable – as it is dangerous. Or it would be if it were true.'

Toil nodded. The manufacture of mage-gun cartridges required a God Fragment and while the Orders had given up their efforts to kidnap mages from these parts, they might well conduct a large-scale raid if they knew of a God Fragment here.

'I know it's true. I've got it on good authority that ship-ments came from these parts that can't be tracked back to any sanctuary. They've supplied enemies of the Divine Orders in Ei Det, Ikir and Olostir and I've no problem with any of that.'

'Why do you want this information then?'

'Because I want them to supply me – or rather, a city I represent. I'm from Parthain and after this business in Jarrazir, the Orders will be shifting their focus. Supply of cartridges will have started drying up already, that's how they work. There are enough competing Orders that they've never been able to entirely cut supply, but if war breaks out the majority will fall into line.'

'You understand, such information would be a close-guarded secret. To betray that would be to betray my own kind. I may disagree with their politics, but all mages are my brothers and sisters. To endanger one is to harm us all.'

Toil shook her head. 'Whatever your creed, anyone fighting the Orders serves your cause. We should be allies in this war and I think events in Jarrazir prove that we're committed. We would hardly have orchestrated all that just to uncover the location of one or two fragments here, not least because they want us more than they want the remaining fragments.'

She helped herself to another cup of wine and sat back, watching Tanimbor as the thin mage considered her words.

'Believe me or not, that's my price. Do you want some time to decide?'

Chapter 21

Toil had to admit she was disappointed. As secret Duegar artefacts went it was bloody unimpressive. As empty rooms went it was still on the dull side. Through the door was a room, circular and six yards across containing nothing beyond a battered armchair and a second doorway. She took a step in so the others could see and then stopped, her innate paranoia taking over.

Before Tanimbor had turned she had her mage-pistol out. Tashen and Layir were quick to follow but when the guildmaster noticed, he merely chuckled.

'Please, Mist— ah, Toil. This isn't a trick. You wouldn't expect me to keep my secrets out in plain view would you?'

'What then?'

He nodded at the floor in the centre of the room. 'If you would stay where you are?'

The floor was smooth, mage-carved stone with nothing at all to indicate the building's provenance. It didn't even look ancient, let alone of interest to a relic hunter.

With a conjurer's flourish Tanimbor drew back the loose sleeves of his coat and knelt to one side of the centre. The air blurred and distorted around him briefly, but then the stone-work itself shuddered and began to sink.

'A Duegar seal?' Lastani breathed, her expression both apprehensive and full of wonder. The others had no such conflict and all braced themselves, mage-guns pointed down at the emerging space.

'You do not need to worry, there are no guardians,' Tanimbor said. Suddenly viscous, the stone dropped down to form a spiral slope around a thick round pillar in the middle half of the room. Toil craned past him and saw the darkness of the space behind.

'How far down does it go?'

'Not far. Not into any great Duegar complex you will be glad to hear, Mistress Sitain.'

'Just Sitain,' the young woman said. 'If she ain't a mistress, I bloody ain't either.'

'Of course. Would you all follow me?'

He led them down the spiral slope, ducking under the lintel and into a narrow dark space. Toil followed cautiously, not wanting to reveal her unnaturally good vision, but in moments a dull glow of light spread around the low room. Tanimbor stood at an alcove with one hand on a mage lamp. It was an oval lump that looked like sea glass but for the glow – nothing like as impressive as the ones she'd seen in the past but possibly even more ancient.

'Allow me,' Lastani said when she followed, touching her fingers to the lamp.

The light brightened considerably. Sitain shot the mage a questioning look as she stepped back and Lastani shrugged.

'The guildmaster is a stone mage. His magic is less than ideal for lending power to a lamp. Ice is little better I confess, but I have power to spare.'

'It doesn't draw any power from the air?' Toil asked.

'Not this sort, it is a simpler type. Hardier, but less impressive than those we saw in the Labyrinth and not so versatile.'

Toil nodded. 'I've left a fair few behind in ruins over the years, assumed the damn things were broken!'

'In future,' Tanimbor said with a smile, 'I would be glad to buy them off you. For now, however, here . . .'

He pointed to the far side of the central post, around which the slope turned. Leading them on a few more paces, Tanimbor indicated a large section of stone that wasn't plain and smooth. Instead there were glyphs cut into the rock, three columns of distinct symbols in a more ornate style than Toil was used to seeing in a place like this.

'Well now, isn't that a surprise?' she breathed as Lastani drifted forward, fingers stopping just short of the glyphs themselves.

'Good surprise or bad surprise?' Sitain asked anxiously.

'Oh good, leastways the bits I can read. Lastani?'

'Hmm? Oh, oh yes it's good. I would need some time, but I believe I can translate it all.'

At that, their host raised a finger and went a little further down the steps. He touched a second mage lamp to create a dull glow then fetched up a sheaf of papers from somewhere below.

'Perhaps these might be of use?'

He handed over the papers and Lastani frowned at them, turning to the brighter lamp to inspect them better. Her lips were already moving as she did so, one finger running over the words of the page.

'This . . . this is respectable work.'

Tanimbor hesitated. 'But?'

Lastani pursed her lips as she continued to scan the paper. 'Respectable is fine for the classroom, as Mistress Ishienne would say. Less so for the library.'

'And fucking lethal in a Duegar ruin,' Toil finished.

Lastani gave her a pained look, enough to remind Toil of the first time Lastani's teacher had tried to do something more practical.

'Ah, yeah, sorry.'

210

Lastani looked away and swallowed hard. 'Nevertheless, you are correct. Perhaps it was a maxim that could have saved her life.'

'Luckily failure has not been punished so severely here.'

'You've tried this already?' Lastani said as Toil gave a snort of dark amusement.

Tanimbor blinked at her. 'Certainly, why else would I call in outside help?'

'Goodness. And there was no effect?'

'None. The magic seemed to just drain away, fade into nothingness. Repeated efforts have not proved cumulative – I believe it needs to be jolted into action.'

Lastani was quiet for a long while. She read through each of the papers very carefully again then compared them to the glyphs engraved on the central column. Occasionally she muttered under her breath, but absolutely nothing else happened for a long while until Toil caught Sitain's attention.

'Drink?'

'What? Now? What about her?'

She grinned. 'Lastani's lost to us for another hour I reckon.'

'And you?'

'Bah, it's above my level. I can read directions, get a sense of warnings and the like, but this is more specific. This is one Duegar mage speaking to those that follow. Paranil's better, he can give her a hand.'

She paused and bent down so her lips were right by the oblivious Lastani's ear. 'And o' course,' Toil added loudly, causing the white-blonde mage to jump, 'Lastani's going to call me before she tries anything, right?'

'Ah, oh yes, certainly.'

'Good then. Wine it is.'

*

'Sanshir?'

The tattooed man scowled as he peered out of the darkened room. His long hair was a mess of tight curls and the stink of sweat and sex emanating from him would have been enough to make her take a step back normally. Instead, Sanshir just looked down and raised an eyebrow.

'Disappointing, I'd heard those tattoos went everywhere.'

Ube's dark skin had whorls of black tattoo across every limb, somehow the man had managed to get a mage to extend that to underneath each of his neatly manicured fingernails – ten individual curls that looked distractingly like claws. Now he was naked, Sanshir was afforded the full view of that artwork.

He gave a lopsided grin that showed the pointed teeth prized among his ancestors. 'Lift it up and you won't be disappointed.'

'So I've heard, but I'm here on business.' She tilted her head to look around Ube. Indistinct shapes moved in the room behind him, three or four people she guessed, lying on a spread heap of rugs and cushions. 'It looks like you're probably all tired out anyway.'

Ube leaned his rangy frame against the door post – perfectly at ease in his nakedness and just as aware that Sanshir wasn't disquieted. The two were rivals and far from friends, but it was too early for posturing. His guards behind her were more keen on putting on a powerful face, but that's what a kaboto's guards were for. It didn't mean Sanshir had to take any notice.

'How can I be of service to the Champion Kaboto of Caldaire?'

'Just a small indulgence.'

'Oh? I was under the impression I'd done that already.'

Sanshir nodded. 'And yet I ask for another.'

'Didn't get the answer you wanted from those mercs last night?' Ube sniffed. 'Shame.'

'I got a different sort of answer,' she explained. 'One that requires more attention, perhaps a little encouragement.'

'Encouragement from a Masts crew? This sounds like there's going to be blood on my streets,' the Kaboto of Aufero said. 'Bad for business, that.'

'There's been a complication.'

He yawned and scratched himself. 'It's too early for all this, oh Queen of the Masts. Give it to me hot and quick so I can break my fast.'

Sanshir hesitated a moment then nodded. 'Fine. An exile of Vi No Le has returned, the Bloody Pauper. It may mean nothing, it may be a threat. I have to assume the worst, but like you say, it's bad for business if things get nasty. I want to set my crews watching his company in a less subtle way, put some pressure on to get them to give up whatever they're planning and get gone from Caldaire.'

'The Bloody . . .' Ube mused. 'Ah, I think I remember. Hey, hold on now. He was your man, wasn't he?'

She nodded. 'For a time.'

'Didn't play well with others, right? Led a coup?'

'Close enough.'

Ube shrugged. 'Thought he was dead. You must've been softer back then. Still – exiles are always bad news. He was part of this Siym business I heard about? Yeah, I see your point. I don't want any of that playing out on my streets. Tooled-up mercs on my turf are bad news anyway, let alone ones with a grudge. It hardly matters if their attention is on Auferno or another district. You have your dispensation. My crews will be all over them too. The usual requirements of course – you know the game as well as I.' He gave an expansive yawn. 'You're not some bravo swinging his dick around, so I don't need to spell anything out.'

'Nor swing your own dick around,' Sanshir pointed out, 'save the flexing and yawns for someone else, Ube.'

He grinned at her, that easy assurance of a man who was comfortable in how powerful and attractive he was.

'If your Bloody Pauper doesn't play nice, you may end up owing me a drink for all these favours I'm granting.'

'I'll have someone send you a whole bottle,' Sanshir replied, managing a courteous smile. 'In the meantime, my lot will behave or they'll pray it's you who punishes them. A pleasure doing business with you, Kaboto Ube.'

There was a balance to the rivalry in Caldaire and while they weren't street gangs competing for territory, failing to offer the respect required could only be met with something violent. Ube was no pushover despite his lazy calm.

He turned back towards his darkened room. 'Yeah yeah, now get naked or get gone, Vi No Le scum.'

She left.

It took an hour, as Toil had predicted, but finally Lastani came up for air. Teshen had, inevitably, pulled a deck of cards from his pocket. He and Layir had engaged in some sort of complex two-player game where half the deck ended up spread across the table. It was one Toil had never seen before and after five rounds of slow progress culminating in a sudden total cascade of cards, she remained utterly mystified.

Sitain and Aben had watched the game with even more confusion than Toil, while Tanimbor had taken to the chair at the window, lost in contemplation of the wild cliff face beyond. It was possible he was merely keeping tabs on Lastani to ensure she was doing no magic, but to keep that up for an hour spoke of a paranoid single-mindedness if so.

'I have it,' Lastani called from the boring room, as Toil had privately dubbed it. 'I know how to revive the mechanism.'

'Mechanism?' Toil asked just ahead of Sitain. 'Mechanism to do what?'

'If the glyphs are to be believed, it is named the breath of life.'

'Oooh, fancy,' Sitain laughed, cheeks flushed after wine so early in the day. 'Bloody Duegar weren't half up themselves sometimes, weren't they?'

'They had a rather dramatic flair,' Lastani agreed. 'Perhaps no surprise from a society underpinned by magical power. There was a degree of mysticism in all aspects of life and for all their mastery, magic was considered an art rather than a science.'

'The breath of life,' Tanimbor commented with a gasp of breath, as though his meditations had taken him to the brink of death. 'To a Duegar, they would not see flair.'

'You know what it does?' Toil asked.

'I suspect,' he corrected. 'There is only one way to be certain.'

'Oh, very reassuring.'

'A relic hunter fears to tread the path?'

'A relic hunter only stays alive by understanding the risks ahead, even if the name does suggest it's not going to kill half the city.'

Lastani raised a reassuring hand and offered over the papers Tanimbor had given her. 'I will take you through it. You understand enough to grasp this, I believe.'

'Careful, Mistress Ufre,' Toil warned. 'All this flattery's likely to go to my head.'

'I'm sure I will have occasion to remind you of your deficiencies soon enough. In the meantime, I am confident I can do this, but I will not be able to do it alone.'

'Time to test the limits of your power?'

Lastani shook her head. 'This must be performed by linked mages, it is a requirement of the work. Whether I or the guildmaster should lead the effort is up for debate, but we need several more at least.'

'How many?' Tanimbor asked. 'I can summon eight or nine right now if you are so confident.'

'Just how sure are you?' Sitain demanded. 'Very sure, kinda sure or, maybe-a-huge-ghostly-monster-will-rip-us-a-new-one sure?'

Lastani scowled. Though she knew the needling was a knee-jerk reaction among the mutually abusive Cards, rather than anyone holding a grudge, the memory remained a raw wound.

'I will be the one standing at the front,' she said in a cracked voice.

Toil heaved herself up out of her seat. 'Come on then, take me through it while the guildmaster rounds up his acolytes.'

Lastani led her down the dark spiral to the glyphs inscribed on the central pillar. As soon as they were out of sight of Tanimbor, Toil motioned for Lastani to keep talking and headed further down.

'Don't bother,' Lastani called after her. 'It doesn't run far.'

Ignoring the woman, Toil continued on down, only to find herself in a low chamber with a second set of glyphs and a single further glass lamp. She looked around the room with a practised relic hunter's eye, but could find nothing that indicated anything hidden and soon returned to Lastani.

'You didn't believe me?' Lastani said when she reappeared.

Toil shrugged. 'Always good to see for yourself. Eye of experience an' all.'

She positioned herself in front of the panel of glyphs and brushed her fingertips over the raised stone lines. They were mage-carved of course, but done with such precision and so well protected from the elements that she could feel the pointed corners to each line.

'These ones I know,' she said, indicating two. 'Those, not so much.'

Lastani nodded. 'Consider them a key – the directions to activate the mechanism correctly. Here, we have the blend of magic required; here, the indication that linked mages are required to match the levels.'

'Levels?'

'Tanimbor will have to do the same at the panel below, they must be done in conjunction.'

'They're the same?'

She nodded. 'Identical. I will need to lead the process, likely the guildmaster already knows he is not powerful enough to manipulate the mechanism properly at such a distance. It's buried deep below us, presumably to ensure only the powerful can activate it.'

Over the next few minutes, Lastani detailed the process required and exactly how she would be doing it and the likely result. By the time Tanimbor had returned with a small cadre, Toil agreed there was nothing beyond Lastani's abilities required. But what convinced her was the very first thing she'd seen here. The hidden staircase was a deft piece of trickery, only a lunatic would feel further defences would be necessary past that. There was likely an older structure over this once, this was just all that remained. She'd be ready to take precautions of course, but had never seen the Duegar put traps on mechanisms. Whether they could do it was less of a concern to Toil than whether they should. Normally she'd be more cautious of the result, but time was pressing and she wanted the information from Tanimbor soon.

The mages filed dutifully down – a ragged procession of seven who were wary and silent around the mercenaries. An old man led them, a grandfatherly figure to whom the youngest, a pale boy of no more than twelve, stuck close to though clearly they were not related by blood.

'Bit young isn't he?' Toil commented to Tanimbor.

The guildmaster inclined his head in agreement. 'Younger than most,' he said, 'but a surprising talent born right here in Cliffbase and one we intend to nurture carefully. The experience will be most instructive.'

'None of these are mages of tempest?' Lastani asked. 'I don't mean to be rude, but their magic might complicate matters.'

'None,' he confirmed. 'We have here stone, fire, wind and lightning.'

The rest were mostly in their twenties, men and women from all around the Callais Sea. Aside from the boy, they all looked rather battered by life, which was no great surprise given they had joined this unconventional guild. Several were barefoot and though they all wore the grey tunics, several had old and stained clothing underneath. Likely they'd been pulled from the kitchens or some other un-mage-like task.

Self-sufficiency or servitude? Toil wondered. She would have loved to speak to one alone, to gauge where Tanimbor lay between generous mentor and dangerous fanatic, but that was tomorrow's problem.

Lastani directed Tanimbor downstairs and described what she needed him to do. Judging by the man's reaction, he'd expected this and his incomplete notes had been as much of a test as anything. The precaution was encouraging, Toil decided, but she reserved her judgement and watched.

The mages formed a chain between Tanimbor and Lastani, the old man offering his hand to her with a courtly bow and an easy smile. At his side the lad looked less at ease, but no more hesitant to participate. Sitain was sent down to stand beside Tanimbor, to balance Lastani's great power at the other end of the chain – and also to punch the man if he did something stupid, Toil hoped.

'Toil, you will not interrupt this,' Lastani instructed her before she began. 'The balance will be delicate, the effort great. I want no talking or touching while I'm working, do you understand?'

Sitain opened her mouth to speak but Lastani cut her off, anticipating her question. 'Yes, of course if some ghostly horror attacks us, that's different. I trust Toil to know which danger would be the greater.'

'You have my word,' Toil said. 'Now get moving. I'd like to get back before Anatin decides to open a brothel or something.'

Lastani nodded and pressed her fingers to one glyph, briefly closing her eyes. Almost immediately the willow tattoos on her skin began to glow, a dull white that soon became brighter than the lamp in the alcove behind. Toil looked past her and saw a second light coming from Sitain.

There was a faint gasp from the boy as the rush of power began to flow through him, the raw energy that linked mages of all types. Toil looked over at where Teshen squatted at the top of the central column, watching the mages owlishly. As she did so, the tattoos on his skin began to glow. Checking her hands, Toil saw her own do the same. The effect on Layir was more startling, his brown skin coming alive with white light.

The tattoos began to tingle warm; nothing alarming but enough to tell her they were becoming a conduit for power. She knew the others would be feeling the same and hoped they hadn't ventured out yet. They couldn't keep the tattoos a secret, but there was no need to provide a light show in the middle of the street.

All of a sudden the feeling changed. The cold rush of movement passing through seemed to envelop her in a torrent. The tattoos became a hole in the world, through which purest energy flowed. She stifled a gasp as itch turned to a furious tingle, just on the cusp of painful and reminding her of the moat around the tree in Jarrazir. That had proved such a surge of sensation only sex rivalled it and as Lastani drew more power she felt her knees weaken. She looked up to see Layir's eyes bulge with surprise, then had to look away as the young man flopped down on to his backside.

She sat herself, thighs pressing themselves tight together. The tattoos ran the length of her body and every part now seemed to be alive with awareness. It was a heady mix of sensitivity and arousal, coupled with a strong sense of the other marked Cards.

Lynx intruded most on her thoughts, the sweet spice of his sweat and great warmth of his body, the power in his limbs and the rumbling, bear-like presence of his mind. Layir and Teshen could have been pressed right up against her too, given how close she felt them. Sharp, youthful eagerness in one, a jagged knife-blade of a soul in the other. Aben loomed behind them both, a reassuring lodestone after their years of friendship.

Then the rest spiralled around her mind. Sitain appeared as a towering presence of night-clouds roiling with uncertainty, anger and warmth too, Atieno a pillar of shifting grey-blue. Acidic and painful to be near yet also sustaining for the power residing within him.

Toil fought to open her eyes again, panting for breath at the effort it took, only to see Lastani calmly moving her hands over the glyphs. Two were lit up, the grooves cut into the stone shining with a frosty light. A third joined it as Toil watched. Somewhere at the back of her awareness she felt something shift deep underground, some change or movement that bypassed her usual senses.

The power pulsed and surged through her, following Lastani's gestures in some way now Toil could watch her, though her thoughts were elsewhere. For all the fascination of watching a mage work, of feeling the activating mechanism she was now linked to, Toil's body had its own focus.

Gods, I hope this feeling hasn't hit Lynx when he's in the same room as Kas, she thought with a crazed laugh that escaped only as a strangled squeak. *Mind you, I'd screw her too right now. I just don't need to feel it going on in the back of my mind!*

Even as she thought that, new sensations blossomed in her head. She gasped, thoughts clearing as a flicker of anger raced through her mind. In the next moment she realised it was not her connection to Lynx though, it was Safir and Estal – the pair apparently wasting no time in engaging in the most desperate and glorious sex.

With stars bursting in front of her eyes, Toil was about to settle back and simply enjoy the second-hand sensations rushing through her, but something began to nag at her mind. She forced herself to straighten and blink away the blur of light that was filling her eyes and watch Lastani finish the ritual. Distantly, Toil noticed it was brighter now, not quite the glare of day they'd arrived in, but every detail was clearly visible.

She looked around blurrily then stopped dead. The light was only coming from their tattoos, but it had not got any brighter. Just as he fainted away and broke his grip on Lastani's hand, Toil saw the old man blazing white down the side of his face. Beside him the boy, eyes wide, was looking at his own shining hands and all the other mages in the link started to realise the same.

'Oh shit,' Toil croaked before slumping backwards against the stone wall and darkness descended.

Chapter 22

Toil blinked and groaned. The world was a blur before her, dim smears of brown and black. She tried to lift her head, but failed at first to make any other part of her body obey. Finally, the heaviness eased and she shifted, hands slapping against the stone until she could right herself.

There was a welt on her head where she must have banged it against the wall. Toil groggily touched her fingers to the lump and found a little blood, but not enough to worry about. The ghost of memory wavered in her mind; the vast surge that had flowed through her body, through her tattoos.

She felt dampness on her skin and between her legs, while her tongue was dry and rasping. Toil tried to speak but all she could manage was a grunt. Even as she tried to right herself, she felt the ghost of sated lust thrum through her body, her limbs shaky and uncertain amid that strange afterglow.

Distantly, Toil felt a pang of something rare in her life – embarrassment, shame even. The connection to the other marked Cards, the torrent of sensation that had become something primal and sexual. Her mind was a tangle of confusion. Unpicking everything was more than she had the strength for right now. Embarrassment at the burning need she'd felt well up through the swirl of minds, their own desperate desires mingling with hers. The memory was uncomfortable and she fought to drive it from her thoughts.

It was something she had little time for in her life. Embarrassment was a poison you fed yourself, Toil believed, shame the cut you let others inflict. She had no use for either except as a weapon to wield. Instead, she focused on the other memory that loomed large in her thoughts, that of the stone tree beneath the Labyrinth.

Toil gasped as the image of the light-tattoos filled her mind – the last moment she'd woken up like this.

'Shattered gods!' she moaned. 'At least we're not bloody naked this time round.'

She hauled herself forward on hands and knees, eyes starting to clear as she sought another body there. It all came back to her now, Lastani's workings and the flare of light from their tattoos just before she'd passed out. From all their tattoos.

The first person she reached was Lastani, barely stirring and half fallen over the old man. Toil shoved her unceremoniously out of the way and grabbed the man, yanking his robe and shirt aside. His brown skin was dry and flaky, peeling under some sort of ailment, but all the same there was the willow-pattern leaves marked in white upon him.

As he started to blink up at her the young boy nearby started to wail softly. He'd recovered his wits enough to see the tattoo on his hands and check the rest of his body. Toil couldn't understand the words, but his confusion and fear were plain in any language.

Soon, more voices started up, filling the spiral chamber with a babble of voices. Toil heaved herself upright and looked over at Layir and Teshen. Both men looked fine, Layir slightly glassy-eyed but she'd have expected nothing less. A cry of confusion came from Aben, left in the study.

'Bet that was fun for you,' Toil called to Layir. 'Assuming you also felt what Safir was doing there.'

He shuddered and covered his eyes. 'Oh gods, I need a drink.'

'Hangover's gone then?'

He shook his head. 'To the deepest black with my hangover, I need to be drunk right bloody now.' He sat up and got unsteadily to his feet. 'Or Sitain could just put me out, I don't give a shit but I need to not be remembering that.'

A howl came from further down the stairs and Toil instinctively went for her gun. Before she found it, however, Sitain staggered into view, if anything looking more sickened than Layir.

'Someone make it stop! Shitting broken gods, I had Deern in my head!'

Toil shivered. Fortunately, the rat-faced man had been a distant presence for her. She wasn't sure if she was going to be able to look Kas in the eye any time soon without some really odd feelings going on, but she realised now that was getting off lightly. Sitain disliked Deern and the touch of men in equal measures. Having a man she loathed getting horny in her mind was going to do a real number on the girl.

She stood and waved the young woman up. 'Go – get upstairs and sink some with Layir.'

Sitain didn't even stop to speak, she just bolted up the slope. Toil worked her way down the line, helping the assorted mages up and checking them for injuries. A few were dazed and bore cuts from falling on to stone, but they had all escaped anything more serious.

'What happened?' Tanimbor demanded woozily as she reached him.

'You got all pretty,' Toil said with a manic grin.

'I always said some o' the Cards were contagious,' Teshen added, following her down. 'Didn't realise it'd be this way too.'

'Turns out it's not only our sense of humour,' Toil said.

'That and the crabs.'

She winced.

'How is this possible?' Tanimbor wondered with his hand up in front of his face, marvelling at the outline of leaves on his skin. 'Am I . . .?' He paused and Toil felt a pulse of magic echo through her body as he drew on his power.

'Hey!' she snapped, clipping the man around the head for good measure. 'Stop playing with it or you'll go blind.' To make her point she slipped a knife from her belt and waved the tip in front of his eyes, but he was too awestruck to be either angry or cowed.

'So much power,' Tanimbor gasped. 'This is . . . remarkable.'

'Just don't let it go to your head,' she insisted. 'Last thing we need is some sort of pissing mage coup going on here. One we get the blame for anyways.'

'We are linked,' he said. Tanimbor reached out to take the hand of the nearest mage, a broad young woman with defensive cuts on her forearm. The eyes of both widened as his fingers closed around hers then let go. 'Touching or not, we are linked. This . . . this is unheard of.'

'Two for the price of one,' Toil said. 'Assuming . . . Lastani, did you get the thing working?'

'I . . . I think so,' came her reply. 'My head hurts so badly I'm not about to try and check.'

'Ah, you got the full taste of Deern getting the horn in your mind too?'

'What are you talking about?'

Toil paused. 'You didn't feel all the Cards in your head?'

'Only distantly, but I had the power of the other mages flowing through me at the time.'

'You missed out on all the bloody fireworks then, it was . . . well it was an experience. Mebbe not one I need to recreate any time soon.' She grimaced and shook her limbs out as though she could get rid of the memory that way.

Lastani leaned heavily against the wall as though she had just imagined having Deern inside her all too clearly. 'Toil, I'm . . . I don't feel well.'

Toil covered the few yards between them in record time, suddenly filled with the sense that the powerful young mage was more precious to her plans than anything else could be. 'Hurts? You about to pass out?'

Lastani looked up at her, allowing Toil to hold her steady. In her eyes Toil saw more concern and questions than imminent unconsciousness. 'I think it will pass. I just need to rest.'

'Can you make it back?'

Lastani nodded.

'Right then, Teshen – grab her. We're heading back to the company.' That being said Toil turned back down the slope and placed herself directly in front of Tanimbor. 'Time to pay up. I want that name.'

'Name? Oh, of the guild that might be able to help your supply needs.' He nodded. 'I make no promises, mind. They may refuse you outright.'

'That's my problem. I can be pretty persuasive.'

The guildmaster paused. 'About the matter of payment, though. Can you even tell me if the job was completed?'

'It's done,' Toil insisted. 'If anyone's able to, it's Lastani and I want paying no matter what the result. We didn't guarantee your mechanism was in perfect working order, lots of the ones by the sea are ruined. And anyways, you got something at least as good in the bargain. How about I charge you more for that bit?'

He smiled wanly. 'And if I refused to pay?'

'I could always try taking back those bits of tattooed skin,' she said. 'Wouldn't be the first time I've had to do something like that, but I hope that's not necessary. I reckon we've both found ourselves an ally here today, no need to mess with that relationship.'

'You make a good point. We seem to be tied together now. Whatever the result, my guild is enhanced by your actions. Speak to the Waterdancer Guild, they are the ones you seek.'

Toil nodded. 'Pleasure doing business with you.' She looked around at all the tattooed mages and felt a profound disquiet at what it might mean, but right now Lastani and the Cards were her only concern. 'Reckon we'll be seeing more of you very soon, but I need to see to my own.'

'Certainly. This mechanism, these tattoos – I have work of my own.'

Toil caught his attention. 'Don't whip it out just to impress any girls or guildmistresses you might run into, understand?'

His gaze turned suddenly frosty. 'I will do as I see fit, *Mistress* Toil, you do not give the orders here. However – I am not a man to act in undue haste, you may be assured of that.'

So much for friends and allies, Toil thought to herself. She set off up the slope to collect the others and start the journey back. 'Guess that'll have to do me. Until next time, Guildmaster.'

Lynx stared down at the sour puddle of food and tea on the floor. Half-chewed pieces of fish and soggy lumps of bread spattered his moccasins. His stomach ached, his head throbbed and the remaining bits of him didn't really know what the hells they felt.

Well that was a waste of a good breakfast.

He could hear voices elsewhere in the lodging house, a bit of shouting, but right here was his own dull little piece of misery and Lynx wasn't planning on leaving it soon. Despite the smell.

I'm starting to regret going back to bed, Lynx thought as he stared down at the floor. *This must be Toil's doing. How does that saying go again? She made her bed and now I've puked in it? Close enough.*

He rolled back on to his bed and lay on the tangled blankets that unfortunately smelled more of him than Toil, looking up at the ceiling of whitewashed plaster. It was pockmarked with holes as though someone had spent a long time lying here in bed, throwing things up at it. Either that or they had some weird rodents in these parts, something Lynx certainly wasn't going to rule out.

After a while he heard more shouting outside and wondered if he should get up. His head had cleared a little and everything else seemed to have calmed down, but there would be talking and Deern out there. He didn't much fancy being around either of those things right now. The memory of images and sensations rolled over him. Lynx decided he probably wasn't ready to be around Kas either, however preferable the idea was.

Instead, he simply lay back and contented himself with knowing this was, for the time being anyway, someone else's problem. Anatin was the commander of the company after all, he probably missed giving all the orders. A good chunk of the company passing out before waking up shudderingly hungover and horny was no doubt familiar territory for him.

His door was thrown open with a crash and several figures barged in, all talking together. Lynx closed his eyes against the voices and when that didn't work, he rolled on to his side away from them. That just earned an insistent finger prodding him in the back until he swatted it away.

'What in the hairy fuck am I standing in?' yelled one of the interlopers. 'Oh deepest black, I thought you held on to yer food better'n that, Lynx.'

'Go away.'

'Oh stop yer whining.'

'What do you want?'

'First of all, for you ta shut up and sit up.'

Lynx did so, scowling at Llaith's grinning face as he did so. Kas's friend, Colet, was next to him, looking disgusted at what was on her sandals, while Varain was so flushed Lynx could tell what was going on with the man.

'Anatin wants you,' Llaith informed him.

'Now?'

Llaith grabbed Lynx's arm and hauled, making little headway until Varain took the other one. 'Right shitting now, master honour or death,' the greying mercenary added. 'All you marked Cards.'

'It wasn't my fault!'

'What wasn't?'

'Um . . . whatever he's pissed off about?'

'I'm pretty sure whenever he's pissed off, it's your fault, my Hanese friend, remember? Come on.'

The pair largely dragged him out of the room while a disgusted Colet followed on behind, muttering about the deficiencies of westerners. A stone stair took them to the main courtyard of the lodging house. There a half-dozen tables sat in the sunshine around a pond, half covered by foliage.

Hummingbirds danced their skittish steps around a spray of pink and white flowers shaped like trumpets. At their arrival, the birds raced away to the raised section at the far end where more flowers surrounded a pair of dwarf apple trees. The air was heavy with the hum of bees, but it was the waspish expression on Anatin's face that concerned Lynx.

Llaith and Varain deposited him at one of the tables where more Cards were assembled, all of them looking dazed and awkward. Lynx caught Kas giving him a hard look and felt his cheeks redden as he looked away. Suth, the new Knight of Tempest, sat opposite him, her calm resolve spoiled somewhat by Varain's lustful regard.

'Finally – that all of them?'

Llaith grunted. 'Except Toil's lot and Atieno.'

'Why didn't you fetch him? He's most likely to get me some answers.'

'You want me to drag a grumpy and scary-powerful mage of tempest from his bed?' Llaith scoffed. 'Boss, you ain't paying any of us enough for that.'

Anatin hesitated. 'Aye, fair point. Right then, which of you idiots can tell me what just happened?'

'Toil happened,' Deern said.

'Fuck off,' Lynx replied. 'That weren't Toil. Must've been Lastani.'

'At whose damn orders, eh?'

'Can't blame Toil for them not knowing what they're on about.'

'But what happened?' yelled Anatin. 'Half o' you just collapsed, while Estal dragged Safir into a storeroom and did things that made him squeal!'

Kas coughed. 'Something magic happened,' she said, 'one whole lot of magic.'

'So? They've done that before and none of you wet yerselves last time.'

She nodded. 'Probably a good sign, hey?'

Anatin hissed and scratched at the stump of his missing hand. 'More magic than they needed to put down a whole regiment of Charnelers or withstand the explosion of a bloody mage sphere?'

'Felt like it to me. Anyone say different?'

None of the marked Cards spoke up.

'How is it I've not seen any part of the city explode then?' Anatin yelled, gesturing wildly behind him.

'Dunno,' Kas said. 'The city's that way though.'

'Eh?' Anatin swung around then looked left and right before realising she was right and he'd been pointing at the open sea. 'That don't fucking matter right now. Explain how this has happened and what it means! Are they under attack? Dead? Has Toil just led a coup without telling me?'

A voice floated down from a walkway somewhere above. Lynx looked up to see the tall mage of tempest, Atieno, looking down at them. The stately black man didn't look his best right now, leaning heavily on the wall with his long hair hanging over his face.

'What did you say?'

'I said, it is worse than that,' Atieno replied.

'Oh shit. How exactly?' Anatin sniffed. 'Other than Deern getting a hard-on right in front of me, that is? If I'm honest, that's one of the things I'm really bloody pissed off about. The look on his face is gonna haunt me for weeks.'

'How?' Atieno echoed. 'Do you remember that little thing we did below the Labyrinth of Jarrazir? The one that's got all the mages and magic-hungry beasts everywhere all riled up?'

'Yeah.'

'Well, we made that worse.'

Chapter 23

Lynx watched Atieno descend the stairway. He looked more stiff and weary than usual, ignoring the babble of noise in the courtyard until he'd reached Anatin.

'Define worse,' the commander said at last, having spent the wait chewing his lip in thought.

'Did any of you see it?' Atieno asked, looked round at the marked Cards. They all shared Lynx's blank expression so he nodded and eased himself down into a spare seat. 'Very well, I will explain as best I can. We believe the Labyrinth served as some sort of, ah, tap is perhaps the best word. It limits the flow of magic into the world.'

'So you opened this . . . tap, and let some more magic out into the world?'

'Exactly. It came in a surge to begin with, but has calmed. However, we, Lastani, Sitain and I, are much more powerful than before. I believe we can access this source, or even that we are the holes in the dam.'

'So what does that mean other than a golden age o' magic?'

Atieno regarded the man severely. 'Other? You believe so much magic worked well for the Duegar?'

'Dunno. For the first few thousand years, maybe?'

'Let us hope we're that lucky. We have changed the face of Urden, that much I am certain of. The attack we faced on the canal might become more common as creatures that feed on magic are strengthened.'

'So more golantha trying to eat my other hand?'

'Maybe.'

'Not so good then. How did we make it worse?'

Atieno shook his head and rubbed a calloused thumb against his temple. 'This is a guess, you must understand. It is what I felt just now, but Lastani and Sitain may disagree.'

'Noted – now fucking spit it out.'

Atieno took a long breath. 'In the lower level, when Bade escaped us on that platform and we found something beneath, there were glyphs.'

'The names o' all the elementals, right?'

'Not all, but yes, eight elementals. Perhaps it was not just a tap, but a lock. When Lastani did whatever she did, I felt her linked to my mind but also several other mages. Some I felt much more strongly than others.'

'I felt some o' the marked Cards more clearly than others,' Lynx pointed out.

'As did I, but the flow of magic was clear and connected to several other mages who I felt at least as strongly,' Atieno replied brusquely. 'I am not experienced in linked magic, as you might expect of a tempest mage, but to have several unknown mages stand out like beacons in the darkness . . . it cannot be coincidence.'

'What sort of coincidence?'

'The eight elementals corresponded to the magic of ice, night, stone, fire, lightning, earth, wind and light. However many elementals exist, I know there are water elementals so this wasn't a list of all types.'

'Oh shit, you think it was a key?' Lynx groaned. 'We only opened two out of eight so far and even that got mages and monsters riled up?'

Atieno nodded. 'Today I sensed a stone mage, wind, fire and lightning link to us – sensed them as strongly as I could feel Sitain and Lastani.'

Lynx counted in his head as quickly as his renewed hangover would allow. 'So six in total? We've just trebled what was unleashed in Jarrazir?'

'No,' Atieno said firmly. 'I'd be feeling more god-like if that were the case, less like something a cat sicked up.'

'Mebbe you would be if we were closer to Jarrazir and it's just not hit you yet.'

The mage managed a weak smile at that. 'Let us hope so.'

To keep the company busy and cheerful while Toil's party returned, or at least griping about something he could control, Anatin announced a surprise weapons and kit check. The mercenaries went to attend to their equipment, and in some cases get dressed, with the usual level of obedience, but Lynx found himself pleased to have a task.

One difficulty of the mercenary life was the boredom. It wasn't the worst part; that would be the bits involving running, screaming, getting shot at and holding guts in. However, for a man like Lynx boredom wasn't great either. A task to focus on was always welcome, even if that job was trying to repair broken kit or cleaning his mage-gun.

One quick check from the walkway told Lynx that no one was rushing back. Indeed, the Prince of Sun was enjoying a cigar with a hat perched over his eyes. That meant Lynx had plenty of time and although he'd scrubbed the dust and dirt from his weapons, he went over the whole process again. The habits of the army life had carried on into his civilian wandering and these days he valued the routine. Though he wore light moccasins here, Lynx also polished his boots, fixed a shirt and got something unpleasantly sticky off his coat in time to be back downstairs, armed and ready for battle, before half of the rest.

For all that Lynx remained the focus of Anatin's ire much of the time, it was doled out only lazily and without real malice. He knew the ageing commander could indeed be a monstrous bully when the mood took him, but here it was more habitual and part of the strange comradeship within the Cards. Either that or a sense of self-preservation kept the worst of his inclinations away from Lynx, whose history was a warning to all superior officers.

When it came to Lynx's turn, Anatin only gave his mage-gun and cartridge case a cursory look. The man knew both would be kept to army standards and quickly moved on to the next, but before he was done with that one there came a shout across the courtyard.

'Atieno!'

They all looked up to see Lastani hurrying forward, face pale and worried.

'Did you feel it?'

'More than I wished,' Atieno confirmed. 'What in the name of all that's shattered did you do?'

'I . . .' Lastani faltered. 'Perhaps we should—'

'No!' Anatin interjected loudly. 'We're all part of this, no playing at secrets here.'

She bowed her head in acceptance. 'Very well. I was trying to activate a mechanism for Guildmaster Tanimbor.'

'The same one we met and none of us thought worth trusting an inch?'

Lastani cast a dark look behind her. 'You can blame Toil for the why. In any case, it required several mages to work in unison and more power than even I had appreciated. Tanimbor summoned all those nearby in his guild and I led the work.'

'The short version where no mention of blame needs to be included,' Toil interrupted, 'is that a whole bunch of mages got linked together the way you three are. They're all now sporting the most beautiful selection of willow-pattern tattoos. What in the deepest black it all means, we're not so sure.'

'There was something more,' Lastani added, almost talking over Toil in her haste. Lynx wasn't sure, but it looked like the two had only recently called a truce on an argument over this.

'More?'

'The Labyrinth, the passageway to the stone tree,' Atieno said.

Lastani nodded and took up the explanation as though they shared a mind, which to Lynx seemed worryingly possible right now. 'The symbols above it, of elementals, must have been some form of lock or seal for the wellspring of magic there.'

Toil looked blank for a moment, her cheek twitching slightly as she processed this new information. 'Oh hells,' she whispered. 'It wasn't open all the way? Now more seals are breached?'

'We don't know how it works or what was intended, but only ice and night were marked there. Tempest was not. I could be wrong, but clearly we got the same impression during the linking. Sitain?'

The young woman wore a helpless look. 'I . . . maybe? Can't say I understood a whole lot of what happened there.' She shuddered. 'And I was distracted.'

'Very well,' Lastani said. 'We must work on that assumption for the time being. If the guildmaster's mages added four more types of magic then only two remain closed. I expect we will soon know the truth there.'

Toil was quiet for a long while, but for some reason Lynx found it all unaccountably funny. He clapped his hands together and gave a laugh traced with bitterness. The sound echoed around the courtyard and startled all those present.

'Now we've got a game on our hands!' he declared. 'Any bets on what happens when it's fully open?'

'A second age of magic,' Lastani said hollowly.

She looked far from happy about it, though from what Lynx had heard of their conversation with the Shard, Lastani was the most powerful mage in all of Urden at the start of this new golden age.

'A new age of magic,' Lynx echoed. 'So more elementals, golantha and their kin, plus the Militant Orders thinking their time to rule has arrived? And we're at the centre of it? Just as well I never expected to live forever, eh?'

'This is what it takes for Lynx to cheer up?' Anatin muttered before reaching for a jug of beer. 'Fucking Hanese madmen.'

Lynx paused, feeling slightly light-headed, but one malicious spark of humour remained in him.

'Don't worry, boss. It's not like things could get worse at this point.'

The yelling and throwing of stuff lasted quite a while.

In the deep darkness of underground, something stirred. Long antennae flickered with bioluminescent light, pale green and blue, first dim then growing stronger. It revealed curved lines and jagged points – shimmering, iridescent plates of chitin that moved with a powdery whisper. Long legs stretched and scraped at the rock walls surrounding it, delicately touching the carapaces of others. Those lay quiet at first, returning to wakefulness only slowly. The first – the largest of them – continued to test and probe, feeling the tiny vibrations that ran through the stone.

Feather-tipped antennae twitched, turning and trembling faintly as they sensed a disturbance. Soft, so soft it was hardly perceptible but there was something still, a change in the air that lay thick and heavy in the great tunnels.

Its legs were spears of oily blackness, mere suggestions in the pulsing glow that ran from its antennae under an armour-plated back to a bulbous hump of a tail. Its head moved, mandibles instinctively reaching out as though there was food within reach. Between the antennae and mandibles stretched ghostly threads of light that scooped at the air and withdrew. What it tasted there was enough to make the creature shift, to lift and turn its long segmented body.

That movement prompted more around it; a sharp indrawing of legs, a curling and tensing of rear segments in anticipation of violence. But the change reached them all, a breath of movement and a shudder of stone that told each creature it was not threat but opportunity in the air.

More greenish light billowed as they came to wakefulness, agitation and alarm flickering in that pattern of light. It settled quickly, replaced with a tremble of anticipation. Long-unused legs reached and stretched, blade-points catching in crevices before heaving their great bodies up. Dozens and dozens of legs flowed into movement.

The open, empty caverns around them began to echo with the sound of sharp tips scraping on stone – a whispering click-clack tread that ran for miles in the silent depths. Round-bellied, eyeless rodents scuttled for the narrow fissures of their breeding grounds, driven there by some urge in their blood passed down through the generations. Far below the sunlit lagoon there were lakes lit by the flowers of trailing vines and algae. There, ghostly islands of moss and slime became abandoned as white-shelled crustaceans climbed the walls and went into the vaulted ceiling.

Through higher caverns and long, broad tunnels, where the stink and heat of guano attracted every scuttling horror, there was a ripple of agitation. The change in the air was enough to trigger uncertainty and ancient instincts. Tysarn took to flight,

the smallest rising in spiralling clouds and then the larger creatures too. Others pushed forward from their breeding caves,
thick limbs and tattered wings driving them towards the safety
of open sea.

The alarm spread further still, far beyond the deep caverns
and the slow-waking beasts. A tremble that had nothing to do
with the air itself, but the currents of magic that drifted through
it. Settlements of Wisp clans, several miles inland, saw all work
halt – every daily task abandoned as the tysarn took flight.

Hands moved in the darkness, urgent words were said
without speaking and soon the ancient wise ones of the clans
were consulted. The news proves shocking, terrifying, but it is
believed without question and decisions cascade from them.
Warrior mages are dispatched to their places, ready to spark
rockfalls and seal off their settlements from the tunnels that
lead into the very depths of the world.

Others, wise ones chosen to represent their people, set off
on a higher path, making for the coast that none in living
memory have ventured beyond. For something has changed,
something impossible to ignore. Now they must risk the fear
and chaos of humanity. The deepest black has once more
become a hunting ground.

Chapter 24

'Head outside, take a look at what's going on.'

Toil's words echoed in Lynx's mind as he belted on his mage-pistol. The day's heat was rising so he just wore a shirt and loose cotton trousers. It was coincidence that there were no company markings on him, but that was probably all for the best.

'And what'll be going on?' Lynx had asked, recognising her tone.

She'd shrugged. 'There are crews watching us. I want to see how closely.'

'Sounds fun for me.'

'I need someone I can trust,' had been the reply. 'Trust not to get pushed around – trust not to pick a fight. There are Vi No Le colours out there, which strikes me as a bad sign.'

'So you want me by myself to see how much they try to push me around?'

'Exactly. They'll know not to push an armed Hanese too far, but one man alone doesn't provoke anything.'

Up in their room, Lynx picked up his battered tricorn and inspected it. The hat was in poor condition, perhaps it was time to find something new.

'Sun's bloody hot here,' he muttered. 'Should be plenty of places.'

Armed with some directions from the lodging house's whiskered proprietor, Lynx headed out into the heavy heat of the street. The pale stone of both buildings and roads meant he was sweating within moments, eyes squinting against the glare. A welcome breeze washed over him, swirling down to mingle the salt-stink of the sea and spices of the lagoon islands.

Less welcome were the faces watching from the shade of a trio of palm trees. Six men and women all with scarves pulled over their heads against the sun, hard eyes, and weapons slung from their belts. Each wore a sash, either around their waist or across their chest, white silk fluttering in the breeze. Despite the heat the Vi No Le crew had leather armour strapped to their arms, knees and elbows – not so much for fighting as clambering around the stone districts of Caldaire without stripping the skin.

Lynx checked his flank. The civilians of Auferno were going about their daily business, careful to ignore everything else. There was a second crew watching, wearing the green of Auferno and split into two groups. Two young men burned bronze by the sun stood on a rooftop with an older black woman. She had close-cropped hair, plain clothing and a crossbow resting on her shoulder. Her charges, by contrast, were shirtless; adorned with fetishes and tattoos.

Three more watched from the open front of an eatery, all heavy-built bruisers with hatchets and long staves, scarred by years of fighting.

This is going to be fun, Lynx thought as he saw a look pass between the crews. Setting off for the street he'd been directed to, his path took him past the seated group of Vi No Le Mastrunners. He had to fight the urge to walk with his hand on the butt of his pistol. As he came level with them, as expected, a stave flicked out to partially block his path. Any resident of the city would know to stop, any visitor would be startled enough to hesitate at least. Lynx stepped neatly around it.

The stave flicked up as he passed, the woman holding it leaning out to slap it painfully against the back of Lynx's calves. Still he didn't stop, taking some small measure of childish pleasure in the scuff of feet he heard behind him.

'Hey you!' yelled the woman in rough Hanese.

That alone almost made him stop, the surprise of hearing his native tongue, but despite a small stumble Lynx carried on. More footsteps came as he reached a narrowing of the street. A wooden stall was attached to the front of a low ground-floor apartment, painted fishes dancing in bright colours down each side to a deep stone trough. A variety of spiny-backed creatures waved antennae inside it, while to one side Lynx saw alarm in the eyes of a plump woman nursing a baby.

A hand descended on his shoulder and hauled back on him, attempting to spin Lynx around. He stepped into the movement and seized the hand as he went, twisting and pivoting to drag his assailant around. The woman was taller but lighter than Lynx and taken unawares. Lynx tossed her to the floor with a grunt, some part of him taking satisfaction in seeing a flash of pain on her face.

Before he could do anything more Lynx saw a hooked spear-like weapon coming at him. He scrambled back and had his mage-pistol out before they could make up the ground, whereupon the women who'd spoken barked a word at the spearman.

'No gun,' she said loudly. 'No fight.'

'You laid hands on me first,' Lynx growled. From the look on her face he could tell she hadn't understood. With a jolt, Lynx realised he'd replied in Hanese. He repeated the words in Parthish, a far more widely spoken language, and she nodded, spreading her empty hands in a placating gesture.

The man with the hooked spear looked less friendly, but it only took a hiss from the woman to make him back off.

Behind them, the Auferno heavies were sauntering forward, apparently happy to leave them to it but wanting to be seen by Lynx at least.

'Stupid to ignore a Mastrunner,' the woman replied. 'Dangerous too.'

'Dangerous to put your hands on me,' Lynx said, lowering his weapon but not sheathing it. 'Dangerous to stand so close together too.'

Her lips tightened at that. Mastrunners didn't use mage-guns, likely she'd rarely seen one fired in anger even, but the reputation of sparkers and burners reached further than their use.

'You are not welcome in Caldaire. You should all leave.'

'Is that the message you were sent to give me?'

She cocked her head to one side. Grey eyes and sandy hair, just like Teshen, but lean compared to the Knight of Stars. 'Listen well. Kabats do not warn people twice.'

'Threats already? You people really are spooked.'

'You've made the wrong sort of friend.'

Lynx frowned. 'What's that supposed to mean?'

'The Splinter is a troublemaker. If you do business with him, the kabats see you the same as him.'

'Who in the deepest black is the Splinter?'

She made a dismissive gesture. 'Tell your commander – if there is trouble, we cut the nephew's throat and your company is marked for death.'

Lynx just stared at her. 'Whose fucking nephew? What's going on?'

'If you do not understand, you have no reason to stay in Caldaire. If you have a second job here, you will end up food for the crabs. Do not be unlucky and stupid at same time.'

'That last bit sounds like us,' Lynx said, more to himself than her, 'but we've got no other job. Our business is, ah, learning – no guns required.'

She took a step forward. 'The Splinter has nothing to teach, but your mages and the exile visited him today. Do you think this will not be noticed? Every boat-captain works for us, every servant, every merchant.'

'That's what you're worried about? Tanimwhatever-the-fuck his name is?'

'That,' she snapped, 'is what will get you killed. Arrange passage to leave while you still can.'

Not waiting to hear his response, the woman and her crew returned to the shade of the trees. Lynx watched them go with a growing sense of unease. He didn't know what bargain Toil had made with Tanimbor, but it was clear the powers-that-be didn't like it.

He stood there until their scowls turned his way again. By that point Lynx didn't much fancy going shopping for a new hat, but scurrying straight back home wasn't so attractive either. He resumed his errand with a new sense of haste, buying the first one he found that would keep the sun off and not bothering to haggle on the price.

With that and a pouch of tobacco in his hand, Lynx returned to report back to Toil and wait out the afternoon heat. When he did reach the lodging house, he noticed a second Vi No Le crew on the northern edge of the square and, inside, several other residents were leaving with their bags packed. As the Cards retreated into drink and desultory games of Tashot to distract them from the heat, Lynx set about explaining what he'd been told.

Toil sat in the courtyard of the lodging house and scowled at the world in general. The coverings had been hauled into place above. The heat was still sapping, but without them it would become like an oven there. Even with the high coverings, heat reflected off the pale stone down into the courtyard, but Toil wanted to be alone as she thought and Lynx had retired to their room.

'Regretting taking the quick and easy job?' said a man behind her. She turned as Teshen walked up and deposited himself in a chair nearby. Like most of the male Cards he'd stripped down and was now bare-chested and barefoot. It was a bit late to hide his tattoos now.

'I'm regretting getting here too fast to gather information properly,' she said. 'Gods, give me a cool, dark Duegar ruin any day,' she added, mopping the sweat from her face.

Teshen grinned. He was sweating too, but seemed no worse for the sudden blaze of summer. 'Helps if you're born to it I guess. O' course, the way it's taken a sudden turn like this means there's a storm building,' he said. ''Cos what we need right now is people getting scratchy and troublesome, eh?'

'We're lovely,' Toil said dismissively. 'How could anyone possibly get upset with us?'

Teshen took a deep breath then sagged. 'Nope, it's too hot for the full list, I don't have the energy.'

Before Toil could do anything more a clatter echoed around the enclosed space. With her thoughts on dark and ancient places, the strange scrape on stone was enough to get her on her feet in the next instant. Teshen was up a moment later, both of them with guns drawn.

She scanned around, heart hammering hard until reason kicked in and she knew there were no black-grey claws reaching from the shadows. A flash of movement caught her eye, however, and Toil turned to see something shatter against the stone wall of one block. The force of the throw cast a dark stain over the wall, red like blood but too thin.

'Someone throwing wine at us?'

Teshen wrinkled his nose and sheathed his mage-pistol. 'Best way to defeat the Cards I'd say,' he said, voice thick with contempt. 'But no, they ain't. This is an insult. Breath it in.'

'Huh?'

Toil did so and the listless breeze finally brought the scent to her nose, the sharp stink of urine briefly overlaying everything else. A third bottle was thrown to break against the wall, again leaving another reddish stain and foul smell.

'This the usual Caldaire welcome?'

'Yup. Piss, wine and sloth-blood. Leaves a mess and the smell lingers.'

'Why?'

'It's an insult. You wait, our host'll be out sharpish to tell us it's time to go.'

Toil looked around at the lodging house. Four squat, stone-built towers rose from a circular compound where a large block of private rooms adjoined the entrance and a narrow rear gate was set into the wall on the far side. A walkway ran around above the rooms that lined the wall, connecting the towers where small, cell-like bedchambers with slit windows overlooked the surrounding streets.

'Does he really think we'd leave a defensible position like this? When he comes, tell him to fuck himself then say I'll pay the next week in advance. Just to keep us all legal and polite.'

The Knight of Stars laughed. 'Yeah, that'll make up for the kabat's people tearing into his home and livelihood.'

'Best I can offer. Unless you think we can't defend this place?'

He shrugged. 'It's why I picked it. They can come in still, the game of Masts started out as practice for boarding ships so don't think these walls will stop 'em. But we're a well-armed merc company. They won't be keen to take the necessary losses.'

As predicted the proprietor of the establishment, one Elisher Jathan, appeared a few moments later. He was a potbellied man with tanned skin and a moustache that had spread down to his jawline. Thinning hair was scraped across his head and a poorly restrained scowl was on his face. He'd clearly been in bed – a lightweight kaftan billowed around him as he hurried forward, revealing more of an outline than Toil might have preferred.

'Mistress Toil,' Jathan called. 'They call for you.'

Toil blinked. She'd been expecting anger, outrage or perhaps even smugness. Anyone who served drinks to the Cards for any period of time was probably allowed a certain satisfaction at the prospect of seeing them in trouble, but Jathan was all business. Either he'd expected this or it wasn't so unusual for the kabats to run strangers out of the city.

'Who does?'

'Eyver of Auferno.'

She glanced at Teshen.

'It just means a Mastrunner crew leader, lieutenant to the kaboto,' he said. 'Not a name.'

'Oh. Shall we, then?'

Teshen inclined his head to agree and they headed through the dim stone hallway to the street beyond. A few faces appeared at the doorways above them, Safir and Estal leading the chorus of swearing at the stink of urine that had interrupted their afternoon's repose. The few other customers of the lodging house only poked their heads out – recognising whatever it was as trouble and swiftly ducking back inside again.

Probably sensible, Toil thought as she stepped into the entrance hall. *It is hot out here after all.*

The air was thick with the smell of smoke and spices drifting through the doorway to the right. It was dim and hard to make out after the glare of outside, but Toil could just see Mistress Jathan and her sister, or lover or some other part of their family unit, hard at work in the large kitchen.

They worked alongside two scowling old ladies who seemed to bear no obvious love for any adult, though presumably they were mother to at least one. It was hard to tell in Caldaire, with marriage considered a silly northern tradition and the bonds of family a more complicated knot. Around them scampered small children, a few of the six or seven little devils who haunted those rooms beyond the kitchen.

The main door stood open, propped by a large stone pot filled with some colourful plants that could be used to barricade it if necessary. Through that Toil saw a small crowd in the shade of the trees beyond, all wearing green to a varying degree with a middle-aged black woman at the fore. They were indeed Auferno Mastrunners, not Teshen's former comrades. Even with the absence of a past grudge, Toil felt a moment of disquiet.

'You know any of them?' she asked as they entered the brutal glare of the sun beyond. Waves of heat assailed them from the stone street. She could feel it through the soles of her moccasins and clawing at the skin of her face even as the weight of the high sun bore down on her head.

'Nope.'

'Good. That is good, right?'

Teshen didn't answer and before Toil could ask any more they had reached the small spray of trees. A broad canopy had been strung from the trees to shade a now-abandoned rug of street-hawker's wares. The locals had occupied almost all the space, but Toil chose to stand aggressively close to the woman leading them rather than stay in the sun.

'You chucked a calling card?' Toil asked, almost nose to nose with the eyver, as she'd been called. They were well matched in height and build, the crew leader maybe a few years older but far from gone to seed. 'I'd return the compliment, but I'm a little parched right now.'

'Kaboto Ube sends me with a message. He gifts you one night in Auferno – no more,' the woman replied baldly. 'You go tomorrow.'

'Why?'

'You are trouble. Trouble is not welcome here.'

'Our job's done,' Toil said. 'There's no more mischief in our plans, just a quiet week while our associates do some light studying.'

She shook her head, all businesslike for the time being but Toil could see threats and drawn blades weren't far away. 'One more night. By high sun tomorrow your time will run out.'

'All 'cos of Guildmaster Tanimbor?'

The woman inclined her head. 'The Splinter is a bad friend to make unless you mean trouble.' She cast a sharp look at Teshen. 'Exiles are trouble, the Splinter is trouble. You will leave Auferno tomorrow.'

'And if we don't? Our mages have business with the Shard.'

'Perhaps no longer,' she replied, 'but mages stand apart in these islands. Your company does not.'

At a twitch of her fingers, two of the Mastrunners behind her raised crossbows. Both aimed their weapons at Teshen. The Knight of Stars didn't move, but Toil could sense the tension in him like a coiled spring.

'We know who you are. Kaboto Ube says Sanshir would be unhappy if you were to die by any other's hand, but he would not. Step out of line and he will worry about apologies later.'

'Ube?' Teshen said. 'Never heard of him.'

'He knows you. He knows your deeds.'

'So do lots of people.'

'Lots of people would like to kill you.'

Before Teshen could reply there was the crack of an icer from somewhere behind them, echoing out from the lodging house. Toil and Teshen spun sharply around and the next thing she knew there was a click and flash of movement.

Teshen gasped and Toil glimpsed a red streak as a crossbow bolt tore between them. There wasn't even time to speak before the Knight of Stars had his mage-pistol out and Toil had enough experience with treachery to be following on instinct. His shot blew the head of the other crossbowman open, a pink cloud of chill air that vanished immediately in the warm air.

Toil's shot took the eyver in the chest and punched her backwards. There was a shout from her remaining crew as shock turned to anger. The nearest woman flicked up her stave, ready to swing, but Toil closed the gap and swiped the empty pistol across her face. A second blow put that one down while Teshen hurled himself at a pair of bronzed, tattooed youths. Years of training gave him the first strike and Teshen had never been an honourable fighter. He grabbed the wild hair of one and headbutted him, using that grip for balance as he kicked the other in the balls.

That won him enough time to stamp on the side of the first youth's knee and throw him in the path of the last Mastrunner, a great lump of a man not far shy of Reft's size. He was slower than Reft, though. The tumbling youth didn't slow him down, but Teshen dodged back from the swing of his hatchet and Toil had plenty of space to stab him in the back. It didn't put the man down, to her disappointment, just seemed to enrage him, but by then Teshen had his long knives out and went to work with swift, savage efficiency.

Toil bent and slammed the pommel of her knife into the head of the trampled youth, thinking he deserved at least half a chance of living. He flopped limp while Teshen wasn't so generous to his wheezing comrade and put a blade in his heart.

They both took a breath and looked at each other.

'Could always have been Himbel,' Teshen said with a bleak laugh. 'Often tries to shoot Deern a few hours into a hangover.'

'Wouldn't that be a bloody stupid way to start a war,' Toil muttered as she started back across the exposed ground. 'Not even we have luck that bad.'

'Bet you a silver isle?' Teshen called after her. Toil didn't respond.

Chapter 25

Lynx burst from his room – shirtless, barefoot, but mage-gun ready. Shouts and crashes came from all around, but it took him a moment to spot the source of the gunshot. His room was on the first floor, leading out on to the walkway that ran all around the compound.

Looking over the edge he saw a body on the floor at the southern end, arms and legs splayed. A shockingly bright stream of blood ran in a widening path from the top of the dead man's head, looking for all the world like a neat trail of red hair. He felt a jolt at the sight. An image of Toil lying dead in some anonymous street came all too readily to mind.

Lynx wasn't a man who thought much of the future. It was foolish to look too far ahead when the past dogged your every step and the present was difficult enough. But still, it took a better man than him to banish all such thoughts forever. Bloody, ignominious death was a risk to every mercenary, but Toil danced above greater dangers still and no one's luck runs forever.

'What happened?' he shouted, trying to focus on the present.

Varain squinted up at him. Shirtless too, the toll of hard years showed on his body; drink and battle scarring his thick frame.

'Fucker came out o' nowhere,' he complained as he reloaded. 'Just dropped down in front o' us and planted one on Aben.'

Lynx looked a little further out. There was Aben, touching his fingers to his lips and looking down at the body.

'He kissed Aben?'

'Kicked me in the face!' Aben said, faintly outraged. He was a big man, hard to put down even with a foot, but clearly it had staggered him. 'Came over the wall there.'

He gestured to the rear wall, twelve feet in height but Lynx could see a small grapple caught on the top edge.

'Don't know about the other shots,' Varain continued. 'Probably not good news though.'

'Others?'

Varain waved a hand towards the far side of the lodging house. 'Outside. Couple more icers.'

Lynx began to walk a circuit of the walkway, checking what he could see of the ground outside. The combination of broad towers and tight-packed, high buildings meant there was little enough out there and no obvious threat. He glanced down at the dead man. An Auferno Mastrunner by the green bands he wore on his biceps and thighs, young too.

Probably just some dumbshit trying to make a name for himself. Instead he lost face – or at least half of it.

The sound of running footsteps made him swivel and aim his gun down, but it turned out to be Toil and Teshen racing inside, shouting as they came.

'Muster!' Toil roared. 'To arms!'

Fuck.

Lynx kept moving, hammering the butt of his gun on doors as he passed, but half the company were already up and out. More than a few were entirely naked, but they were all armed which was the important thing.

'What's going on?' Anatin yelled, fumbling to sling his gunbelt on to one shoulder. 'Who's dead?'

'Some local shitbird,' Varain replied. 'Jumped the wall and went for us.'

'Fuck 'im then.'

'Bad fucking timing,' Toil shouted. 'We were talking to a Masts crew just as it happened. They were giving us a warning, next thing we knew a gun went off behind us.'

'They dead?' Anatin shook his head as he realised who he was asking. 'Never mind. Fuck.' He looked around at the assembling mercenaries. 'Sun and Stars hold the walkway. The rest o' you get your kit and come relieve us. I want a full muster in two minutes, understand? Toil, is the front door shut?'

'Blocked it with that bloody great flowerpot.'

'Good. You sure this wasn't a planned hit?'

'Doubt we'd have made it back inside if it was.'

Anatin nodded. 'That gives us time to get ready. Someone barricade the rear gate. Teshen, go talk to our host and make sure he doesn't get any funny ideas or has an exit we don't know about. He stays out o' sight with his family if he knows what's good for him.'

Anatin looked around at the watching faces of his company. There was a slight, twisted smile on his face, as though he'd finally found something he could get properly angry at.

'Boys and girls, looks like we got ourselves a siege – so get fucking moving!'

The mercenaries of Blood, Snow and Tempest all raced back to their rooms.

The afternoon dragged on, hot, heavy and interminable. With his sword and pistol belted to his waist, shirt tucked in to avoid snagging, and a cartridge case hanging heavy on his stomach, Lynx felt like ten years had been added to his life. The hangover had gone, but the oppressive heat radiated out from the stone walls all around and precious little of the sea breeze came to ease it. Inside, it was cooler because of the thick stone walls, but still warm and unpleasantly stuffy after half an hour stationed at a window watching the street below.

'This good or bad?' he muttered to Llaith who stood at the room's other window. 'I can't see anyone at all out there.'

They were on the top floor of the tower assigned to Tempest. The buildings beyond it stood on lower ground than the lodging house, which meant there was less risk of attack this side, but he still kept a weather eye on every open window.

'No one's shooting at us,' Llaith suggested, drawing on the stub of his cigarette. 'That's good.'

'Or they're getting ready to attack in numbers.'

'Or just trying to work out what the fuck to do,' Llaith countered. 'You heard Toil – they were giving us a warning when that wanker jumped the wall by himself. Likely the kabat don't know what's gone on. Mebbe the boy was alone, mebbe he had mates with him who're saying how he was just stealing in ta find some sort of trophy. Anyway, it's too hot to fight – better to make us stew in our juices for a few hours.'

'What does the kabat know?' Lynx mused. 'He sent a crew to warn us off and it went south. Mebbe someone's told him about the gunshot that sparked it, mebbe not.'

'There's a hot-head in every crew,' Llaith added. 'Anyone can start a fight for a stupid fucking reason. I dunno what Teshen's reputation was back in the day, but he ain't a fool and who chooses ta take on more'n twice their numbers? Doubt it'll add up.'

'But the kabat's been given a bloody nose on home turf, can't back off after that.'

'Aye, s'pose so. Shit.'

'Enough with the gossiping,' Suth called as she entered the room. 'See anything?'

Lynx turned to look at the compact gunfighter, who was wearing two pairs of mage-pistols. 'Not a damn thing,' he said. 'Streets are empty. No one's come near the place.'

'Nor this side,' Llaith confirmed. 'Toil got a plan?'

Suth scowled. 'Not that she's sharing. Turns out the lieutenant she killed also warned us about getting cosy with that
mage, Tanimbor. Sounds like he's been making enemies all
over the city, stirring up trouble and the like. Just the sort
of man who'd want to make friends with a crack mercenary
company, no?'

Lynx snorted. 'Great, we're going to die because of a misun-
derstanding. Sounds about right.'

'I've seen it happen more times than I can count,' Suth
said. 'Must come a close second to plain old shitty luck on
the list of easy ways to die.'

'What now?'

She jabbed a thumb towards the door behind her. 'I'll take
your place here. You go sidle up to your woman, see if you
can get more out of her than I did.'

'Reckon that'll work?' Lynx ask sceptically as he moved to
obey.

'Doubt it, but if we don't keep swapping positions people will
fall asleep in this heat.' The Knight of Tempest crouched by the
window, peering out through the aperture at the buildings beyond
as though expecting a sniper to take a shot at any moment. 'Take
a turn on the walkway after, move someone else on.'

'Aye, sir.'

Lynx headed out on to the open walkway, just six yards
in length and only enough to link the two rooms at the top
of the tower to the stairway. The air wavered in the slanted
shafts of afternoon sunshine and Lynx paused to take a swig
of water from his bottle before descending.

There were Cards stationed on every side of the lower
walkway, avoiding making obvious targets of themselves as
they patrolled. Lower down, in the courtyard where no archer
or gunman could see, Toil and Anatin stood with Payl, Anatin's
lieutenant, and the two mages whose opinions Anatin cared

about. Sitain reclined a few yards away, close enough to listen but resting her eyes.

If anyone did attack, Lynx knew it'd be Sitain's job to run towards them and put down everyone in front of her. She was a fierce young woman, but no sort of soldier. He could only imagine how it was playing out before her eyes right now.

He joined the company's officers without saying a word. They had got to the point of working out how much food was in the lodging house, which to Lynx sounded both a bad sign and overly optimistic that things would last that long. It wasn't long before Anatin broke off their conversation and gave Lynx a look.

'Want something, soldier?'

'Suth just asked me to come down, see what the situation was.'

'Same as it bloody was when she last asked,' Anatin snapped. 'This ain't our city, we don't control what comes next.'

'What about you mages?' Lynx asked, turning to Lastani. 'Can't you get your friend the Shard to do anything?'

'We're stuck in here because Toil took a job from her biggest rival,' Atieno pointed out. 'The Shard may be less friendly towards us now.'

'So? Fucking persuade her.'

Atieno pointed towards the main entrance. 'By all means walk out there with a sign saying "mage" hung around your neck, see how much protection it gives you.'

Toil cleared her throat. 'Atieno is, um, hesitant to rely on the protected status of mages in Caldaire. However, Lynx does have a point. The Shard's our best option, we just need to get access to her.'

'They'll be sending someone to negotiate soon,' Anatin said firmly. 'Even if they raid their kabat's arsenal, no one will want to breach these walls while we're ready.'

'Teshen said they'll come at night,' Toil added. 'They don't know how well some of us can see in the dark, which means we'll likely fight them off but spill a whole lot of blood in the process.'

'But whoever sent that crew you killed, they'll be along to tell us exactly what they plan on doing if we don't surrender.'

'And that's not an option, right?' Lynx said, checking around at their faces. 'Right? It's not like they'll accept an apology at this point, is it?'

'None of us are dying over this if I've got any say,' Anatin declared, 'and don't worry, we're not at the point where I clock Toil in the side of the head and hand her over. We're still a ways from that yet.'

'Good to hear it's still an option,' Toil muttered, prompting a cruel laugh from Anatin. 'Makes me feel all warm and fuzzy, loyalty like that.'

'Hey, mercenary, remember? Taking money from strangers to kill other strangers. Warm and fuzzy doesn't come into it.'

Toil sighed. 'In any case, the Shard wants to be friends with you three and she's a politician. Politicians like friends but only get a hard-on for someone who owes them a favour.'

'Why do I get the feeling you're selling us to the Shard?' Atieno asked.

'I'm not. We're in this together, whatever Anatin says, and you're part of my plans. If the Shard wants you as a pet, I'll talk her down or shoot her in the head. Either way I'm not leaving the Mage Islands without you, understood?'

'Bloody fanatics,' Anatin sniffed, but the mages at least looked mollified.

There came a whistle from the walkway above, followed by a shout of 'Boss!'

Varain's battered face appeared a moment later, almost scarlet in the heat. 'Someone's coming.'

257

'Wearing green?'

'Aye. Alone, looks like he wants ta talk.'

'About bloody time.' Anatin nodded towards Toil. 'Get going then.'

'Me? You're the commander.'

'Haha, nice fucking try. This is your fault and you're paying our wages. You get to go out there and be the one they shoot if the conversation goes bad.'

'Alone?'

Anatin gave Lynx a crooked grin. 'Nah, there's always some other dumbshit ready to stand in the way of danger, I reckon. Still, it's his choice. What are you, Lynx, a proper mercenary or some fool hero?'

Lynx's heart sank.

'Is there a third option?'

Chapter 26

The man was tall and lean with a great mass of braided hair bound up on top of his head and loosely covered by a scarf. He wore a light, loose wrap belted at the waist with a pair of curved long knives. From what Lynx could see of his dark skin, the man seemed to be mostly made up of tattoos and corded muscle, all wrapped around a core of simmering rage. He barely looked at Lynx. His attention was solely focused on Toil and not in a good way.

'You're the one?' he called as they neared him.

He stood on the edge of the shade, just a few paces clear of where the blood lay dry and cracked on the dirt street. The sun was still high and searing, past its zenith, but the snakes of heat that wavered through the air clearly hadn't got the message yet.

'I guess so,' Toil said with a respectful nod. 'Kaboto Ube?'

'That's me,' he confirmed. 'And aside from being a thorn up my dick, who're you?'

'Toil – officer of Anatin's Mercenary Deck. This is Lynx, one of my men.'

'No exile? From all I've heard, the Bloody Pauper was never shy of taking his bows.'

She shook her head. 'I told Teshen to stay inside. No need for the distant past to clutter up the present any more than it already has.'

'Huh.' Ube scratched his cheek as he inspected her, as though certain there was a key to all this that he could fathom if only he looked hard enough. 'Tell me what happened. Persuade me I shouldn't just have those walls pulled down in fire and thunder.'

Lynx realised the man's Parthish was better than Lynx's own – the rich rolling sounds of his accent sliding neatly around each syllable. The kaboto was a fighting man, but he'd been well educated too.

'Bad luck is what happened. Some fool climbed the wall and surprised two of ours so they shot him.'

'And that was reason enough to kill my friend, was it? Her name was Kivrei, in case you were interested. I'd known her twenty years.'

'Not reason enough, but the gunshot surprised us all. One of her crew fired a crossbow at us – we didn't wait to find out if it was a mistake. Where I'm from you only get one chance when a meeting goes sour. I doubt it's much different here.'

'That's a cold and bloody way to live.'

Toil nodded. 'Lets me live, though.'

'For the moment. So what am I meant to do about you? Even assuming I believe a word of what you just said, I've got six dead and just piss in the wind to show for it.'

'I don't know your laws.'

'No, you don't.'

There was a long moment of silence, during which Lynx realised the longer this went on, the hotter the fires were going to burn.

'What do *you* want?' Lynx asked, trying not to sound confrontational.

Both turned to look at him as though the dog had just sat down at dinner. He squinted at Ube through the unbroken sunshine.

'There's nothing can undo what happened,' Lynx continued. 'No apology that'll make it right, but still we're sorry for it. We never intended for anyone here to die, never meant any trouble at all in Auferno.'

'You reckon apologies are worth shit here?'

'I figure they're still worth saying,' Lynx persisted. 'Better'n forgetting to.'

'And now?'

He shrugged. 'Any of them got families?'

'You think you can buy absolution?' Ube snapped.

'No, but life's a hard mistress who don't give two shits about grieving. Money doesn't fix things, but it can stop more misery from piling on top.'

'We take care of our own,' Ube said dismissively. 'Keep your money for your own funerals.'

'Does it need to come to that?'

The Auferno man paused. 'Sometimes it always comes down to blood. Here's my offer – I believe it was a mistake and so one of the guilty pair walks free. The other does not. Your company leaves the city tomorrow or things get nasty.'

'One of us dies?' Toil said. 'You asking me to choose?'

'Nah. He's the exile, he's the one who shouldn't have come back here in the first place. He's the one the kabats know as a killer.'

'Then they should know Teshen isn't exactly the public-spirited sort, likely to just give himself up.'

'That's your problem. You've got until nightfall to deliver him.'

Toil shot Lynx a glance he couldn't interpret. 'There may be a way to get what we all want, but I need something from you too.'

'You're in no fucking position to negotiate!'

'You want us all out of the city,' she replied calmly, 'but the mages with us have unfinished business.'

261

Ube gave a brief, barking laugh. 'Spirits of the deep, the Splinter? Are you stupid, woman?'

'Not Tanimbor,' she said, shaking her head. 'The Shard. They've got business with her, that's the only reason we've not yet packed up.'

'You think she wants to deal with you now she knows you're cosy with the Splinter?'

'That's our problem – if she doesn't, we're done all the sooner.'

Ube shook his head, his carefully restrained anger for a moment eclipsed by surprise. 'This is the Mage Islands,' he said finally. 'Mages go where they like. So long as they don't fuck with the kabats, they're not subject to our laws. I'll even provide an escort.'

'That won't be necessary.'

He bared his teeth and Lynx noticed the slight points that gave him a feline air. 'They'll get an escort. If I don't hear they were delivered safely to the Shard's Rest, they lose all privileges and I lose my patience with all of you.' He pointed towards the lodging house behind them. 'Now fucking jump to it. I've got a hundred Mastrunners thirsty for your blood and as soon as I get bored waiting, they'll get it.'

The pair hurried back inside, glad to be out of the sun. They spent a while blinking at the ghostly shapes emerging from the gloom until their eyes adjusted.

'Well?' Anatin demanded through the inner door, his remaining hand on his pistol as though fearing the worst.

'Lastani, Atieno,' Toil called, ignoring the Prince of Sun for the moment. 'He'll let you out – go to the Shard, see if you can get her to intervene on our behalf. Whatever it takes, you understand?'

'And if we cannot?' the tall mage of tempest asked.

Toil gave him a crooked grin. 'Then you stick to the mission as best you can. I still want to know all I can about these damn tattoos. Come the morning, I want you back here with good news in your sticky little hands.'

'What about the rest of you? What about Sitain?'

'Sitain I need here, she's our jester in the hole for any fight. I've bought us a few hours, enough to get to nightfall.'

'What happens then?'

'Either we send Teshen out to be executed or get ready for a fight. Anatin's the company commander, the choice is his o' course.'

Anatin snorted. 'Why Teshen and not you?'

'Obviously I tried to offer myself over instead, but they seemed pretty keen on stringing up Teshen. I'm guessing he's made more enemies round here than I have.'

'Aye well, you've only been here a few days,' Anatin said. 'They've not got to know you yet.'

Toil nodded. 'It could be he's making some point to the Kaboto of Vi No Le too. I didn't push him on the details, man was pretty fucking angry.'

'I can see why. Seems we've made a mercenary of you, Toil.'

'Don't go soft on me,' Toil scoffed. 'I'm the one saying we get ready to fight, remember? Ube wasn't interested in having a discussion, but you're welcome to go and change his mind if you like.'

'I reckon anyone leaving here who isn't a mage is getting shot.'

Toil beamed at the two mages as they set off to the door. 'Me too, but don't worry, you two. I'm almost completely sure they won't kill you.'

Lastani and Atieno walked hesitantly out into the bright sunshine of the street. To their relief, absolutely no one killed them. They stumbled forward to the shade of the trees where Ube still lounged. The man had procured a drink and seat from somewhere. Under the hot afternoon sun, the commander of the enemy forces was perched on a wooden stool and sipping something pungent from a cut-open coconut so far as Lastani could tell.

'You the mages?'

'Ah, yes, sir.'

He raised an eyebrow. 'Sir, is it? Definitely not local mages then.'

'No, we're from—' Lastani stopped as Atieno put a hand on her arm.

'He doesn't care,' the tall man advised. 'Just prove you're a mage.'

She nodded and swept her arm through a high arc that cast a dusting of frost over the kaboto. The man raised his drink at her, appreciating the moment of cool on a hot day.

'And your friend?'

'I'm a mage of tempest.'

'No demonstration needed then.' Ube waved one hand and a pair of Mastrunners trotted forward, golden-skinned siblings by the look of them with ritual scars down their arms and wicked, multi-bladed weapons that Lastani had never seen before.

'These two will escort you to the Shard's Rest. If they don't report back soon, I'll be very unhappy at the world, understand?'

'We understand.'

He waved them away and the male half of their escort gestured for them to get moving. Auferno was deathly quiet in the afternoon heat and with armed crews prowling, so they made good time across the district. The mage on guard at the Shard's Rest was unknown to them, but she seemed unsurprised by their appearance and ushered the pair in without even confirming their abilities.

Inside, it was cool, unnaturally so – a sudden slap that swiftly turned into relief. Atieno groaned with pleasure at the change in temperature as they were directed to the Court of the Shard itself. It was only then that Lastani noticed the buzz of sound coming from behind the double doors and she hesitated as she crossed the hallway.

'You can't be surprised?' Atieno muttered into her ear. 'If what we suspect just happened, ah, did happen – they'll all know it.'

'Already? We're a long way from Jarrazir.'

'It was quite a jolt of power. You might have a better handle on it, but Sitain's leaking magic like an incontinent toddler.' He paused. 'I'm barely holding on myself. If things get nasty, you don't want to be anywhere near me, understand?'

She gave him a startled look. 'Is it really that bad? I know there's a huge flow of power, but still . . .'

'You're a very powerful mage,' he said with a weary smile. 'Well schooled and disciplined. I'm an angry old man who's been holding back all his life, who's never been able to even practise a whole lot.'

'How bad?'

He shrugged. 'If someone put a knife in me right now, it'd be a miracle if I only turned the entire Shard's Rest inside out.'

Lastani gave a cough of surprise and alarm. 'Let's, ah – let's make sure it doesn't come to that,' she said in a hoarse voice. 'Please.'

She took a shaky few steps forward just as one of the stewards appeared from a side room. She'd seen him on her last visit, a middle-aged man with a cleft lip, attending the Shard, but hadn't actually spoken to the man.

'Mistress Ufre?' he said with a small bow. 'They will want to see you immediately.'

'Who will?'

'All of them.'

The doors opened and a strange combination of cool air and angry voices rushed out to greet them. Lastani blinked at the court as the clamour rose for a moment then waned. Directly opposite her sat the Shard, half out of her seat with one hand raised. She had been in mid-shout when Lastani came into view, but it was forgotten in an instant. Many of the room couldn't see the newcomers and continued to argue until the Shard slammed her fist down on the table in front of her.

There was a blur around the woman's hand as she did it, a tiny sliver of magic that turned the thumping fist into an echoing boom. The voices stopped almost immediately, but the Shard was already staring straight at Lastani. With one pudgy finger she beckoned for the Cards to enter her court. Lastani took a breath and walked forward, trying to ignore the swish of heavy doors closing behind her.

'Now perhaps we will get some answers,' the Shard declared. 'Mistress Ufre, now would be the time to explain yourselves.'

The Guild Court was full – every tier of benches occupied. Taminbor, the so-called Splinter, wasn't there but aside from him, every guildmaster had to be present. In her shock she didn't respond immediately, instead staring around at the faces watching her. The Mage Islands had its ancestors in three major tribes of the area, but it was a trading port and former pirate haven too, so the sheer variety of faces looking back at her was astonishing to a Jarraziran.

'I'm waiting,' the Shard called. 'What madness have you done now?'

'Done?' Atieno replied. 'I'm sorry, Shard, but you're going to have to narrow that down a bit. We've, ah, been rather busy.'

'Do you think I give two shits about your escort picking a fight with the local kabat? As representative of the greatest gathering of mages in the Riven Kingdom, that does not concern me.'

'The magic bit then?'

'Indeed.'

Lastani caught up with herself and shook the dazed sensation from her head. Atieno was being argumentative, she realised belatedly – whether that was a result of the changes they'd wrought or just spending time around the Cards, it wasn't what they needed.

She cleared her throat and touched him on the arm. 'Perhaps I may?'

'Please do.'

'How much do, ah, do you want me to say here, Shard?'

The woman ran a hand over her bald head in a frustrated gesture. 'I think we are beyond worrying on that front.'

'Very well. We believe we may have accidentally increased the level of magic in the world.'

'Again,' the Shard said in a level tone.

Lastani hesitated. 'Ah, yes. Again.' For reasons she couldn't explain, she added 'sorry' a moment later then immediately regretted it.

'How?'

'We attempted a ritual,' Atieno broke smoothly in. 'Linking our powers together. It produced unexpected results.'

The Shard glared at him a long while. 'This would be while you were making friends with Guildmaster Tanimbor?'

Her tone was more than frosty and judging by the sudden stillness on the benches, Tanimbor wasn't any more popular among the rest.

'The guildmaster asked me to consult on a problem he had.'

'And you happily obliged him?'

'Why would we not?'

The Shard gave a snort and gestured around the room. 'Because he is a constant source of trouble. Because you and your company of drunken idiots could do with some powerful friends in this city, but are more interested in upsetting the balance of power. There your tendencies are aligned with

Tanimbor's.' She waved her hand dismissively before Lastani could reply and continued speaking. 'When you say you have increased the magic in the world – how? You did so before, but you were in Jarrazir then, in the Labyrinth itself.'

'The ritual – it required us joining with several other mages. Mages of other disciplines than the three of ours.'

The Shard was quiet a while, blinking repeatedly as she sorted the information she already knew in her head. 'More mages. Some fools had unwittingly pulled the stopper out in Jarrazir, but more power was needed to open it all the way?'

Lastani could see the woman wanted no input from them and the muttered questions from the other guildmasters also went ignored by their appointed leader. 'You discovered the tree beneath some sort of chimney, if I recall? There were symbols there.'

'Yes.'

'Elementals, correct? How many?'

'Eight.'

'Was tempest one?'

Lastani glanced at Atieno and shook her head.

'So two of you aligned to those symbols. Two out of eight was enough to cause a measurable increase in magic across the continent,' the Shard mused. 'Elementals are almost synonymous with the magic they embody, it is an obvious key to use. How many did you add to that list today?'

'Four more.'

Without warning the Shard snatched up a large silver goblet that stood to one side on her desk and hurled it across the room. It bounced off the floor with a great clatter and crashed into the wall beside the now-closed doorway.

'Four?' she yelled, suddenly incandescently angry. 'You've just doubled – no trebled – the effect of—' She stopped and went very still before pinching the bridge of her nose. 'That's not even the bad news, is it? Shattered gods . . . You damn fools. You linked with at least four mages. You were linked to them when this happened. Last time this happened, you became connected to the Stone Tree and the power of its reservoir.'

She looked up. 'And thrice-damned Tanimbor was one of the mages you linked to, wasn't he? With all that, why are you here? My intervention to save your friends? Further access to our library?'

The Shard paused and thought for a moment longer. Then the hint of a smile crept on to her face, one laced with anger and malice, and she looked up at Lastani. 'This work you did for Tanimbor, did it involve an ancient mechanism? Tell me, do you know anything of this city's history? Have you ever heard of the razing?'

Chapter 27

'Movement!'

Lynx followed Braqe's finger. All he saw was the flicker of a dark shape ducking into a doorway, but that was enough. He shuffled back to look over the walkway rail, about to call down when there came a hiss from the far side of the building.

'Four closing,' Kas called from the opposite walkway. The lodging house was quiet and her voice carried easily.

'Movement here,' Lynx added.

'Get ready,' Toil replied in a louder voice. She stood on the ground floor with a knot of Cards, ready to support whoever was getting the brunt of the attack. 'Watch for decoys – they know they're out-gunned and this is home ground.'

Braqe grunted at that. For a moment Lynx thought she was going to start snapping away like the little ray of sunshine she usually was, but then he realised her eyes were fixed off to the side.

'What is it?'

'Bugs are coming out to play,' she said with a nod. 'North.'

Lynx felt his breath catch as he realised what she was on about. The hot day had kept the tysarn away and only now were they emerging to feed. With sunset complete and a cloudless sky, it was the cool white light of the skyriver that shone down upon the swarm rising from the hellmouths. Three swirling columns of creatures, thousands upon thousands catching the moonlight as they rose high into the sky.

'Just one more thing that wants to eat us,' Braqe commented, cutting through the sense of wonder Lynx was experiencing.

'You're a poet at heart, woman,' he muttered.

'Don't need dreamers when we're trying to stay alive,' she spat back. 'This is what your lot are born to do so get ready for it and watch my back. You ain't here 'cos I like the look o' you.'

'Fuck you too, Braqe,' Lynx whispered.

Out of the corner of his eye he caught a faint, lupine grin appear and vanish on her face. He drew his sword and laid it on the stone floor beside him. One flick of the thumb reminded him that he had an icer in the pipe, a second revealed the burner in his pistol.

'Damn city-fighting,' she said while Lynx checked. 'Least the houses round here cleared out. For a moment I thought they were going to attack as everyone was leaving.'

'If this were a Charneler city . . .'

He didn't need to finish the sentence. The Militant Orders were well known for using civilians as cover, but Auferno was a tight-knit community. Friends and relations of the Masts crews would be in those houses. The sharp crack of an icer broke the night and Lynx watched a white trail pass overhead.

'And shit, they brought guns,' Braqe commented. 'Have at 'em then.'

Lynx knew it was a speculative shot. He levelled his gun and followed the trail back to an open stairway running up the side of a house.

'Bad choice,' Lynx whispered. The shot had revealed the shooter's location, but there wasn't much room to shift position. His mage-blessed eyesight didn't show a whole lot, but there was a huddled shape, moving like it was reloading a mage-gun.

He pulled the trigger and the figure on the stairway was hurled backwards to crash against the wall behind.

'Another fucking amateur who doesn't get time to learn lesson one,' Braqe said. 'We ain't seen the last of that tonight.'

'Aye. Let's just hope they don't show us what they're good at,' Lynx replied as he shifted right and reloaded.

She gave a grunt and hopped up, looking over the wall at the street below. In one movement Braqe brought her gun around and fired at someone down there, prompting shouts and scrambling feet. From the tower beside them came more icer-shots. Then Lynx was up and searching. An arrow flashed past, barely seen in the gloom, then he picked out a creeping figure and fired. The attacker spun around and fell, howling in pain, while Lynx ducked back down.

More return fire came, arrows and an icer clattering uselessly against the stone tower. Lynx couldn't even tell if it was meant for them or the Cards at the windows, but he figured it was mostly to keep their heads down. From somewhere behind came more gunfire, then off to the left as well.

Teshen had his suit manning the wall where he thought the main attack most likely to come, but no need to hold back when you had the advantage of numbers. He heard boots stamp their way out of the tower towards him. Suth appeared at their side a moment later ahead of two mercs from Blood, Himbel and Ulax. Tempest were under-strength and anyone climbing the wall on Blood's side would find Reft waiting.

'How many?' Suth barked, taking one quick look before she ducked down behind the wall.

'Four in the street,' Lynx said. 'I got a sniper from the block over there.'

Suth nodded, edging up and back so she could scan the rooftops without exposing herself to the street. 'One more there, see him?'

Lynx brought his gun up. 'Balcony on that high block? Yeah.'

He took aim and fired. Suth didn't wait to see if the man was dead. The distraction was enough for her. She stood, mage-pistol in each hand and fired once, twice at the figures down below. An arrow flew up and nicked her shoulder, but the small woman barely skipped a beat. Discarding one pistol, she drew the next and fired in one movement.

'Two dead,' she reported, dropping back down and tossing one pistol to Himbel.

The company surgeon scowled as he juggled the weapon, then righted it and went about loading for her. Just at that moment the gunfire elsewhere increased. Lynx looked over and saw furious bursts of light flashing in both directions on the Snow walkway. He waited a moment but they seemed to be giving as good as they got.

One of the defenders crashed down, the back of his head blown out by an icer, but Lynx couldn't see who it was. The remaining Cards switched to earthers and sparkers then, unleashing a devastating fusillade that ended the attack in moments.

'I could see to that arm too,' Himbel grumbled, but Suth just shook her head.

'Just a nick,' she said as Braqe ventured up, looking for a target. She fired in a hurry and threw herself back.

'Fuck – Lynx!'

The tone of her voice was enough to make Lynx drop his gun. He pulled his pistol and popped up to see half a dozen Mastrunners racing forward with grapples. The burner's flash illuminated a woman's shape before she burst into flames and yellow light exploded across the street. It engulfed three or four in that instant, dead before they knew what hit them. The blast threw the others back and he heard screams of fear and pain as he dropped out of sight.

There was no return fire, the only clatter of gunshots came from the other stretches of walkway. Suth ventured another look once she had two pistols loaded again, but even with her mage-blessed eyes she didn't see anything worth taking a shot at.

'That's a hard lesson,' she commented as she dropped back down. 'Someone's screwed this up.'

'Too many proud fighters used to doing it the Mage Islands way,' Lynx agreed. 'Plus they couldn't know about our eyes.'

She glanced back at the other walkways where the defenders were coming to the same conclusion and the gunfire was petering out. 'Long may that last. The next attack'll be more serious.'

'What's next then?'

'They need cover to get up to us, smoke or fire probably.'

'Firebombs?'

'That's how I'd do it. Their snipers aren't going to cut it. Even with every mage-gun in Auferno we'd take them in a straight fight and no kabat will leave themselves unprotected.'

'Not when folk like Tanimbor might be stirring up trouble among their rivals.' Lynx nodded. 'Too many pirates round these parts.'

'Himbel, tear up a sheet for rags, the rest of you drink something. We don't have much water, but it might be we'll need to cover our mouths.'

The surgeon scurried away as Suth held her hand out to Lynx. 'Stand down for a bit, I'll take a watch.'

'I'm fine.'

'Rest your eyes,' she insisted. 'It's the marked Cards that'll make the difference here. To smoke us out they need to get close and we can see better than them.' She looked up. 'Those awnings kept the worst of the sun off and I reckon they'll do for the skyriver's light too. It'll be full dark soon. After that they're hardly seeing anything in these shadows.'

Lynx looked around at the other walkways. They were similarly covered, but the long curve of the skyriver meant half of

Teshen's side was illuminated. The danger had already been highlighted, given there was a wounded Card slumped on the walkway. While Kas helped the man away – Rubesh, Lynx guessed from the shock of blond hair – several others were pulling bed-frames from the rooms. These were set up against the wall and covered in sheets to put the Cards beneath in shadow once more.

'Let's hope they don't take our awnings,' Lynx muttered, glancing up.

'Quite a throw if you're close enough for a firebomb,' Braqe said. 'And if they've got a burner, they'd shoot it at us not the awnings.'

'Guess that's the good news.'

She nodded. 'Until those fucking mages find a way out for us, that's as good as it's likely to get.'

'Yeah.' Lynx glanced again at the black smear of blood from the dead man. 'How many more dead before Anatin changes his mind about sending Teshen out?'

'Thought that was against your code.'

He nodded slowly. 'I ain't voting for it, but I'm not in command. Anatin's loyal but he ain't all that loyal.'

'We're going nowhere tonight,' Suth said with finality. 'We just need to last until morning.'

'And then what?'

'Then they count their dead and have a long hard think about coming at us again.'

'There'll be too many dead to let them back down.'

Her face hardened. 'Damn right, but we'll get our mages back in the morning. If we have to cut a path through this city with Lastani and Sitain clearing the way, so be it.'

'That's one long hard walk to the canal.'

'Got a better idea?' Suth asked.

Lynx was quiet.

'Yeah, I thought not. So we're cutting a bloody swathe through this city or we're dying.'

Braqe gave a snort. 'When did we all get so loyal?'

'Some time deep underground is my guess.'

'Cards o' the deepest black. Let these fuckers come.' She raised her voice to an expected shout. 'You hear that? Fucking come, we'll kill you all!'

Lynx blinked at her.

'Feel better?'

'Yup.'

Darkness fell. It wrapped Sitain in velvet folds and the pressure in her head eased a little. All day it had been building, the steady sensation of a storm – except she knew it wasn't the weather. The oppressive day had only worsened the sensation. It was unpleasant and exhausting, but there was something else that tired her. The wellspring of magic deep inside. The tattoos that pulsed with power. Pressure had been building and even as the heat of the day had begun to ease, she'd feared her head might explode. Quite literally perhaps.

It was hard to deny Atieno's assessment. The newly tattooed mages were enough of a clue, but all through the day she'd felt a weight closing in. A great tidal wave of power radiating out from Jarrazir. Only nightfall had eased it, the embrace of her magic's embodiment. The power was still there, but it had broken over her and now she swam in that sea. Now it was obedient to her.

Sitain sank back into her seat, in the central courtyard of the lodging house. She hadn't been aware of standing, but suddenly she was. She closed her eyes and immediately opened them again. She wanted to sleep, but who could sleep like this? In Jarrazir she'd felt power unlike anything she'd known before. It leaked out of her like smoke from a thurible. But living that way had changed her, had cracked her bones and stretched her muscles to reform her into something that could contain more than any human should.

I wonder how Tanimbor's mages are doing? she thought idly, luxuriating in the tingle and rush of vast, lazy power. *Will they survive this? I wouldn't have, not this much power all at once.*

She looked up at the sky, hidden by the dark canopies strung between towers. They made no difference to her. Sitain could see the line of the skyriver almost directly overhead, a blade of light thinner than she remembered from growing up, north of here. The stars too – their light hidden but revealed to her still and more besides. She sensed movement, circling and spiralling like birds of prey hunting. But she knew they weren't birds and nor were they hunting.

With a little concentration and a thin flare of night magic, she counted three, then seven, then a dozen far above her – dancing in the thermals of Sitain's mind. The numbers made her gasp. Never before had she seen this many. Never before had she attracted more than three at any one time and now . . .

Two more drifted into her perception, cutting a wider path but orbiting those that danced and gently closing to join them. Sitain smiled and sent more flares of magic up into the sky – unnoticed by her mercenary comrades as they chattered somewhere on the fringes of Sitain's body. Her soul rose into the sky and the Falesh, the night elementals, welcomed her as a giver of life.

Chapter 28

'What's that?'

Lynx turned and squinted. 'Looks like smoke.'

Suth snorted. 'I can bloody see that, what's it doing over there? Aren't they supposed to be smoking *us* out?'

Lynx peered down what he could see of the street. There were a few figures watching, Mastrunners no doubt. They kept a wide perimeter within which no one moved. He couldn't see more attackers, but he raised his gun anyway.

'They seem to be doing it wrong,' he said at last.

'Somehow that worries more than reassures.'

There was something burning a hundred yards away at least. It sent up a great column of dirty smoke into the night sky, but what use was that? There were none of the shouts that he would expect if this was someone screwing up, no panic or anger. Just smoke, too far away to be of use and too controlled to be a mistake.

'Now I'm worried too,' he admitted.

'Stop whining, the pair of you,' Braqe said. 'If you want to be concerned about something, how about the fact our jester in the hole is stoned out of her shitting mind?'

She pointed behind them, between two fat balustrade supports. There in the courtyard below was Sitain, sitting limp in a chair and staring blankly up at the sky. With his unnatural vision, Lynx was sure he could see a faint smile on her face.

'Hoy, Toil,' he hissed. 'Fuck's up with Sitain?'

The woman glanced around and scowled. 'Dunno.'

She went to shake Sitain then stopped dead. The air around Sitain seemed to be glittering darkly, a faint flicker of movement that could be easily dismissed if you'd not seen a shadowshard before.

'Something's going on out there,' Suth added. 'They've set fires, but well clear of us.'

'Same here,' reported Teshen. 'Looks like they're coming soon.'

'How?'

The man hissed in irritation. 'Where are we again? Forgotten that detail?'

Lynx blinked for a moment before realisation hit him. *Shit, the Mage Islands. We're not the only ones who can call on mages for support.*

'Wind mages,' he said aloud.

Down in the courtyard, Toil fetched a cup of wine and tossed it over Sitain. Lynx couldn't be sure, but he thought he saw something neatly slice through the water, cuts like a dozen razors, before it splashed down on Sitain's face.

'Guh,' the young woman said muzzily, blinking up at Toil. 'Wassat for?'

'Get ready,' Toil ordered her. 'We're about to be hit, we'll need you soon.'

A lazy grin appeared on Sitain's face. 'Want me to put 'em out now? Reckon I could do half the district.'

'Missing us out?'

Sitain laughed. 'Sure, I'll definitely give that a shot.'

'Wait for my order then.'

'Spoilsport.'

Lynx went back to sentry duty, crouched at the outer wall in the security of the shadows. There was more movement out there, figures creeping closer then vanishing behind buildings.

Auferno's streets weren't as much of a tangle as some districts, but this was a multi-level city shaped by the whims of mages. There were plenty of places to hide and approach in safety.

The closest building was a squat lump, two storeys high, with a bridge across the roof to its neighbour and another to the taller one behind. That was a curved block of four levels, a rock shelf wide enough for carts occupying its near side that led to a hump of land behind. The fires were burning past the right flank of that. He could see figures illuminated in the light while three bridges spread fingers across the low scattering of houses between the block and a string of shore-front compounds.

Teshen's prediction was soon proved right. The smoke rising from the fires abruptly twisted into a spiral in the still night air, whipping around in a tight knot that whirled with unexpected ferocity. Lynx couldn't see the mage doing it and wasn't sure what he'd do if he could, given how they were hoping for the Shard's benevolence. They watched the spiralling ball of smoke spin drunkenly towards them, making jerky progress but all too soon looming large.

'Ideas, anyone?' Suth asked.

Lynx turned. 'Sitain, could you take out everyone on the ground?'

She peered up at him. 'Not all in one go. Remember the barracks in Jarrazir though? I could do that more than once.'

'Toil, smoke's coming. Best you get up here while you still can.'

The woman nodded and Anatin quickly gave directions to their small team who waited down in the courtyard. Quickly they spread to cover different sections of the wall – there would be no meeting the main assault if they couldn't see the stairways properly. As Toil headed up towards Lynx's section, Anatin remained at Sitain's side, talking softly to her while the young woman nodded.

'What's the plan?' Suth asked once Toil reached them. She kept one eye on the cloud of smoke, fast approaching, as they all started to wet rags and tie them over their faces.

'When it reaches us, we wait as long as we can while Sitain does each side in turn,' Toil said, her face taut with concern. 'Puts down anyone outside the walls without knocking us out as well. No wind mage will be able to hold that smoke for long.'

'Gives them plenty of time to put burners over the wall. Hells, any sort of firebomb would do the job. Doesn't need to be magic.'

'We hear any movement, we drop a grenade over the side. I don't think there's a book of tactics for this shit. If in doubt, blow something up.'

They fell silent, watching the smoke. Breathing through his rag mask, Lynx felt suddenly alone as the world seemed to fade away and he was left with just the sound of his breathing. One by one, buildings were swallowed by the cloud. Still he couldn't see the mage, but as the fear kicked in Lynx knew he'd not hesitate if he did catch sight of them. Consequences were for the living.

'Take a deep breath and follow my lead,' Suth said, taking one last check of her pistol, opening the breech to reveal the painted head of a burner cartridge and closing it again. They all filled their lungs and Toil primed a grenade. Then the cloud hit them.

Lynx closed his eyes as the warm air swarmed all around him. The still night air was transformed into a roiling storm, spun like a gale by the wind mage to keep the smoke together. Somewhere behind him he heard Anatin shout, over the sound of the wind tearing past his face.

He felt the tattoos on his skin grow warm. All of a sudden Sitain became the only thing Lynx could feel; a great iron mass that contorted the fabric of the world. By the grunts he heard,

Suth and Toil had been hit by the same, but in the next moment there was a vast punch of magic racing past, under his feet.

If there were bodies falling in the street, Lynx didn't hear them. His attention was still on Sitain, bubbling with such power it almost drove the wind from his lungs. She moved on, towards Reft's station, while Lynx fought the urge to gasp for air.

Just a little while longer, he urged his unwilling body. *Just one more heartbeat.*

Someone submitted nearby, puffing out hard before coughing furiously a moment later. Lynx's lungs were burning now, screaming for air as panic began to fill him and dark spots encroached on his vision. Still he fought it. Even as the walls started closing in and the stink of coal-dust filled his nose. Even as the grit filled every pore and the weight of shackles dragged at his ankles. Even as the light faded to a memory and fear and hunger gnawed at his belly.

There was coughing all around him, he felt an elbow clip his shoulder and he staggered, then the crack and roar of a burner cut through the night. Moments later a deeper boom shook the ground under him. A bright orange flash seared the air past his closed eyes. Still Lynx fought, but then the wind abruptly faltered and vanished.

He dropped to his knees, feeling his strength failing. Only the power humming through his tattoos kept him conscious. He lasted two final heartbeats then submitted to the roaring need inside him and blessed, smoke-cursed air rushed in.

Lynx immediately started to cough furiously, but the second breath and the third were better. The smoke lingered but they were out in the open, high and exposed in a shoreline city. Every breath he took was improved and the blackness filling his eyes began to fade again.

Distantly he realised Toil had thrown her grenade over the side. There were cries and screams overlaying the sound of flames, and the wheezing and retching of his comrades. The stink of vomit assailed him. Through bleary eyes he saw Toil doubled over, coughing uncontrollably – the rest of them no better. Suth had one hand up on the wall for support, but she was in no condition to fight.

The mage had lasted longer than any of them had expected. Distantly he realised there had probably been two. Lastani had said such things were a trial of strength. A wind mage would encourage the air towards a ship through affinity as much as anything, gently direct its force into the sails perhaps. To generate something and direct it on a near-still day was a different order, power only the marked Cards could muster for long.

He struggled his way to the wall and peered over. The flames had died down already, with little to burn in a city made of stone. There was blurred movement all around and it took him a while to work out what was what. By the time he did so, arrows and icers were flashing up to meet him.

Lynx dropped back as chunks of stone burst from the wall. There were cries of the dying out there too – the terrible power of a fire grenade was a shocking thing to behold, even for a veteran. The survivors would be all the more stunned, but Lynx didn't mean to give them time to recover. Instead he put his gun above his head and fired a sparker blind, in the direction he'd seen some of the enemy.

Reloading, he fired again in the other direction then chanced a look up. More gunshots came, but he hardly noticed as the first of half a dozen Mastrunners were scaling the walls. He shot one with his pistol, hoping to dissuade them while the rest of the defenders coughed their guts up, but more crossbow bolts kept him down.

A third sparker took several off the tower wall, but then the first one clambered over the low section Lynx stood at.

He hurled his mage-gun at the woman and the wooden stock cracked against her head, throwing her back. She almost fell, but somehow held on. It was enough time for Lynx to find his sword, lying where he'd left it, and he threw himself at her.

He drove the tip into her sternum and shoved her clear of the wall. She fell screaming while Lynx felt an arrow score a furrow in his upper arm. He reeled away but forced himself forward as more Mastrunners appeared.

They were swift climbers, terrifyingly so. Lynx had been in sieges so he'd seen how fast men scaled ladders, but these bastards were using little more than the natural flaws of the rock itself. A grapple clanged over the far side as he watched, but Lynx was too busy trying to cut the head off a large man with a tall mane of hair. His blow was neatly deflected but Lynx turned that into a shoulder barge.

He shoved the Mastrunner sideways, trying to smash the pommel of his sword into the man's face but somehow getting caught in a grapple instead. The man fought like Teshen, limbs like willow that felt solid when you hit them, but which could twist around and whip back at you in the next moment. Lynx rode a blow then found himself shoved backwards. Just as the man was about to run him through, Suth recovered enough to put an icer through one eye. The back of the man's head exploded in chill gore.

Lynx lurched forward as the man's weight dragged him back to the wall, almost getting a spear through the face in the next moment. Suth shot that one too as Lynx fell on to his backside, disentangling himself from the first corpse. More Cards were rising, but on shaking limbs, and more Mastrunners appeared at the wall, sliding neatly over. Among them was the kaboto – Ube. Lynx found himself face to face with the man. He saw the look of utter fury settle directly on to Lynx as a hooked axe was raised.

'Shattered gods!' Lynx heard Suth gasp, but he couldn't tear his eyes away.

Enfeebled by the smoke his arm went limp as he caught Ube's blow on his sword. Ube took a pace forward as he tugged a second axe from his belt and readied a killing blow. Lynx felt the cold hand of death settle upon his shoulder and found he had no fight left for those last moments. But Ube never reached him.

Chapter 29

Ube flew abruptly sideways. Something massive ripped him from the wall in a blur of movement. Lynx barely saw it happen. One moment the Mastrunner was about to kill him, the next he was dragged howling into the night. Great wings swept through the sky, folding in their up-stroke to clear the space between the towers.

'Down!' Toil yelled, bearing Lynx to the ground. More Mastrunners came over the wall, but now they were looking around for this new threat. In the panic and chaos of night they could see almost nothing, but Lynx saw more shapes darting forward. They swooped with a speed the commando in him might once have admired, if he hadn't been so stupefied. One man was hauled away. The other had his head torn off in a fountain of blood that sprayed hot and sticky across Lynx's face.

A crash followed in the next moment as one of the creatures snagged a wing on the high canopies and ripped it clean off. Newly loosed ropes and metal pulleys lashed the wall, then the beast's claws latched briefly on a stone tower as it fought to stay in the air. Lynx had to throw himself aside to avoid a long limb that tore a furrow in the stonework and he kept rolling to try and get clear.

'What's going on?' he heard Toil yell.

The darkness was a blur of confused movement, even to Lynx's eyes. Flocks of small tysarn flashed around in sweeping arcs, some pursued by larger ones, some trailing in their slipstreams. Screams and shouts came from all directions, then the crisp detonation of icers. White streaks tore up at the huge tysarn still struggling with the canopies. Some punched right through its wings, others disappeared into the beast's flesh. The tysarn didn't seem to notice the impacts as it writhed and snapped at the ropes entangling it. Before it could free itself, however, Lynx was aware of a sudden pulse of magic.

Felt more than seen, a great burst of night magic flew up from the courtyard floor. The tysarn simply folded up and dropped, shaking the ground with the impact. As Lynx stared in astonishment, more tysarn began to fall, the small insecthunters pattering down like hailstones from the sky. A few larger beasts fell too, one ripping a section of the canopy away, others bouncing or slithering off those remaining.

One hand over his head to protect against the falling reptiles, Lynx looked around. The screams were mostly coming from outside, the shouts from inside the perimeter. It seemed the Mastrunners were having the harder time of whatever this was.

'Didn't Teshen say they were no threat?'

'Look at the size of it!' Toil exclaimed, pointing. 'We're all lunch to something that big. Shattered gods, how does it even fly?'

She had a point, Lynx realised. The tysarn was far bigger than the ones they'd seen in the sky before, more than double their length. This one's body was five yards long, its neck adding a few more. Claws the size of daggers tipped the end of each winged limb, the larger fore pair spanning fifteen yards he guessed.

'Teshen!' Toil yelled. 'You there?'

The shaven-headed man turned, crouching behind the wall like the rest of his command. 'Yeah!'

'What's going on?'

'Fucked if I know!' was his reply. 'Never seen one this big fly. Mostly they swim, take you off the shore but this . . . fuck!'

Lynx checked his arm. The bleeding didn't seem bad, the wound more of a discomfort than anything. That done, he scrabbled for his mage-gun and reloaded it. The Mastrunners seemed to have broken off, but there was a greater threat now.

'This may not be the time,' Lynx started, 'but when weird shit happens, it's usually our fault.'

Toil looked round. 'You think we caused this?'

'It's the sort o' thing we do.'

'Stick to making sure—' she broke off as a mid-sized tysarn, a couple of yards across, swooped and Toil was forced to duck. Lynx snapped off a shot but missed and the tysarn swept off into the night.

'Shit!' Toil yelled. 'They've gone mad!'

'Time to hide?' Lynx suggested.

'And leave the wall open?'

Lynx gestured above them. Dark shapes streamed through the sky, coiling above the lodging house or breaking off to dart away across the district. There was gunfire and voices coming from all parts, Lynx realised. He didn't bother poking his head above the parapet. The sound was enough to tell him this wasn't restricted to the lodging house – even if some of the tysarn seemed to be circling it like vultures.

'Is anyone coming through this?'

'Dunno – want to take that risk?'

Lynx crawled to the outer wall and sat with his back against it. He was well below the parapet and had his gun pointing across the open space to the walkway beyond, where other Cards were doing something similar.

'Pretty exposed out here,' he commented, aiming his mage-gun.

A big tysarn appeared in the gap between towers, but then broke off and wheeled in the direction of the Shard's Rest. Lynx thought for a moment that he'd somehow scared it off, then a booming detonation erupted from the opposite side. There sat Reft, white skin faintly glowing in the light of the skyriver. The dark path of an earther roared over Lynx's head and struck something with a terrific impact. Lynx felt the hammer blow shudder through the air then a large body slammed into the stone on the other side of the parapet.

The whole building trembled, jolting Suth so hard she half-slipped between support posts. She only just grabbed one in time to stop herself falling into the courtyard. Toil hauled her back while Lynx checked around to see whether they'd lost anyone.

'Smoke did us a favour,' he said. 'We were all on our bloody knees when the tysarn came!'

'Yeah, when there was magic all around this place,' Toil said. By the tone of her voice Lynx could tell she was thinking furiously, but he left her to it and resumed his watch for monsters.

'So what now? We just sit here?'

Toil crawled over to him with Suth not far behind and the two women took similar positions, backs to the low wall and legs outstretched.

'I . . . Deepest black, damned if I know.'

'You're the one comfortable around swarms of monsters.'

'Fuckers don't fly underground.'

'How's it different?'

Toil shrugged. 'Something stirred this lot up,' she reasoned. 'This ain't normal or no one would live here. A pack of maspids won't stop hunting you till they're all dead, that's how Lady Dark plays.'

'Maspids aren't drawn by magic, are they?'

'No,' she admitted. Toil flopped on to her belly and crawled to the edge of the walkway. 'Hey, Sitain, you dead?'

There was a long pause before an irate voice replied, 'No, she ain't. Nor am I.'

'That you, Anatin?'

'Yup. Anyone else notice a fucking great dragon fall on me or did Varain spike my drink?'

'We saw it. Ah, Sitain, is it just sleeping then?'

Anatin growled. 'She says yes. Hit her head so she's a bit wobbly. As for the dragon, gimme a minute.'

Lynx and the others joined Toil in time to see Anatin start to clamber over the scarred rubbery membrane of the tysarn's wing. He drew his mage-pistol and aimed it at the creature's head before giving it an experimental kick. Nothing happened so Anatin got a bit closer. The head was a yard and a half long, wedge-shaped with a long mouth of jagged teeth.

Eye slits longer than a hand span curved around its head – whitish protective ridges above and below – allowing the tysarn to see forward like a raptor or both sides like a prey animal. Anatin put his foot on the beast's head and fired an icer right into the open eye. The eyeball exploded in a gout of dark liquid, spattering up Anatin's tunic. The tysarn spasmed momentarily then fell still.

'Dead now,' he announced, giving the tysarn a last kick for good measure. Before he could say anything more, gunshots rang out behind him.

They all looked over to the high terrace at the far end where Lynx had been eating breakfast not so long ago. Payl and the rest of Sun had been defending that. The outside ground was more open there, providing a clear view of the Callais Sea and a killing ground for any attackers. He doubted if anyone had done more than take pot shots to keep the defenders spread thin, but now the terrace served as a space big enough for a tysarn to land.

Its wings were half-furled, clawing at the mercenaries that scrambled under tables and hacked at anything within reach.

Lynx put an icer into the tysarn's flank, as did someone else from the far side. It screeched in pain, but didn't let up its assault. The tysarn snatched up one man who couldn't scramble clear in time and bit down. He howled as he was lifted high before Teshen got it with an earther.

The shot broke its shoulder and half-tore the fore wing away, spraying gore across the terrace. A few more shots came from the beleaguered group, icers bursting wildly up as the tysarn flailed. The movement made it harder to aim at and a second earther flashed wide. The near miss made the creature thrash even more furiously and the injured man's shrieks went up a notch. The rest of the suit were pressed up against the side walls, trying to keep clear, while the tysarn went berserk amid the wreckage of tables, chairs and the clusters of stepped troughs.

Lynx tried to take aim, but the tysarn never stopped moving. He was about to give up and take a gamble when Toil put her hand on his shoulder and shouted. Lynx looked up and saw a pale shape streak in from the side, a hatchet in each hand. His mouth fell open at the sight of anyone charging the huge creature. It was double Reft's height, but the Knight of Blood didn't hesitate.

With one hatchet he hooked on to the tysarn's wing and pulled himself bodily up into the air, chopping down as the beast turned his way. As it snapped at him, he scored a long slash down its neck and the hatchet taking his weight ripped down through its wing. Reft ducked and wrenched himself free, cutting at the tysarn's leg as he rolled away. As it made to follow, Teshen appeared from the other side. He took the same approach, stabbing at whatever he could reach before running clear.

Pulled both ways, the tysarn left itself open to Reft chopping a hatchet – in any other man's hand a decent-sized axe – into its rear wing. The hatchet lodged and he abandoned it, scoring a hit on the ruined fore wing with his second. This time he planted his feet and hauled at the beast with all his incredible strength. Somehow Reft managed to pull the wounded tysarn slightly off balance, enough to give Teshen time to vault up the other side and stab one long knife into its other shoulder.

The tysarn flailed with its remaining strength and knocked Teshen flying. The bald man was agile enough to roll with the blow but still he landed heavily and slammed into the inner railing, while Reft was hauled off his feet. Wounded on both sides the tysarn momentarily sat back on its haunches and Lynx took aim.

Before he could fire, a trio of arrows slammed into the tysarn, right where he'd expect its heart to be, and at least one of them hurt it badly. It raised its head and gave a long ragged roar, weaker than earlier but Lynx ignored that. He let out a puff of breath and steadied himself before firing.

The sparker caught it in the throat and enveloped its head in a crackling ball of sparks. For one long moment the tysarn juddered in the throes of agony then two icers tore in from Lynx's right. Both struck home and punched its head back – catching the brain and leaving it to flop backwards over the terrace railing, dead at last.

'Knights!' roared Anatin from down in the courtyard. 'Count your Cards and get everyone down here – fuck this fight. Only dead men'll come over these walls tonight.'

The Mercenary Deck didn't need to be told twice. They grabbed their wounded and raced down to the safety of below.

Chapter 30

The night passed not exactly in peace, but in the close confines of those weathering a storm. The Cards kept watch for another attack throughout, even though such a thing would have been lunacy. The deep stuttered calls of the tysarn continued all night, the occasional shriek of their victims dwindling as the hours passed. Mercenaries occupied every one of the ground-floor rooms surrounding the courtyard. Much of these were stores and workrooms so it was little imposition, but they also barged into the private quarters of the extended Jathan family.

The youngest Jathans had been both fascinated and terrified by the stranger foreigners from the outset, while the elders were all entirely incensed by the imposition. Lynx kept to the long, open-sided hall that occupied one flank of the lodging. It meant he had to watch a flock of smaller tysarn feast on the flesh of their larger kin, but small stone rooms filled with unwashed and bloodied bodies brought back unwelcome memories.

The older Jathan ladies had hissed and grumbled at the feasting tysarn, clearly wanting to harvest some parts of the corpses for their own purposes. It was only when a larger one dropped down that they gave up. This tysarn was a yard in length, no great threat and oblivious of the levelled mage-guns as it ripped open some sort of egg-sack to feast on the contents. Seeing that, the old ladies gave up their efforts and sulkily retreated to their own rooms.

The strangeness of the night meant that none of the Cards were even drunk by the time the sky started to lighten, despite a few mugs of beer emerging to slake the thirst of some. Only a handful managed to catch any sleep either. When the first glow of dawn began to illuminate the district, two dozen faces crammed at the narrow windows to get a proper look at the streets beyond.

Lynx and Toil chose to venture up on to the walkway instead, Kas and Teshen close behind. Auferno was deserted and at last the cries of the tysarn faded. It looked almost peaceful after the violence of the night, strangely so to Lynx's mind. With such violence normally came scattered, smashed bodies and a mass of scars from mage-cartridges, but not so in this city of few guns.

'The young roost during the day,' Teshen commented, pointing to the mountainous hellmouths at the heart of the lagoon. There were no majestic spiralling flocks now, just a smear of shadow against the lightening sky, pouring back inside. 'Most of the rest will do the same after that I'm guessing.'

'Where are the bodies?' Lynx wondered as he looked out over the rail. 'Have they all been eaten?'

'The people? Yeah,' Teshen confirmed. 'The biggest ones will take a person whole, but three or four of the juveniles will make short work of a body too. Given how many tysarn were out there, I doubt there'll be much to return to the sea.'

'Movement,' Kas said, reaching for her bow.

She didn't nock an arrow, however, as the group heading towards them were walking with a total disregard to their safety. Lynx had only been in the city a few days, but he recognised the bearing of a group of mages by now. As they came closer, Lynx picked out two figures within their number and let out a puff of relief. One small, pale and white-blond, the other tall dark and limping.

'That's a piece of good news,' Toil commented, seeing the pair too. 'The face on that women leading them, however . . .'

Lynx had to agree. A sturdy black woman in a multi-coloured robe marched at the head of the group, fifteen in all he counted. The woman had the bearing of an empress, but not the sort who ruled with a gentle, benevolent touch. She wore the fixed expression of someone who was profoundly angry with the world in general or the Cards in particular, but wasn't going to waste time indulging in yelling or abuse.

'This'll be fun for you,' he muttered as Toil started back down the stair. 'Good luck.'

She cast him a baleful look and headed down while Lynx, Kas and Teshen sat on the walkway with their feet dangling over the edge, ready to watch. By the time the delegation had arrived at the barricaded front door, half of the Mercenary Deck had joined them. Llaith had already rolled a half-dozen smokes to greet the morning. He and Lynx puffed merrily away as the mages emerged into the courtyard.

The sight of the tysarn's corpse greeted them. Lynx could see the woman – the Shard he guessed, given her fancy colours and escort of taciturn mages – briefly consider the beast before dismissing it. Behind her, Lastani and Atieno lingered like chastised schoolchildren, but clearly no worse for the previous night's drama.

'What a mess,' the Shard declared. 'Foolishness and savagery for no good reason.' She turned to Anatin and Toil. 'Now, which of you is in charge here?'

The pair exchanged looks and Anatin shrugged. 'Angry people are your department,' he said. 'I just deal with the paying customers.'

'To be fair, I'm often the one making them angry,' Toil countered.

Anatin nodded, forced to agree with her. Just before the Shard lost her patience entirely he stepped forward and offered an ostentatious bow.

'Commander Anatin at your service, Mistress. Might I assume I am addressing her magnificence, the Shard? Chosen of Mages, Arbiter of Caldaire and voice of all wizardly wisdom?'

She rolled her eyes, but Lynx could see the idiotic display of toadying certainly hadn't hurt matters. 'You missed a few titles,' the Shard said at last. 'But at least you realise my time isn't to be wasted by a rabble of unwashed gunslingers.'

'Certainly not, your magnificence. How may we be of service to you this day?'

'By doing exactly what I say, when I say. This idiocy has gone far enough, it ends now. Assuming you do want to live to see another sunset?'

Anatin bowed again. 'Indeed, your munificence. Big game hunting's something of a hobby and last night was so much fun, I want to try and beat my tally.'

'Listen and obey then,' the Shard said. 'Tomorrow morning you will be leaving Caldaire. You may send a group out to gather what supplies you need and find a barge. They will be unarmed and escorted by one of my mages at all times. If anyone wanders off or misbehaves, they'll die and five more of your number will see the same fate.'

'Tomorrow?' Toil asked.

'You have work to do today – and tonight too. Mistress Ufre here has informed me about the work you performed for Guildmaster Tanimbor. I have allowed myself to be persuaded that you are sufficiently stupid and blithely ignorant enough to have meant none of this. That you took a job from a man without understanding the implications is just one thing you will receive the benefit of the doubt on.'

'That's us,' Anatin piped up, jabbing a thumb up at the mercenaries watching from the walkway. 'Look at the bastards. The ones grinning at you are the blithely ignorant, the ones still drinking are the sufficiently stupid.'

The Shard did just that. Deern waved back, a wide grin on his face, and raised a mug of beer to claim both titles. Her expression soured.

'For the sake of ending this conflict without further bloodshed,' she continued after a pause, 'I have taken much on faith and will not scrutinise matters further. However, that is contingent on you rectifying the balance in the city.'

'Balance?' Toil said. 'Oh, I think I see where you're going here. Fancy a few new tattoos do you?'

The Shard shook her head. 'Not I – I am an earth mage and Lastani tells me that seal is still closed.'

'Does it really matter at this point?'

She gave Toil a level look. 'I'm the ruler of mages facing a new age of magic – and I've just said no to a huge increase in my own power. What do you think?'

'Fair point. A few of your trusted comrades then?'

'Just so. Today – tonight you may be too busy. Tysarn don't feed off magic, but they are attracted to it. Normally this is no great problem, but the Riven Kingdom has been flooded with enough power to leave them drunk on the stuff. Then some towering fool decided to rile them up by turning on an ancient mechanism.'

'Ah yes, about that. What did we do, exactly?'

'You don't even know?' the Shard asked, eyebrows raised. 'Have you at least worked out that you're to blame for last night?'

'Seemed too much of a coincidence otherwise.' Toil paused. 'It's appreciated by the way, you not screaming that in my face as soon as you walked in here.'

Lynx felt a nudge from Kas as the company scout whispered breathily in his ear. 'Your girl's learning diplomacy at last. Turns out she does listen to you after all.'

'Cold hells, how about that, eh?' he muttered back. 'Does that mean I win a prize or something?'

The Shard cleared her throat, glancing back at Lastani for the first time since walking into the courtyard. 'The mechanism drives fresh air through the great tunnel to ensure it is breathable for the tunnel's entire length. My records suggest the tunnel is not the only Duegar construction, however – their work is woven into the entire cliff for at least twenty miles and below the lagoon itself for an unknown distance. A trading hub of their own, likely equivalent to Caldaire in terms of importance.'

'Shit,' Toil breathed. 'A sealed system because of all the water, and Duegar cities were so much bigger than ours . . .'

'So big, in fact, that while previous attempts have stirred up the tysarn that live inside – something our histories call "the razing" – they have likely never had the power to reach the deepest parts.'

The Shard looked at Lastani again. 'With your new-found strength, you may have sparked a cascade of those remaining parts of the system. We do not know if the mechanism will sustain itself as the Labyrinth of Jarrazir does, but the jolt has been enough to agitate the tens of thousands of tysarn that use those tunnels for breeding.'

'And they're attracted to magic?'

'They appear to enjoy the residual effects of it,' she said with a slight shrug. 'We do not entirely understand why. It is not a source of nourishment, but they are drawn to it – experiments suggest a narcotic effect. Some of those we saw last night will have rarely flown in recent years, having grown too large, but during the razing they are stirred to greater effort.'

'Is that what you want us to do tonight?'

The Shard inclined her head. 'If the razing comes upon us tonight, I expect your mages to expend your power, high into the sky. It may draw the tysarn away from the rest of the city, it may not, but you *will* make the effort.'

Her voice didn't brook any argument, nor did it bother with mentioning possible consequences of that action, but Toil nodded all the same. If the Cards knew what sort of threat they might be facing, they could at least prepare for it. The Shard getting them out of the city without more violence was worth that.

'Did Lastani tell you my price for Tanimbor?' Toil asked.

'She did not.'

'I asked for a name, having heard a rumour that there was a mage guild skilled at cartridge-making in the city. It might not be I get to pay that guild a visit, but I was sent to try and hire their services. If they chose to take their expertise to the city-states of Parthain, starting at Jarrazir perhaps, then they would be handsomely rewarded.' Toil hesitated. 'Perhaps a generous commission could also be paid to the appropriate kabat of Auferno, by way of some form of recompense?'

The Shard stared at Toil a long while. Lynx wasn't sure if she was enraged by the woman's audacity or genuinely considering the implications. Eventually she nodded. 'A message could be passed on,' the Shard conceded. 'Now – I will leave nine mages here for you, Mistress Ufre, to perform some linking spell with, while I go and ensure your safe passage.'

'Nine?' Toil queried.

'Yes. Do you have a problem with that?'

She paused. 'Nope, it's your business so long as Lastani is happy.'

The young mage nodded her head. 'A simple linking may be all that's required, we will have to test and adapt.'

'Can you guarantee it'll work?' Toil asked, clearly imagining how the Shard would react to a surprise like that.

'No. I . . . I believe it will, but we are working from limited knowledge.'

The Shard raised a hand. 'If the linking does not work, you will attempt a spell. There is, in our archives, a Duegar mechanism that can be used if you need to operate something to drive the magic. Some of my finest mages will be part of it, I am confident they will be able to attest to your efforts.'

'You want to start now?' Toil asked.

'Unless there's a reason not to?'

A small smile crept on to Toil's face. 'No, no, that's fine. I just, ah . . . wanted to check.' She spun around and sought Lynx out from among the onlookers. 'Lynx – our bedroom, now! Sitain, fair warning. If you want to knock Deern out first, now's your chance.'

All around them, the marked Cards scrambled towards their vacant rooms, several dragging comrades along too. Lynx had his shirt off before he even reached the stair and Toil was close on his heels.

Chapter 31

Despite everything, after the ritual Lynx and Toil both fell asleep. Lynx woke first, but was slow to stir in the heavy afterglow. A night of no sleep had left him weary and sluggish even before Lastani's latest ritual had sent a lightning bolt through his body. He couldn't tell how long it had gone on for, but neither he nor Toil had been for stopping when the crackle of sensation and connection had started to fade from their minds.

Unlike last time, the other Cards were only distant presences as Lastani drew them all together and began to churn magic through their minds. The new mages were only pinpricks of light in the darkness, Tanimbor's group a cluster of stars in another part of the sky. Each was discernible if he focused on them, but Lynx's interest had been elsewhere. It was the marked Cards he could sense more strongly, while Lastani, Atieno and Sitain were the trinity of suns eclipsing them all.

The sweat lay thick and greasy on his skin. With a flicker of surprise Lynx realised it was likely afternoon, the air laden with heat once again. He shifted on the bed. Toil grunted but didn't wake. With difficultly he eased his large frame off the bed and pulled on a pair of loose trousers before finding a shirt. Heading barefoot to the door, his hand touched the latch as a sleepy voice spoke from the bed.

'Sneaking out on me? Not very gentlemanly of you.'

He smiled and turned. 'And there's you looking all prim and ladylike.'

Toil swept her hair back out of her face and tugged the sheet up a little. 'That's just rude.'

'If I liked prim, earlier would've been a whole lot less fun. But you looked like you might catch an hour more sleep if I left.'

She sighed. 'There'll be lots to do. What bell is it?'

'Dunno, but someone else can do it. You're not the company quartermaster. Let Foren do his job for once.'

'It must be past noon, I can't lie here all day.'

Lynx leaned back against the door jamb. 'Oh I dunno, I like the idea o' that.'

'You can get those thoughts out of your head, I'm sore and tired so I ain't going to wait for you.'

'Worth a shot.' He shrugged. 'I'm after coffee and food, want me to bring some up?'

Toil shook her head. 'I'll be down in a minute.'

Lynx gave her a mock salute and headed outside. Llaith was passing at that moment and glimpsed inside, his eyes widening to saucers. The ageing Card had a reputation for surprising smoothness and sophistication around high-born ladies and expensive courtesans. Yet here he was taken by surprise and made a choking sound as he tripped over his own feet. Llaith was half-heading over the guardrail before Lynx grabbed him.

'Shattered gods, take a breath,' Lynx said as he pulled the door shut behind him.

'Sad to say I did, my friend,' Llaith replied. 'That's quite a stink o' sweat and sex coming out o' there.'

'And the rest of the company's smelling like roses in this heat?'

'Some of us better than others,' Llaith protested. 'So you finally dragged yourself away? The others are about the same. Teshen's the only one been up and out this last hour.'

'Any news?'

Llaith gestured to the courtyard behind. 'See for yourself!'

Lynx looked past him and saw four of the Shard's mages talking there. Two were shirtless and the willow-pattern tattoos were plain to see against their brown skin. 'Well I guess that's good.'

'You don't sound so happy, my friend.'

'Aye well, I know how her indoors thinks,' Lynx said, prompting a smile from Llaith. 'If we can create a dozen super-mages, why not a hundred? Why not an army who can advance under shields and tear through anything the Militant Orders can throw at them?'

'There are worse ideas,' the older man said, though he didn't look exactly eager. 'Lastani's been flat out since the ritual, though. I doubt she'll be so keen to do this many more times.'

Lynx nodded. 'What's the food situation?'

'Supplies? Foren's still out getting it sorted. Ah, right. That's not what you meant.' Llaith laughed. 'There's something cooking away down there, no damn clue what it is except it smells like old fish. I doubt you'll care much, just watch your step around those old biddies. A bad night's sleep has made 'em nastier than the prince o' hangovers.'

'Fish?' Lynx thought for a moment. 'It's always pissing fish round here. Guess it'll have to do.'

Together they headed down. After a short while of being polite and looking suitably chastened, Lynx was offered a bowl of something even he was suspicious of, while Llaith secured a large pot of coffee. Only as he was sniffing the food, trying to work out what was in it, did he notice that the enormous tysarn was missing from the centre of the courtyard.

'Don't worry,' Llaith said, heading for a shady spot at the far end. 'We chopped it up and dragged the pieces away once Lastani was done. Didn't want it stinking up the place – nor give those old girls ideas about what to feed us.'

Half of the courtyard was bathed in sunshine now, the complex array of awnings strung between the towers tangled and ripped. Several had been torn away completely in the fight and most of the rest would need to be replaced. The sky beyond had long wisps of cloud running from the horizon against the deep blue.

To a paranoid eye, Lynx thought, *those could look like they were all running towards this city. Not sure I like where that thought leads, though.*

He sat next to Llaith and gingerly tasted the bowl. It was a soggy pile of yellow-green rice with what looked like fat knobbly grass and lumps of fish – far from enticing, but the flavour was hot and sour with the sharp salty tang of the sea.

'Good hey?' Llaith said approvingly. 'We all were surprised, but it turns out as mean as they are, they're proud too. And o' course, they don't know how much of last night was actually our fault. We've decided to keep it that way.'

Lynx nodded his agreement, too busy to speak. They continued in silence until the bowl was empty and Lynx could start allowing the coffee to ease the dullness in his head. Just as Toil emerged from their room, a dull thump echoed out through the courtyard. Everyone turned as the sound came again, clearly not a gunshot, but it took Lynx a while to realise it was someone thumping on the heavy door to the entrance hall. Presently a bemused-looking Varain wandered out of the entrance hall ahead of a line of elderly mages, five in all and the youngest of whom was certainly not a day under sixty.

'Toil,' Varain called, 'you got visitors.'

The Princess of Blood peered at the group for a few moments then realisation struck. 'The Waterdancer Guild?'

The elderly white man leading the mages, three shades of blue stripes running down his white sleeve, bowed. As they spread out behind him, Lynx saw the others had the same stripes, though most wore flowing blue robes.

'The Shard,' their leader said in broken Parthish. 'She send message.'

'Most obliging of you to come,' Toil said as she hurried down the steps to the ground floor. 'I thought you'd want me to come to you?'

The leader glanced back at one of his mages, a tall woman with rusty-red skin and neat black curls of hair spilling over her shawl. She in turn glanced at another wearing the red headscarf of a Casteril Mastrunner, though he was as old as any of them.

'We do not invite outsiders,' the woman said. 'For our safety, you understand?'

'I do. Did the Shard tell you what I wanted?'

She inclined her head. 'We are here to negotiate.'

'That takes five of you?' Toil scratched her cheek. 'Ulfer's broken horn – something tells me this is going to be a long afternoon. Lynx, fetch me coffee.'

The five figures halt well short of the yawning tunnel entrance. Up ahead the light of day is oppressive to behold, far more intimidating than the restless shift and dart of tysarn in the black waters nearby. Three of the Wisp delegation are old and stooped, comprised as all reason and custom dictates of one of each sex in their species, xeale, female, and male. Their age makes them no less adept mages than the pair of tall warriors who bring up the rear, but the journey has been long. The halt is born of need as much as apprehension.

The leader wears a plain white robe that glows faintly in the darkness, while the others are dressed in the more usual wrap cloths covered in detailed geometric patterns. With a gesture of one crooked hand, the stout xeale who is the appointed representative of their clans breaks the wary regard they have fallen into. Xe orders xir companions to make ready, all too aware of how fearfully the sunlight is regarded. It was used as a most terrible punishment, back in less civilised times, and their oldest myths considered the sun some world-ending demon.

The xeale is the oldest of the group. Xir upper arm joints are near-fused by age and make a mockery of the name xe was given at birth – Turran, the whisper of smooth water flowing. The slender male at the rear hurries to attend xer. He fixes a long, hooded cloak around the small xeale's shoulder until Turran is almost hidden from view and fastens it securely. All the others do the same and are soon waiting for the male to put on his own.

One of the elderly trio moves to the edge of the canal while they wait. They have travelled a mile or more along the wide towpath that runs the canal's entire length, studded with obstructions after so many centuries of disuse. She peers down at the water, head drifting slightly from side to side to employ all four eyes. The surface of the water trembles under the movement beneath, only just visible to her night-adapted eyes, but when a shape explodes up from the surface she is prepared for it.

A fat coil of water surges up to intercept the leaping tysarn, slapping into the side of its head with the force of a hammer. It is a battle-scarred beast, no more than three yards long but with tattered rear wings that have left it unable to fly. Before its jaws can reach her the tysarn is hurled sideways and crashes into the side wall of the canal. The Wisp mage bobs her head, speaking-finger darting forward and back twice before she turns away.

Satisfied? signs Turran, the light of xir speaking-fingers hard to make out against the glare of daylight.

Yes, she replies. *That one was dangerous. It has followed us overlong.*

Still you tire yourself, playing with wildlife.

She makes a gesture and covers one speaking-finger, prompting xer to turn away in feigned outrage. She knows xir humour well enough and signs gentle laughter.

Come, Turran signs to xir companions. *We should not wait.*

Is it safe? asks the taller of the attendant warriors.

There will be discomfort, xe acknowledges, *but we cannot know if there is time to wait.*

Do we really owe them this?

The comment brings a sharp rebuke from the female elder. *It is not owed,* she signs sharply, *yet we would be the lesser without acting.*

Chastened, he steps back until she folds her speaking-finger into the palm of her hand. Then, with a bob of the head, he advances past the rest – long, fluid strides taking him swiftly towards the mouth of the canal tunnel. His agitation is clear, the loose stones on the ground swirling and skittering as he passes.

The others follow, each of them faltering as they reach the edge of the sun. There are more tysarn in the water there – large, restless and irritable though none try to attack the Wisps as the smaller rogue had. Soon the delegation stands at the canal mouth where the ancient channels for Duegar traffic remain only as broken-off chunks of stone. Beyond it are the crude dwellings of the humans, stone boxes with their odd, tilted ceilings. Smoke rises from many, the clatter and noise of the city causing each Wisp to tighten the skin around their ears and dull the oppressive sensation.

Behind those small streets of dwellings are large, more impressive ones. Great blocks that rise up like cliffs, decorated in colours that lack anything pleasing to a Wisp eye. Markings of danger and threat where there seem to be none, stone that reflects the cruel heat of the sun. It is a daunting prospect to enter, for all that they have each prepared themselves.

They do not speak. Each of them have their eyes almost entirely closed against the harsh daylight. There is no way they would be able to see the light of a speaking-finger and follow its movements. Fortunately they agreed much earlier what they would do, all that they could do under such circumstances. The water mage reaches out to the lapping waves below and gathers a column of glittering water, so intense it pains her to bring it closer.

Once settled, she inspects the narrow, silver-sliver fish caught within it and ushers them away before she tightens her grip on the water. That done she steps forward on to the column and her companions follow. Once they are settled she carries them all across the narrow strip of water there. One large tysarn follows their path, drawn by the movement, but she bumps at its snout with a twitch of her magic and the creature drifts clear again.

There is one long channel cut through the rock shelf where the humans have established themselves. She drives towards that until she finds a section where a stony beach leads directly to a street. There a cluster of humans stare in astonishment, huge mouths hanging open then flapping madly. Most are young, smaller even than Turran. They dart back and forth with crazed gestures as the group approaches. When the delegation reaches the shore, the humans scatter. The Wisps step on to deserted dry land, though the two warrior mages are careful to advance not too far in case panic prompts violence.

They wait a few moments, allowing the water mage to recover herself after such exertions. Faces appear constantly from around corners, vanishing as quickly as they come, while ripples of sound seem to spread out through the district. Only once do they see more than that, when a tall human mage in a billowing grey robe emerges to look at them. It stands still for a long moment. Finally, it runs a hand the colour of cured leather back through its hair then extends both hands towards them.

If it notices the calm response of the warriors to its hostile movement, it makes no sign. Instead, the human bobs its upper body in a faintly repulsive, unnatural fashion and hurries away. Turran takes that as reason enough to move on – that their presence has been noticed by a figure of importance. The only logical conclusion would be to summon their chieftains. Until then the delegation needs somewhere appropriate to wait. Somewhere away from the terrible glare of the sun.

They walk, slowly so as not to frighten the scampering humans and wearied by the weight of heat. The burden of that is enormous, even more than expected. Turran finds it almost overwhelming at times. Only the abundant water their mage can draw the filth from makes it bearable, but still it takes them a long while before they reach a market square. There a strange inverted building offers sanctuary, a peaked square roof supported by pillars and open on every side.

The humans flee as soon as the delegation comes within sight. To an underground-dwelling race it feels absurd to have a roof with no walls, except they eagerly embrace the shade beneath. Passing between stalls where strange fruits and fish have been abandoned, they take position in the very centre where mats and crates have been piled.

It takes only a moment to arrange the mats so they may all sit comfortably. As best they can, they divest themselves of their protective cloaks – letting the strange, uncomfortable movement of the air cool them. More faces appear around corners, one human even summons the courage to walk right out into the square.

Long-haired and skin burned brown, it comes to within two paces of the shaded sanctuary, but seems reluctant to step out of the sun as though protected by its light. It makes some noises, hands flapping uselessly for all that they try to see some scraps of sense in its gestures. It is not a mage, they know this, and so it cannot be of any real importance.

The warriors watch it carefully all the same. It has no magic but carries weapons of steel. There is no real threat unless more come, but it makes no effort to draw its weapons. After a long while it goes away again. The noise it makes with its mouth continues even after it has turned away, but they realise now that is how all humans are.

Once it is gone, no more approach. Many peer at the delegation around corners, out of windows, but none address them. They are frightened and awed, this much is clear, but even the younglings keep clear.

Under the shelter, surrounded by the sounds of waves and shrieking, winged creatures that have no fear of the Wisps as they feast on the abandoned fish, the delegation waits.

Chapter 32

When the message came, Toil had been pacing the courtyard like a leopard in a cage. Her meeting with the Waterdancer Guild had gone surprisingly well, albeit expensively. She wasn't looking forward to the reaction of Su Dregir's First Lord of the Treasury, but there hadn't been much room to negotiate.

For a while the argument between mages didn't disturb the clatter of her thoughts, even when the shouting started. Only when her name was mentioned and Lynx yelled over did any of it filter through.

She looked up to see the confrontation growing heated and hurried over. There was a mage in a grey robe, one of Tanimbor's guild, arguing furiously with one of the Shard's own. What they were saying was anyone's guess, but Teshen was nearby and listening. She concentrated on his face in case it betrayed anything. When naked surprise appeared there, Toil was shocked. Alarm stirred in her gut as she went to Teshen's side and pulled him aside.

'What's going on?'

'I . . .' The cold-nerved killer appeared to be lost for words until Toil gave an angry hiss. 'It's a message for you, from Tanimbor.'

'That much I guessed. What's got them so riled up?'

'He ain't won many friends these past few days,' Teshen said. 'The Shard wants him well clear of everything until we're gone.

They're flexing authority, testing loyalties now he's suddenly so much more powerful.'

'What does he want with me? Not Lastani?'

Teshen stared at her. 'No, it's you he wants. The mage says there's some Wisps sitting in a Cliffbase market – just sitting there and waiting.'

'What?' Toil almost yelled. 'Wisps? Here? They've just walked into a fucking human city?'

'That's what he says.'

'Impossible!'

He gave her a level look. 'You're telling that to someone who grew up here?'

'That's . . .' Toil gave up. She was lost for words too. Chances were that she'd had more contact with Wisps than all but a handful of people alive, but how did Tanimbor know that?

When she asked Teshen that, he shook his head. 'That one says he's sent a messenger to the Shard as well, a few other guilds too. He's got no one who can speak to the Wisps, but he remembered you saying you were a relic hunter.'

'So he figured I was worth trying,' Toil finished. 'Well he's in luck – assuming the Shard actually lets me out of here.'

'She will,' Teshen said, half-distracted by the ongoing argument.

'Sure of that?'

'A fucking Wisp just appeared for the first time in Caldaire in . . . I dunno, centuries? For all the academics and experts the guilds can boast, I doubt any of 'em will have actually had a conversation with a Wisp.' He nodded towards the pair of mages. 'Want me to interrupt?'

Centuries at least? Then the day after every tysarn roosting in the caverns goes batshit crazy, some Wisps appear. There's no way this is going to be good news, Toil realised. 'Yeah, get in there, Find me something useful to do.'

312

With a combination of shouting louder than everyone else and looking every inch the dead-eyed killer he was, Teshen managed to attract their attention. The mages were startled enough to listen and that quickly turned to astonishment when Teshen informed them Toil could speak to Wisps. Realising the Shard still needed to approve anyone leaving the lodging house, Teshen sent the messenger on to give her that extra piece of news. After that came a frustratingly long delay, but at last the Shard herself appeared. She marched in ahead of a gaggle of rather dishevelled and frightened-looking academics, if anything even more angry than last time.

'You can speak to them?' the Shard demanded without preamble.

Toil raised a small pot she'd retrieved from her pack. 'They speak with hand gestures, their fingers glow in the dark and this stuff does pretty much the same job. I learned a few years back when a job went wrong and I got hurt. A forage party came across me and helped me out, I spend a couple of months with them in the end.'

'How convenient for Tanimbor.'

'That after dicking around with a Duegar artefact with the help of a relic hunter, some Wisps turned up?' Toil shook her head. 'Coincidence will always turn to conspiracy if that's what you're looking for.'

'Perhaps so. Either way, I will be coming with you.'

'Not scared it's a convoluted trap?' Toil said with a snort. 'I mean, if you reckon the Splinter in your backside planned all this, it could be the best way to lure you on to his territory.'

'My title protects me,' the Shard said. The look on her face told Toil she had indeed considered the possibility. 'In killing me he shows all mages in the city he cannot be trusted, that he is their enemy. And, after all, most of my trusted advisers are linked to your mages and his – they are too valuable to risk.'

There's a twisted logic to that, Toil was forced to admit privately. *Gutsy too. She knows her enemy's more powerful than she is personally, but she won't let that scare her.*

'Guess we should be off then. Teshen, Paranil, Lastani – you're with me.'

Just as they headed to the door, Toil saw a second newcomer, this one loitering in the shadows of the hallway. She'd clearly come in with the Shard but had held back, happy to make her own entrance once the Shard had said her piece. There were flashes of the flamboyant style preferred by Masts crews, but understated – coloured stitching rather than the cloth itself, weapon sheaths with intricate leather tooling but no silver decoration. Only the white sash around her waist stood out.

'We meet again,' Toil said as the woman came forward. 'Sanshir, right?'

'I'm surprised you remember,' she replied. 'You were all very drunk.'

'I'm a woman who appreciates the value of making an impression.'

'What are you doing here?' Teshen interrupted, slightly awkwardly.

'Cold waters, you have been away so long.' Sanshir gave a small shake of the head. 'I am the Champion Kaboto of the city.'

'That make you the Shard's bodyguard?' Toil asked.

'The city's bodyguard,' Sanshir clarified. 'Caldaire has no army and the Court of the Kabats speaks with many voices. When there is a threat to the city, the crews need to work together, under one person.'

'The Wisps aren't a threat to the city, I'm certain of it.'

'I am glad to hear this, but I will come anyway. Times are tense, what with the giant tysarn eating people on the streets. At some point, my kabat may ask me who is to blame. I would not wish to be in any doubt there.'

The Shard held up a hand. 'Right now, you both answer to me – understand? And I say there will be no more blame and violence until I am satisfied. These are the Mage Islands – we are in charge here.'

The two women conceded without a further word. To Teshen's obvious astonishment, Sanshir presented him with her arm as the Shard moved to lead the way. When he didn't take it, the kaboto only gave a soft laugh and padded along after, leaving the Cards to catch up.

Toil grinned. *Men, they're all fucking idiots really.* She gave Teshen a patronising pat on the head and followed Sanshir.

The journey was swift and unimpeded, taking little over half the time it had when Toil had gone to meet Tanimbor. The Shard had even brought a wind mage to speed their journey across the lagoon in a personal barge – a long, sleek craft painted from curling prow to stern in all the bright colours of her coat of office. It was hardly necessary, but Toil knew that if ever there was a day to flex the power of her position, this was it.

On the journey, Toil noticed the red flags were out on the warning stations. She couldn't see any tysarn in the water, but people were taking no chances. There were no fishing coracles out, nothing small enough that a hungry tysarn could overturn and all traffic on the lagoon was lessened. Only the guard boats around the spice islands seemed to be unaffected and the armed guards in them didn't look at ease today.

Guildmaster Tanimbor met them at the dock, to Toil's surprise – compounded by the fact he was almost deferential in his manner. Guild rivalries and intrigue were one thing, but it was plain the appearance of these Wisps had rattled him. Clearly sleep-deprived and wearing rumpled clothes, he looked more like a scarecrow than power broker.

At that thought, Toil looked up. She'd found herself avoiding it last time, but now there was no way she could. The huge pale cliffs loomed behind the district, pockmarked with ledges and caves far above the height where waves could have carved such things. She saw one or two large tysarn basking in the sun but still looking agitated. Others flew in high circles above the cliffs, some lay on the grassy scrub above and complained in deep resonant grunts.

There was no violence, but still the beasts were stirred up and the need for sleep couldn't dim that. Most would have fed last night – the death toll remained a guess but it was in the hundreds at least. She imagined they should be sated, but Toil noticed more movement and noise than last time. The dark maw of the canal tunnel looked empty at least; a huge black arch more than twice the height and width of any of the dozens of caves there.

And underneath, Toil reminded herself, *some whole damn Duegar complex taken over by tysarn, a breeding ground for them and impossibility for me. Who knows what's lost to the tysarn down there, covered in millennia-worth of shit and guarded by ten thousand carnivorous little bastards – assuming you get past the giant ones first?*

'Guildmaster,' the Shard acknowledged in a neutral tone as she stepped off the barge.

Four of her mage-guards had hopped off as soon as it touched dry land, watching for threats, but Tanimbor had been careful to limit his own escort to one mage. There were two local militia types overseeing the dock more generally, thugs with cudgels in any other language. Both had scratches and bandaged wounds that spoke of their night's activities.

'Shard,' Tanimbor said.

'You requested my assistance?' Toil enquired.

His cheek twitched, but he made no comment other than to incline his head. 'Wisps are beyond my expertise,' Tanimbor admitted, 'but I know they would not leave their caverns without good reason.'

'And I'm guessing your district got ripped through last night,' Toil said. 'Which means you're desperate and can't handle any more bad news without help.'

He inclined his head again. 'That is so. The people of this district were hunted like deer. My mages did what they could, but tysarn are attracted to magic. We have barely begun to count how many are missing.'

'We will assist you,' the Shard said stiffly. 'I will ensure the kabats help beyond their own borders. This is not a matter of districts.'

Sanshir didn't add anything beyond a small nod, but it seemed to satisfy the guildmaster.

'I thank you. Now – our guests. Shall I lead the way?'

The Shard nodded as the others disembarked. Toil had a good look around before they set off. Work had ceased on the dock as people stopped to watch, but the presence of people was a reassuring thing, even if many bore some sort of injury and half had grimy tear-streaks on their cheeks.

Broken awnings and the faint stain of blood on stone showed people had likely died here, but for all the shock of last night, the citizens were indeed getting on with the daily activities of life. They kept close to the buildings, however, that much was obvious – children and adults alike glancing up at the sky from time to time. Just as they set off across the short dock, a gull appeared unexpectedly, swooping low over the buildings. The sight was enough to make most of them start. Fire and chunks of stone leaped into the hands of several mages before they realised it was just a bird.

Despite that interruption, they made good time across the district. It was only a few minutes before Tanimbor pointed ahead, down the street to a deserted market square. Toil glanced at Teshen and saw the man also had his hand on his mage-pistol. She gave a nod of approval and put a friendly arm around Paranil's shoulder, easing the bespectacled academic back. He glanced up at her and blinked, but realised what she was about a moment later.

Mebbe the end times are upon us, Toil thought with a grim smile. *It's taken bloody years of working for me, but finally even Paranil's become more than a wide-eyed innocent.*

Even before Jarrazir, Paranil had been on several hunts in Duegar ruins alongside Toil, all of which saw violence in one form or another. He'd been useless and bewildered the entire time, his survival bordering on miraculous despite Toil and Aben's best efforts.

Is it hanging around the Cards these past few months, she wondered, *or a sign of how serious the danger is these days?*

She dismissed the thought and advanced with Teshen at her side. Toil gave the Shard just enough space to be gunned down before they came into the crossfire, but not enough to be impolite. When nothing happened, Toil upped her pace only to stop dead a few moments later. It was true. There, ahead of them, sheltering from the bright afternoon sunshine was a group of five Wisps – sitting patiently on mats while raucous gulls feasted all around them.

Toil was the first to get over her surprise, being most comfortable around the underground race. While the clan she'd spent time with lived over a thousand miles away, she knew they shared a common language and that was what her hosts had taught her.

The nuances of even that clan's language were beyond her, in some respects literally because she didn't have enough joints in her fingers, but it was underpinned by a simpler version. That was what the clans used to speak to each other. Life underground was dangerous enough without considering every other Wisp anything but an ally.

'Do you want me to go ahead?' Toil asked, pulling her pot of white paste from one pocket.

'I . . .' The Shard hesitated. 'Have they been drawing?'

They all advanced another step and saw there were indeed slates on the floor before two of the Wisps, twine wrapped around the edges and chalk drawings made on the surface. The drawings were markedly different. One showed a Wisp offering a plate of food, a traditional greeting, alongside glyphs of greeting, but the other showed something monstrous and came with a warning.

'They didn't expect anyone to be able to talk to them,' Toil suggested. 'They're skilled artists though, and I'm guessing one of your academics can read a bit?'

By way of reply the Shard turned to one of her companions, a tall greying man with a prominent forehead and wire-rimmed spectacles. He wasn't a local, judging from his pale skin. More likely the Greensea, which meant it was a good thing Lynx hadn't tagged along.

'Ah, well – yes,' the man said. 'Of course, the pictures help.'

'A greeting and a warning,' Toil said. 'I don't recognise the picture on the second slate, but I don't much fancy meeting one.'

'How well can you read their language, Gre Feir?'

The man pursed his lips. 'Well enough,' he said stiffly as one of the Wisps picked up the greeting slate and began to erase what had been written. 'I'm sure my abilities will be entirely sufficient.'

'Guess that's me dismissed then,' Toil muttered, giving the man a dainty curtsey before winking at Paranil. Before the Wisp could finish a new drawing, she stepped smartly around the mage and went to kneel in front of the elderly third who was clearly leading the delegation.

Greetings, eldest, she signed while splutters of outrage happened behind her.

The Wisp blinked at her. *May the light guide you,* xe signed in reply. *I am surprised.*

We are all surprising, Toil signed, only noting her mistake when xe gestured gentle amusement.

I fear my news will not be welcome, xe signed, after a pause to allow xir amusement to dissipate.

Toil lowered her head in acknowledgement, though the human gesture would be lost on xer. *Unwelcome in the light is better than surprising in the dark.*

It is so.

The others watched in silence as Toil haltingly conversed with the Wisp. The strangeness of the scene meant they waited without complaint or restlessness. If it was even a surprise when Toil briefly broke off, rocked back on her heels by what she'd heard, there was no indication. Or perhaps the shock Toil felt numbed her to all else around her. The deepest black held no terrors for her, not in the way they did for Lynx. She knew there was horror down there and she had no wish to die in some Duegar city-ruin, but it didn't haunt her dreams. Not even after her first trip, when Sotorian Bade had left her to die in the dark.

Even so, she felt the news like a punch to the chest. Toil was not quite so heartless as the Cards imagined, not quite so callous as Lynx often feared. The image of what might happen to this city touched even the closely guarded part of her soul.

'Oh fuck,' she gasped. 'Golantha.'

Chapter 33

The human is still a long time. Turran watches its face, trying to fathom what it is thinking. From what xe knows of humans, the males are the larger and more likely to be warriors, so xe assumes that is the case here.

His signing is endearingly simple, possessing a childlike charm that reminds Turran of xir children. Especially for males, those years of awkwardness when their limbs are still growing render conversation either mystifying or adorable. The human sadly does not look adorable, from what Turran can make out against the glare. Still, his efforts are commendable and quicker than drawing.

His – admittedly shaky – accent is dimly reminiscent of somewhere Turran recognises from travels in xir distant youth, but cannot place. That he knows the signs for the darkest lights suggests a story all of its own perhaps, but Turran is just content the seriousness is understood. The golantha are close to myth even for the clans, but a myth they know can be stirred to life all too easily.

How long?

The darkest lights sleep in the deepest black, far below our clan domains. We do not know, but we sense the stirring.

The air does this?

The Duegar artefacts have agitated all creatures of the black. The tysarn will settle in time, but the darkest lights will hunt. There is change in the air, there is new nourishment for their kind. The scent leads here.

I . . . I understand. They come. Tonight?

Perhaps. They move fast.

Many?

Turran closes all four eyes to emphasise xir sadness.

How many?

The clans have not seen them in generations, we cannot say. They hunt the elementals of the depths when they stir, but the writings speak of sleep lasting decades. Not dozens, not one.

You have danger, coming here?

Water protects us.

The human pauses and looks around. Turren waits.

Will it protect us? he asks eventually.

I do not know. They will not follow us out on to water – but you are so many. Your islands are close together, they can cross.

They want only mages? the human signs, almost hopefully.

The darkest lights kill all in their path, xe replies. Your mages must save you.

How?

Pitfalls, snares, light – these are not elementals, they are creatures of flesh and bone, but magic too.

I fight one, he confirms to Turren's surprise. In Shadows Deep.

Shadows Deep?

A city in north. Two gorges, one open to the sky, one deep and home to darkest lights.

Ah, I know of the place – where the Whiteshadow clans live. You fought one?

We drove it from the bridge with guns. It falls far.

There is no place to fall here, Turren signs with sympathy. The water does not kill them. Perhaps the deep waters beyond this city, we do not know.

322

This is it? he asks, pointing at the drawing on the slate. *It is not the same.*

This is how our histories describe them, but it is not perfect. The darkest lights come in many forms.

What can we do?

You are many, you have your guns.

Not many. This is not a city of guns.

Then flee.

The human is still again for a long while. *I thank you for this warning. I know you have danger to come here.*

We must come.

Now you must go. This is not your fight.

We will be safe. Our stonecaster will hide us in the cliff until the way is clear. Do you speak for the city?

The female behind me, in many colours. She speaks for the city. I will tell all.

Xe signed acceptance. *We will return to the dark. May the light guide you.*

Toil signed her thanks once more and returned the farewell. Stiffly, she stood and turned to face the Shard, her throat gone dry after news like that.

'What is it? What's golantha?' Sanshir demanded. The fierce woman glared at Toil and Teshen both, as though this was some plot she couldn't fathom.

'The golantha,' Toil said haltingly, 'are the biggest horrors Urden has to offer. The kings of the deepest black.'

'Monsters or children's stories?'

'Not stories,' the Shard said. 'Warnings – ones the Wisps know to take seriously.'

'We've seen one,' Teshen added. 'In Shadows Deep. Damn thing chewed through a few companies of Knights-Charnel as it tried to get to us.'

Toil scowled. 'But it didn't look like the picture they drew. I've read wildly different accounts in my time. The name "golantha" is used for any sort of huge magic-hungry monster of the deepest black.'

'That's not encouraging.'

'It gets worse,' Toil said. 'There I stirred one up and we were lucky to get out alive. But now? Now there's a few coming and the best snacks will be standing right next to us.'

Teshen glanced towards the cliffs. 'Oh screaming shits, our mages – hells, all of the marked Cards will taste of magic now!'

'What exactly are they?' the Shard demanded. 'I have read brief mentions of such things, but . . .'

'What exactly?' Toil said in a hollow voice. 'Gods-in-shards . . . Likely they'll be more'n twice the size of the biggest tysarn – a monster of flesh and magic that drinks in half the magic you throw at it. The one we saw had four legs and huge horns, a tongue like a dozen glowing whips and all wrapped in shadow 'n' flame.'

The Shard went rigid – not through fear, Toil realised after a moment, but with the effort of controlling a volcano of rage.

'How many?'

'They don't know. These things live in the very depths. They're the reason even Wisps fear the deepest black. Not dozens, they're too big for that, but several.'

'How did you find yourselves facing one?' the Shard asked.

Toil faltered. 'Ah, well. We needed to cross a chasm and there were Charnelers holding both bridges.'

'So?'

'So I dropped a grenade off the edge to see if there was anything down below, willing to be stirred up.'

The Shard's face was a mask. 'So it was your fault then, too?'

'Yeah.'

She nodded and glanced up at the caves of the huge cliff looming over the district. 'Guildmaster Tanimbor – it sounds like these things will be coming for your mages first of all. We will of course offer sanctuary elsewhere.'

'They'll kill anything in their way,' Toil broke in, 'but magic's what they feed off. The Eldest said they won't swim so we can evacuate some to the other islands—'

'But they are huge and will move around Caldaire with ease,' Sanshir finished. 'Gods-in-shards, you have brought this city nothing but ruin. And now your creatures of chaos have returned with you.' This was directed at Teshen, who had no response, but Sanshir didn't wait for one.

'Guildmaster,' she said in a loud voice, 'we must evacuate Cliffbase entirely. Have your mages give the orders. Every man woman and child must go to Vi No Le. There is one bridge between the districts. We will destroy that so they cannot cross and establish our defences at Si Jo Island.'

'Give up An Vir too?' Teshen asked.

Sanshir nodded. 'We evacuate that, the shoreline is too large. Si Jo is smaller and easier to defend. Shard, the Court of the Kabats must order out every Mastrunner and mage-gun they have – the guilds too. Anything that can hurt these things needs to be on Si Jo. We will have a small reserve in Casteril too, but if they can cross the cliffs there is no stopping them.'

She pointed and they all looked at the great cliff that over-looked a long stretch of water before reaching the canal mouth. Large parts of it were sheer sheets of rock that offered no space for nesting birds let alone something massive to climb, and there were no caves within a hundred yards of the canal.

'You're hoping, what, twenty yards of water will stop them? Cats don't like to swim either, that doesn't mean they won't get their feet wet if they need to. These things might be able to reach all the way across!'

'It's still the best place to defend. If they can swim we cannot fight them. Perhaps the wider channel between Cliffbase and An Vir will stop them, but we cannot evacuate the whole city to the other islands. We must be ready to fight.' She paused. 'And of course, we will have the experts beside us.'

Toil laughed. 'Experts? We faced one and barely got away with our lives. Anatin lost his hand down in Shadows Deep and some friends too. You ask this and it's an even chance between him shooting your face off and going head first into a barrel of brandy before nightfall.'

'Nightfall?'

Toil nodded. 'They're creatures of the dark, just like the Wisps. They'll come at night.'

'This night? Tomorrow night?'

'No way to know. The golantha live in the deep, far further down than Wisps, but they're big and fast. Mebbe it cancels out.'

She tailed off and all present found their eyes turning north towards the Etrel Cliffs. The tysarn, the biggest of those who could still fly and were safe from the predations of all but their huge, sea-bound kin, emitted great croaking bellows as they shifted anxiously on their perches. More voices echoed from inside the caves, hollow and distorted sounds, but not the usual lazy calls of previous days.

'Is that normal?' Toil asked. 'Or do they sound pissed off to everyone else too?'

'What could piss off a hundred tysarn?' Teshen said. 'Other than us, that is? Ulfer's broken horn, nightfall it is.'

'Tonight?' Anatin demanded, a scowl on his face and a beer in his hand. 'And you want us to do fucking *what*?'

'What do you think?' Teshen replied.

The commander of the Mercenary Deck gestured around at the courtyard. Most of the Cards were mustered – if lounging

326

around and panting in the hot weather counted. Foren, the company quartermaster, had done a good job in acquiring supplies and a liberal sprinkling of promises had secured them berths on barges leaving early next morning.

There was chaos at the main canal dock, Foren had reported, with every scheduled departure eager to leave as soon as they could afford it. The cost of passage hadn't been that steep in the end. Many barges were only half-full of goods and happy to offer space if it meant the journey would be in profit. Seagoing ships were proving harder, all the wealthy of Caldaire determined to escape to the other islands of the chain.

Toil's new friends at the Waterdancer Guild had also come through for them, albeit at a steep price. Ammunition was in scarce supply in the city anyway, but the kabats were buying up sparkers and burners in particular. Given Caldaire was largely mage-carved stone, the place wasn't as flammable as most cities.

Toil hadn't been so heartless as to withhold what they'd seen in Shadows Deep. There the golantha had shrugged off most mage-shot as it fed on the magic, icers and earthers having a greater impact – but she'd still secured what she needed direct from the source. Prices were quadruple what you'd find anywhere on Parthain, but even Deern was happy to fork out if it meant staying alive. The results weren't impressive though. The Cards were the best equipped troops in the city, but there simply weren't enough mage cartridges available.

'The kabats need us to fight,' Toil said as Anatin and Teshen glared at each other. 'They need every mage-gun they can muster on that defensive line if they're going to stand a chance.'

'Yeah, that's where you've lost me,' Anatin snapped. 'What's the first rule of mercenaries?'

'There's so pissing many of them,' Toil said wearily. 'Just tell me which one you're on about.'

That at least prompted a small, nasty smile on Anatin's face, but the Prince of Sun was both sober and entirely serious now. 'The one where both you and the person paying you needs to be alive at the end of the day. If you're going to get paid, that is.'

'The Shard's good for the money – and in case you weren't properly listening, they weren't looking for much discussion here. They expect us to fight.'

'More fool them, then.'

'You're just going to sit back and watch it play out?' Teshen growled. Normally he was on Anatin's side in any moral argument, but Toil saw that a threat to his home was pushing some buttons.

'That's bloody exactly what I'm gonna do!' Anatin yelled back. 'And I'm ordering all you fuckers to do the same, understand?'

He looked around at all the watching Cards to make sure it was clear he meant the whole company, gesturing with the stump of his arm to make his point further.

'You lot listening? We've faced these fucking horrors before, some of us anyways. The rest o' you have heard the stories. I'm in command here and one reason for that is I don't piss your lives away for no reason. Not often just for profit either. We're mercs, we're paid to fight and I'm the one who decides if the pay is worth the fight. If you shitstains didn't trust me on that, you'd have left the company by now.'

'And you're going to tell the Shard that?' Toil asked.

'If I have to. This damned fool line of defence she an' Teshen's girl have planned, it ain't going ta work! You hear me? I ain't putting the Cards – some of whom I like an' the rest who make me money – in a line like that.'

'You think it'll break?'

'Hah – you don't? They ain't all like Teshen, I'll put all the money I've got left on it.'

'They're tough,' Teshen said, 'and Sanshir's a strong leader.'

'They're tough against each other,' Anatin scoffed. 'In a

game where hardly anyone gets killed, compared to any of the shit we've been up to.' He waved his stump in Teshen's face. 'They're not a gods-shattered army, they're fifty or a hundred tiny little groups. Most don't have mage-guns and none have the first fucking clue what they're really dealing with.'

Anatin cast around at the watching Cards. 'How about you, Lynx? Ain't you always the first to sign up to dumbshit hero work?'

There was a moment of quiet then Lynx cleared his throat. 'I ain't keen,' the big man replied at last, 'but I'll not stand back and leave them to die. Not if I think I could help.'

'Fine then – how about I make you a deal? This line's got to last the night, right?'

'Yeah.'

'How about we give it five minutes then? We hang back and find somewhere good to watch the whole thing. If I'm wrong, seven blackest hells, I won't even ask for payment, on my life! I'll march down there with the rest o' you to do my civic duty.'

'Five minutes?'

'Five – Fucking – Minutes!' Anatin roared. 'That's my wager. Sanshir an' her line'll be smashed open in the first shitting assault and I won't be standing there when it does. I'll be ready to run in the other bloody direction, well ahead of the rest.

''Cos it will break, you know it will, Teshen. You saw that damn thing in Shadows Deep. Here there's more'n one, limited ammunition and no mile-deep chasm to knock 'em down.'

Toil looked around at the faces, but she knew the answer even before she did. She felt it in her heart, the truth to Anatin's words. How many mage-guns would Sanshir be able to muster, a hundred? Mages too – certainly more than they'd had in Shadows Deep, but that had been a confined space. They had been able to lure the beast, predict it. Out here, the damn things might come any way they want.

'Blackest hells,' Toil muttered. 'Fine. Five minutes.'

Chapter 34

Teshen fought the urge to run. He wasn't a man prone to great emotion, so this homecoming had been a strange mixture of electric memories and the haze of intervening years. Here and now, however, he wanted to run. To feel the blood pump until his heart ached. To be reminded of the young man who'd once walked these streets. Raced with his whooping, savage kin through the alleys and across rooftops.

He walked Vi No Le's streets again, something he had thought he would never do. In younger days he had haunted them as part vengeful spirit and part nobility. But Sanshir wasn't at his side and that was both good and bad.

Sanshir and he together had been glorious and relentless – a combination even the famous feared to go up against. When the proud went to put them in their place, the proud ended up broken. But now . . . now he walked. On the lowest streets, overlooked on all sides, he walked as one whose glory was two decades past. Slow and vulnerable in some ways, greater in others.

Teshen glanced back at his comrades. The once-handsome face of Anatin, as nasty as he was charming, and Safir, who'd have been a hero of legend in some earlier age. Kas too – a woman he could trust his life to as utterly as once he had Sanshir, but sharing little else with her. Kas was an archer and he thought of her as a bow, master-made and all the more beautiful for her craftsmanship.

Sanshir was a dagger blade – no less incredible in the forging, but you could never forget that cutting edge, never avoid it. That was why they had been so good together, so intense in their relationship. They had both been fascinated by the danger of the other and the equal they had found. How it might have lasted, Teshen could never see, but it had been intoxicating. Until his treachery.

And mebbe that was just part of our relationship. That unspoken friction. It was always going to tear us apart, some way or another. I was just the one to run headlong at that breaking point.

He looked past Kas. Reft the quiet monster, Llaith who was more like Anatin than he liked to admit. Even the newcomer Suth, who was glorious just like Sanshir, and remorseless, relentless Toil. Many of the Cards were background noise to Teshen. He had never had time for those who were unexceptional, but Anatin had assembled a remarkable crew and its light attracted more. Few employers had ever fought at their side as Toil had, but Teshen saw a kindred spirit there.

He wasn't as broken as Lynx, but with the wisdom of years Teshen knew how important the crew was to him. Back then it had only been Sanshir. The rest hadn't really mattered, for all they had fought side by side and toasted the fallen together. Perhaps age had mellowed him. Perhaps he understood himself more fully and had found what he had always needed here. Not riches, nor fame. Luxury meant little to him, worthy causes even less. Toil and he differed there. Her cause was everything and she would do terrible things in its name, but Teshen had never cared.

No, he needed the company of monsters and heroes, a crew of the extraordinary within which he fitted. Nothing else was worth standing beside and that, it turned out, was all that mattered to him. To stand and face the world. To challenge the odds with a pantheon at his side.

With one hand on his long knife, the other on the butt of his mage-gun, the Bloody Pauper smiled and walked the streets of Vi No Le once more.

Lynx watched the sun reach the horizon. Orange light spilled across the sea and cast gold feathers of cloud across the sky. Above, the skyriver bore a gilt edge while below, the shadows reached long fingers across the city. He shivered despite the warmth that lingered in the air.

The memories of days spent in Shadows Deep merged with older, more mundane horrors. The desire to help, to not sit idly by, clashed with those images. The golantha hurling itself across the chasm, the crack and crash of stone as it tore through the empty hallways in its pursuit of them.

Occasionally, he dreamed of it. The creature of flame and shadow chasing him down the open street that overlooked the great rift and on to the bridge. Footfalls so heavy they shook the ground and took his feet from under him. Flickering tongues of light that lashed at his heels as he stumbled on. The enormous strength and fury of the creature, the exhaustion and helplessness he'd felt when he stopped to face it.

Shadows Deep had kept him from arguing with Anatin. Lynx suspected that even Anatin had been surprised at that and part of Lynx hated himself for his meekness. A small voice at the back of his head claimed he would stand up when the golantha came. That when they were first sighted and the line wavered, he would walk up and join them, but Lynx wasn't certain.

The fractures in his soul and the demons that scratched away at his mind would play their own part, Lynx was only too aware. That he was not always in control of his mind was a spectre constantly lingering at his shoulder, but never more so than at times like this. And so he and all the other Cards had followed Teshen up into the high-reaching warren of Vi No Le district.

It was the tallest of all the districts, three huge tors on Xi Le island, and two lesser piles on now-deserted An Vir. Hollowed out by generations of mages, the smallest of those was ten storeys high with a network of raised bridges connecting them to the smaller blocks skirting them.

Teshen had led the company unerringly through the great warren of the district's largest island, Xi Le, where even Kas would have got turned around. It had almost come as a shock when they emerged into the evening sun on the other side, where the narrow, layered streets ended abruptly at a long, thin plaza on the shore.

From there, two bridges led on to the small stepping stone island between Xi Le and An Vir, called Si Jo. Aside from one kabat's home, a quartet of copper-sheathed domes on the lagoon shore, Si Jo was much lower. The best view was offered from the shallow roof of a warehouse, less than a hundred yards from the narrow channel where Sanshir would lead their stand.

Civilians continued to flee through the streets while the fighters of every district assembled ahead with whatever weapons they had. If anyone wondered why these foreign mercenaries were not marching forward, no one bothered to ask in their haste – the uncertain threat of sundown eclipsing all other thoughts.

The Cards spread out in silence, some lying on the warm stone roof and others with their legs dangling over the edge. Lynx could see the low district of Cliffbase and An Vir island were largely deserted now, but not entirely. Some refused to leave, others could not and had been abandoned to cry piteously in the quiet darkening streets. Behind were the great cliffs where the tysarn roosted and above which many now circled – lit by the sun in the west, bright and warm in the day's last light.

333

It made the two dozen or more caves look all the more forbidding and dark, but Lynx knew they still had a short while. The sun was falling between the outer islands of the western chain and its light lay slanted across the cliff face. Only sunset itself would release the promised horrors from their prison.

'Not long now,' someone said uselessly.

There was one bridge remaining across the channel between Si Jo and its larger neighbour, An Vir. The rest had been demolished, both this side and all those between it and Cliffbase, to only limited protest. The Shard's authority had proved enough to sway the argument when people refused to believe huge monsters of ancient myth were advancing on the city. He could see mages fussing over the high stone bridge that remained, clearly preparing it as a trap for anything trying to cross.

'Where did the Wisps go?' Lynx asked Toil, suddenly remembering he'd not asked before.

'Somewhere on the cliff itself,' she replied. 'They're all mages, they'll wait until the golantha are distracted then slip in while their backs are turned.'

'Distracted with killing all of us,' Anatin said. 'Still, they gave us the warning I guess.'

Toil nodded. 'They risked their lives to do it.'

'Unless this is all some sort o' Wisp practical joke,' Anatin chuckled. 'We realise at sundown their whole clan is watching us shit ourselves and laughing at us!'

'I hope so. Losing face is better'n the alternative.'

Anatin raised his stump. 'Preaching to the converted there, missy.'

The shore of the island was a gentle curve around from the east that came to an abrupt point not far ahead of where the Cards were sitting. The remaining bridge was just fifty yards short of that point and as a result, the bulk of Sanshir's command were stationed there. The Cards had arrived too late to see all of the preparation work done in An Vir, but the mages had clearly been busy – undermining buildings, blocking streets and using every trick they could think of to channel any attack where they wanted it.

The regular troops were confused and apprehensive as sunset loomed, growing fractious as a result. Their fighting was normally done on the move, pack-hunting tactics and feints instead of a standing defence. There had already been fights between rival crews, some clearly unwilling or unable to believe their orders. Sanshir had apparently ordered the destruction of every barrel and bottle of booze on the island to limit this, but how long the détente would last come nightfall was anyone's guess.

The kabat guards, the only ones armed with mage-guns, were slightly better disciplined but only barely. The longer they watched, the more Lynx recognised the sense in Anatin's orders. He still felt a coward about it all, a betrayer of the code he tried to follow, but he had no illusions. He *was* afraid, terrified of the thought of more than one golantha, and seeing all this, the commando in him saw a rabble ripe for shattering.

If it doesn't hold, Lynx thought to himself, *all us marked Cards are going to want to run fast, not just the mages. I'm guessing we're all on the menu now.*

He felt a nudge. It was Llaith offering him a smoke, which he took gratefully. The ritual of lighting and puffing was a balm as much as a distraction, familiar movements that helped to quell the turmoil inside him. As he smoked and the breeze snatched each puff away like an angry spirit, the last of the sun's light sank into the sea.

'No elementals,' Sitain said in a whisper from further down the line. 'Not one, even here.'

'Even around you?' Lynx asked.

'Nowhere,' she replied, pointing. 'Must be a sign the Wisps are right.'

There were mages down in Sanshir's rabble, either brightly coloured or in dark coats depending on the habits of their guild. Lynx couldn't see them at this distance, most swallowed up by the mass of troops down there, but he'd seen many arrive. Tanimbor's cadre had been first to take their place, so Teshen had reported, and half a dozen of the Shard's own led a unit of fifty. There should be elementals of all kinds buzzing around the small island, drawn to the mages of their particular flavour, but perhaps that flavour was what kept them away. The creatures that hunted magic would have elementals as their natural prey.

'We should be down there,' Atieno muttered to himself, not for the first time. 'Not sitting here too far away to help, too close to escape.'

Lynx didn't think Atieno sounded any more convinced than he was. For all that Atieno also wore a Vagrim ring, he'd had a lifetime of avoiding battle, from unleashing the strange corrupting power inside him. It made this no simple decision for either of them.

A treacherous voice at the back of his head reminded Lynx he should lead the way down, show the others what was expected of them. He was the soldier, not Atieno. Rarely had he let himself be swayed from what he thought was right. He felt a sour taste in his mouth as he watched others get ready to fight.

'You won't make the difference,' Toil said; the voice of Lynx's grubbier angels. 'They've got a hundred or more mage-guns, four hundred Mastrunners, maybe a hundred mages too and what, ten of those are marked? It's not people who'll get to decide how this fight goes.'

'And I know you ain't much for following orders, you and Lynx both,' Anatin added, 'but this is one o' those times when I need them followed. For your good as well as mine. I'm willing

336

to let a lot o' shit slide from all you idiots, but we're working and I'm in charge. That means you damn well do what I tell you or your friends could start dying.'

A sigh seemed to rise up from the patchwork army ahead of them, a shiver that acknowledged the encroaching dark. For the Cards, the light was still good enough to make out most of the scene ahead, but down on the ground it would be very gloomy. They had planted torches all along both shorelines of course and long tails of flame pointed out towards the lagoon where a large gun- and mage-laden boat bobbed fifty yards from the shore.

'What's that?' Kas asked, pointing at the shadow-smeared cliff ahead. Lynx followed her finger but saw nothing at first. Others hissed, a few cursed, but it took him a long time before he worked out what was attracting their attention.

Then he saw it, a flicker of movement at one cave mouth. Not the spreading of a tysarn's wings, the beat at the air as they stretched their limbs and pushed off, but something altogether larger and more tentative. Lynx glanced to the side and saw a thin column of small tysarn emerge from the hellmouths in the centre of the lagoon. It didn't look like as many as before, but he had no idea what that meant.

At one of the larger caves, not far above the water, there was a sudden commotion and flurry of movement. Three enormous tysarn crawled out into view, bellowing furiously. They were as big as the ones who'd attacked the lodging house – as big as Teshen said they got before being unable to fly. Two reached out with their wings and began to gather the air, while the last continued to crawl across the shelf of rock.

The first two heaved themselves up with heavy strokes of their wings, their great bulk dragging them down to brush their tails across the water before climbing. More than one of the Cards hefted their gun and kept a wary eye on those, but most watched the third. It made no attempt to fly, for all that it was also looking to get away. Instead it crawled on its four wings, making for the safety of water.

But something was wrong with it. Its movements looked heavy and sickened, one of the larger forewings unable to push forward properly. When it did reach the edge of the ledge, it seemed not to notice – just kept on going and flopped over the edge to tumble into the sea channel below.

Lynx found his gaze darting between that ledge and the cave that Kas had pointed out. The earlier movement hadn't resolved into anything more, but then almost in unison a shape appeared in the fading light from each dark entrance. He found himself recoiling at the large head that emerged, just a head but one the size of a tysarn. At that distance it was hard to make out much more, even with his unnatural night-sight. But when Kas – the keenest-eyed of the company – hissed and instinctively drew back he felt a chill.

There was no veil of shadows that flickered with inner fire around this golantha, as there had been in Shadows Deep. This one was entirely different. It was hard to make out but it emerged as though tasting the air, strange flickering movement surrounding it. Long, slender legs reached forward from a blunt shape Lynx could barely make out. There was a jagged tangle of something at its face, no eyes or mouth that he could make out, and all overlaid by a greenish flicker that danced around it.

As he tried to picture the golantha from Shadows Deep, he realised it looked nothing like this – that had been more dragon-like, with clawed feet and a horned head. This one he saw nothing recognisable in for a while, until he remembered what else lived down there.

Even as he thought that, Toil gave a moan.

'Oh screaming hells, that's one big bug!'

It really was big, Lynx saw. Massive compared to the tysarn that had plucked people off the walkway even. Both of the shapes to half-emerge from the caves seemed of the same type, but how long that dark body went back was anyone's guess.

Faint flickers of light illuminated it, random bursts of greenish yellow running down its length and casting a slight haze around its head. Then a pulse of light seemed to well up from somewhere inside it. The light flowed outwards to trace the lines of its lower body, creating an after-image of many long, angular limbs and terrifying, twitching mandibles. The upper part remained dark, but from that glimpse Lynx guessed its back was armoured in some way and Kas seemed to agree.

'See that?' she called. 'Plated back, the light beneath?'

'Like that damn thing that bit me in Shadow's Deep!' Sitain moaned. 'And killed Olut – but shattered gods, how big is that?'

'That thing was just a centipede grown big,' Toil warned. 'Golantha are creatures o' magic as well as flesh. Might be it's got some extra surprises all of its own.'

The creature came further out on to the shelf and the Cards gasped as one. It was huge – longer than the golantha they'd faced and with a dozen more legs emerging from beneath its plate armour back. The rear third tapered, but ended in a bulbous lump it kept slightly raised as it quested at the edge of the rock shelf with long whips of antennae.

The antennae left a faint trail of light as they moved, resembling fronds drifting on a sea current then twitching back. There was a mass of mandibles behind those, six or more lit up by the strange glow and all in movement. They reached out to the air and Lynx couldn't shake the sense of anticipation he saw in those gestures – nor the memory of the last golantha's glowing tongue-threads that had hungrily gathered up every mage cartridge it could find.

The other one was half over the shelf it had emerged on to, lumpen tail held high as it anchored itself against one corner of the cave mouth. It twisted left and right as it sought purchase on the cliff face, but soon found enough to move down and disappear from view.

'There's rocks down there,' Teshen said. 'Not much, but if they don't mind getting wet they can pull themselves along from one to the next. No boats can use that channel.'

'More!' someone shouted, pointing. 'Oh Veraimin's breath!'

It was true – another had emerged from a different cave and a fourth followed the boldest as that one vanished behind the jutting towers of An Vir. Each was as big as the first, each unnervingly swift and lithe.

'You count four?' Kas asked the group in general. There were murmurs of agreement, but Teshen shook his head.

'We saw four,' he said. 'There are more caves behind An Vir. We've no idea how many are coming.'

'Aren't you a little ray of sunshine?' Anatin said, almost ripping his jacket as he tugged his hip-flask out. He took a long swig and then another.

'If they reach us, don't be precious with your ammo, boys and girls. Hard and fast is the only way, keep shooting after you're sure you're in range!'

Chapter 35

Lynx tried to follow the movement of the golantha through An Vir's streets, but the tors and blocks obscured everything. Flickers of movement would catch the eye only to disappear when Lynx tried to focus on them. The largest streets had been lined with lanterns, small points of light that afforded some sense of the layout to his mage-enhanced eyes.

The minutes stretched on. The darkness deepened. The tysarn circled. Lynx could feel the anticipation in the air, but An Vir remained still and silent.

'Has the water stopped them?' Lastani asked after a long while.

'Mebbe just looking for a way around,' Toil said. 'Hunters take their time.'

She pointed at the boat, off-shore. 'Wouldn't they have spotted them? But if they have crossed it, surely we would have heard something? The mages have seeded An Vir with traps.'

'It's likely they can sense the traps and avoid them.'

'Or eat 'em,' Lynx said. 'If anyone's going to build a trap for me, I like to think they'd make it out of bacon.'

The idea seemed to startle Lastani. 'They're taking their time, dismantling the traps on the way?'

'Why not? They've got a fight ahead of them. Nice to have a snack beforehand, keep the strength up. A little trail of appetisers leading to the main course.'

On the shoreline, the mages clearly agreed, either that or some scout had sent word. There was a shudder in the channel between islands and for an awful moment Lynx thought the golantha were going to erupt from it. Then the water began to part and his tattoos started to glow as the linked mages put their strength to work.

'What're they doing? Clearing the damn way?'

'Exactly that,' Lastani said, pointing. 'Look, they're dragging a wall of water each way, a blend of earth-magic and water-magic.'

'Let's hope the beasts ain't as fast as they look,' Anatin muttered. 'Or clever.'

'They're beasts,' she insisted. 'Presented with an easy path to a great source of food.'

'Beasts ain't stupid.'

'Nor do they think too hard,' Toil chimed in. 'Something that big isn't likely to be in the habit of hesitating. If you're the scariest thing around, you're rarely cautious.'

'That right, Reft?' Anatin called with a half-laugh.

The big man nodded and gave a wide grin, displaying none of the fear the rest of them seemed to have. His pale, hairless skin took on an even more ethereal quality in the moonlight. For all the Lynx had seen Wisps up close and knew they were nothing similar to human, it still gave him pause.

With the magic humming inside him, all of the marked Cards possessing a faint shine in the gloaming, Lynx watched the darkness ahead. Unexpectedly, there was a brief burst of light from one of the streets, oil spilling from a lamp as something knocked it flying. A great moan rose up from the assembled army and bursts of mage-light swept over the far shore, searching. Lynx saw the line shudder as men and women recoiled from the sight, but somehow it held.

A golantha had emerged from a side-street, perhaps kept away by the lights, and it moved tentatively into the open. Antennae quested across the road-mouth, ten yards or more long. Those it brushed back and forth over the ground, touching doorways and balconies as it investigated its surroundings. When it advanced, it moved just a few yards, antennae flicking forward like fishing lines – casting out ghostly spider-threads of light which were then gathered back in to its mandibles. Whatever trap had been laid there, faint pops of light appeared in the air then were drawn in and consumed.

He could see no eyes, nothing beyond a repulsive, shifting tangle of overlapping mouthparts. The legs seemed all the more massive now; a shorter, thicker upper part that hinged into a lower section three times the length. The golantha planted legs on buildings on either side of the island's wide street and tasted the air.

Behind it came a second, drawn by the taste of magic and with less caution. That seemed to make up the first one's mind and it surged unexpectedly forward. They moved with deceptive speed, segmented bodies that rose and fell with fluid grace as they crested a boathouse built right at the edge of the land and continued on into the now-empty channel.

A volley of gunshots rang out, a stuttered boom that lit up the night air with icer lines. The first creature was hit at least twenty times, icers slamming into its armoured body and sparkers bursting in a brief haze across its mouth. Veteran of too many gunfights, Lynx realised the sparkers vanished far faster than normal – even as the golantha shuddered under the massed impacts. Antennae and mandibles both embraced the jagged burst of lightning and ripped the magic from the air. But then the water hit.

A massive wave slammed into the side of the golantha, sweeping in from the right as tonnes of water were released by the mages. Already halfway across the channel, the huge monster was unable to resist that sort of power. Lynx saw it tumble before the churning waters closed over it and bore it away – under the high stone bridge and beyond. Off to the left, the other wall of water held until the first reached it. When they met a great explosion of spray burst fifty yards up into the sky then the greater momentum carried it on. The torrent drove out into the open sea where a churning white wave fanned out wide over the dark water.

The second golantha had only managed to get half of its body into the channel when the water came. It too was hammered sideways, its front half pulled from the ground by the force of water, but the rear legs still gripped the shore. For a few tortuous seconds Lynx saw it fighting the enormous power of the water. Then something broke and it began to slip.

This golantha wasn't swallowed by the tumult, however, having resisted the initial impact. Instead, it was dragged along the shoreline until it reached the stone bridge that spanned the channel. It slammed into the far end of the bridge and was almost dragged underneath, but somehow found purchase.

The bridge itself crumpled under the impact, already weakened by the mages. Great chunks of stone crashed on to the monster's back, others tumbled towards the sea. Some were gathered up by the assembled stone mages. Those were dragged to the near shore as the golantha fought to right itself, twisting and slashing at the crumbling stub of bridge.

Mortar flaked away as grey-white magic swarmed around the stone, then chunks the size of a man's body were hurled at the golantha. They were accompanied by more gunfire, icers casting flashes of white light while burners spilled briefly over the roiling waters and the light mages cast flares up into the night air.

Lynx watched the beast shudder under those impacts, but even the huge pieces of stone clattered off its armoured back without causing any great damage. The burners spilled across it all too briefly, a flash of light then drained of magic.

One huge piece of stone was hoisted, no doubt by a marked mage or some sort of linked group. Whatever the source, the golantha felt the power from across the channel. It darted forwards, antennae and pincers slashing at the air. The greenish threads seemed to tug at the magic and unravelled it in one movement.

The stone fell and people screamed. A gun went off and sparks burst over one section of the defenders, then a cartridge case exploded. The burst of light illuminated a shower of blood and several of the light-flares winked immediately out.

'Get ready to move,' Anatin shouted.

Lynx hefted his mage-gun, preparing to advance on the horrors, only for Anatin to point into the streets of An Vir. There were more coming, three huge dark shapes outlined in flickers of pale green light.

'Shitting gods!'

The defenders saw them a few moments later and the gunfire started. It barely made the golantha hesitate. One slewed sideways and ascended a housing block, a few deft steps of its dozen or more legs taking it ten yards above street level. There it only attracted more of the gunfire, but most of that clattered harmlessly off the creature's back-plates. But one earther cracked its chitin armour while another snapped a leg and demolished the balcony it was using for a foothold. The golantha faltered, instinctively coiling in on itself as it was hurt, but their respite lasted only moments. It dropped with a great thump and made for the ruined bridge as the first pulled itself on to the shore.

Grenades were thrown and the far shore momentarily vanished in a sudden, furious display of fire and lightning. Lynx winced at the brightness and clearly so did the golantha, but in moments the light was gone.

Even as they reared up, away from the light, they drained the magic feeding it. Another flopped heavily forward into the water and drove through – just its antennae held high above the surface for a few seconds. Then it emerged with terrible fury on the other side. At point-blank range the gunfire could hardly miss – Lynx couldn't count the icers that slammed into it – but the golantha didn't seem to care.

Once across, the huge creatures simply waded forward into the ranks, not trying to kill. Broader than an elephant and twenty yards long, each barged through the crowd and laid waste to everything in its path. The Mastrunners were armed with every pole-arm and axe they had, but few even scored a blow. The golantha were too big, each leg a barbed and spear-tipped tree trunk. They tore through thee ranks like a siege weapon.

The only thing that slowed them was bursts of light as the city's mages attacked, but none of their efforts seemed to hurt it. Each attack drew the target's attention and the golantha snapped up mage after mage, holding them broken in its mandibles as it drank the magic from their bodies. It didn't take long for the mages to stop. A last few hurled chunks of stone then more earthers roared out. Those seemed to hurt it, but by then there were four golantha across and the army was overrun. It was over and the Cards were already running ahead of the rout.

'No tastier treats than us!' Deern yelled, drunk on terror or just drunk, as they piled down the steps to ground level.

There was crazed, panicked laughter from some of the other Cards. Lynx felt it bubble up inside him too, but he was too focused on keeping his feet to let it out. Down at street level it felt suddenly darker, a confusing array of roads ahead of them, but Teshen ploughed forward without hesitation.

Shadows lurched from every corner, dark jagged shapes that made Lynx's hands clamp fearfully around his gun grip. They were all experienced enough to keep fingers away from triggers, but even in this mad flight he could hear sporadic gunfire and screams from behind them.

The whoosh of wings made them all flinch as a large shape swept overhead. Someone fired an icer up at the beast, the rest offered just curses as the tysarn passed by. Lynx looked around.

'Oh screaming spirits, not the tysarn too!'

They were all flying low over the district now, apparently unafraid of the golantha. Even as Lynx watched, he saw one plunge down behind a nearby building. Someone shrieked in fear and pain as it landed, the sound continuing for several long seconds before being cut abruptly off.

'Drawn by the blood!' Toil yelled. 'They're not the golantha's prey.'

'Fucking bully for them,' Anatin shouted back. 'Move, you bastards!'

Teshen stood at the end of the street, mage-gun propped on his hip and waving them forward. As Lynx stumbled forward, Teshen levelled the gun and fired at the sky above them. The white streak of an icer punched through a descending tysarn and the creature crashed dead through the door of a nearby building.

Lynx barrelled on, almost shoving Toil out of the way in the process. The Cards ran out into a square with a vine-draped arcade around the inner face. There Anatin called a halt and demanded a head count. The Knights of the company reeled them off swiftly, Lynx's finishing last because Atieno was last to enter the square.

The ageing mage was struggling, he could see that, and Lynx offered the man a shoulder as Suth finished the count. There were two missing, somehow lost in the rush, but before Anatin could decide if there was time to look for them, Kas gave a yell.

A huge shape appeared over the rooftops and shock hit Lynx like a punch. At a distance it was massive. Up close the golantha was vast and all the more terrifying. He could hear the swish of its antennae as they swept above the square and the air shimmered with sickly green light. The twitching mass of mandibles made him physically recoil as much as the large main pair of pincers that reached round from the lower side of its head. Three yards long, each ended in a curved spike longer than Lynx's falchion.

In that glow the tattoos of the marked Cards seemed to blaze. The mages became bright beacons, casting jagged light. The sheer variety of prey seemed to surprise the golantha and it hesitated, turning from left to right as it tried to make sense of the scampering figures. At the base of each antenna was a glistening block slightly lighter than the rest of its body – looking for all the world like a dozen mismatched cobblestones. With a jolt Lynx realised they were its eyes and his hands were already moving. His icer struck just to one side of the eye, but four more shots followed then a pair of earthers rocked it backwards.

The golantha heaved up, but seemed to roll with the blows like a seasoned brawler. Before anyone else could fire, it bent over the rooftop and snatched Lastani up in its pincers. The young mage screamed in pain, white-blond hair blazing in the strange light. Magic began to stream from her body. Lynx felt the strange tug inside him as it began to flow and the air grew colder.

He realised the golantha was feeding as she screamed, drinking in the magic that roared through her body. One pincer had gone through her thigh. Lynx could feel the pain in her cries as blood welled up fast and black in the stark light. He reloaded, backing away to some pretence of cover, while Reft raced forward. The Knight of Blood launched himself off a stepped planter at one end of the vines and hammered a hatchet into the pincer pressing bloodily against Lastani's back. It was hard enough for the weapon to lodge, but the golantha ignored it as Reft dropped and rolled away.

348

Just then Lastani's cry took on a note of fury. The air around her shimmered with power, an icy haze that was being drained by the feeding golantha. In that moment she seemed to remember she was the most powerful mage in the Riven Kingdom. Anger eclipsed pain and Lynx felt a great jolt forward as the draw of magic intensified. All around him the marked Cards stumbled, fumbling as they reloaded. Their tattoos went from shining to an eye-watering intensity.

The chill in the summer air turned ferociously cold. The air began to glitter with ice crystals and Lastani's hands blazed with power. She didn't try anything clever, just hurled power at it with all the strength she had left. The golantha recoiled now, faltering in its greedy efforts as a hoarfrost burst across its head. The ice moved rapidly, Lastani put every ounce of her strength into the wild stream of magic – more than even the golantha could absorb.

For good measure, some of the Cards off to the sides fired into the underside of its head, clear of Lastani. The shots seemed to pain it more now. An earther tore a chunk of flesh out and one of its great legs went limp. The golantha tried to turn and flee, to shake Lastani from its pincers, but ice now coated its head. Its eyes were blind and it seemed disorientated, too confused to know how to escape, while all the time Lastani continued pouring her energy into it.

A second earther sent chunks of ice flying as it buried into the creature's side. The golantha flinched away from the impact – clumsy in its movements, but still its limbs were huge and powerful. With one sweep of a leg it brushed Lastani away and she fell in a spray of blood. As soon as she was out of the way a wave of earthers hammered it, three or four wrecking the antennae and mandibles of its mouth before it was able to pull away.

Himbel and Sitain ran to Lastani. Himbel had a belt in his hand ready to tie off the leg, but then he faltered. Lastani clutched at the wound only feebly, her mouth working but only a hoarse croak came out. Blood flooded over the stone floor of the square. Her leg had been almost entirely torn off.

'Shit, Sitain! Help her!'

Himbel had to grab the stunned mage by the collar and shake Sitain before the shock faded. She gaped wordlessly at Himbel for a moment then realised what he meant and placed a hand on Lastani's head. One brief pulse of magic and the young woman flopped still.

'We can't stay!' Anatin roared.

There were other Cards down, several crying in pain from where they'd been batted aside by the golantha. Each was grabbed and hauled away, Teshen shouting directions from the rear of the square. Lynx went to grab Sitain and pull her back. The young woman resisted for a moment then looked pleadingly up at him.

'She's dead, or as good as,' he said, more roughly than he intended. 'We can't bring her.'

'But the tysarn!'

He nodded and knelt at Lastani's side. The blood still flowed from her leg, but when he put his fingers at her throat he couldn't find a pulse. 'Sorry, girl,' Lynx muttered. 'You didn't deserve this life.'

Someone knelt beside him, offering forward a mage cartridge. It was Anatin, a burner in his fingers. Lynx took it with a nod and folded Lastani's hands around it.

'She was one of us,' Anatin said. 'I ain't leaving her to be lunch.'

Lynx got up, one hand under Sitain's armpit. 'You want to do it?' he asked, offering his mage-pistol to her. As she stared at it, Lynx pulled a sparker from his cartridge case. 'Damn things aren't much use anyway against these monsters.'

Sitain looked away and shook her head so he pushed her in the direction of Teshen where the rest were already moving.

Loading the gun, he saw an approving nod from Anatin before the commander followed, chivvying Sitain on with his usual gentleness.

Lynx followed, stopping at the edge of the square and looking back. Lastani almost looked peaceful there, alone on the ground while all seven hells continued to rage in the streets beyond. Finding he had no last words, Lynx fired the sparker and was halfway gone by the time the burner ignited.

Chapter 36

The Cards crossed to the largest island of Vi No Le without further incident. The screams and explosions on Si Jo continued, but not even Lynx thought about turning round. Across the rooftops raced groups of Mastrunners, colourful and ragged, heading for the great warren of Xi Le. They moved faster than the Cards, leaping across narrow alleys or using archways to cross the wider ones. It was more dangerous though, as tysarn of all sizes danced and wheeled above the city.

Lynx saw one woman not attacked, but simply caught up in a flock of the small scavengers. Her balance thrown at the wrong moment, she fell heavily from the edge of a building. Her head caught on a water trough with a sickening crunch. The tysarn swirled and fluttered away in confusion then returned as the smell of blood drew them back.

Other Mastrunners were picked off by the larger beasts, the frenzy of last night reasserting itself. The biggest dived on swept-forward wings then furled their rear pair and snatched at the fleeing humans with expert timing. Those two or three yards long hunted in packs chasing people down. Of the golantha there was no sign. Lynx couldn't even say if the one Lastani had tried to freeze solid was dead or not, only that he wasn't going back to find out.

'This way,' Teshen called.

He ducked into one street and headed for a long, shallow ramp that led to one of the honeycombed tors. It was big enough for pack-sloths to climb several abreast, but the enclosed streets meant the tysarn were unlikely to pursue them. Lynx was blowing after the sprint away, but as more Mastrunners crossed the bridges between islands, he was glad they'd been ahead of the flood.

There were people here still, terrified faces at windows and doors – even some kids running around the narrow streets. Their faces were a strange mix of terror and elation, the chaos of what was happening driving all sense from their heads.

Teshen led them up two levels. Lynx looked around in wonder as he found himself on an open street of eateries and workshops, the shuttered frontage of a bookseller of all things facing them as they emerged. Teshen wasn't interested in that, only the views it provided. Between the organic curve of support columns and buildings, Lynx could glimpse the lagoon. Lights on boats dotted the water, even a few flashes as those on board fought off tysarn. The opposite shore proved a strangely serene counter-balance to this eastern flank, lamps and mage-lights outlining Casteril's streets.

The Cards barged a handful of locals from their narrow vantage point behind one deserted eatery. From there they had an almost unfettered view of Si Jo – the light of the moon and skyriver enough for all of them to gasp at what they saw.

The islands were largely dark, aside from small fires burning and what few lanterns remained. Cliffbase was barely visible in the gloom. Given the lack of chaos in Casteril, Lynx guessed the hundred yards of open water between Cliffbase and the Duegar canal had proved enough to dissuade the golantha.

'Look!' Teshen said, pointing to the lagoon side of Si Jo.

One golantha there was lit up by flames, a stuttering burst of sparkers describing its long armoured back before the magic abruptly vanished. There were pockets of resistance all across the island, just a few hundred yards in length, but most of the Mastrunners were dead or running.

'Another,' Kas shouted. This one was still by the scene of slaughter, picking its way through the shattered corpses of the shoreline. 'It must be feeding from cartridge cases.'

Lynx felt his guts tighten. He remembered all too well using a cartridge case to lure the golantha of Shadows Deep out on to the bridge.

Gods, I really am a fool, he reflected. *Now I've had time to think about it properly, would I be that brave again?*

'There's one in An Vir,' Suth said. 'Must have found another trap the mages left for them.'

'That's three, and one washed out to sea, if the gods are more merciful than Safir's always saying,' Anatin added.

'If we're trusting that bunch of smashed-mosaic cretins,' Safir replied, 'we'll be chewed-up lumps by morning. But if they could survive the open sea, they'd be swimming in the lagoon by now.'

'So we need to lure the rest to the shore?'

Teshen snorted. 'Any ideas how?'

There was silence. If anyone felt like chiming in with a suggestion, the mood sunk even lower when the head of a fourth golantha emerged from behind a large building – dusted white in the moonlight and obviously injured, but more than a match for the intemperate tysarn that had decided it was a potential meal. Winged beasts swirled all over the small island, most of the tysarn population apparently drawn by the scent of blood.

'How are we doing for ammo?' Anatin said at last, physically shaking himself from the stunned vigil they'd fallen into. 'This ain't a spectator sport, boys and girls, we're still in the game.'

'Barely,' Lynx said. He was peering into his cartridge case as he spoke. 'I hope we've got more earthers in reserve. Those things took more'n a few hits and they're still going. I've got three.'

Several others said something similar and Anatin snorted. 'It's more'n we had back in Shadows Deep, but I'm starting to regret coming to a city so far from a Militant Order sanctuary.'

'And most o' the city's ammunition is now just a late-night snack,' Teshen agreed, pointing at the butcher's yard of Si Jo. 'Best we go find Toil's new friends at the Waterdancer Guild before we go monster hunting. After this, the Shard will tell 'em to make us anything we want. Profit's no use to the dead.'

'Hunting?' Sitain exclaimed. 'We're the gods-burned prey, not the hunters. They're after us!'

Teshen shrugged. 'We might as well take the fight to them.'

'Five!' Kas broke in. 'Not that I want to upset you all, but there's five of the little scallywags.'

She pointed out over the city and counted the golantha off one by one. The last was a smaller creature from what Lynx could see, but still at least fifteen yards long.

'Call it four 'n a half,' Anatin said. 'Lastani's mostly done for one I reckon.'

'And she's dead now,' Lynx reminded them. 'Maybe Atieno could take another down the same way, but that's quite a price to pay and there'd still be three left.'

As they watched, one of the remaining golantha smashed into a large building complex surrounded by five narrow towers. With a jolt Lynx realised it was a temple to Insar. White bursts of icer fire streaked into its flank from one of the towers, but the god's protection proved empty. With a flick of its head the golantha smashed the tower to the ground and returned to its burrowing.

When it couldn't bludgeon its way through the stone walls it curled its bulbous tail around instead. Lynx didn't see what happened but there was a blur that seemed to cover the whole near side of the building.

The stone roof of the temple had been decorated with black stones, imported from gods-knew where and arranged to outline a prayer to Insar that shone in the moonlight. Under the attentions of the golantha, the rooftop blurred and the message was erased. Wisps of smoke started to rise from the rooftop then points of white light appeared all across it.

Without warning, snakes of red light burst out over the surface and merged with the brighter spots – growing in intensity as smoke started to pour from it. The fiery light lasted just a few seconds, but then the golantha renewed its attack on the temple roof. This time the stone simply crumbled under its assault, great chunks of stone flaking away as it tore it open and started snatching up the mages cowering within.

'What in the deepest black was that?' Toil breathed. 'Oh hells.'

'Recognise it?' Anatin asked.

She shook her head. 'No. Maybe – I dunno. You've heard of stonecarver beetles?'

'Aye – Veraimin's burning eye, they do that?!'

'No, but they spit some sort of chemical that softens stone, makes it possible to tunnel in it. These things, shit. I've heard Wisp tales of creatures like stonecarvers, ones that use heat instead. Never seen anything like it myself, until now.'

'So we can't hide from these unholy bugs o' the deepest black?'

Toil looked around at the vast structure they were within. Xi Le was the tallest part of Caldaire, sporting three tors like small mountains that had been carved out by mages over a dozen generations and more. The one they were currently in had to be two hundred yards across and upwards of sixty high.

'They could fit down this one street,' she said, 'but not the rest, and this place is huge. How long would it take them to dig their way to us? Would they bother if our mages don't give them reason?'

'They can sniff us out!' Sitain almost wailed.

'But this is the Mage Isles,' Toil pointed out. 'There are mages everywhere. Got to be easier prey elsewhere, no?'

'We'll make a mercenary of you yet, Toil,' Anatin said drily. 'But the night's got a long way to go still.'

'You want to go bang on the Waterdancer Guild's door, hope they've got something in reserve?'

Anatin shook his head and looked around at the street they were on. 'Nah,' he said slowly. A grin crept across his face. 'I think Teshen's got the right idea, or the back half o' one anyway.'

'Fancy sharing?'

He nodded. 'We go with the tried and tested method. Boys and girls, madmen and monsters – it's time we took charge of the situation.'

'How?'

He flashed a smile at Toil, the old rogue in him coming to the surface even in these desperate circumstances. Anatin shrugged his shoulders and straightened his jacket then set off down the street. He made for a slope that led to the higher levels of the great stone tor.

'In the finest traditions of the Cards,' he called over his shoulder. 'Someone hold my beer, I'm gonna try something.'

After ascending one level and moving up to the next, Lynx had worked out Anatin's plan. Varain was still asking about the beer, in case someone had magically found some on the way, but that soon petered out. The running and ascending was taking its toll on many of them as Teshen led the way up.

The streets soon became narrow and unpleasant, just one of decent width on each level from what Lynx could see. The rest were cramped, dark and suffocating to Lynx's mind. Mage-stones marked the occasional crossroad, but more often the

357

ceilings were crisscrossed with thin threads that glowed faintly bluish. It was nothing like enough to shine a light, but even in the darkest parts a person could see the direction of the tunnel.

'What's with the cobwebs?' Deern grumbled as they filed down an alley just two yards across. 'Funny-looking spiders there.'

Lynx looked closer and realised Deern was correct. There were thin white insects standing within the strange overlapping threads, some sort of small, boring caterpillar to Lynx's untutored eye.

'Mages bred 'em centuries ago,' Teshen replied. 'At least, that's what folk said when I was a kid. The threads are sticky, anything gets caught and they'll all wander over for a meal. They're no bother to people, unless you . . .' He sighed. 'Deern. You've already put your hand in one, haven't you?'

'Wasn't I meant to?'

Teshen just shook his head and kept on walking. The intermittent sounds of the golantha faded into the distance as they marched higher. Near the top of the tor, the levels narrowed significantly. To Lynx's surprise, they came out on to one open section that occupied the whole level and displayed a sudden degree of opulence.

'What's this?' Anatin asked, looking hopeful.

There were stone mage-carved tables all around the perimeter of the room, wide window spaces on the lagoon side and narrow, slanted slits on the seaward side. Intricate mosaics dominated every wall, beautiful renditions of sea battles for the main, and ornate iron lanterns hung from hooks in the ceiling.

'A high hall,' Teshen said, wrinkling his nose. 'A fancy pub to the likes of us. Rich folk use it, mingle with their own kind and look down on the rest of the city.'

'Never got an invite?'

Teshen gave a small grin. 'Killed someone here once, does that count?'

'Bloody does in my book,' Anatin said. He turned to a wide doorway opposite the entrance. Above it was a painted sign, perhaps in deference to tavern tradition, portraying a flat basket piled with small orange fruit.

'Reft, if you'd be so good as to knock?'

The big man did just that. The echo of his fist thumping on wood ran around the wide room, but elicited no response. He tested the handle just to be sure, but it was locked fast.

'Forgive me, my friend,' Anatin added after a moment. 'I did actually mean kick the shitting thing in.'

Reft shrugged and did just that. It was a fairly solid door and the first two kicks didn't do much. Just when Anatin was drawing his pistol to put an earther through it instead, the lock burst and Reft yanked the door back.

Before anyone could enter there came a shout from upstairs, a man's voice that sounded more indignant than threatening. Anatin cocked his head at Teshen.

'Who in the deepest black do we think we are?' Teshen translated. 'And don't we know who *he* is?'

'Hoi, you up there!' Anatin yelled. 'You speak Parthish?'

'Of course!' came the reply. 'This establishment caters to the cream of mercantile society.'

'Good. Where's the beer?'

'Are you mad? Who are you to come here and make such demands?'

'The fella who's about to walk up these stairs with his gun at the ready. Anyone shoots me and you'll all burn, I promise you that.'

True to his word, Anatin loaded a burner into his mage-pistol and led the way himself. The rest of the Cards followed eagerly, but at a slight remove in case anyone did accidentally shoot. Before long, most of them had filed out into an elegantly divided space where the stonework was finished in polished wood. There were two sections for private parties, a bar with a glittering sea-glass top and an open storeroom displaying stacked bottles and even a few small barrels.

Occupying the foolish position between the Cards and alcohol was an old man with dark skin and a white beard. He was flanked by a pair of pale-skinned thugs who could have been Teshen's younger brothers at first look. They were smartly dressed in white shirts and headscarves all embroidered with a concentric circle device that, Lynx guessed, was the establishment's emblem.

'What is the meaning of this?' the old man demanded, but his indignation was cut off by a man emerging from one private section.

'Commander Anatin?' he said in a quiet, breathy voice. The stranger was a few years younger than the proprietor, with light brown skin and long black hair poking out from under a plain blue headscarf. He was bigger than either of the guards and still looked every inch a fighter, but wore a devotional pendant to rival any high priest's.

Anatin paused half a beat then, to Lynx's surprise, gave a deep and florid bow. 'The one and bloody only. At yer service, sir.'

'Is that why you disturb me, to offer your service?'

'Just came looking for a drink. We didn't know you were going to be here.'

'You came looking for a drink – here?'

'Something like that.'

The man gave a fastidious sniff and two more grey-clad guards emerged from behind him, three more from the other private section. The three men and two women had mage-pistols in each hand and a murderous look in their eyes.

'In these confined parts, we all die if it comes to a confrontation.'

Anatin raised his hands in mock-surrender. 'We ain't stupid . . . well, I ain't anyway. We're not here for a fight, didn't even know you were here, Kabat. Ah . . . no disrespect, but afraid I don't even know your actual name.'

'Jo-Sarl,' Teshen said in a quiet voice beside him.

'Then like I said, Kabat Jo-Sarl, I'm at yer service. Though, come to think of it, I had come here with something in mind so maybe I could be at yer service afterwards? Assuming any of us are alive by then?'

'What are you here to do?'

'Something really bloody stupid.' Anatin grinned. He pointed with his one remaining hand at the proprietor without taking his eyes off Jo-Sarl. 'First of all though, I'd like this man to start us a tab. It's been a shitty evening so far and I think a dozen bottles might take the edge off things.'

Chapter 37

'Anyone else find that weird?'

Lynx looked around at the other members of Tempest as they settled at one of the stone tables and he started pouring amber beer from a jug.

'Weird?' Llaith puffed out his cheeks. 'You're gonna have to narrow it down it bit there, friend.'

'The kabat. He didn't even blink the whole time Anatin was talking.'

Lynx glanced instinctively back at the door to the upper room, but there was no one there. The murmur around the room had prevented his words from carrying anyway, Varain in particular becoming voluble now there was beer at hand.

'Didn't move, didn't blink – nothing. Like a statue he was.'

'I'd have probably slapped myself to see if I was dreaming,' Llaith said. 'Given what's going on and what we're about to do.'

Lynx took a long drink and gave an appreciative sigh. 'Shattered gods, why don't we get this stuff more often?'

''Cos it's a quarter-isle a pint!' called Himbel from the next table.

The company surgeon was looking almost cheerful now, something that didn't exactly detract from the strangeness of their situation.

'My advice – as your physician o' course – is to make the most of it and hope Foren don't have a heart attack when he gets the bill.'

'Shame the kabat's sticking around,' Llaith added. 'Makes it harder to run out on the bill when the most powerful man in the city's bloody watching.'

'We pull this off, he'll let it slide,' Lynx said. 'If we don't, they can pin the bar tab on our graves, if there's enough left to bury. Probably a fitting memorial anyway.'

The older man cackled. 'Aye. Here lies Anatin: leader of men, gambler of lives, lover of sarcastic women and defaulter of bills. We commend his soul to any god able to prise his purse from his cold, dead hands.'

Lynx went to the window and peered out. This high it was chilly, the windows open to the elements. It was full dark and even with his unnatural eyesight he could make out little detail of the unlit islands. Casteril's lights still looked undisturbed.

Only a few lamps had been lit, barely enough to see what they were loading into their guns. As he watched, Lynx realised he could just about make out the dark shapes of at least two golantha, still prowling the wrecked streets below. In the confusion and chaos, with tysarn swarming above, he imagined a lot of mages and soldiers with mage-guns had holed up somewhere quiet, hoping to let the storm pass.

'Drink up, my heroes!' called a voice from the doorway.

They all turned to see Anatin with what looked like a bottle of brandy in his hand, grinning madly as he addressed the company.

'The finest of soldiers, the great heroes of Caldaire!'

'Where?' called someone.

'Oh yeah, they couldn't make it so we're stuck with—'

Anatin hesitated then blinked down at his hand. The tattoo on it had started to glow, a steady outline of white in the gloom. Quickly it turned brighter and Lynx felt his own do the same. Somewhere above them, Sitain was pulling all the magic she could manage and casting it out into the night sky.

Part of Lynx wanted to smile, picturing a few luckless tysarn that might fly straight into that stream of night magic. Just a few days ago he'd idly thought the massive lizards looked majestic as they flew above Caldaire – those double pairs of wings like some strange dragon-butterfly. Recently his feelings towards them had significantly cooled. He didn't smile, though. It was hard to find any sort of mirth here, except perhaps at the bottom of a cup. He drained his beer, just to check, but even that didn't seem to work.

'Everyone ready?' Anatin asked, suddenly serious and sober.

There were grunts of agreement. Men and women slapped the breeches of their mage-guns in instinctive reminder. The room was occupied by Tempest and Stars, with a few extra hands from Blood. Upstairs with the two remaining mages was the rest of Blood, no doubt all keeping their cartridge cases as far from Sitain as they could, just in case. The suits of Sun and Snow were on the level below and it was there Anatin was heading, to be with his own suit.

Man doesn't give two shits about the suits normally, Lynx thought all of a sudden. *He leaves that to Payl. Gods – that can't be a good sign, even Anatin's nervous. This was his bloody idea!*

He kept those thoughts to himself as Kabat Jo-Sarl followed Anatin out of the stairway. The proprietor was long gone, having muttered something about his inventory before scampering away, guards close behind. Jo-Sarl hadn't been in such a rush, but there was no need for him to be present for what was coming. A few more guns wouldn't make the difference after all, and he didn't have anything to prove to anyone.

Especially when most of his crews and Holding guards just got slaughtered. His lot have lost enough already.

'Luck to us all,' Anatin called over his shoulder as he headed down. 'I'll get Safir to say a prayer.'

'Tell him to be quick about it,' Suth said from another window. She was looking down and pointed. 'They've taken the bait.'

Anatin didn't respond, just hurried on down. Teshen was the one to raise his voice in response, being the highest-ranked Knight in the room.

'Remember the plan. Keep your cool unless you get a face full of monster. Wait for Reft to start and pick your target. We don't have much ammo so make sure of every shot. Questions?'

There were none so Teshen nodded. 'Cases in the middle of the room. We won't be in a long fight here and best we don't smell any more delicious than we need to.'

Lynx hesitated at that, it went against the grain, but eventually he saw the sense – even as his skin glowed with power. No need to make the damn things pause here. He pulled the earthers and one sparker for good measure, tucked those into his belt and dumped the near-full cartridge case behind them. Most Cards had an earther to hand and he offered one of his spares to Braqe when he saw her load an icer.

The woman gave him a tense look. She'd hated him from the first moment she saw him and the time in between hadn't lessened that much. Braqe was one of many people in this life who'd seen the Hanese commandos up close and personal. She'd lost friends and family to them and Lynx served as a constant reminder of that.

'I'll save the icer for you,' she said finally and took the cartridge.

It wasn't much of a thank you, but he knew he wouldn't get anything more. Pride and hate might not always eclipse sense, but they would steal its words. He grunted in return and looked away.

Lynx had to lean out of the window to see the ground. Suth was already doing so and when she noticed him, she pointed to the shore-side base of the tor.

'There, see it?'

Lynx did. The golantha was already climbing, while two others behind it turned their heads up, antennae waving at the air above. From here the greenish haze was barely visible, just affording a sense of the beast's body. Lynx couldn't make out any more detail, but he was in no great rush.

'Can you make it do this yourself?' Llaith asked, tapping the tattoo on Lynx's hand that glowed brightly.

Lynx shook his head.

'Shame, you two together would be useful if we've run out of candles.'

Something thwacked against the back of his head and clattered to the floor, a wine-jug stopper of all things. Llaith turned, rubbing the back of his head, to see Kas give him a little wave. She wore a light jerkin embroidered with a Madman of Stars playing card, tattooed neck and arms exposed to cast their light over the woman beside her.

'No need to throw stuff,' he grumbled at her.

'Sure about that?' she replied.

Lynx blinked at Kas, struck by the sight of a mage-gun in her hands more than the bright willow-pattern shining from her dark skin. He'd never seen her carry one before. Even in the most desperate battles she preferred her bow.

She gave a mock tip of the hat to Lynx, calling, 'Luck to you,' before turning back to her own window.

The Cards were spread around the room, half of which had large open windows. The seaward side had only narrow, angled slits that kept the worst of the breeze away. Sitain was above them on the lagoon side of the room. Lynx realised he could sense this now. The magic flowing through him had spread some sense of awareness to his surroundings, with Sitain a fizzing spark in the centre of that.

The pull of magic was strange – he could feel it flowing

out, but not where it came from. It wasn't the tattoos, they were just some conduit from what he could tell, but it didn't leave him fatigued as it welled up and surged away. On the contrary, Lynx found it invigorating, but to his inexperienced senses it was coming from some part of him that seemed inexhaustible so far.

'That's two,' Suth commented, dragging Lynx's attention back to the present.

'Which one?'

'The small one. Lastani's is at the base, thinking about it.'

He looked down and saw the first golantha had ascended a fair way already. The huge creatures were taking their time and ascending with care, but given their size and the two dozen massive legs, it wouldn't take them long to cover the climb.

'You know what'd really piss me off?' Suth muttered, not taking her eyes off the beasts.

'What?'

'We know nothing about these things,' she said. 'What if the fucker suddenly sprouts wings and flies?'

Lynx gave an instinctive shudder. 'If that happens, I'm blaming you,' he advised.

The nearer golantha moved steadily closer. The skyriver's light picked out the lines of its body more clearly now. There was an oily, iridescent sheen to the plates on its back that Lynx hadn't seen before. Its great legs hauled it steadily upward, body pressed close to the uneven ledges and rough walls of the tor.

'Pull back,' Suth said, spreading her arms and taking a pace backwards. 'Let it pass.'

None of them needed much encouragement. While there was a certain fascination with watching it come, the golantha somehow looked bigger when it was heading straight for them, its whole body unveiled in the moonlight. They crept back a few paces, guns at the ready but fingers off the trigger. In a tall stone building, the last thing they needed was panicked earther-fire. Anatin's gamble was big enough already.

They collectively jumped as a huge spear-like leg flashed into view and hooked on the corner of the window. For a moment nothing more happened and Lynx had to fight the urge to shoot at the leg itself. Clearly it was finding footholds scarcer here, almost at the very peak of the tor, but with so many bloody legs, even if he did shoot this one off, the victory might be short.

A dark shape surged forward, eclipsing the skyriver's pale blade and the scattered stars behind. Lynx glimpsed pincers and crooked mandibles then they were gone, replaced with a dull underside that filled the entire window. Flickers of greenish light surged down its ridged belly, swirling like smoke across water. Lynx felt a strange dryness on his skin – the golantha drinking magic from the air as it flowed to Sitain.

He felt a moment of panic as the dryness became a heave, an arid storm that veiled the marked Cards, but before he could do anything there was a booming gunshot. They ran to the window, Suth leading the way with both pistols levelled. She'd wrapped bandages around each wrist in anticipation of the heavy recoil from earthers, but for a moment they could see nothing more than its hard carapace belly to shoot at. Then there came more gunshots from above.

The golantha shuddered under the impact. The rippling light turned jagged and stuttering as it was driven back. Lynx fired almost at point-blank range, aiming to one side of what he could see and hoping it would be close to a leg. The earther slammed into it with incredibly force – a fist of darkness that buckled and split what it met. Then a sharp crack came above followed by a bright flare of light – sudden and shocking.

Llaith fired as Lynx reloaded, targeting the same spot and winning a gout of blackish gore. The golantha reeled and a leg flashed into view as it scrabbled for grip. Suth shot that on instinct, her mage-pistol kicking back so hard Lynx heard the gunslinger yelp with pain. The light above burned on. Clearly, Toil had borrowed Anatin's preferred little trick to ruin the night-sight of enemies, hoping it worked even better on cave-dwellers.

As Suth fired again and Lynx heard a crack echo out from the leg, he realised the golantha should have drained the light-shot's magic by now. His tattoos continued to shine and Lynx realised Sitain had turned her magic on the beast too, following Lastani's example as best she could. Clearly the combined assault was distracting it so he stepped forward, hoping to catch sight of where it was gripping below. The beast obliged by rearing away from the battering it was taking, just as a new assault from the level below started.

The Cards of Sun and Snow fired again and again as Lynx's comrades battered at its belly. He couldn't see anything of what was happening above, but a leg was blown clear off beneath them by someone. The golantha thumped hard against the tor's outer wall, thrashing furiously to keep its precarious grip. The light that had confused it now faded and the damn thing was still there so Lynx risked putting his head right out.

There – off to the left he saw another leg with a secure hold. He didn't dare miss so he fired at the shoulder. If he missed as it moved he'd probably still damage the thing. It twitched just as he fired, but turned into the shot by accident. He caught the joint just where it met the body and the whole thing exploded in a shower of gore.

The golantha gave a strange sort of chittering screech, a sound the likes of which Lynx had never heard before. It was soon drowned out by the boom of more earthers as the Cards pressed their advantage. A huge pincer flashed down as it dipped to protect the wound, a blade two yards long flashing across Lynx's face. It scored the stone and held, but another gunshot above made the whole thing shudder.

'More!' Lynx yelled, drunk with terror.

He only had one earther left, but someone else fired into the centre of its belly and drove the beast further back. Just as he clicked the breech of his gun shut, Lynx suddenly noticed the golantha rear up, away from them. From where he stood he could see that wasn't good. The monster turned its lumpen tail inwards, underneath itself. He remembered what had happened to the temple and his stomach gave a lurch.

'Now! Now!'

He scanned for a target, anything that wasn't moving. For a moment his mind was a whirl, the shuddering twitching golantha just too massive for his head to take in all at once. And then he saw it. A leg, to one side of the lower level – the Cards below probably couldn't see it without leaning dangerously out.

'Suth!'

He didn't bother to point, didn't even aim at the golantha. Its foot was hooked on a jutting balcony – solid stone and enough to take a considerable weight all on its own, but earthers were made just for that. Lynx pulled his mage-gun tight into his body and checked his breath. One moment of calm and then his eyes settled properly on the target – the hooked chitinous blade that held it there and the stone beneath it.

Lynx fired and the blade-foot vanished along with a chunk of balcony. It was as though a great weight had suddenly slammed on to the golantha. It lurched down, clawing and scraping at the tor's flank as it fought the pull of gravity.

'Someone shoot it!' Lynx bellowed.

When he looked back the others were all just staring at him blankly, gun breeches open. Time stood still. The only movement was the golantha, fighting for purchase and rearing up again, and the rising horror in their faces. Then a figure flashed into view, vaulting the stack of cartridge cases and sliding along the smooth stone floor all the way to the window.

Teshen had his gun already levelled. He whispered something, but the words were lost to the breathless panic in Lynx's heart. Then he pulled the trigger. His earther struck the golantha just beneath its head, at the base of its great pincers, and smashed it back.

For a moment it seemed like it would hold, then its remaining strength failed and it started to topple. The scrape and crack of legs bending and breaking from where they gripped the stone was the only sound as it arced back into the open air.

Then it was falling – no longer a creature of horror, now just twisting tonnes of armour and legs rushing towards the stone below with shocking speed.

Chapter 38

For a long while Lynx simply sat on the floor, unwilling to move. His bones had been reduced to jelly, the reality of what they'd just faced hitting him in that moment of calm. Others had gone to the window – had whooped and cheered as they watched it fall and declared the beast dead. Part of Lynx didn't want to look in case it turned out to be a lie. In case those dozens of legs twitched once more then heaved themselves up again.

Teshen reported the second faltering at the first's demise. It wasn't climbing any longer and seemed unsure what to do. What intelligence the golantha had – and surely they had to have some, these ancient horrors of Duegar myth – meant they did not swarm forward like unthinking beasts. But nor did they know how to respond, it appeared.

'They're just standing there,' Suth commented. 'You reckon they're thinking?'

'Even animals think,' Teshen said. 'Probably not used to seeing their own dead. The sight of one spread across the street has to give even the nastiest horror of the deepest black a moment's pause.'

'Let's bloody hope so. We can't have many earthers left.'

Lynx exhaled slowly, trying not to picture what would happen if the second golantha pressed the attack. 'Anyone got a drink?'

'Anyone dead?' shouted Anatin as the commander emerged from the stairway.

'No,' Teshen reported.

'No,' Toil added, emerging from the upper stairway.

'Shattered gods, I could get used to hearing that,' Anatin said. 'Drinks are on me!'

Lynx heaved himself to his feet. 'Sure those things aren't coming up?'

'Reckon not. They ain't stupid,' Teshen said. He didn't keep his eyes off them all the same. 'First the water trap then this.'

'They've fed well,' Suth added. 'Why take the risk?'

'That's good enough for me,' Lynx said. 'Someone point me in the direction of booze.'

The remaining Cards appeared from both the levels above and below. They seemed evenly split between exhausted and elated, but all had the energy to find a seat as those from above carried armfuls of assorted bottles.

'You two,' Anatin ordered, pointing mostly at random. Eventually his finger settled upon two of the lower-ranked Cards. 'Yeah, you – stop trying to hide. You're on first watch. If those things move, shout.'

He settled down and took a drink, then pushed himself upright again. 'All of you, listen up! So long as those things remain out there, we take it slow, understand?'

'Slow?' several Cards echoed, aghast.

'You heard me. We're only safe at dawn when they've crawled back into the deepest black. Until then, any Card who can't aim their gun gets the usual punishment.'

That quietened most of the Cards, that and the sight of Reft cracking the knuckles of his huge hands.

'So who finished it off?' Toil asked after her second cup of wine.

'Teshen,' Laith said, nodding over at the man. 'Swooped in at the last moment. Honestly, it were heroic. I went all weak at the knees and girlish.'

Lynx refilled his cup. The wine here really was excellent and doing a fine job in helping him feel normal again. Just as he swallowed, the image of the golantha's pincers lunged to the fore of his mind and Lynx gave an involuntary shudder. He threw back the next cup and went for more, heedless of Anatin's warning.

'Just as well you weren't here, Toil,' Llaith added. 'Lynx felt the same and you probably don't need to see that.'

'Not with Teshen anyway,' Toil said. 'Layir now, that could maybe work, but Teshen? I'd start to think Lynx had got an unhealthy interest in troublemakers.'

Llaith spat out a mouthful of wine. 'Hah, yeah,' he said, wiping his mouth. 'What a mistake that'd be.'

'Movement!' called the Card assigned to the nearer window, Colet. She leaned further out of the window. 'One of you with the weird eyes, come take a look. I think they're leaving.'

Before Lynx knew what was happening, Llaith and Toil had each raised one of Lynx's hands.

'Well volunteered that man,' Anatin smirked. 'Go on then.'

With a shake of the head Lynx did just that. Colet leaned close and pointed. 'That's one, right?'

He nodded. 'And there's the little one. Where's the one Lastani iced?'

'Round there I think,' she said, pointing.

'Ah yes. Curled up to die, with any luck.' He scanned around. 'We're missing one.'

'Maybe in there,' Colet said, 'down the big street they attacked from.'

'That's three heading back the way they came,' Lynx called over his shoulder. 'It's promising.'

'Good!' Anatin shouted back. 'Now just stand there until you see 'em crawl back into the cliff.'

Muttering curses, Lynx returned to the vigil, but Toil brought him another cup and touched Colet on the shoulder, indicating that she should go back to the tables. The green-eyed woman gave her a look of slight surprise but didn't wait for an explanation.

'Is this better?' Toil whispered to Lynx after he'd pointed out the ones still in sight.

'What?'

'Fighting these horrors above ground?'

He managed a smile at that. 'Sure, better.' Lynx winced. 'Not exactly good, but I'm certainly glad we're not underground again.'

'Don't say I never listen to your requests,' she said with a smile. 'But . . . better? You're good right now?'

He rubbed a hand over his face. 'Ah, I guess so. Terror's chased all the demons away, or something anyway. That's healthy right? I mostly need sleep at the moment. Too drained for much else.'

'We all do. I'd like to work out a plan first though.'

'Plan?'

'For dusk tomorrow.'

Lynx shook his head. 'Shattered gods, Toil. Can't we get past this night first?'

She shook her head. The fatigue was obvious in the dark rings around her eyes, but he knew she wasn't one to give in to tiredness. 'I like to have a plan. Won't get to sleep without one.'

'So we'll go see your new friends and gather a load more earthers. Enough to finish off three of the bastards this time.'

'They can't produce many in a day,' Toil said. 'Not enough given how many we used on that bastard.'

'Ah shit.' Lynx was still a long moment then turned around to look at the whole assembled company. 'Hey, you lot! Can anyone think of a plan for the other three golantha? One that doesn't rely on us finding a few hundred earthers in a city that just got 'et by magic-hungry monsters?'

There was a long moment of quiet. Eventually, Toil muttered, 'Really? You're just throwing it out to the group?'

'No idea's too stupid right now.'

'You sure about that?'

He grinned. 'Heh, that must've been the drink talking. Still, some aren't total idiots and they're all survivors. There's loads of experience and killer instinct in this room, even if it's been somewhat preserved in spirits.'

Toil waited a while. 'I wish Lastani was here. Girl didn't have much common sense, but she could approach a problem with a clear head. I can use a mind like that, sharp and bright and ready to be turned to purpose.'

'Well she ain't here,' Lynx growled. 'She's dead and much as she deserves more, we can mourn her if we survive the week.'

Toil paused. 'Yes, Lieutenant.'

'Don't take the piss.'

She gave him a look that he couldn't interpret, but there was no joking there that he could see.

'I'm not,' Toil said at last. 'I just . . . no, nothing. Forget it.'

The silence around them continued. The longer it went on, the more a sense of gloom seemed to descend over the mercenaries. Just when Lynx was about to give up and get back to drinking, a hand was raised.

Everyone turned. The patrician face of Atieno tightened under the scrutiny, but he didn't hesitate.

'No earthers?'

'I can't believe we'll find enough in time,' Toil confirmed. 'Or get enough made.'

'Then I may have an alternative.'

'But you're only bringing it up now?' coughed Anatin, slamming his palm against the stone table top. 'Dammit man!'

'It's ah . . .' Atieno hesitated. 'It is not a good alternative.'

'We're all out of good ones,' Toil said with a wolfish grin. 'Stupid and fucking insane ideas are all that's left to us. Fortunately that's our strong suit.'

'Then I need to see your friends at the Waterdancer Guild.'

Dawn came all too soon. One moment Lynx had given up on his fitful attempt to sleep, listening to the snores of his comrades, the next there was a glow of light at the window. The Cards had settled down quickly; too weary to drink hard, too drained to play any more than a few desultory hands of Tashot.

Toil had burrowed into his lee, working herself into a space that was apparently comfortable and drifting straight off. Visions of claws and mandibles kept interrupting Lynx's own efforts, however. Each twitch was rewarded by Toil's elbow or chin pressed deeper, like a cat objecting to its owner's comfort, but something akin to sleep took him until first light at least. When the rising sun became too insistent to ignore, Lynx went to search upstairs for something to eat.

A tankard of beer slaked the morning thirst, but if there'd been any food it hadn't lasted the night. He was about to give up and head downstairs when instinct prickled at his neck. Fingers tightening around the tankard, Lynx turned to discover it was only Sitain, watching him from under a looted window drape.

'Morning,' he said, the words escaping as a croak that prompted him to take another swig of beer. 'How're you doing?'

'How do you think?' she said, sitting up. There was a defiant look in her eye, as though she was just daring him to comment on the tears streaking her cheeks.

'You two were close.'

'Close enough. She wasn't just some dumb-fuck merc. That's rare in my life right now.'

He let that comment go. This morning wasn't going to look pretty to any of them and he was used to Sitain's particular brand of cheeriness.

'What now?'

'Now?' Sitain stood and brushed herself down. Even with the new clothes her recent pay had bought, the young woman looked bedraggled. Hair plastered and greasy, cheeks thin, eyes bloodshot. 'Now we go find a way to kill these things.'

'Just like that?'

'What else do you want? My life ain't my own, that much has been made clear, but those things need to die. If I can help, I will.'

Lynx nodded. He didn't much care for the look in her eye. It had something of Toil's sharpness about it, but in a more fragile package. She was right though, they had a job to do. The time for worrying about what had been broken could wait.

'Got anything left after last night?'

'I'm tired. Dead tired, if I'm honest, but I'll manage. Come on, let's get them moving.'

Rousing the rest of the company turned out to be nothing a few kicks couldn't fix. Before the sun was much higher the Cards had gathered their kit with a minimum of complaints and started down the various flights of stairs through the tor. A few faces met them on the enclosed stone streets, more at the window-openings of apartments, but the district remained subdued by the time they reached what passed for ground level in Vi No Le.

There they paused, some unspoken thing passing between them as the Cards stared down the half-open avenue towards Si Jo. No one much wanted to go and inspect the destruction, but a moment of silence was spared all the same. Lynx could see the bones of shattered buildings from where they stood; jagged walls, thin trails of smoke and silence broken only by the harsh cry of scavenger birds.

'Come on,' Anatin ordered after a short while. 'Time to get back to the lodging house and see if any of our lost lambs made it home.'

With Teshen in the lead, the Cards tramped back to Auferno. They did their best to ignore the cries and laments that slowly built across Vi No Le's islands. Even at the high bridge that crossed the main channel into the lagoon, between Nquet Dam and Auferno districts, they avoided looking back at the battered islands behind.

Auferno mourned too, home to the Shard's Rest and many guilds, but it wasn't as brutalised as Vi No Le. There the events of the last night took on a more surreal quality in Lynx's mind. It was like walking out of a nightmare – not quite into wakefulness, but at least a dream where he could pretend for a while longer.

Most of the Cards slunk back to their beds once they reached the lodging house, watched by the disappointed owners who'd clearly hoped they'd died in the fighting. They didn't speak when Anatin threw himself in a chair and asked, remarkably politely given his bloodshot eyes and heavy limbs, for some hot food to be brought out.

Lynx lingered, seeing the Knights of the company join their commander without a word. Soon he was waved into a seat by Anatin, alongside Kas, Atieno, Toil, Llaith and Aben. Neither Card who'd gone missing, Crais and Sethail, were waiting and no one seemed optimistic.

'Guess we need a plan,' Anatin said at last. 'Atieno, are you sure about what you said last night?'

'Sure enough.'

'That's all I get?'

The tall mage ran his fingers through his dark beard as he thought. 'You want more?' He shook his head. 'I have nothing to offer, only my belief.'

'And if it doesn't work?'

'Then I will be dead. Everyone nearby too.'

'But come nightfall, we won't be left standing with our dicks in our hands and only harsh language to throw at the monsters?'

'Ah, I see. No. If it works, we will know. Any mage in the city will be able to tell you so. Perhaps the marked Cards too. It . . . ah, it will not be a good thing.'

'No good things here,' Anatin muttered. 'If you're willing to risk your life, I'll take that guarantee.' Anatin looked around at the assembled mercenaries. 'Now – assuming it does all work, we'll be limited to a few. A strike team up against those monsters. Is that a problem for anyone?'

No one spoke, but Lynx could see Aben looking round.

'Aben?'

The big man shrugged. 'I'm Toil's man,' he said. 'I ain't arguing if she ain't. I just follow orders.'

'And now you're following mine.' Anatin scowled, the sparker-scar on his cheek twisting further under the expression. 'I don't much give a shit about anyone's opinion now. We've got blood in the game and I for one don't much want to run away.'

'Sure about that?' Payl asked softly. 'We're ordinary mercs, most of us anyway. Get paid and live long enough to spend it.'

He turned to face her. Payl was his right-hand woman and the pair were close enough he wasn't going to take her words the wrong way. Her young lover, Fashail, had been killed on the wall when the Mastrunners attacked. Lynx could see grief like a ghost in her shadow, but one she wasn't ready to acknowledge yet.

'Mebbe I'm getting old,' Anatin said. 'Mebbe hanging around some o' you fools has rubbed off. I ain't taking any more blame for this shit-storm than I have to, but between friends . . . hells, we're in it and who else is there? This ain't our home, this ain't our fight really, but I ain't a monster who'll turn his back either.'

'Don't worry,' Toil said, leaning forward. 'We can dress it up in self-interest later. The pay, the fame, the favours it'll win

– whatever means other merc crews don't point and laugh, but this is a fight we need to win. This city's gone otherwise.'

'How kind of you,' called a voice from the courtyard's main entrance.

They all turned to see a figure lingering in the shadows of the hallway. She stepped forward – it was Sanshir, Teshen's former lover. Her clothes were torn and bloodstained, her face bruised and further darkened by simmering fury.

Anatin sighed and stood as he recognised her.

'Now's not the time for this argument.'

Sanshir paused. 'I just presided over a massacre. I saw good men and woman torn apart in front of me. Friends of mine killed almost by accident. You may be the arseholes who started it all, but I've got better things to do than blame you right now.'

'Why are you here then?'

'You took one down, what else? Half my crews are dead so far as I can tell, including my best. Insar alone knows what mages survived that, but you managed to take one down. I've seen its body. We can't get too close for the tysarn feeding on it, but it's dead. If you're the best tools for the job of saving Caldaire, you are what I will use.'

Anatin nodded. 'We've got a plan – of sorts anyways. We used near enough all our earthers to kill that one. The things are too clever for the same trick twice an' it took one hell of a beating. If the second one had climbed up, we'd be dead.'

'Tell me your plan then.'

Anatin hesitated. From behind Sanshir, one of the owners came out carrying a great glazed pot, sky-blue in colour and containing what turned out to be rice porridge.

'Join us – we'll tell you as we eat. After that we're gonna hold a gun to some mage's head. All in the interests o' saving your city, o' course.' He grinned.

Chapter 39

'Is anyone else stuck on all the ways this plan could go wrong?'

Lynx's question was met with mostly silence and scowls at first. It was almost like that wasn't the most helpful thing to say at this point. Finally, some people started to shake their heads.

'Nope.'

'Not me.'

'I was trying not to.'

'It's not like we could make things worse at this point, 'cept for us ending up dead.'

That last comment from Sitain brought a round of scornful looks. She reddened slightly. 'What? How could it get worse at this point?'

Lynx raised a finger. 'Firstly, being dead isn't popular in the Cards, what with us being money-grubbing thugs who prefer getting paid to fighting. Secondly, these are creatures of magic an' we're basically going to throw some new magic at them. It might be we end up faced with something even more horrifying than we did yesterday, instead of a pile of insect-mush.'

'That's not going to happen,' Atieno said from the far end of the table.

They were seated around an oval stone table at one end of the Waterdancer Guild's central courtyard – five Cards plus Sanshir and three senior mages. The mages seemed a genial lot, all in shades of blue and white, with a fat woven belt bearing their guild colours, but looked shocked by their losses.

The guild itself was beautiful. This was one of the oldest in the city and while it was small, it occupied a prestigious position on the lagoon shore. The stone had been sculpted with a level of artistry normally reserved for palaces. Every doorway and window bore intricate decoration, while the stone floor itself contained swirling patterns like a branching river. Stone archways ringed the interior of the courtyard in typical local manner, detailed with leaves and creatures of all types and supporting a canopy of pungent wisteria for most of the sixty-yard perimeter.

There were troughs of water and a snarl of wooden hoops at the other end from the Cards where the mages practised their art, but any lessons had been cancelled in light of last night's calamity. The senior mages with them, led by a man with pale, bluish-tinted skin and crazed white eyebrows called Ustirtei, were all very old. Clearly they had sent younger, stronger mages in their stead to the slaughter. The weight of mourning and guilt lay heavily upon their shoulders.

Lynx suspected under any other circumstances, the Cards would have been thrown out of the guild's grounds by now – whatever the threat, whoever it was accompanying them. Instead they were too dazed and shocked to argue much, leaving Sanshir to treat their cooperation as assumed.

'How long will it take?' the Vi No Le Kaboto asked.

Atieno spread his hands helplessly. 'The theory is simple – the basic magic I could perform now, with assistance.'

'So how long?'

Atieno didn't reply, only cast a look towards the three guild mages. Ustirtei blinked at them, as though waking from a bad dream.

'I . . . this is not known.'

He broke off and turned to his colleague, a leathery old man with crew tattoos on his eyebrow and cheek. He still wore a red Casteril headscarf over his shaved head, though it had to have been fifty years since he'd run with any crew of that district. They exchanged a few rapid-fire sentences then the second man nodded.

'This thing is unknown,' he said. 'For this we must test. It would be weeks before we would normally be ready.'

'We've got a few hours.'

The man stared at Sanshir, open-mouthed. 'This is madness!'

'This is our best option,' she snapped back. 'Many have died already – the city will not survive weeks.'

'Surely there's a way to estimate,' Toil broke in. 'You've produced weapons before. You must have a process whatever ammunition you're producing.'

'This is not ammunition!' the man shouted back, his cracked voice betraying the weight of fear and loss. 'This is heresy and madness! This is more risk than we can ask of any mage. The process is not simple even if this man was not involved. To use an unknown process, one written about only as a warning to others, is already a great danger—'

'More risk than heading out at sundown and trying to fight the golantha?' Toil said, interrupting.

'I . . . both are more than we can ask of any mage.'

'One's going to happen come sundown,' she replied, sounding calm and matter-of-fact rather than angry or threatening. The subject at hand meant anything more was unnecessary. 'Whether you want it or not, that's beyond your control. The only question is whether you want a shot at survival.'

'We should evacuate the city,' Ustirtei muttered at the other man's side. 'Flee where they cannot pursue.'

Toil raised an eyebrow. 'The whole city? You want to ask tens of thousands to pack up and leave in the next few hours. Can you magic up boats? A bridge to the mainland?'

'Not everyone is in danger, from what you tell us.'

'Oh right – so just you and your friends need to run away? Leave everyone else where they are, hoping the huge monsters don't lay waste to the whole city on general principle?'

Sanshir stood and put her hands on her hips, the pommel of a long knife just below each one. 'You are not leaving. I need you to give this city a chance of survival – your knowledge and your God Fragment. If I have to surround this guild with every Mastrunner left in the city, I will.'

Atieno held up a hand. 'How long does each cartridge take to produce, once you have everything ready?'

'A few minutes only,' the man replied.

'And how many can a mage produce in a day?'

'The process is taxing, for the lead mage most of all. Who would that be? You?'

Atieno shook his head. 'I cannot be in contact with the God Fragment myself – nor anyone with these tattoos. It might crumble to dust.'

'Then it must be one of ours . . .' He shook his head. 'How does this even work? The lead mage is always the one to shape and focus the power, to determine the characteristic of the cartridge.'

'We will find a way. Perhaps a mage of tempest for me to work through. How many?'

'A mage is tired after ten cartridges.'

'How long before it becomes dangerous?'

'For this, it will be dangerous from the start. For a normal mage, mistakes depend on experience and a mage of tempest has none. We do not have one in the guild!'

Lynx looked up at that. 'Didn't we meet one? That woman at the healer guild, Sirr or something like that?'

'Olen Siere of the Shudoren Guild?' Sanshir said, standing. 'I know of her. I will bring any tempest mages they have there.'

Anatin pointed at Reft. 'You and Lynx go with her. Take a few more guns plus Sitain with you. We're not at home to asking in a friendly way, not today.'

'That won't be necessary. They know me.'

He shrugged. 'The buggers are no use here anyway, and like you said, they know you there. They know you're not a fool or a trigger-happy madwoman.'

'I do not understand.'

'They know what you're capable of, you're one of them. My lot look *exactly* like trigger-happy crazies who'll shoot anyone getting in their way and don't give a shit what mess they leave behind. Folk hesitate in the face of strangers with guns. It's harder to argue with us.'

She considered the point. 'It will not be necessary,' she said, 'but it will not hinder me either. Are there any other mages you need?'

'Stone, wind, light and ice,' Atieno said, 'along with Sitain.'

They all looked at the guild mages, who shifted uncomfortably. 'We can provide those,' Ustirtei admitted.

'Then do whatever you must to get ready. I will be back soon.'

The threat of violence proved unnecessary. In the great bowl of the Shudoren Guild there were injured everywhere, mages and Mastrunners lying side by side while the healers worked frantically to save those they could. Lynx had been in enough field hospitals to know how lucky these people were, mage-healing not normally being for common folk, but it remained a hellish sight.

Many of the mages looked exhausted. They had worked through the tail end of the night after the golantha retreated and the Mastrunners of every district started to drag their friends here. It was all rough and ready work, Lynx saw. Many of the staff there were performing normal surgery too – the magic used to patch up injuries before stitches and bandages could be usefully employed. Siere, when they found her, was grey-eyed and sluggish even after Sanshir outlined what was expected of her.

The mage did not speak for a long time, even when Lynx fetched a cup of brandy for her, guessing the woman had barely stopped all night. He fitted it into the stiff, clawed fingers of her right hand, where the skin was more grey than brown – product of her strange, corrupting magic. Siere sipped at the brandy gently, staring glassily at Sanshir but at least finding time to think.

'You need me for making cartridges?' The old woman pondered that for a long while before finally the reality clicked into place. 'Cartridges?' she exclaimed in a louder voice. 'No! Impossible, I am a healer!'

'Not today,' Sanshir said. 'The best thing you can do for these people is to come with us.'

'I know what you intend – it cannot be done. I am not strong enough and I am not such a fool as to try.'

'We have a strong mage,' Sitain said. 'We need you to be the conduit for the work.'

The tiny mage shook her head with such force that in her fatigued state she almost tipped sideways off her seat and Lynx had to steady her.

'It is too much, the magic is too wild. For any mage to draw that much they would have to be . . .' She tailed off as her eyes came to rest on the willow-pattern tattoos on Sitain's skin. 'He is like you,' Siere said baldly.

'I, yeah, he is. He's strong enough, but the last God Fragment he touched crumbled under his fingers.'

'How do you know this one will not?'

'We don't, but we have to try.'

Siere bowed her head. Lynx watched Sanshir restrain herself as Siere remained still for a long while. The anger inside her fought for release, like a rat clawing its way out, but the kaboto would not let her guilt-laden exhaustion rule her. She remained quiet until Siere spoke again.

'This may kill us all,' Siere finally said in little more than a whisper.

'This may be our only chance,' Sanshir countered in a gentle voice, though her knuckles were white.

'You do not know what it is you ask,' Siere said, her protest sounding weak but worryingly heartfelt to Lynx's ear. 'This thing, it is terrible. It is an affront to life itself. Once released into the world, you do not know what it may do.'

'According to Atieno it's no great secret. Most tempest mages know of it, if they get old enough. You could do it easily, couldn't you?'

'I would never do this.'

'But it's within your power. It's where all the stories come from, isn't it?'

She bowed her head again. 'There are always some who choose the darkest of actions,' Siere said. 'Many of us believe the invention of mage cartridges was a terrible crime against the world, but you would go further still.'

'Someone will anyway,' Lynx said. 'Something this powerful, some bastard will work it out soon.'

She reached out and took his hand unexpectedly, the one which bore his Vagrim ring. Siere squeezed the finger around the ring, pointedly.

'Do you believe that means an action is justified? That because the evil men of this world will do something, you may also?'

Lynx hesitated, thrown by her accusation, and took a breath while he thought. She did have a point. Could a Vagrim so easily make this choice? What did his vows mean here?

He was a man used to making a stand, to refusing the easy choice, yet he'd not even questioned Atieno's thinking. And perhaps that was the reason why. Atieno was a Vagrim too. He followed the same path as Lynx and surely had spent hours and days over his life pondering this very thing.

'I believe mage cartridges are just things,' he said at last. 'Not good, not evil. But if I could choose to make them impossible, I would. They inflict horror, of that I'm certain, but they're not evil themselves. If I had been there to stop their inventor, would anything now be different? Was it a rare stroke of genius that created them or the natural result of science?'

She let go of his hand. 'It is so. Still I fear this.'

'We all do. And perhaps others will hear of what we attempt and be inspired to new efforts, but there's more magic in the world now. That cannot be undone and sooner or later, one or more of the bastard Orders will no doubt revive what past efforts they made.'

Siere stood. 'I will fetch my colleagues,' she announced.

'Colleagues?'

'If I am to do this, it is better I use mages I have worked with before. Safer for all of us.' She gave a feeble smile. 'If it must be done, I mean to see it save our city.'

'If it's any help, you may be stronger than ever, afterwards. That hand might feel better too.'

Her eyes widened briefly. 'The tattoos?'

Lynx shrugged. 'Seems like they're a by-product of any linking ritual.'

Siere was quiet a while then shook her head. 'If that were the only reason, it would not be enough. But you are correct. There is another.'

'Let's go save the city then.'

Chapter 40

Sitain dozed, shrouded by the hanging flowers of wisteria, enveloped in a bubble of sound as bees droned all around her head. Beyond that she could hear the babble of mages, no more intelligible and of less interest. The day's heat was rising hour upon hour and the sun had now reached its zenith. Sitain could find no strength to keep her limbs moving, no will to force her thoughts in line.

The fatigue of the previous night sapped her, but each time she felt herself sinking into sleep, something jerked her awake. She could do nothing but keep her eyes closed and her thoughts drifting, hoping that some rest would result. The heady scent of wisteria hung thick in the air and provoked a bittersweet memory.

It had grown up one sunny wall of her childhood home – the cottage her family did still live in, Sitain assumed. Her Hanese mother had always loved that spot, to sit in the sun there – enveloped in that scent and bathed in warmth. Sitain could almost sense her mother at her side, the press of her shoulder against Sitain's.

Her heart ached for that gentle presence again, so patient and loving for all that she'd been too frightened to speak when the Charnelers had come for Sitain. Rarely had her mother been at peace, not entirely, but with her eyes closed in that sunny spot there had been a glimpse of what might have been.

Sitain let herself sink back into that memory and draw what strength she might find from it, but her fears remained. Fear of mistakes, of failure – of success too.

As the time dragged past, a small boy brought cups of weak wine as often as he dared. Sitain had been puzzled by it at first, but eventually it dawned on her that he was a novice in the guild, not a servant. He was a night mage and shyly curious – of the tattoos that made her so powerful as much as anything. She had no answers for him, though, no wisdom to pass on. The boy probably knew more of magic than she did, but seemed content to sense her well of power and wonder.

At last it was time and a pulse of power came from Atieno as he flexed his magical muscles. The sensation, through whatever the link was between them, snapped Sitain to wakefulness. She came close to jumping from her seat at the jolt. A sly look from Atieno, across the guild courtyard, told her that had been deliberate. Sitain took a few wobbly paces, gravel floor proving treacherous underfoot until she found her balance, and glared at the man.

Showing off for the old lady? Sitain wondered, as though he could hear her. *Aren't you a bit old for that?*

She shook her head. An old man was still just a man.

'It's time, Sitain,' Atieno called. 'For a test, at least.'

She stretched and started over. 'Time to see if you're going to break their precious toy?'

The pained looks she received suggested they'd been discussing that very point.

'It will be kept in a metal frame so no mage touches it during the process,' Atieno explained. 'Toil has had to guarantee to replace it if that is not enough to stop it crumbling.'

'The promise of more marked mages wasn't tempting enough?'

Atieno looked weary. 'Not after half of those Lastani created were hunted down by the golantha.'

She paused and cocked her head at the tall mage.

'Have you had any rest? Any food?'

'I have eaten.'

'And rest? I'm not saying you've got time for a nap, but take a few minutes to clear your mind, no?'

He forced a smile. 'Thank you, I will be fine.'

'Good, that's my mothering all done for the day. Where do you want me?'

The leader of the guild mages, Ustirtei, gestured.

'Come.'

He led them down a wide stairway into the bedrock of the island, each guild mage collecting an oil lamp at the bottom of the stairway. Below ground a long corridor ran left and right. As they set off down the right-hand path, Sitain realised it followed the shape of the paths above, in the courtyard. Before long they came back around to the far end where a heavy iron-bound door stood.

There was a sort of guardroom to one side where a woman stood to attention at their arrival, but made no effort to interfere. Ustirtei removed a key from his belt and unlocked the door. The ageing mage gave the guard a look at that point and she nodded, reaching behind a panel in her small room to give something a tug.

The guard watched Ustirtei open the door and continue through. Sitain wasn't the only one to glance up as she crossed the threshold. Ustirtei's colleague in the Mastrunner headscarf, whose name had turned out to be Luverno, explained as she did so.

'A security arrangement,' Luverno said with a smile. 'One we will have to redesign now so many outsiders are here.' He gave an apologetic look towards Siere as he spoke, but the healer did not appear to take offence.

'You trust each other that little?' Sitain commented.

'A God Fragment is a valuable thing,' he said. 'It is the only one in Caldaire and is greatly desired by our rivals as well as the Orders. You are the first outsiders to come here since we acquired the fragment.'

Inside was a wood-panelled antechamber that they filled before the first door was locked again behind them. Only then did a bell chime from somewhere unseen and Luverno produced a second key for the next door. That brought them into a wider room perhaps ten yards across where a great hump of stone jutted out from very centre of the floor.

It was shaped, Sitain realised, like a strange V-wedge, pointing towards the door with the tip half cut away so there was a narrow shelf there. On this side of the stone were stacked boxes of machine-worked brass cartridges and a table bearing trays of porcelain balls on one side, dull glass discs on the other. Six sturdy stools occupied the floor on this side of the stone wedge.

'So where is it?' Sitain asked, peering round.

There was a heavy steel door set into the wall on the left, while the far end was, rather worryingly, just blackened stone with deep cracks in it and flaked shards littering the ground. Off to the right was some sort of small dumb-waiter arrangement, presumably to remove viable cartridges in case of catastrophe.

'The fragment? Locked away.'

'We're not ready for it yet,' Atieno added. 'First we practise.'

'Practise? How bloody long is that going to take? We've only got until nightfall.'

'And we have hours until then. Before we can make any cartridges, I need to be sure I know what I'm doing – what we're all doing.'

'This is how all mages learn the craft,' Luverno added.

Sitain scowled at that. She'd been destined for this work perhaps, once, before the Cards, or maybe to live as a servant of sorts, attending those permitted to make mage cartridges and envious of their servitude.

'Does it take long?'

He gave her a pained look.

'I'll take that as a yes,' she snorted.

'When we train novices, we do so slowly. Atieno is a more experienced mage. I am . . . optimistic.'

'Oh me too,' Sitain said. 'Really bloody optimistic. So we're going to practise on some glass beads and hope he doesn't accidentally kill us before he works out what he's doing?'

'Correct,' Atieno said before the others could respond. 'Do you have a problem with that?'

She hesitated. 'I guess not.'

'Good. Now – you are almost untrained, you have no experience of linked working or anything beyond basic magery. Please just listen and do as you are asked from now on. This will be dull but difficult and dangerous.'

Sitain nodded and Atieno inclined his head in thanks before gesturing to Ustirtei. The old man immediately set about directing mages to the wooden stools laid out before the central block of stone. Sitain was placed on the left of the small healer mage, Siere, while one of the guild's own took position on the other side. She guessed he was a light mage, there to balance her out, and a second took a place behind him.

Man needs a bit of power to balance me out, she thought with a smirk of childish satisfaction.

Atieno took position behind Siere while two more flanked him. Sitain watched them all for a moment until she noticed Siere reach a hand towards her. She put the tiny hand into her own and took a calming breath. Siere's skin was cool and smooth like porcelain. Gently she opened herself to the woman, as Lastani had taught her, and tried to relax. This was going to be a long afternoon.

'Remember,' Atieno said loudly, 'we may become linked. I will only be drawing small amounts at first, but you may still find your skin marked like ours, your power greatly increased.'

It was strange, uncomfortably so, when the magic was teased out of her. Sitain wasn't in control of what was going on and could really only glimpse it in her mind. That she sensed she had the ability to break the link at will, to wrestle control back from either Siere or Atieno, didn't comfort her much. It was too much like someone using her arms on her behalf, an extension of herself now obedient to another's will.

Dimly, at the back of her mind, she could feel the marked Cards. There was a yawning gap in her awareness left by Lastani, the shining presence of Atieno and Tanimbor's mages unable to make up for the loss of that brightest star. The sense of Lynx nearby was no compensation, a strange mixture of doglike patience and juddering emotion. Still, Sitain had to admit to herself it was a more comfortable presence than some of the others.

Suth appeared strongly, Teshen too – both of them knife-sharp and cold like steel. Toil was a blazing fire of determination that caused everything around her to smoulder. The relentless-ness of her frightened Sitain, more so than the dispassionate killers or even Deern's restless latent anger. Its scale and capacity overshadowed the others and burned all it touched.

As Atieno embraced the magic, however, her sense of the marked Cards faded. Instead, something new rose up, the shifting presence of Siere and then the other mages joining their ritual. Sitain opened her eyes and saw as well as felt the influence of the tree spread – not fast this time, not riding the vast power Sitain had commanded, but stealing steadily over them. The marks of willow leaves appeared faintly on their skin, little more than a suggestion but it was enough.

Atieno broke off and looked around, allowing the other mages a few moments to wonder at the changes. He exchanged a look with Sitain and the young woman forced a grin.

'Looks like it's going to be gradual,' Sitain said. 'No passing out, hopefully. No images of horny mercenaries running through your heads.'

'We will continue this way,' Atieno confirmed.

It took a moment to get the others concentrating again, but they were experienced mages and aware of the severity of matters so before long Atieno had resumed the link. He held it for a while. Sitain could feel him gently probe the powers of each mage – manipulating it, drawing it out and getting a feel for how it reacted to him, then retreating. Only when he'd done that with each of them did Atieno start to gather the strands together.

'Shit!' Atieno exclaimed a few moments later, cutting through Sitain's reverie.

She opened her eyes, not even realising she'd closed them. The aftertaste of magic hung in the air, bitter and sharp, while the stone wall ahead now bore a jagged ash-grey scar.

'What happened?'

'It just got away from me,' he replied, not looking her way. 'Such is the way with tempest magic. Another.'

Ustirtei stepped forward, a hearth brush of all things in his hand. With a few deft strokes he fussily brushed away at the central shelf in the V-shaped rock then produced a small glass ball which he set there. That done, he stepped sharply away and left Atieno to try again.

Siere placed two fingers on the ball, both greyish and dead-looking but now with a pattern traced across them, while resuming her hold on Sitain's hand. The other mages placed their hands on her; Atieno's palms flat against her back while the light mage rested a hand on her shoulder. Sitain didn't know what discipline Atieno's two attendant mages were, but they also put hands on his back. Before long Sitain felt threads of her magic slowly play out like a reel unspooling.

She closed her eyes and focused on the sensation, finding nothing worth looking at. The night magic and light opposed each other, turning slowly in unison, while a core of roiling tempest magic merged with more sedate types within. She guessed at stone and wind there; one solid and sluggish, the other elusive and quick. The longer she looked, the longer she was amazed – not at the complexity of the working, but at the control required of Atieno.

She could sense Siere guiding him a little, perhaps the others lending a steadying hand as well, but the work was done by Atieno. His was the controlling force that kept each element in movement as he brought the five together. Again it failed, the tempest core seeming to dart away and tear into the stone magic. Atieno only sighed and tried again with a new glass ball.

The next time she tried to assist him, but her efforts brought about immediate disaster. Fortunately for them all, it was early in the process and only a scrap of magic had been drawn. Not enough to escape Atieno's grasp and put them all out, but still Sitain felt her cheeks burning as it brought reproving looks from all directions. They tried again, then again and again until Luverno called a halt.

'I can continue,' Atieno said, looking up.

'A few minutes,' the mage insisted. 'Stand up, walk around. You may forget about your body when working magic, but your body has not forgotten about you.'

It was clearly a lecture he had delivered many times and the other mages were already up – stretching their backs and muttering to each other in their own language. Sitain reached out and patted Atieno on the shoulder.

'Come on, old man, do what teacher says.'

He gave her a baleful look, which Sitain ignored, so was left with no alternative but to comply. Sitain went to investigate the brutalised wall, brushing a few fragments of stone from the fractured sheets of rock. The other mages stood and set about properly inspecting the emerging white tattoos on their skin, still very faint but a definite pattern of willow leaves.

'None of this was you,' she commented when Atieno went to join her. 'That's good.'

'We are not at the dangerous part yet.'

'True. Ah, sorry about trying to help back there. I should've known better.'

Atieno nodded. 'It is natural, but do not allow it to happen later.'

'I won't.' Sitain gave him an askance look. 'All going about how you thought?'

'It is.'

'Still confident we'll be ready?'

His hands tightened briefly, but Sitain didn't think it was anger at her – rather the reminder of what was to come.

'I believe I can do this. I . . . I realise there is much depending on it.'

Sitain nodded. 'One lap around the room then. Keep the blood flowing then we get back to it. They're stupid bastards in the main, but our friends won't die for lack of us trying.'

He nodded. 'So they're your friends now, are they?'

'Until I find some better ones, sure,' she said, smiling briefly. 'Life ain't fair on that front, but when is it?'

'Fair isn't for the likes of us,' Atieno agreed. 'Let's just do what's right instead.'

When they returned, it took an hour before he got it right. As the minutes ticked by and Sitain fought the urge to grind her teeth with impatience, she could sense the fatigue building even as Atieno's workings became more and more deft. Finally, they were rewarded with a small glass ball sitting in the palm of Siere's hand.

It was dark – not quite black but a heavy, threatening grey that seemed both solid and possessed of some shifting, restless quality. Sitain felt uncomfortable just looking at it. The utmost care Siere took to handle it told volumes, but they were far from done. A second was made, then after a break three more. There were failures too. Three of those ripped sections from the stone wall behind the shelf and the last required other mages to be fetched to shore up the bedrock before they could continue.

Finally, there were five, almost identical, balls of dark glass each in their own divider on the table behind. Ustirtei inspected each one in turn very slowly as the mages checked the progress of their tattoos. He turned the balls with a wooden tool he'd produced from a pocket, reluctant to touch them with his own skin. Finally, he pronounced them satisfactory, but there was a grey and fearful look on his face as he did so. Atieno looked similarly pleased with their success, but he didn't hesitate before asking for the God Fragment to be brought out. It was time to create something altogether more powerful and terrible.

'So that's it?' Anatin looked up at Sitain. 'Is this a pissing joke?'

She pointed at the cartridges set snugly into a steel-frame box. 'That right there's a bloody minor miracle.'

'Really? 'Cos it looks like you two had your thumbs up your arses for half the day then knocked a couple out in the last half-hour.'

Lynx glanced up at the darkening sky. By his guess, they had maybe half an hour of decent light left before the city was the playground of monsters again. The whole Mercenary Deck stood behind Anatin, armed and ready for battle and disturbingly quiet by their standards.

'Have you got any damn idea how to make mage cartridges?' Sitain demanded. 'No? Well then, shut the hells up. Atieno risked his life doing this – all our lives most likely. Damn stuff is tricksy like you wouldn't believe. Any flaws at all in the glass, even ones that'd be fine for a normal cartridge, meant the thing wouldn't charge, went off halfway or started to degrade almost immediately. The fact he managed to do it all is a testament to his power an' the skill of the mages here.'

'Oh aye, right bloody heroes you are, eh?'

She shook her head. 'I did crap all, just sat there and let him draw on my strength. I don't know about any of this, but I got to see first-hand the difficulty of the job. You all should be giving him big manly hugs or whatever it is you lot do to express gratitude. He's still working, by the way, well after the point even the Militant Orders would have thought it unsafe to continue pushing. You might get more cartridges in time to use, but here's the chance you asked for.'

Sitain had raised her voice to almost a shout. Anatin wasn't one for proper respect towards officers, but there was a limit and they could all see she was skirting it.

'Here's our chance,' the Prince of Sun mused. 'Ten shots to take down three golantha. How many earthers did it take to kill the last one? Or rather, knock it off a wall and let the fall kill it?'

'These aren't earthers,' she insisted. 'Not even bloody close. Ask any mage, they won't want to go near them.'

'Ten shots,' Anatin said, only half listening. 'Guess we should spread our precious cargo then. Let's say five teams of two, a Mastrunner for each team to pass messages and guide. The rest of the company stays holed up in some dark corner as back-up.'

He turned to face the Cards and started to point.

'Teshen, you're up. Reckon you and Sanshir have one more run in you?'

The man's face went taut. The play of emotion was hard to read, but eventually he gave a cautious nod. Sanshir was similarly closed off, but signalled her agreement by shouldering her mage-gun.

'Good – as for the rest. Kas, Safir, Suth, Reft. Toil, I take it you won't be backing down?'

'No chance – unless it means leaving out a better shot than me. This isn't about ego.'

'Yeah, but the best shot may not be who we need. We don't have much luxury to miss, so you'll be taking your shots so close you're wetting yerselves, even you, Suth. Understand? Good. This is about getting the job done any way we can. We can't outrun or outclimb these things so Aben and Lynx, you're also in. The last spot goes to Deern, in the interests of using bastards who'll get the job done right.'

He raised a hand as several Cards protested. 'Enough, this ain't a discussion. Layir, if we were facing men you'd be in, but you're young and hot-headed which I don't need now. Varain, Colet, we've only got one shot and neither of you aim so well these days.'

'The tattoos won't be a problem?' Toil asked Sitain.

The young woman shook her head. 'So I'm told. If Atieno and I aren't drawing magic at the time, you shouldn't stand out. He's going to stop work at nightfall.'

Lynx cleared his throat. 'And the plan? These things won't fall for the same trick twice, they've shown that much.'

'Mebbe so, but don't give 'em too much credit. They're still dumb beasts.'

'So're maspids,' Toil pointed out. 'Those are smarter than dogs all the same and can plan around dangers.'

Anatin nodded and pulled the stump of his arm tight against his body. 'Point taken. First of all we give 'em what they're out there to hunt.'

'A mage?'

'Some sort of magery,' he confirmed. 'Not Sitain's "look what a big wand I've got" from last night, but something of a different flavour. They want mages, we must still be able to find some of those.'

'And we ambush them on the way? What if they sniff us out?'

'We'll need a few mages, something to distract 'em. Hit one and run, lead the others into a second trap.'

'Pick somewhere with two main routes for them to use,' Toil suggested. 'Two teams on each with one assigned to take the first shot so we don't waste these. Whoever kicks it off will get the attention of any remaining golantha. They need an escape route and the second pair to watch their back. That leads to the fifth pair with an ambush ready further back with the bulk of the Cards.'

'Always planning, ain't you, Toil?' Anatin said in a voice that sounded half irritated and half pleased.

'It keeps me alive,' she replied with a shrug. 'Normally it's just Aben backing me up. Teshen, Sanshir – reckon you can find suitable locations?'

Sanshir nodded. 'Most of the district will be deserted.'

'Time to move then,' Anatin announced.

The Cards he'd picked each walked up to select one of the precious mage cartridges. Lynx looked at his before putting it in his case. The cartridge was plain and unremarkable, its end sealed in wax rather than fired clay and unmarked by a designation.

'Guess the mages are going to have to come up with a symbol for them,' he commented as he safely stowed it, clear of the others so he wouldn't mistake it. The contents of Lynx's case looked pretty forlorn now. A couple of icers and one earther were all that remained. Anything else wouldn't be much use and would only make him a more obvious target.

'Let's hope there's no call for it, after today,' Toil muttered as she took hers.

The rest of the company had the same, a few shots plus any remaining earthers. A couple more had been scared up by Sanshir's boss, Kabat Jo-Sarl, but most of the city's stock were gone. What was left had been collected up by Foren, a terrifying collection of burners and sparkers under normal circumstances, but now they were a last resort. In Shadows Deep they'd used them as a makeshift bomb, but it wasn't far off like throwing bucketsful of water at a man. He might be overwhelmed eventually, but up to a point he was just thirsty and waterproof.

'Let's just hope these damn things work,' Deern said. 'Did you even test one?'

'Test one?' Sitain said, almost startled. 'When we've only got ten? You want to pull the trigger on yours, just let me get out of the way first.'

'You've not even fucking tested them?' Anatin roared. 'Oh broken gods and shitweasel priests! This just gets better and better.'

'We've tested the magic,' Sitain snapped back. 'That's as good as you get unless you want to risk one shot per monster. Atieno warns there may be misfires, it's far more likely than you'd normally get, but we can't help that. The effect of the magic on any tiny flaws in the glass core means that's inevitable – and for pity's sake don't drop the bloody things because they're far more likely to blow up. I've no idea about range but you're getting as close as you can anyway.' She paused and pulled something from around her waist. 'Here, there's this as well. A last resort sort o' thing.'

Toil took the belt from her. 'Mage balls?' she asked.

Sitain nodded. 'The ones we didn't test. There's five left. Not powerful, nothing like the cartridges, but . . .'

Toil nodded and strapped the belt around her waist. 'Better'n nothing,' she confirmed. 'Let's go be heroes.'

Chapter 41

Sanshir ushered the ambush group to the docks where a long, narrow barge sat waiting for them. They didn't wait for the rest of the company but set off immediately. A second boat would bring the rest of the Cards plus a few co-opted mages – each boat boasting a water mage to see them across the lagoon as fast as possible.

The shadows had all merged into one by that point, a dull darkness settling over the lagoon. A long stream of small tysarn rose up into the evening sky from the hellmouths. Their numbers were much reduced from previous days, so far as Lynx could see. The frenzy of their larger kin perhaps, one that had built like a tidal wave since Lastani had inadvertently triggered it.

'Hear us, our gods,' Safir suddenly called out, standing high in the prow of the boat. 'Let your spirits come forth to guide us in this hour of need.'

Sanshir turned to watch him, startled by the outburst, while Teshen and Kas both solemnly bowed their heads.

'This city of faithful servants stands on the brink of destruction, oh most powerful of beings. Without your blessing, all will come to ruin here, but before we get to the begging, let's talk about blame, eh? Lords of Earth and Darkness, Ulfer and Insar, which one of you pricks is going to claim these golantha as your own? Or were these horrors just the product of some idiot drunken bet?

'Veraimin, great god of light and all forms of fiery bluster, I . . . well probably this one isn't on you I guess. But don't think that means we're friends. Catrac, master of passion and invention – ten bloody cartridges, just ten. Is that meant to be funny? Some sort of pissy lesson for us maybe? Either way, don't think we've forgotten it was a Duegar artefact that sparked this whole mess off.

'Lastly, Lord Banesh. Let's just hope your servant Atieno hasn't shit the bed in such a catastrophic way as you did, back in the day. Otherwise we're all fucked and anyone who survives is coming for whatever little pieces are left of you five bastards, that I promise. So we pray.'

'So we pray,' most of the Cards intoned in response. Sanshir just rolled her eyes and looked away.

They cut across to Xi Le island in a matter of minutes and soon disembarked at an abandoned dock. There was debris scattered across the northern part, where a building had been shattered. Blood was everywhere, but as Lynx crept forward he saw the long claw of a tysarn wing-tip through one empty doorway. A cloud of insects and smaller tysarn danced up as he moved, but soon settled again, unwilling to leave their meal.

'We've not got much time,' Sanshir reported. She'd been looking up at the nearer tor where a light was flashing. It was followed by whistles, staccato bursts of sound that echoed around. The Cards instinctively raised their guns, feeling surrounded, but Sanshir simply whistled an acknowledgement and beckoned.

'Three coming, approaching Si Jo,' she reported. 'What's left of my crew are spread throughout this island. With luck they'll be ignored if they have no mage cartridges.'

'Tell us where to go,' Toil said in a brisk voice.

The kaboto scanned around, catching Teshen's eye briefly but whatever passed between them in that look was lost to

Lynx. As she did so, slim figures raced towards them, first two then another five emerging like foxes breaking cover. They were all young, four boys and three girls, the oldest looking no more than fifteen.

They sported the usual crew markings, the girls with long twisting braids tied with white cloth and the boys in white headscarves. Novices, Lynx guessed, but likely ones who'd been on the Si Jo shoreline. The look in their eyes suggested as much.

'Your guides, one for each pair. They'll keep you from getting lost and track the golantha.' She paused then pointed at the water mage who'd brought them. 'You, stay here. Start working magic – when the other boat arrives, link with the other mages and do something to attract the golantha.'

'Attract them?' the mage asked, aghast. Her hand went to the small curve of her belly and Lynx realised with a jolt she was pregnant. The mage was a round-faced woman whose pale skin and northern accent showed she was a recent arrival in the city, but she wore the Waterdancer Guild robes.

'Wait, she's got a baby,' Lynx said, but Sanshir just shook her head.

'Doesn't matter, we're out of time and need a mage to serve as bait. That's you, but we'll be the ones between it and you. If you get hurt, it's because I'm already too dead to give a shit about anything ever again.'

'But—'

'Lynx,' Toil warned. 'She's right. Being further away doesn't help the baby if we fail.'

'I will do it,' the mage announced before Lynx could object further. 'I knew many who died last night. I will not hide away.'

Sanshir nodded. 'If it goes wrong, you can probably escape across the water anyway. Tell the rest of the mercenaries to occupy Vars Holding.'

She pointed a little way south towards a blockish complex of buildings, piled like bricks with gaps left between each. It was the highest ground on this stretch of the shore, but dwarfed by the tor ahead.

'Now for us.'

She paused a moment and surveyed the ground to the north. There was a wide market space abutting the dock, leading to the tor that dominated their view; a lopsided hump of rock much lower than the one they'd used last night. A great avenue ran down the centre. Lynx could see lanterns had been lit within though most of the dwellings looked dark and abandoned.

The shore side on the right was the lower – an abrupt, elongated hill that projected out to warehouses and palazzos on the shorefront – while the seaward flank bore four great shelves of streets like levels of a ziggurat. Past that was an interconnected sprawl of smaller blocks, several of which were topped with temples. Two blazed with light, great bonfires or firepits that seemed to be trying to defy the darkness, or at least its creatures.

The sight gave Lynx a flicker of hope that the city wasn't yet entirely cowed, but the island was largely dark and abandoned. Beneath the temples was a chaotic tangle of dark streets, cut through with raised roads and looking more like a puzzle than a place people lived.

'One pair on each side of the Under-Avenue,' Sanshir called, pointing at the road that ran right through the tor and reminded Lynx of the Duegar road they'd followed to Shadows Deep.

'If it comes around the shore side, have someone fire a light bolt,' she added to the mage. 'It's unlikely though, these creatures prefer the darkest places. Teshen and I will go inland into the Ve Ho maze with one pair, we're more likely to need to move fast.'

As she spoke more whistles came, a frenetic burst of sound that each of the Mastrunners cocked an ear to before glancing towards the tor.

'Okay, Lynx and I will take the dark tunnel,' Toil said. 'Kas and Suth, you're best with Teshen. Safir and Aben, you're with us. Reft and Deern, you're the back-up team.'

Sanshir nodded and pointed west of where they stood, an elongated dip that was dotted with greenery. 'The Low Gardens. Take position on the far side, you'll get a good view of anything trying to cross.'

Without any further instructions, Sanshir loped off with long, easy strides towards the nearest of the beacon temples. Teshen waved Kas and Suth forward and they raced after her, one of the youths trotting alongside. Another gestured to Deern, keeping a wary eye on Reft as he did so, and they set off, while the four remaining Cards headed for the tor.

As they went, the whistles came again and their guides upped the pace without saying a word. The urgency in those sounds made the Cards match them and soon they were entering the gloom of the Under-Avenue.

About thirty yards in, Toil slowed her pace and hissed at their guides. The avenue was ten yards high, spotted with puddles of light from oil lamps but mostly pitch black as the last of the daylight vanished. It was built for strength, not beauty, from what Lynx could see.

The ceiling was bare and marked with sooty stains, with only the occasional patch of glowing threads they'd seen the previous evening. The click of bats echoed through the avenue. Lynx could sense more than see the flicker of movement as those or small tysarn flashed past overhead. Out of instinct they scouted the path, checking the couple of larger tunnels that led off this one, but the streets of the tor at least were empty.

Lynx didn't want to think about how many people were hiding in their homes, hoping to ride out the violence. The avenue was lined with shops, taverns and eateries, all shuttered or simply abandoned, while a tier of apartments hunkered above those. There was only a narrow walkway in front of the apartments and only rarely were there stairways to reach it. More often it was simply a case of steps chiselled into a sheer face.

'These are empty?' Toil asked one of their guides, a boy with a scar-twisted lip.

He shook his head. 'Workers, poor people,' he said by way of explanation. 'Some go, many cannot.'

'Find us some that are empty,' she ordered. 'We might as well try to avoid them getting killed.'

While the guides raced up the steps to the narrow walkway above the protruding shop-fronts, Toil pulled a grenade from her jacket pocket. She set it on the rutted road, a little way towards the open air. From the red pin, Lynx could tell it was a fire bomb.

'Distraction?' Lynx guessed.

'Give 'em something to sniff other than us,' Toil confirmed. 'Better than throwing the damn thing, anyway. Safir, Aben, you take right, we'll be on the left. Let me take the shot unless you're in danger, okay?'

'And after?'

'It'll turn our way if it's not already dead. Lynx gets a shot then. After that we'll be running. You decide whether to shoot or not. Regroup with the Cards after, however you decide to play it. In the meantime, let's keep it down in here. I've no idea how well those things can hear, but we'll be pretty exposed if they notice us. You two,' she added, pointing to the young Mastrunners with them. 'No signals back unless we have to, okay? You can tell us what's being passed on, but quietly, understand?'

The pair nodded, one placing his fingers over his mouth to pantomime the order. Lynx thought about asking their names given they were risking their lives too, but instinct stopped him. Their names would make them harder to forget if this went wrong, make the guilt more real. Without names, the memories faded faster.

'Yes, boss,' Aben added with a nervous grin and banged his fist against hers. 'Luck to you.'

'Luck to us all,' Safir added, offering Toil a florid bow. 'Princess, Stranger – see you on the other side.'

They parted, but before they could take their assigned sides – only twenty yards apart but immediately feeling like there was a gulf between them – more whistles were relayed from behind.

'The boat is come,' their guide whispered.

Toil nodded to acknowledge that before the young man took a quick run up at the nearest wall. There was no path that Lynx could see, aside from the steps that he ignored entirely. Apparently there were enough footholds that the Mastrunner could do it without needing his hands.

Lynx and Toil didn't attempt to follow, instead hauling themselves up the chiselled steps to join him on the walkway above. There they waited, looking along the empty tunnel then inspecting their options. After a while spent in quiet contemplation of the task ahead, another signal was passed down.

'On Xi Le shore,' the young boy hissed.

There was fear in his eyes now, his voice wavering. Lynx could tell he was reliving the moments when the golantha last reached that shore and, awkwardly, he reached out and squeezed the kid's shoulder.

'Time they paid for it,' he said. The young man just blinked at him and gave a curt nod before trotting off down the walkway. He wasn't running now – Xi Le was a big island and the golantha wouldn't yet be making a beeline for the Cards. They had a few minutes at least. Time enough to check out some more of the tunnel and make sure they weren't going to get any surprises.

They didn't walk the full length of the tunnel, just enough to be certain that there was nowhere for anything to pop out unexpectedly from. Whether or not the golantha entered at the far end or elsewhere, assuming it did so at all of course, they'd see it coming.

'Hold here,' Toil said after they retraced their steps almost to where the grenade sat. 'This looks like what we want.'

Lynx looked around. There was a narrow path cut through the rock at right angles to the main avenue. There would be little more than shoulder-width for him there, the tunnel very faintly lit by the hanging threads of whatever insect it was they'd tamed here. Still, it was too dark and narrow for Lynx's liking and he immediately backed away.

'No, no I don't think so,' he muttered, staring at the elongated tomb.

'You've got a little time to get used to it,' Toil hissed. 'I'm sorry, but there won't be any other escape path bigger than this.'

'Maybe I should go swap with Deern,' Lynx replied, edging towards the steps. 'Yeah, that's a better idea.'

'Odds on Deern knifes me in the back, first chance he gets,' she replied conversationally, setting her mage-gun carefully down and taking hold of Lynx's jacket. She brought her face right up to his to force him to take his eyes off the narrow path.

'Look at me, Lynx. Focus.'

He tried to, but the tunnel was a shifting, looming mass of darkness behind and his heart started to boom in his ears. 'I . . .'

'You can do this. There's no time to switch and I need you beside me.'

'I don't think I can.'

She kissed him, just softly. 'Yes you can. You're stronger than this.'

He shook his head, fighting the urge to rip her hands off him and shove Toil away. His hands tightened into fists as spots of light began to burst across his eyes, but Toil just continued to talk in a calm voice – relaxing her grip on him as though seeing what he fought. Instead of holding him, she rested her palms on his chest, letting them rise and fall as he took quick breaths.

'Not sure I am,' Lynx said in a small voice, his throat so tight he could hardly breathe.

'Yes you are – not for your own sake maybe, but you are. You won't let others down even if it breaks you. This much I know.'

'Finding it hard to even stay upright,' Lynx gasped, 'let alone think about others.'

'Thinking's not what you need,' Toil hissed, glancing over her shoulder. 'This thing is coming to kill us. Your body knows what it needs to do.'

Distantly, Lynx heard the sound of running feet, but he couldn't connect that to anything real. There was the faint smell of Toil, sweat and night jasmine, overlaying the stink of the city. That stirred a distant part of his mind, but the darkness intruded on it all. It swarmed forward, swamped his senses until Toil was just a dim shape moving in front of him. For a moment he couldn't even hear her, but then she slapped him across the cheek and a flare of white-hot anger surged through him.

'Focus!' she hissed as loudly as she could. 'Damn the tunnel then, we'll find another way out. Breathe, Lynx! It's coming!'

'I . . .'

He tried to say more, but his throat was so tight it came out as a growl. The sound itself made him stop, hesitate and see himself once more. His right hand was clamped around Toil's arm, knuckles white and suddenly he could see the grip was hurting even her. With an effort Lynx unpeeled himself and sank to his knees, panting.

'Gods, man,' Toil said, rubbing her arm as she knelt at his side. 'I forget how strong you are, when you let yourself be.'

'Sorry,' he slurred, trying to still his shaky hands.

'Worry about that another time.' She looked back again and fetched up her mage-gun. 'Hey, Lynx.'

He managed to look up, the anger still bubbling inside but at the moment it was only the balance between that and blind terror keeping him upright.

'Yeah?'

'That thing you had a few days back, in the market before the siege. Fried squid was it?'

'I . . .'

She nudged him with her arm and slipped his long gun from its place on his shoulder. 'Come on, think. Squid?'

'Yeah, squid.'

'What did it taste like?'

'Um. Hot. Really hot. Made my teeth ache.'

'Breadcrumbs?'

He shook his head. 'Dunno what it was, not bread, not batter. Sweet though. Crunchy.'

'Smoky too,' she said. 'I could smell it on you when I took you to bed. Taste it on your tongue, in your sweat.'

Lynx nodded.

'We should go get more of that. What do you say, tomorrow?'

'Tomorrow?'

'Yeah, tomorrow. Fried potatoes, squid, bread soaked in garlic oil. What do you say?'

'Sure,' he said, slightly drunkenly. 'Sounds good.'

'Then we better make it to tomorrow.' Her voice took on a more commanding edge. 'So take hold of your fucking gun and load it, soldier.'

His hands moved even as his brain wallowed in treacle. Breech clicked open, one hand sliding down to flip open

413

the cartridge case lid. A moment's hesitation at the unfamiliar emptiness of the case, the smooth glyph-less top of the cartridge. Then he pulled it out and slid it home, snapping the breech shut a moment after Toil did the same.

'Here it comes,' she whispered, nodding towards an open doorway nearby. 'You stay here.'

Lynx lay flat on the walkway, muzzle over the edge, while Toil advanced to the doorway and settled inside. Out of the corner of his eye he caught a flash of movement as the others took up firing positions, but his attention was on the shape advancing swiftly through the gloom.

It was hard to tell in the darkness, but Lynx guessed it wasn't the one that had killed Lastani. Rogue flashes of green fluttered the length of its body, muted by the great plates of armour, but it looked uniformly dark and uninjured. Its legs seemed to ripple forwards in groups as it walked, antennae twitching but showing little wariness. Lynx's heart lurched suddenly as the golantha paused and turned to the far side of the avenue.

There was a lamp burning above what Lynx guessed was a tavern. He could see the faint outlines of benches and tables before they were scattered by the golantha moving. It raised itself up, mandibles and front legs hooked on to the walkway while it quested forward with flicks of the feathery glow. After a short while it slipped back down, satisfied there was nothing there, and continued on towards them.

Lynx felt his guts clamp tight. The golantha moved with remarkable speed and it was so flexible it could whip its whole huge body from one side of the avenue to the other in a heartbeat. Then it paused again and flicked its antennae directly forward, down the rough surface of the road. Ghostly trails of green danced out through the air and vanished. Almost immediately it started up again, moving faster and with clear intent.

Lynx fought the urge to turn his head and check where the grenade had been left. It didn't matter. Either the thing would end up dead in their sights or it'd sense their handful of cartridges and attack. They were clearly not blind, so any movement might catch its attention.

Hardly daring to breathe, Lynx watched the huge creature glide forward. Twenty yards away, ten. Then it was almost level with them, armoured back a few yards away, while the golantha's legs were almost close enough to touch with his gun muzzle.

Toil swung her mage-gun around, clearly not wanting to move until it was too close to miss. The golantha twitched and coiled back as she did so, turning to face them just as she pulled the trigger.

Nothing happened. For a moment the world went black around Lynx as panic enveloped him. Toil looked down at her gun, aghast, cocked and pulled the trigger again. Still nothing. Then the golantha was rearing up, alive to the danger and ready to strike. The air blossomed sickly green, illuminating every sharp angle of its body and huge pincers. It was all the jolt Lynx needed. He rolled and brought his gun around, no time to think about whether it would work.

He fired.

Chapter 42

The recoil slammed him backwards. A roiling eruption of darkness tore from the mage-gun and hit the golantha in its side, just below the head. Something exploded, green light flashing wildly as the creature coiled under the impact. The sound of the shot was muted, deeper than the boom of an earther, but one Lynx felt jangle through his bones.

Where the shot had hit it, the very air looked fractured – the glow of the golantha's strange light ripped apart. The golantha let out a terrible hissing screech, louder than the gunshot even, and thrashed as a strange hushing sound filled the air. On the far side Lynx heard shouts. He couldn't make out the meaning before another gunshot went off and the darkness smashed into its plated back like a grenade.

The golantha bent backwards under the impact, this time caught in a moment of agony. Lynx could see what happened all the better now as a cloud of darkness seemed to erupt around the impact site. With his mage-touched eyes he could see enough to feel a sense of horror. His breath caught as he watched the creature twist and shudder. Where the shot had hit it, the armour had proved no real defence – there was a ragged hole in its back and again the hushing sound filled the air.

'Again!' Toil yelled, hurling her useless dud cartridge at the golantha's head in anger.

Aben stepped out from the doorway he'd been hiding in, gun level. Lynx glanced back down at the golantha, still half-paralysed from the second shot. He was about to shout when he saw the golantha's tail start to curl forward and he remembered what had happened to the temple the previous night.

'Now!' he shouted.

Aben fired in the next instant. The shot caught it at the back of its head and the armour exploded. The light faltered and the golantha was slammed to the ground, pinned by the blackness that had hit it. All around the impact point, chitin started to shudder and crumble. A cloud rose up – not blood or anything like that, Lynx realised. It was dust, flesh reduced to something utterly lifeless.

The wound spread in all directions and as Lynx watched he saw the others were still expanding. The golantha tried to lift its head once more, but faltered then fell limp. The aura of greenish light dimmed, the ghostly threads flickered and died. A shuddering, twisting wreckage was all that was left, the expanding ruin of its wounds shrouded in a haze of dust as they continued to expand horribly.

Lynx felt his gorge rise. He had seen a lot of injuries in his time, but there was something about this that turned his stomach. The very flesh seemed to collapse into nothingness, not just burned or something, but destroyed utterly. The very air around it warped and tore as the magic worked its hideous path through the corpse – slowing but still eroding the body until the head part dropped away from the rest and finally all fell silent.

'Shattered gods,' Lynx whispered, staring down at it.

'The ruin of gods,' Toil intoned. 'The last act of Banesh.'

'Dark magic.'

For a while they could only stare at the withering corpse. The last time they'd seen one up close it had been a blur of panic and desperation. Now it was still, the size seemed all the more impossible.

In the grey-edged gloom of his mage sight, Lynx couldn't make out much detail beyond the shape of the creature; huge jointed legs, more than a score on each flank, dull plates of chitin and great pincers longer than a man's leg, now lying limp.

Finally, the magic was spent, leaving the golantha a pitted ruin with huge chunks of its body reduced to dust. Lynx could taste it in the air, dry and lifeless. He spat, but the dust was all around and he couldn't get it clear.

'Cards!' their guide suddenly yelled.

Lynx looked up in confusion then realised the boy must have heard Sanshir use the word. The youth was frantically pointing down the tunnel and Lynx's heart gave a jolt. There was a large shape moving in the dark, a faint ghostly white in the scraps of lamplight.

'Deepest black,' Toil gasped. 'We're all out.'

'Run away?' Safir asked the group at large.

'Run away,' Aben agreed.

They waved their guides back, took one last look at the approaching creature, and took to their heels. It seemed like an age before they covered the remaining ground to the tunnel entrance. Lynx could almost feel the huge pincers bearing down on them, but they clattered out into the pale light of the moon without incident. Their guides outstripped the mercenaries easily, pausing only to issue a volley of whistles. The sound was taken up above and ahead, repeated on to the rest, before another call came and the guides turned.

Lynx stumbled to a halt as he looked right with them. A dozen narrow streets all led into the warren on the far side of the tor, about fifty yards off across this empty market ground. A figure was running their way, Sanshir, but just as Lynx thought she was abandoning the others the kaboto veered sideways.

With two hopping steps she propelled herself up towards the roof of a building. One-handed she swung up off a beam, spun around and landed on the roof to bring her gun up.

While Kas and Suth appeared from a different alley, Sanshir fired at something in the streets behind them. The white blade of an icer flashed through the night, but he couldn't see whether it hit. Sanshir didn't seem to care, she pulled another cartridge. Kas and Suth didn't look back, they were running with every ounce of strength remaining to them. Ignoring Lynx's group the pair veered down the side of the market towards the entrance to the Low Gardens where Reft and Deern waited.

Sanshir fired again and reloaded, likely coming close to her last shot Lynx realised. As she did so Teshen appeared on a different rooftop, vaulting the peak and running down the other side at breakneck speed. Without breaking stride he jumped across to the next house, the tight jumble of buildings offering an easy path across the warren. Something thumped down on to the building behind him and Lynx flinched, seeing the unmistakable bulk of a golantha swarm up with remarkable agility.

Sanshir fired again and scored a hit on the creature's head, but the icer didn't seem to hurt it. It did make the creature pause, however, and flick around towards Sanshir. She abandoned her gun as soon as it did and ran off to her left, away from Lynx. Teshen dropped down and carried on, his own mage-gun in his hands. The golantha started up towards Sanshir, responding to her attack, and crossed the first two buildings in two flicks of its massive body.

It was the smallest of the beasts they'd seen last night, but still big enough to lay waste to an army. Now Lynx watched he realised it was faster than the others too. There were injuries on it, deep furrows scored through the plates on its back that seemed to be smoking in the pale moonlight, and the broken stubs of two or three legs scraping along the ground. Clearly they had managed to get some shots off with the dark-bolts, but hadn't scored direct hits.

As he ran, Teshen raised his gun and drew a bead on the creature. Belatedly Lynx resumed running, realising Teshen would overtake him in seconds. The golantha closed on Sanshir, but just as it came within a few yards Teshen set his feet and fired. The icer went high over its head, but again it reacted to the buzz of magic. Toil, Aben and Safir were already out on the other side of the market ground and Lynx joined them at the far side just as the golantha slewed around.

'Cold hells,' Safir growled, loading his gun. 'Run, you fucker!'

Lynx felt a cold sense in his belly as Safir said that. Teshen was in the open ground now. He could move fast but he had no cover at all. The four of them loaded the last cartridges they had, but in that time the golantha had crossed half the market. They fired as one, three icers slamming home into the beast's carapace while one went high.

This time it didn't even pause, so intent it was on its prey. Just as it lashed forward Teshen threw himself sideways. Rolling, he came up with long knives in hand as a huge pincer flashed just past his head. Teshen slashed at it then dodged – always moving.

Lynx reloaded with an earther and took aim again. The golantha was large enough he didn't have to worry about shooting too close to Teshen. He fired, Safir following a moment later. The earther roared against its carapace and visibly rocked it, but other than a cracked dent it wasn't hurt. Teshen took advantage of the distraction though, hammering one long knife right into the joint of its pincer. That done he turned and ran once again, this time heading away from the golantha while Toil and Aben fired at its face.

The golantha swung around, almost impaling Teshen with one of its legs, but he escaped by a whisker. Then he stopped and Lynx realised the other, larger golantha had scuttled out of the Under-Avenue to cut off his escape. Checking around, Teshen dived aside as the vengeful smaller one lunged for him. Somehow he managed to elude its stabbing grasp and came up cutting furiously. Lynx saw him score a hit, but the golantha didn't notice.

It swung around and used its huge bulk to swat him to the ground. Beside him, Lynx heard Safir moan with horror. Its injured pincer, still impaled with Teshen's knife, was moving awkwardly, but the other was more than enough.

The golantha punched that right into Teshen's gut, forcing a howl of pain from the man. It lifted him up, impaled and trying to crush him but its injured pincer wouldn't allow it. Astonishingly, Teshen continued to slash at the beast's face with his remaining knife. There was a spray of fluid as he tore open one of its eyes, but then the golantha pulled him closer and bit into his face with its mass of mandibles. Teshen jerked and fell limp.

'Run!' Toil yelled at them, seeing the Knight of Stars was dead.

She grabbed Safir and Lynx by the shoulders, dragging them back until their wits returned and then stumbled after her. There was no time to check if the golantha were following. Lynx glimpsed his hand as he ran, trying to ignore the roaring sound of blood in his ears, and felt a flicker of relief that his tattoos were not shining.

Round one corner, on to a wide street that led up to the building Sanshir had directed the Cards to. Off to the right were Kas and Suth, waiting at the entrance to the Low Gardens. They waved them forward with frantic gestures.

'What happened?' Toil roared as they got close.

'Bloody misfires,' Kas shouted back, 'two of them! If Teshen hadn't drawn it off, we'd be dead right now.'

'It got him,' Safir said, the anguish clear in his voice. 'Damn thing killed him.'

'Fuck!' Kas shook her head and glanced behind her then started running up towards the Cards. There was a long stepped slope up to the odd angular blocks Sanshir had pointed out – open ground that offered no cover.

There was no time for anything else. Up ahead, Lynx could see Anatin calling them forward, the windows of the central stone block bristling with gun muzzles.

'Move, you bastards!' Anatin yelled with rare urgency.

Lynx fought the urge to look over his shoulder, but he didn't need to when Anatin's eyes widened and the commander physically recoiled.

'Deepest black, two of them!'

'Reft and Deern are ready,' Kas gasped as she stumbled to a halt.

Running inside, Lynx turned and saw the faster golantha just thirty yards away. He yelled for some ammo and Foren shoved an earther in his hand.

'Hold!' Anatin bellowed as loud as he could, Payl doing the same at the other end of the room.

The remaining Cards huddled at the windows of what Lynx now saw was a wide gallery hall, long tables running its full length and dark doorways leading off behind. He loaded and brought his gun up. When the golantha reached the base of the slope leading up to the hall, Anatin roared the order and the whole company opened fire. Seven or eight earthers smashed into it, rocking the golantha backwards while icers peppered its side.

The impact stopped it and made the creature curl its legs up to its body, but just as Lynx felt a surge of elation, the golantha wriggled. It moved groggily, stunned by the volley, but then its legs stretched. The wounds from the dark-bolts were clear now it wasn't moving. A chunk had been gouged from its side where the broken legs were, but it had a dozen pairs left and those started it moving forward almost immediately.

The golantha closed on them as Cards on all sides yelled for ammo, but Foren just shouted back that there were no more earthers left. A hush fell over the company, the blood draining from their faces, as they saw the golantha turn its bulbous tail end towards then.

It never had the chance to unleash the strange chemical sting they'd seen before. A black hammer blow struck it in the side and folded it in on itself. The golantha screeched in pain and turned, only to have a second dark-bolt strike it directly below its head.

A gout of grey dust burst up through the air and the golantha spasmed. Lynx gasped. The shot had nearly cut it in half, ripped right through the golantha even before the terrible magic started eating away at its insides. The strange hushing sound echoed over the stone ground as the beast fell still, half-disintegrating before their eyes. A cloud of dust lifted up like its soul being carried away.

Lynx looked left. There was Deern, leaning against Reft with his mage-gun smoking gently in the night air. The rat-faced mercenary made an obscene gesture at the dead golantha then grinned at his comrades. Sanshir stood beside them, surveying the corpse with a scowl. Deern stepped up on to a low wall and took an extravagant bow as the Cards cheered.

Toil pushed her way forward, bodily shoving Haphori out of the way to step out into the moonlight.

'There's fucking two of them!' she roared, stopping their celebrations in an instant. 'Two! You just used our last dark-bolts!'

'Eh?'

As Deern replied, his partner put a meaty hand on his shoulder. The small man turned, his mouth falling open as the slower of the golantha heaved its way forward. Its once-dark carapace had a whitish sheen to it, one that showed up its oily iridescence in the moonlight. Lastani's ice magic had left it permanently marked somehow – scarred by a furious torrent of energy which even a creature that fed on magic couldn't handle.

The eyes on its right-hand side were a ruined mess, torn flesh and congealed blood, or whatever the golantha had instead perhaps. Its mouthparts were similarly brutalised, one antenna missing and the other casting just a ragged light. Two legs on the near side trailed limp, another seemed to be missing entirely. Even the great curves of armour on its back were cracked and holed, while the light that pulsed through it was jerky and fitful. Everything about what was left seemed intent on vengeance, however.

'What do we have?'

'Nothing,' Foren shouted, holding up a handful of burners and sparkers from the bag they'd kept back.

Safir grabbed a burner from the man and loaded it. As the golantha started to heave towards the aghast trio at the Low Gardens, Safir fired. The streak of fire raced down the slope and burst over the golantha, but the beast didn't even draw back. If anything it seemed to relish the brief cloud of orange flames. The golantha turned into the impact and flicked its remaining antennae, sweeping the fire up in a net of green threads that waxed bright as the flames vanished.

The sight was enough to make Sanshir, Reft and Deern turn tail, but by then the golantha had turned towards the source of the burner – where it could no doubt sense the remaining mage cartridges.

'Lastani hurt it,' Lynx said. He looked around. 'Who's got an earther? Come on, one of you shitweasels has held back. Time to be a hero.'

He was met with only blank faces, but then Anatin himself gave a cough. The commander reached into his cartridge case and pulled out a single small cartridge – pistol size, but even in the weak moonlight Lynx could see the symbol of Ulfer inscribed.

'Last resort,' Anatin said by way of explanation. 'In case I had no more running left in me.'

Lynx grabbed the cartridge and loaded it into his own pistol, lying empty in its holster at his hip.

'Last resort,' he said, bending low over the bag of remaining mage cartridges. They were the ones that hadn't proved to be of much use in a fight, that might only make a man smell more like magic to the beast. Burners, sparkers, several dozen surplus icers plus a few fire grenades. 'Shit, I've been here before, ain't I?'

'You're doing *that*?' Toil asked, taken off balance.

'Is there another choice? I don't see Sitain waving any more dark-catridges anywhere.'

To that, she had no response. Lynx didn't look at her, he didn't think he could bear it. There was no time for a final kiss or any bold words. The golantha was slow, but not that slow. Lynx plucked a sparker from the bag and tossed it to Suth.

'How good a shot are you?'

The woman caught it and cocked her head at him even as she slotted the cartridge into her long gun.

'Good.'

'Get ready then.'

Lynx scooped up the bag and was about to set off when Toil suddenly shouted.

'Wait!'

He paused to see her frantically tugging off a spare belt around her waist. It took him a moment but then Lynx remembered the mage balls Sitain had given her – weak, but five of them and dark magic. She placed that in the bag and he nodded as he set off out of the door, not trusting himself to speak. The golanatha was less than thirty yards off and heading straight for them. From what he could see, its tail was undamaged – it could wreck the whole building as they tried to escape through it.

Lynx didn't stop, didn't want to think about what would be coming next. The world closed in around him, terror eclipsed by determination. For a few long seconds his mind simply watched with surreal dispassion. All Lynx could feel was the groan of his knees, the pound of his feet on stone, the huff of hot breath as he sucked in all the air he could.

Exhaustion was a looming spectre, fear a pursing hound. In front of him the golantha reared up, ready to gather him in with its twisted, bloody pincers and mandibles. Every step seemed to make it bigger and more mind-numbingly horrifying, but Lynx turned his eyes to the ground. Every last scrap of sense he had left was desperately counting down the steps. Five, two, one.

He swung around, not trying to stop the sprint but turning it into a spinning movement. His foot twisted underneath him and Lynx felt himself stumble, but momentum carried him around. The weight of the bag hauled at his arm as he brought it in a long circle. Lynx caught a glimpse of the Cards spilling out of the great hallway, Toil and Suth fighting their way clear. Suth had her mage-gun at the ready. Lynx glimpsed the muzzle rising as the bag dragged him back around and towards the monster.

He found himself tipping forwards, his balance gone, feet no longer underneath him. He was falling, flying towards the feet of the golantha but the bag was everything. Lynx let it slip his fingers as he saw the creature appear in his blurred vision. The bag rose up in an ungainly and wobbling arc through the night air.

Just ten yards between them, Lynx and the monster. He fell and hit the ground hard, bounced and rolled over. Couldn't stop himself going, sliding on the shallow slope as the crack of a gunshot rang out.

The jagged, angry roar of a sparker raced over his head. Through blurred vision Lynx could see it, could smell the burned air and feel the prickle and hiss of its claws on his skin. It caught the bag dead-on, high in the air as the golantha reached to snatch it. Just a moment's difference but one that seemed to last for ever to Lynx. Then the bag exploded.

Everything went white. Fire and lightning swallowed by a cloud of fury incarnate. He felt the hammer blow against his back, throwing him back the way he came.

Lynx scrabbled at the ground, instinct screaming to get away from the terrible flames. He could see nothing but that brightness – hear nothing beyond the great elongated detonation of cartridges and grenades. There was heat and the stink of scorched flesh, but he couldn't even tell if it was his own. Eventually he came to a stop, lying on his back and staring up at the sky. Some strange instinct kicked in, a voice roaring in Hanese.

Press on, push through!

Some nameless sergeant, probably long dead, but the words were in Hanese and his body obeyed like a whipped dog. He pushed himself upright and took a few staggering steps. The golantha was a blurred shape, raised high in the air and swaying. Light and swirling dust filled the air. Lynx felt the patter of rain or something on his face as ghostly trails of heat swept across his face.

He pulled the mage-pistol from his holster and raised it just as the golantha screeched. Still he couldn't make out anything, but right now he knew he didn't have to. The great shape was too big to miss, a dark lump shot through with shuddering flashes of light. He raised the pistol, both hands wrapped around the grip to keep it steady, and fired.

The earther kicked backwards so hard that he fell again, barely seeing it strike. A gout of something exploded from whatever had been left of the golantha's face. Even amid the blur, Lynx saw it convulse under the impact.

Icers followed it; three, four, five white blades of light slamming into its face. The whip-crack reports filled the air, gore and dark dust bursting up into the night sky. The golantha tipped sideways and slumped. Lynx felt it hit the ground, the impact shuddering through his body as he flopped on to his back. The mage-pistol fell, forgotten, and only one flailing hand stopped him from cracking his skull on the stone ground. The golantha shuddered and twitched, death spasms scoring the slopes with its spear-like legs before finally going still.

'Got you,' Lynx whispered to the dead beast. 'Lastani got you.'

The sound of feet echoed distantly behind him. Lynx kept his eyes on the golantha, as though fearing it would rise again. Strong arms slipped under him and hauled him up, the arc of the skyriver sweeping overhead as he went.

'You mad bastard!' a voice yelled.

Lynx blinked. It was Toil.

'Someone had to,' he croaked.

'And that someone's you?'

Lynx nodded. 'Yeah.'

'Fuck.' She looked away and Lynx saw several of the Cards approaching the corpse, guns at the ready.

'Is it dead?'

'Looks like it,' Llaith replied. 'Either that or it's bloody good at pretending.'

'Make sure!'

'Shoot it in the face!' someone added, but Llaith shook his head.

'It ain't got one left,' he reported, looking close. 'It's dead.'

Lynx felt the final ounce of strength drain out of his body and he sagged. Only the combined muscle of Aben and Toil kept him upright. Then Reft appeared and pretty much tucked Lynx under his arm like a puppy.

'They're both dead,' Lynx said, dazed. 'That's good. Too tired to go again. Anything to drink round here? Water even?'

Toil laughed, incredulous. 'After this, I think the finest chefs in the city will be yours to command.'

Lynx's stomach gave a lurch as the jangle of terror and exhaustion there recoiled at the idea. Some distant part of his head was more receptive, but his body wasn't taking orders from that yet. The whole idea was more than it felt capable of right now.

'Too tired,' he sighed. 'Let's get pissed and just see what happens.'

Toil laughed and took hold of his head, cupping his face and kissing him painfully hard.

'Fine, let's get pissed.'

Chapter 43

Lynx thought about opening his eyes, but decided he'd regret it. Quite a lot of him hurt in a surprising number of different ways. It was unlikely a view would improve matters.

The deep ache of overtaxed muscles vibrated like a drum through his body, the hot sharp sting of scorched skin singing like a fiddle across it. Trumpets blared inside his skull too, while the state of his guts was more the discordant jangle of collapsed buildings and shattered windows.

Glimpses of the previous night flitted through his mind. The blood and destruction were impossible to drive out, however hard he tried. Everything that followed was a blur, a dull haze compared to the sharp memory of gunfire and horror.

Teshen. It was impossible to forget that sight, Teshen fighting to the last – Lastani too.

More of a mercenary that she'd have ever thought, Lynx reflected. *Takes true fighting spirit to go down the way Lastani did.*

The bed jolted suddenly as a boot connected with the side.

'Come on,' said someone above him, 'time to get up.'

Lynx groaned.

'Wha?' he managed before his head protested.

'It's morning,' Toil informed him.

'So?'

'So get up. Sanshir's back.'

Lynx thought about that for a while. Nothing about it seemed to suggest he needed to get out of bed.

'So?'

'Just move. There's food, laid on special for the hero of the hour.'

'Who's that?'

'You, ya damn fool.'

'Oh.'

Lynx was quiet for a while.

'What sort of food?'

Toil gave a snort. 'Smells like pork.'

Lynx make a determined effort to get up, but his wobbly muscles had a number of contrasting ideas on that front and none were willing to work together. He mostly slithered off the side of the bed on to a reed floor mat. Lynx lay there for a while until Toil started to kick him in the shoulder – not with real malice, but certainly enough to be annoying.

With an effort he got both arms to work together and pushed himself up, muttering curses under his breath as he did so. Toil watched him with what he suspected was cruel amusement until Lynx had righted himself and managed to sit on the side of the bed.

'So the hero thing didn't last long, eh?'

'Even heroes can be annoying,' Toil said. 'I've met a few, my tolerance is low.'

Lynx scowled and grabbed at some clothes to pull on. After a bit of effort he stopped trying to fit into Toil's trousers and found some of his own.

'Not going to help?' Lynx asked eventually.

Toil just shook her head. When finally he had trousers and a shirt on, Toil turned towards the door then paused as Lynx sat back on the bed.

'What is it?'

'Just . . . ah, takin' a moment. The whole city's grieving and my head's all a-tangle.'

Who else did we lose? Lynx asked himself, appalled that he couldn't recall their names. For a while he felt like the true bastard some people saw him as, but eventually faces loomed in his memory.

'Crais and Sethail,' he exclaimed at last.

'Never found,' Toil said, misinterpreting him. 'We can only guess what happened, but likely it was the tysarn.'

Lynx nodded absent-mindedly. He'd not known either really, Crais being the only one of the pair he'd even exchanged more than a few words with. A stocky man, balding and freckled with a loud voice and uncomplicated appetites, Lynx hadn't taken to him but he'd been popular in the company. Sethail had been a quiet youth, but showing promise.

'Ah gods,' Lynx said. 'Sethail joined the same night as me.'

It seemed a long time ago to Lynx now – waking up in that cell in Janagrai and needing a job to get him out of town. He hadn't been the only one to join up that night. Fashail and Sethail had been shop apprentices until the Cards swaggered into town. Cousins too, kin to look after each other. And now in the space of a couple of nights, both were dead. Fashail in the fight at the lodging house, Sethail lost in the press as the Cards fled the golantha. Killed by tysarn most likely.

'There were three of them, that first night,' he recalled. 'Cousins. One didn't go through with it, thought better of a life of adventure. Now he's the only one alive.'

'That's the life,' Toil said stiffly. 'It's cruel, but that's the way it is. We all got lucky when we were young, stayed alive long enough to get good. Plenty others weren't so lucky.'

'Yeah, I know. Still – it makes a man think when he wakes up, sore but alive, the nightmares still fresh in his head.'

'Come on,' Toil said, beckoning. 'It's company you need, not quiet. Company and food.'

Rather unsteadily, Lynx followed her outside. A cool breeze drifted over him as she opened the door and Lynx squinted around, for a moment thinking that she'd woken him not long after dawn. Finally, he realised that the low rumbles he could hear weren't his stomach, but thunder from the clouds over the mainland. The flash of lightning was visible over the long wall of cliffs. A few desultory spots of rain fell, but they were more than welcome after a searing few days. The heavy grey clouds hiding the sun seemed a blessing as Lynx walked unsteadily down to the courtyard.

Many of the Cards were eating, a few already drinking again too. Lynx had no idea what time of day it was, but instinct told him it was late morning at least. He certainly couldn't face another drink, not after last night, but most of the company were up and about. If it had been early, the courtyard would be mostly deserted.

He was ushered to a table by one of the cheerless old ladies who ruled the lodging house, tiny and unsmiling even as she set a pot of coffee down in front of him. The other of the harridans emerged from the kitchen door a few moments later. In her arms was a round clay dish so big Lynx could see her strain under the weight. That too was set down on the table and the lid removed to reveal a great cloud of steam and delicious smells.

Lynx snatched at the nearest plate. He was already digging out a portion before he'd even worked out what was being offered. There was a sweet, peppery spice overlaying the heady smell of pork – whatever else was included, he was willing to fight even Reft for it.

Llaith dropped heavily into the seat opposite Lynx. The ageing mercenary looked bruised and old, but there was a smile on his face and a smoke hanging from his lips. Sitain appeared too and joined Toil on Lynx's right, while Kas, Himbel and Safir took the remaining seats. Lynx had started by the time anyone else managed to get a portion, almost moaning with delight at what he'd found. Some sort of dumplings filled with salty white cheese, fried with the heavily spiced pork and all baked together with about two dozen eggs. For a while he couldn't even see anything beyond the plate.

Once Lynx slowed, he looked around at the rest of the company. There was a buzz of chatter coming from a table on the other side of the courtyard. Craning his neck he saw the stern face of Sanshir. The kaboto was almost unrecognisable beneath several dozen black teardrops painted on to her cheeks in addition to the smile she wore.

'What's going on?'

'Local tradition,' Llaith explained. 'Knowing the dead, she called it.'

'Eh?'

'She turned up mebbe half an hour back, asking to hear stories of Teshen's life in the Cards.'

'Holding a candle for him all this time, eh?'

The comment provoked a playful punch on the shoulder from Toil. 'She loved him once. That leaves a mark whatever comes later. Go over, listen to her.'

Lynx did so, fetching a second portion for the journey. He positioned himself behind a small gathering of Cards all focused on Sanshir.

'Why the Bloody Pauper?' Anatin asked as Lynx arrived. 'He never told us that.'

Sanshir inclined her head. 'No family,' she explained. 'People say here, "with family close, no person is poor", but Teshen was an orphan.'

'You're telling that ta the wrong crowd,' Anatin said. 'A bunch of well-paid loners, that's this lot.'

'Family by a different name,' she said with a dismissive flick. 'Also, if you kill during Masts, you pay their family out of your winnings. Teshen preferred glory to money.'

She broke off and spared Lynx a nod. 'Good morning. My kabat sends his thanks.'

'Ah, sure. He's welcome.'

'He also wishes your company to go away soon.'

Lynx nodded. 'No argument here. Um, Toil said you were here to know the dead.'

'Yes. When we die, our family and friends gather – tell stories. No person is just a son, a friend, a lover. We often do not see each side, so to remember them we ask for more. You were his family, I was his past.'

Family eh? Yet for a while I couldn't even remember all their names. Lynx grunted. 'And the paint?'

She touched her cheek, her smile vanishing. 'For each of the dead. To paint more than one is a great sadness.'

He had no reply to that. Both sides of her face were covered with the black teardrops, he guessed two dozen at least. She was the Kaboto of Vi No Le, most of her friends would have been within the crews who had fought on that shore. Most of her friends would likely be dead now.

'Do you have a story for me?'

Lynx hesitated. 'I . . . no. Didn't know him well enough. Lastani neither – or the others we lost.'

'They were not your family?'

'Guess they were,' he said, uncomfortable.

'Then tell me.'

Lynx looked away. 'Let someone else speak, I've got nothing.'

'We've all been speaking,' Anatin said, eyeing Lynx through a cloud of cigar smoke. 'She's heard our stories. Even the one about the wrestling contest out Aldath way, which frankly I still half don't believe an' I was there beside the man – just as naked and just as blue.'

'Doubt there's much I can add then.' Lynx shrugged. 'I stood beside each of them when things turned nasty, was glad to have them there when it did. None of 'em were perfect, no person is, but I was glad to know them and stand with them.'

Sanshir nodded. 'They have told me of Shadows Deep, of Jarrazir and the years before. Now I tell you of another Teshen, the young man who was born Tekeil Shenqin.'

She paused after saying his true name out loud, as though just that had exorcised a ghost of her past. The first tale was an amusing one, a young Tekeil hiding in a gaggle of prostitutes long enough to evade a kabat's guard, before she moved on to his Masts victories and other bloody deeds.

Later, when she was done, Sanshir pushed herself up from her seat. She looked weary as though such memories drained her more than the running and fighting ever could. She wrapped a white shawl around her shoulders, mourning cloth and Masts allegiance both, and left as silent as a ghost while the Cards were left to remember their dead.

Lynx nudged Anatin as the group broke up. He was reluctant to break the solemn hush that descended in Sanshir's wake, but felt compelled to speak all the same.

'Anatin, I . . . well. I guess I owe you an apology.'

The commander of the Cards raised an eyebrow. 'Aye, it's likely that ya do, but what for this time? Just tell me it's for somethin' I already know about. Don't reckon I could face one o' your surprises this morning.'

Lynx gave a cough as he felt a pang in his chest – something halfway between amusement and guilt. 'Don't worry. I just wanted to say you were right. About joining the fight on the shoreline, that is. We lost people these last few days, but . . . Shanshir's the one grieving all her friends.'

'Aye, there's that,' Anatin said. He took a deep breath and nodded, looking away to the rumbling clouds over the distant cliffs. 'Doubt there'd be a company after that, true enough. It's funny really. Doesn't feel like we got off lightly, but we did. Given what we faced anyway.'

'Yeah, we did an' that was down to you.' Lynx coughed. 'Anyways, seemed worth saying. You made the right call. I was wrong.'

Anatin scowled and heaved himself up. 'No good choices there,' he said. 'But some better'n others even if you're not the man to see that.' He looked down at Lynx, the pain visible in his eyes just for a moment. 'You did all right these past days though. I reckon we're both too old and tired to drag up disagreements now. Let's forget the apologies and just keep on living, eh?'

He didn't wait for a response, just headed away in a cloud of cigar smoke.

Lynx watched Anatin head up to the high terrace that looked south across the sea. The man clearly needed some time alone so Lynx shifted seats to join Toil.

'What now?' he whispered as she rested an arm on his shoulder, leaning heavily against his large frame.

'Now?' Toil ran her fingers through her hair. 'Now we get ready to go.'

'Where are we going?'

She laughed. 'I'd thought this job would be a good break, I truly did. Useful for me too, I'll not deny it, but a rest for the company. Now I see we're going to get into the shit wherever we go, most likely.'

'So . . .'

Unexpectedly she leaned in and kissed him.

'So now, we face the fact there's a war brewing. There's news of fighting in the north, the Sons of the Wind have razed a town and fortress of the Knights of the Sacred Mountain.'

'That's our business how?'

'Because they're turning on each other. They know the magic has changed and they're getting ready for the last battle.'

'The what, now?'

She smiled. 'These fanatics, they've always got some dogma they'll protect with their lives, some prophecy they think will make it all worthwhile. That's one way you can tell they're the bastards who need to be shot.'

'We're in the realms of prophecy now?'

Toil puffed out her cheeks. 'Mad ramblings might be more accurate, unless you believe gods are like jigsaw puzzles and can be put back together again. Either way, they see an end coming and they want to be the ones standing on top of the pile when it comes.'

'A pile of what?' Lynx wondered. 'Skulls? Broken cities?'

'Whatever it takes,' she agreed. 'So it's time for us to get back to the war before it becomes one. Maybe we can stop it tearing the whole Riven Kingdom apart.'

'It can't be all down to us, can it?'

'No, we've got allies – we're looking for more. The eastern states are no friends of the Orders, we just need to persuade them in time that the danger is this great. But we're right in the heart of it now, these tattoos prove that much. There's no escape for us so we might as well charge in with all guns blazing.'

'Once we find some more ammunition.'

Her face darkened. 'Yeah. Atieno may need persuading on that front.'

'I didn't mean that!' Lynx protested.

'I know, but it may yet come to it. The Militant Orders are bigger than Su Dregir and all the Parthain League, whatever that looks like by now. First stop is Su Dregir – we take stock and report in. The Archelect may have some bright ideas on where we go next. Reckon I'm getting above my pay grade here.'

Lynx sighed and shook his head. 'Aren't we all at this point?'

'True. Starting to feel like the responsibility is ours though, doesn't it?' Toil nodded towards the nearest group of Cards. 'Even this lot are feeling it, don't you think?'

'Yeah, I reckon so. Some of them at least. That's a lot to ask of anyone though.' Lynx scowled. 'That's a lot for anyone to appoint themselves to.'

She gave a soft laugh. 'Stopping a war across the whole of the Riven Kingdom? Mebbe something far worse? Even my arrogance has limits – just don't tell anyone that. But we're the ones with the key painted on our skin. Might be you and I need to nudge the rest of the company into doing the right thing.'

'Shattered gods. That's a lot to hang on us – on this of all mornings.'

'I know. Sorry. But you of all folk know that life's not fair. That sometimes you need to step up and do what's right. I'm not making any decisions now, but I don't see many paths from where we're at. Not ones that leave the Riven Kingdom and all the rest of Urden free of total domination.'

'Gods, Toil!' Lynx gasped. 'You really mean this, don't you?'

Her voice took on an urgent tone. 'You saw what Atieno did down in the Labyrinth – he destroyed a God Fragment! That's *never* been done before. Never. It was considered impossible. Drop a mage sphere on one, the biggest earth-bomb you can find, and you can't even scratch it.'

Slowly Lynx nodded. 'Aye, and Atieno crumbled it to dust by accident. Crap.' He was quiet for a long while. 'Are we leaving Caldaire today?'

'Tomorrow.' Toil gave him a weak smile. 'There's still time for that squid I promised you last night.'

'Finally some good news!' Lynx paused. 'Jigsaw puzzles, you say?'

'Huh? Oh, aye. Don't worry about it. Probably fine. I'm almost certain.'

'Almost?'

Toil forced a smile. 'Pretty sure. I mean, sort of. I doubt our luck is *that* bad, right?'

'Oh right. Yeah. What's the worst that could happen, eh?'

'Precisely.'

Lynx shook his head. 'Screw you all, I'm going back to bed.'